MW00635118

BATTLE FOR FOREVER:

ANCIENT AMONG US

EDWARD SAVIO

BABELFISH
PRESS

SAN FRANCISCO

BABELFISH PRESS
237 Kearny Street, Suite 9179, San Francisco, CA 94108

Copyright © 2019 by Edward Savio

All rights reserved. No part of this publication may be reproduced, distributed, or transmitted in any form or by any means, including photocopying, recording, or other electronic or mechanical methods, without the prior written permission of Babelfish Press, except for brief quotations in connection with a literary review.

ISBN-13: 978-1-63124-017-1

This is a work of fiction. Names, characters, corporations, places and incidents in this novel are either the product of the author's imagination or used fictitiously. Any resemblance to actual events, locales, organizations, or persons, living or dead, is entirely coincidental and beyond the intent of either the author or the publisher.

Babelfish Press and the talking fish logo are trademarks of Babelfish Press.

For reprint permission: permission@babelfishpress.com
All other information: info@babelfishpress.com

FOR SPENCER & JESSE
AND JESSE & TYLER

Because you are my best audience
and my toughest critics.

FLIGHT

"WE'VE BEEN PROGRAMMED BY EVOLUTION—
FIGHT OR FLIGHT. BUT ALL WE'VE EVER WANTED
WAS TO SOAR."

—UNKNOWN

I Get Upgraded To Worst Class

Futuo!

χέζω!

該死的!

Sorry. I had to let that out.

It's probably not the best time to bring this up, you probably have your own problems to deal with. Depending on where you are, things could be pretty desperate. But if you're still with me, and not against me, there are things you need to know.

If you *are* against me, I'm going to ask you—politely—to stop reading. If you don't, I'll come find you.

I won't kill you, I promise. I'll just slather your body in honey and shove you in a bear cave—politely.

Let *them* take care of things.

Maybe you can tell, I'm getting sick of being polite.

You may have heard bits and pieces of the story from others. That's the problem when things get fragmented. There are a lot of people telling a lot of stories, each one a little different, and each time the story gets told, it becomes a little bit more of a lie.

That's one of their weapons. Misinformation. Because when too much information becomes unreliable, all information becomes suspect.

I'm going to try to set the record straight.

My name is Alexander X, the tenth in my family of that name, but at the moment, I'm known as Alexander Grant. Four days ago

I turned fifteen hundred years old. It seems like I've lived another thousand since then. I'm a high school junior at—

I…don't…know where I'm from at the moment. I don't think I'm from anywhere.

But at least, now, after a very long time, I know who I am.

I remember reading this book that begins: *The past is a foreign country: they do things differently there.*

I know that's true because I guarantee you you'd feel a lot more out of place standing in whatever town you're in, in whatever country you're in, in the year 1341 than if I dropped you in the middle of a North Korean military parade during a monsoon tomorrow afternoon.

The storm that's coming…North Korea may be *the* vacation spot on the planet.

That's because the population in that country is accustomed to starvation, deprivation, and essentially living in the nineteenth century. Most of you…aren't prepared for what's coming.

I'm sitting on a plane, fastened into a seat in coach—a middle seat, mind you—watching dozens of Special Forces troops moving toward the aircraft.

The wide-body jet we're on has been rolled to the far end of the tarmac, more than half a mile from the terminal.

That's so people in the airport don't get killed if things get a little messy on board once they storm the plane.

There are at least fifty foil wrappers at my feet. My friend Daniel Lang is, at the moment, opening his fifty-first piece of hard candy. I'd slap him if I could. But I don't dare make any quick movements. Spotters watching us are in constant contact with the soldiers approaching the aircraft who are heavily armed with automatic weapons and itching to take down anything that seems suspicious.

The girl I've been crushing on since the beginning of sophomore year, Phoebe Amara, is on the other side of me, trying to keep calm. She's holding my left hand, squeezing the blood out of my palm. It's the most pleasant thing that's happened all day.

Perhaps, I should explain how I got here, strapped into seat 24B with at least three Special Forces teams storming our plane.

You may know some of it already. If you do, forgive me. I don't really know what information is getting through. Whatever you've heard, it's almost certainly wrong.

I've spent my life trying to remain anonymous. Telling you any of this is against everything I've ever been taught. But they've broken the rules, so now I have to.

When I finally find my father, if I survive this, he's either going to wrap his arms around me and hold me tight, or he's gonna wrap his hands around my throat and choke me to death.

Even though he loves me, it's about a fifty-fifty chance, either way.

∞

The water taxi skimmed across the surface of Massachusetts Bay, the boat rolling over the waves like a car on a poorly paved road after too many years baked in the desert sun. It was a rhythmic motion, a constant up-and-down that I found relaxing. Night was still deciding when it would give way to the day. In the distance, there were the faintest hints of light peeking over the water's gray horizon in the east. It would be about an hour before the sun would appear. Hopefully, we had enough time, but not too much, before the first overseas flights took off from Logan Airport.

That was our goal now. Get out of the country. Forget saving the world or protecting a hundred plus years of technological advancements. Just get on a plane and leave.

It sounded so simple.

Nikolay steered the boat around Deer Island. He was smiling. It wasn't the stack of fifty-dollar bills I had given the Russian boat pilot for helping us, although that had improved his mood considerably. No, he relished being in the middle of the action. I'm not sure he would've felt the same way had he experienced everything we'd gone through at Wonderland Park. But I was glad for his help and extremely grateful he hadn't abandoned us on Revere Beach to fend for ourselves.

"I love America," he muttered happily to himself in his thick Slavic accent.

To the left, the approach lights of the airport's main runway extended into the bay. Nikolay aimed the boat toward them.

The rush of excitement that coursed through my veins after surviving the explosion at the abandoned dog park and our fight to get away from Elam Khai was beginning to subside.

I hadn't beaten him. I had, at best, postponed his plans.

Briefly.

The heat of the flames, the narrow escape, the thrill and the terror of it had unlocked something deep within me, caused me to rip off my shirt, bare my flesh, reveal the warrior that had been kept hidden under layers of trendy clothes, softened by years of comfort, and reined in by my father's wishes and by a kinder, gentler society.

The cold air felt good on my skin. I was finally beginning to cool off. I didn't want to put my shirt back on. I wanted to feel this free forever.

Nikolay glanced up at me from behind the wheel. "You sure you're not Russian?" he said. "You know, we do dis in Saint Petersburg during da winter for fun. Of course, every year, a few of us die of pneumonia."

Phoebe tried to give me back my jacket. "He's right. You're going to make yourself sick."

I stopped her from removing my coat, which had a hole under the arm from the spear the Scotsman had fired at me on the roof of the Old State House. "You need it more than I do."

I looked out over the gunwale at the water rushing past. At some point, my eyes lost focus on each individual ripple and wave, and the water blurred into a uniform sheet.

The Scotsman.

In the end, he had saved my life.

I glanced away from the hypnotic water.

The approach lights towered over us as we passed the narrow pier which held them. We were under the glide path of the main runway, and a midsize jet roared overhead. Puffs of smoke rose up from the tires as the plane touched down.

The airport was only a few hundred yards away, but it was three miles to the ferry dock and an unprotected mile long bus ride to the terminals.

We'd be vulnerable until we got past security.

Phoebe studied me. "You okay?"

It was a simple question, and yet I didn't know how to answer it. If I was truthful, my response would be: No, not at all. I've had people try to kill me before. I've been in battle. I've been choked. I've been threatened. I've even been kidnapped. But I've never felt so deeply betrayed.

My father had lied to me. Or, at the very least, not told me the truth. I needed to know why.

"What happened back there?" Phoebe said, her eyes on the plume of smoke five miles to the north. Wonderland Greyhound Park was still burning. The smoke reflected the glow of the flames, as if someone had taken an orange pastel chalk and rubbed it across the black sky.

I stared at a navigation light as it blinked on and off. Green. Darkness. Green. Darkness. The thought of explaining everything she missed exhausted me. I told her the only thing that really mattered.

"I found out who I am." I didn't know how to begin telling her, so I just came out with it. "My father is Mark Antony."

It felt strange to say it. Foreign.

Daniel scrunched up his face, his eyes becoming slits. I don't have any idea why people think this expression helps them decipher something they can't understand with a normal face.

"Your father is a former Latin pop star?" He shook his hips, imitating a stage show. He was still feeling the effects of whatever drug they had given him, although, he was steadier on his feet than he was before—until, of course, he started doing that thing with the hips.

I stared at Daniel.

"No. My father is—was—Mark *Antony,* Julius Caesar's friend and second-in-command, a Consul of Rome, and a member of the Second Triumvirate."

"So, *not* a pop star."

"But he sort of was a rock star," said Phoebe. "Consul of Rome. Part of the Second Triumvirate." When I gave her a look, she shrugged. "I kind of had a thing for the actor who played him on this show."

It annoyed me that my father was not that much older than me when he presided over Rome. While I got scolded for coming in third at a chess championship.

It was embarrassing.

It highlighted the differences in our generations. They got to rule the world. I had to endure a century and a half of high school.

I hate to sound like a whiny-ass six-year-old, but...*I want my own army!*

I guess I don't really want my own army. It's a lot of work. But I do feel compelled to lead. To command. Maybe it's the consequence of my father constantly testing me on battle tactics and strategies, the by-product of centuries spent studying every style and school of martial arts. It's what I've been trained to do. And apparently, it's what I was born to do.

I've been in battle. I've seen the horror of it too many times. I don't revel in the glory of war, or even talk about war the way my father does, that is, when you can get him to talk about it at all. Maybe I don't feel that sense of pride because I've always appeared too young to be given a command. If I'd been born a few hundred years earlier, I'd be leading soldiers at my age. Okita Soji was defeating his teachers at twelve, leading Samurai at sixteen. At seventeen, Joan of Arc commanded the armies of a nation. But boys and girls don't get to lead soldiers into battle in today's world. Instead, they play at war while sitting on the couch. I don't even like playing First Person Shooter games. They dull the senses. Because they lack the one thing that makes war *war.*

Fear. True fear. For one's life.

"Weren't you listening at the dog track?" I asked Daniel. "Battle of Actium? Mark Antony vs. Octavian? My father against Elam Khai? Hundreds of ships at sea?"

"Not ringing a bell. I was too busy trying not to die."

As if it had just hit her, Phoebe glanced over at me. "Your father... was Mark Antony?" I couldn't tell if she was impressed or nauseous.

"That's *one* of the people my father's been."

I needed to know them all now. Everyone he had ever been. No more hiding. No more secrets.

"He was in love with Cleopatra," Phoebe said.

"Yes."

Pretty much, most of what I know about Cleopatra VII Philopator, I learned from books, which pretty much means I don't know very much about her at all. In my experience, the person you read about, and the person *in person* are vastly different.

I've never had a conversation with my father about Cleopatra. That's not exactly true. I had one. And it was more like a tiny fragment of a conversation. I asked him if he'd ever met her. He told me he had.

"What was she like?"

"She was a Pharaoh of Egypt." As if that said it all.

Whenever my father gave me answers like that—short, succinct, conversation ending—it was usually a waste of time to attempt to pry anything more out of him.

Engel mentioned her in passing one day. Looking back on it now, my very, very, very old friend immediately tried changing the subject. But I continued pressing Engel until he finally relented.

"She was everything you've ever heard. And like nothing you've ever seen." Engel, closing in on nine thousand years old, had a wistful, dreamy look, like he was some infatuated teenager. "She was stunning. Yet, I don't know if I'd call her pretty. Hers was an attractiveness enhanced by daily contact. The persuasiveness of her conversation. The sound of her voice. A beauty magnified the closer you got. She was powerful. Strong. Clever. Cunning.

Not a warrior, but she could wage war. She was a leader. She was mesmerizing."

Apparently so.

Get a room, Engel.

Why hadn't I seen it then? My father's nonchalance, his lack of interest in someone who by every account was captivating. It wasn't indifference. It was pain.

"Didn't Mark Antony have children with her?" said Phoebe.

"Three of them," I said. "She married her brother first, then Julius Caesar, and then Mark Ant—I guess my father—after Caesar's death."

"She married her brother?" Daniel cringed. "That's disgusting."

"*That's* disgusting," I said, motioning toward the residue of vomit and saliva running down his chin. "The Ptolemaic Dynasty kept their bloodline pure by marrying amongst themselves." I turned to Phoebe. "Julius Caesar fell in love with her first. She gave him his only son."

It was difficult to connect the two. My father. Mark Antony. Even as the words were coming out of my mouth, I couldn't wrap my mind around my father having children with a Queen of Egypt. That he *married* a Pharaoh.

It was also difficult to accept that my father had been so ruthless. After they took control of Rome, Antony and Octavian proscribed many powerful members of the elite class, which is to say, my father and Elam Khai murdered hundreds of patricians and plebeians, replenishing the treasury with the plundered wealth, which allowed them to pay their soldiers and maintain control of the republic. Some of what I know of Mark Antony is so incompatible with the man I know as my father that it violently conflicts with my image of him.

"Cleopatra was smoking hot, right?" said Daniel.

"Cleopatra was dead five hundred years before I was born."

Phoebe sensed my disillusionment. "You didn't know, did you?"

I shook my head.

"There's probably a good reason why he didn't tell you."

"I'll have to ask him when I find him."

Maybe the reason my father never told me was because he knew I'd have this reaction.

"I'm sorry," she said.

It was her apology that pulled me back.

"You have nothing to be sorry about." I stared into her eyes. "Nothing. At all. That was amazing what you did. That woman was twice the size of you."

"I was lucky you gave me the flare gun."

"You did a roundoff back handspring into her jaw."

Phoebe scrunched up her face, slightly embarrassed. "Eight years of gymnastics," she said, downplaying her heroics.

"It was awesome. We couldn't see anything except when the flares went off. What happened?"

Phoebe got a faraway look in her eyes, reliving it. "Somehow the woman got free of the dog pens we'd trapped her in. I was hiding in the bushes. At about nine minutes, I crawled out and got ready to fire the flare. That's when she saw me." Phoebe swallowed hard before continuing. "She got her hands around my throat. I couldn't believe how much it hurt not being able to breathe. All I wanted to do was give up. I thought, *I'm going to die here.* And that's when I got mad at myself. I was acting so…weak. I closed my eyes like you said. And then, I fired. She was blinded for a moment. Which gave me the chance to escape." She shook her head as if she didn't believe it herself. What she had done. She glanced at me. "You knew that would happen, didn't you? The explosion."

I waited before answering.

"Hoped."

She nodded, absently. "Don't you think you should've mentioned that? You told me I was alerting the police. I would've never fired those flares if I knew I was going to blow up the roof hanging over your heads."

"Which is why I didn't tell you."

"I could have killed you."

"But you didn't. You saved us."

She turned away, as if my gratitude made things worse. When her gaze returned to me, there was a fire in her eyes. "You mean, you had a good reason not to tell me something?"

I got the point. I had done to her what, perhaps, my father had done to me. Maybe there *was* a reason he hadn't told me all his secrets.

"I still don't understand how the flares exploded," she said.

"When I first got to the dog park, I maaaay have opened the valve on a rather large propane tank on the roof. What people don't realize is that a mostly empty fuel tank is more dangerous than a full one. Propane is heavier than air, so the gas pooled along the surface of the roof. When the flares got close, the gas ignited, traveled back into the fume-filled tank and—BOOM! I told you the police would show up as soon as you fired the flares. I didn't say *why*."

"You both could have died."

I put my hands on her upper arms and held them firmly. "Daniel would be dead if you hadn't set off that explosion. You understand? Dead."

The truth of that struck her. She inhaled involuntarily.

Daniel was throwing up over the side. "I hate boats."

I walked over and patted him on the back. "I think this has more to do with what they gave you," I said. "Do you have any idea what it was?"

"No. But I felt like I was going to die."

"You *were* going to die. That was the whole idea. Elam Khai was going to kill you."

Daniel threw up again, and Phoebe and I had to move away from the stench to avoid hurling ourselves.

We were approaching the western edge of the airport where the land made a sharp right turn into a cove. A fifteen-story hotel overlooked the water. Just beyond that was the Logan Airport Ferry Terminal.

I asked Nikolay to cut the engines.

We drifted.

Nikolay extinguished the running lights.

The only sound was the water lapping against the hull. For a moment, it felt as if we were the only ones out here, birds were chirping from somewhere unseen, but then the outside world intruded, the whine of the jets, the rumble of ferries. Normally at this time of the morning there was more activity. Ferries would be crisscrossing the harbor, repopulating downtown with workers and tourists. But it was Sunday.

The lower floors of the hotel were lit up as the staff readied breakfast. Lights dotted the upper floors. And every few minutes a new window would brighten.

Maybe I was being reckless. Elam Khai had grabbed Daniel at Airport Station. He knew our intentions. He might be at the airport right now, waiting for us again.

At the moment, we were an anonymous boat in the dark harbor. We'd be vulnerable the second we stepped onto the dock.

I could just catch a glimpse of the ramps, covered in blue canvas for the winter. I tried to remember the layout. There was a circle driveway in front used by buses making the loop from the dock to the subway station, then to each of the terminals.

Since I had ditched the backpack with the tracking device, Elam Khai would no longer know for sure where we were coming ashore. The boat terminal was an obvious choice, which is why I chose it. But if he was here, we'd be at our most exposed point.

"What are you thinking?" Phoebe asked.

"D-Day."

Phoebe looked at me curiously.

"It's what they called the start of the massive invasion by American, British and Canadian troops to retake France from the Nazis in World War II."

"I know what D-Day is. I just don't understand what that has to do with this."

Daniel quickly ducked behind the gunwale. "Are we worried

about people taking the high ground and picking us off with machine guns?"

"The landing ramp is a bottleneck. If anyone is waiting for us, we'd have nowhere to run." I turned to Nikolay. "Can you get me closer to shore?"

There was riprap all along the water's edge, protecting it from the waves and boat wakes. The sloping rock barrier was made of jagged boulders roughly the size of a Mini Cooper.

"Not so close," Nikolay said. "Doze rocks angle out under de surface. I'd run da boat aground on dem. You have to swim."

Standing on the bow with my shirt off was defiant, fearless, maybe a little crazy, but diving into the frigid water was just plain stupid. In forty-degree water, it takes about eight seconds to start lowering your body temperature. Your muscles freeze up. It's difficult to move, to breathe. Most people don't die of hypothermia, they drown because they can't stay afloat.

There was a break in the riprap.

"What's that right there? That vertical wall?"

"Maybe a drain."

"Can you get close to it?"

Nikolay looked at me. "Is too high."

"Let me worry about that."

Daniel interrupted clearing the foul taste from his mouth by repeatedly spitting over the side to say, "Besides not getting shot, what is our plan?"

"Fly to London. Greenwich. Try to find my father."

"You don't think it's going to look a little suspicious getting on a transcontinental flight without luggage?"

"We'll buy luggage at the airport."

"No, that won't look suspicious. Yeah, I'm going to Europe for—I don't know—*ever*, I'll be fine with this cute makeup bag I got at the gift shop."

"I have luggage," Nikolay said, showing me to the hold. Stuffed into the corner, next to a stack of life jackets, were four pieces of mismatched luggage. "People leave dere bags behind all da time."

Two backpacks. Two suitcases.

I unzipped the smaller suitcase and rummaged through it, while Phoebe and Daniel searched the larger one. I picked through the contents. There didn't appear to be anything that would get us arrested, detained, or sent to some secret foreign CIA detention center.

I emptied the cash and contents of the bag Nikolay had given me into the black North Face with shoulder straps.

"Whoa." Daniel held up a pair of underwear big enough for Phoebe and Daniel and me to fit in at the same time. "I do not wanna be around when this person comes looking for their bag."

Nikolay waved his hand, motioning for us to take them. "Ven day com back, I give them many hundred dollars for dere trouble."

I grabbed the flashlight mounted next to the wheel. "I'll signal you if it is okay to pull in."

"And what if it's not?" Daniel asked.

"Then...I will *make* it okay."

Nikolay smiled. "I like you veeeeery much. You are fright'ning boy."

He meant that as a compliment.

Nikolay started the engine, and slowly piloted the water taxi toward the cut out in the riprap. As we neared the shore, I slipped on my shirt.

Phoebe removed my jacket and handed it to me.

"I told you, I'm fine."

"Maybe, but it's not normal for someone to be walking around at six AM. on a Sunday in late November wearing only a button-down shirt. It's barely above freezing."

I thought about it for a moment. "You're right."

"Of course, I'm right." She picked a loose string off the sleeve of my jacket and kept her eyes lowered. "Be careful."

I lifted her chin, forcing her to look at me. "I'm going to see you in a few minutes."

She nodded. I could tell she was worried. She took my hand and slid hers into it. Her fingers were warm, her skin soft. And for a second, I let myself enjoy her touch. I felt like I should say something, but I just squeezed her hand, then let go.

I gazed out over the bow, scanning the shore for anything out of place. I put my hand on Nikolay's shoulder. "I can't thank you enough, my friend. I hope your wife is not too angry with you."

He laughed. "My wife..." He tapped the stack of cash. "She sees diss, she won't care if I ever came home agane." He was quiet for a moment, keeping his eyes on our target. "Who are you really?"

"Just someone who is very grateful."

He laughed again, but this time with more sadness laced into it. He fumbled around in his pocket, pulled out his wallet, and found—buried under credit cards and licenses and receipts and various scraps of I-don't-know-what—several mangled business cards. He liberated one and handed it to me.

"I give dese to people who may need a ride in da futures, so day ken reach me directly. If you com back, you call me. I vould very much like to hear da story of vhat happened."

I stared at the card. "Of course."

He smiled and patted me on the back, satisfied he would see me again, then went about maneuvering the boat between the rocks.

I stepped onto the bow. I motioned for Nikolay to inch the water taxi ahead, holding my hands five feet apart and then slowly moving them closer together as the boat pushed forward until I thrust out my palm for him to stop.

I retreated a few steps, got a running start, then launched myself off the bow.

Avoiding the algae-covered high water line, I tic-tac'd off the concrete walls where they came to a ninety-degree angle, then grabbed at the top. I hung there for a second, bounced my feet twice, then pulled myself up.

I was on land.

I waved to Nikolay as I sprinted toward the fence that lay between me and the hotel parking lot. I hadn't gone ten steps before I ripped up Nikolay's business card, knowing I would never use it. It's not that I didn't want to know him. It was simply too dangerous having his information on me. If Elam Khai were to find it, I couldn't risk my uncle taking retribution on the man who'd made our escape possible.

I scattered the shreds as I hit the fence and popped over it.

- TWO -
Unfortunately, You Can't Check Your Emotional Baggage At The Gate

I navigated the parked cars, weaving between gas-guzzling monstrosities and ridiculously tiny eco-friendlies. Passing the front entrance to the hotel, I caught a heavy whiff of bacon, banana bread, and pancakes. The aromas reminded me that I hadn't eaten, and my stomach immediately began to growl, kicking my guts, urging me to detour inside. I resisted, increasing my speed until the scent of breakfast receded.

As I came to the end of the building, I pressed myself against the brick wall and peered around the corner. Just as I remembered, a circle drive looped in front of the ferry terminal. The black sky in the west yielded to a touch of color directly overhead. It was still early, but the area was well-lit. I scoped out the roof of the terminal, then the side wall of the building.

Brick. No rooms looking out.

I ventured into the open and checked the roofline of the hotel, then slowly spun around, sweeping my gaze over the area.

Nothing.

I made my way to the glassed-in waiting area, putting my hands to the window to look inside.

Empty.

I pulled on the door. It was locked.

My senses on alert, I descended the covered ramp to the floating dock. Not a person in sight. No ambush. No danger. And yet, my pulse was rapid as adrenaline surged through me.

It was almost a letdown not finding anyone to take my anger out on.

I checked one last time.

Clear.

I felt uneasy. That's what happens when the ground under your feet is unstable. I'm not talking about the rise and fall of the dock. Elam Khai had ripped away my sense of security, caused me to question every decision, to be uncertain, to doubt. That's how an enemy controls you. Without ever being present. Without looking you in the eye.

Maybe Elam Khai figured I would come ashore at some random place along the water, which is probably what I should have done. Or maybe he thought I'd given up on leaving through Logan and decided to find another way out of town. A car, a train, a bicycle. Zigzag toward any one of a dozen other airports. Hopscotch from place to place, taking a slow, circuitous route to wherever. Throw Elam Khai off the scent.

Patience is difficult for me, even after a thousand years of practice.

Elam Khai is patient.

I hesitated. I couldn't come up with a reason to delay letting Nikolay pull up to the dock any longer, so I slipped the flashlight from my pocket to signal to him that it was safe.

I was about to flick on the light when I caught a shadow at the edge of my peripheral vision. Something on the roof. It moved ever so slightly. Some*one*.

I froze.

I was under an overhang. After not shifting, not breathing for thirty seconds, I slowly leaned forward. There, peeking over the edge of the awning was something that looked like the tip of a giant ballpoint pen. I could almost reach up and grab it. I instantly knew what it was: the business end of a rocket-propelled grenade launcher.

A stream of inaudible swearing followed as I mouthed curse after curse. The launcher was pointed toward the harbor. The water taxi was just out of sight, blocked by the hotel. I snuck to the other side of the overhang to make sure there weren't more rockets lying in wait. It looked clear. But a person doesn't cruise around town with a battlefield weapon by themselves. A team—two, three—that was more likely.

The overhang was nine feet off the ground.

Jumping makes noise. Noise brings attention. Attention leads to people aiming deadly weapons in your direction.

My elevated heart rate was burning through the oxygen in my lungs faster than I could quietly take it in. Whoever was operating this weapon would see the water taxi as soon as it approached. My friends would be in the crosshairs.

I had one chance. And I had to fully commit to it.

Tensing my muscles, I jumped up, grabbing the tip of the launcher. My goal was to pull it off the roof, which I did, yanking it down with my weight. I also dragged the operator with it. They both landed with a thunderous crash on the metal gangway.

I lunged, hoping to catch the man before he regained his balance. I slammed my shoulder into his chest, knocking him off his feet. He slid down the gangway, making a rata-tat-tat sound.

His hands never came off the weapon.

He rose to his feet. I was several yards away, dead in his sights. He went to fire. The only reason he didn't launch was because the weapon had gotten turned around and was aiming the wrong way. I rushed him as he struggled to flip the launcher in my direction. I got a hand on the RPG, preventing him from pointing it at me. Cyrillic letters were visible on the tube. It was surprisingly light.

The man churned his legs. He was short but powerfully built, and I began to slip on the damp ground. He pushed me under the awning and against the building.

I hit hard.

The metal frame of a window dug into my back, sending a sharp pain through me. A glint of sunlight preceded a blade thrown at my head by a second man. My body instinctively moved out of the way, and I grabbed the bone handle just before it hit the wall behind me. I thrust the knife at the man holding the RPG. He spun to avoid being stabbed in the chest. The cutting-edge sliced the arm of his jacket. I pulled back from my lunge and heaved the blade at the thrower behind me. It all happened in a split second. The sharp tip pierced his right arm, the one I was aiming at. Unfortunately, my attacker was left-handed, which became clear as another blade whizzed my way. It missed wide, pain affecting his aim. He had to suspend his attack to staunch the blood pouring from his wounded arm.

RPG Man slammed into me, knocking the air from my lungs. I struggled to breathe. The startling pain reminded me of the fight in the woods. It felt like I cracked a rib. At the very least, cartilage had torn away from my sternum.

He aimed the RPG at me, determined to fire. This didn't seem like a winning strategy. For any of us. We'd all go up in the blast. All three of us. There was a moment when he abruptly, tangibly realized this. In that hesitation, I charged at him, hoping his self-preservation would bring him to his senses. Instead, I saw his thumb flip the safety switch, and his finger pull the trigger. I flailed, swinging wildly at the launcher, but my reaction was late. The slender explosive blasted out of the cylinder. Thrashing about, I must have grazed the barrel, deflecting it just enough so the munition swooshed past my ribcage, trailing smoke behind it. The knife thrower hit the ground when he saw the missile heading his way. For a second, all three of us watched the path of the warhead, wondering what it would hit. A moment of camaraderie.

The projectile smashed through the back window of an SUV. I closed one eye, waiting for the concussion of the blast. One. Two. Three.

Nothing.

Four. Five. Six.

Still nothing.

I was turning back to RPG Man when a third knife whizzed past my neck just above my shoulder. Knife Thrower came for me, and I rounded with my leg, kicking him in the side of the head. He dropped to the cement, unconscious. Adrenaline surged through me as I realized how close my life had come to ending. But this wasn't the time for existential angst. RPG Man swung the launcher, catching me just above my ear. I staggered from the blow. The RPG-7 was a formidable weapon, apparently, with or without its munition. There was a ringing in my head, like a thousand alarm clocks. Engulfed by nausea, I toppled, the wall of windows catching me before I crumbled to the ground. My mouth found the taste of metal as my lip dragged on the frame, cold, damp, vaguely of seafood. Pain can shut a body down, or it can spur it into action. At first, I couldn't move, then I got angry.

I pressed the launcher against the building with my hip. As the man tried to wrench it free using both hands, I slammed my fist into his unguarded cheek. His head snapped back. He reacted quickly, jamming a hand strike into my windpipe.

"Don't make me do this," I said, my voice barely a squeak from the leopard punch.

He seemed amused by my plea. I felt a pain in my stomach. Not from a punch, but from the sickening feeling of knowing what I had to do. I swung the launcher around and caught him in the chest. I kicked and kicked and kicked until he stumbled against the storage shed a few yards away from the terminal. I smashed his body into the door until it gave and he fell through it. Pails, mops, large bottles of cleaning fluids tumbled down on top of him.

I dragged the other man inside the shed. I taped their hands, ankles, and mouths with duct tape I found hanging on a nail. I wrapped tape around the wound on Knife Thrower's arm, arresting the bleeding.

These were not Elam Khai's men. Incinerating me with an RPG wasn't part of my uncle's plan. My life was not in danger. My body, a few limbs maybe, but my life, I figured I'd get to keep that. These two had no reservations about killing me. And Elam Khai's people didn't give up so easily. These two were mercenaries. Shoddily trained ones at that. But who had hired them?

I looked into their eyes. There was no recognition on their faces. They had no idea who I was. I briefly regretted duct-taping their mouths shut. I wanted to ask, who they were working for? What was their purpose?

I patted them down. Found a few more knives on the one, a cell phone on the other. It was old school like the one I had with me. No GPS, no Wi-Fi, no frills. It didn't even have a passcode. Finally, I came across a sheet folded in quarters. A color photograph printed on plain paper. The image was of a wide-body passenger jet, painted white with a thin, undulating blue stripe forming an elongated sine wave. A logo midway down the fuselage read:

"You were protecting this plane?" I asked Mr. RPG who was the more coherent one at the moment. He wasn't sure how to answer, whether one way or another would keep him alive or get him killed. I moved closer to his ear. "If I wanted you dead, I wouldn't have taped your friend's wound." I asked again, "Were you protecting this plane?"

The one I had knifed in the arm shook his head, no.

My lungs emptied and I didn't breathe in for—I'm not sure how long. I already knew the answer, but I had to ask it anyway. "You were sent to take it down." I pointed at the plane in the photo.

Knife Thrower looked at the other one, then over at me, and then…he nodded. I felt ice rush through my core, as if someone had pumped liquid nitrogen into my heart.

I had thwarted an attack on a jet full of passengers of an airline I'd never heard of.

Looking at the photo again, I noticed many of the windows were filled in. Not a commercial jet. A very expensive private jet.

As I continued to stare at the plane, my vision going out of focus, my eyes crossing...I saw it for just an instant. I blinked, and it was gone. But the image was burned in my mind. The letters of the ONYX logo, the stylized O, the N, the Y, the X, stacked on top of one another, forming the symbol worn by Eternals who had come of age. But I knew this plane didn't belong to just any Eternal. It was owned by a man flirting with the edge, barely restrained in his desire to reveal himself. This was Elam Khai's plane.

Could my father have sent these men? Is that why Elam Khai wanted me? For protection?

No.

We have only one rule. We do not kill each other.

My father wouldn't attack his brother like this. Even if it weren't forbidden, this was cowardly. My father may not be exactly who I thought he was, but he's not a coward.

And then the truth bore down on me.

I had saved Elam Khai. From whom, I didn't know. But I had saved him.

It reminded me of an event that took place in the early years of the twentieth century. Before the First World War, before I embarked on the *Titanic*. Something that still haunts me. I'd been traveling Europe for several months, and on a cold February day, I met a starving young artist on the streets of Vienna. A pale, baby-faced man with a swoop of black hair. He wasn't begging for money or asking for help. He was just sitting on the frozen ground, staring into the distance with piercing eyes. It looked as though he was suffering from exposure, frostbite, and malnutrition, and that he might not survive another night in his threadbare clothes. I bought him some warm food, gave him my coat. It was a simple act.

The artist thanked me. He told me his name was Adolph.

In 1938 as Hitler terrorized Europe, I told the story to a friend at the high school I was attending in Indianapolis. I lied and said it was my father, and that the frail man had given my dad his last name, which the man hadn't done. My friend thought it was the most wonderfully terrible thing he'd ever heard. Years later, that friend became a bestselling author, and he put the story in a novel, having the protagonist's father do what I did. Save Hitler by giving him his coat.

Had I just done it again?

Saved a man who would tear apart the world?

This all might have ended when Elam Khai's plane took off.

Then again, I might've been on the plane by then. A small price to pay.

The shed door was half off its hinges and I dragged it into place, wedging it into the frame to create a tight fit. I picked up the knives and tossed them—plink, plink—into the water.

Leaning on the rail of the gangway, I could just barely make out the water taxi hiding in the darkness. I considered turning and leaving. It would be easier for me to move, easier for me to disappear without them. I had left Braeden behind because he would have slowed our escape. It doesn't matter that he told me to do it. I left. When I could have saved him, could've dragged him to a hospital.

I didn't. And now he was gone. He was my step-brother. One I never got to know. I wouldn't leave Daniel and Phoebe until I knew they and their families were out of danger.

I signaled three long flashes toward the south, letting Nikolay know it was safe to approach.

Safe.

What a relative term.

I waited.

The quiet seemed deafening.

In the distance, two Police helicopters hovered over Beacon Hill. They were joined by a ring of news choppers slowly circling counter-clockwise outside the perimeter. Smoke rose into the night sky beyond the capital. It was pink and orange and looked beautiful, and it disguised the horror below.

A single helicopter hung in the air over Wonderland Park. Two explosions in Boston in one night. Airport security would be on high alert.

After a few moments, the water taxi pulled alongside the floating dock. A lot of banging and swearing followed, all of which echoed loudly in the quiet cove, as Phoebe and Daniel stepped off the boat and rolled the luggage up the ramps, making a clack-clack-clack-clack clatter so thunderous, I had to cover my ears.

I stayed at the top of the gangway. Mostly so I could keep watch, but also because I didn't want to look into Nikolay's eyes.

Daniel handed off the large suitcase to me. "A little anticlimactic, don't you think? No people trying to kidnap you or kill us. Frankly, I'm a bit disappointed."

I nodded. I could swear I heard muffled thumping coming from inside the maintenance shed.

"Alexander?" Phoebe said.

I had zoned out for a moment. "What?"

Phoebe was looking in the direction of Wonderland, toward the hovering helicopter. "I said, do you think the State Police might have caught Elam Khai?"

"I think that's…unlikely." Elam Khai was here, somewhere. With a plane ready to follow us wherever we went. "We're exposed. We need to get behind security as quickly as we can."

I could see the terminals *right there*, three hundred yards away, but it was a convoluted mile-long route to get to there.

Letters stenciled on the glass told us the waiting area didn't open until seven AM on Sundays, which probably meant the buses didn't start running until around then.

A cab pulled out from a driveway to the left, empty except for the driver. I ran out from under the awning, frantically waving my arms, but the car didn't stop. I yelled after it. No use. I swung around in frustration, and that's when I saw—partially blocked by a building—a sea of white taxis.

"This way," I said, pointing toward the cars.

"I don't think they're allowed to pick us up from there," Daniel said. "They've been waiting in line, hoping for a fat fare to Nashua. They're not going to want to take us from here to the terminals."

"I've got two hundred dollars says they will."

"Why weren't you throwing money around like this when we went out to eat?"

"You never paid for anything. I always paid!"

"True. But we ate at really crappy places."

"I just thought you had an aversion to good food."

"No, I felt guilty you always picked up the check. So, I chose the cheapest places. If I'd known it was nothing for you to throw down a couple of Benjamins for a taxi to take you twenty-five feet, I might've suggested, you know, some nicer establishments."

"We make it to London still breathing, I'll take you out for a thick, juicy steak."

"You are unbelievable, you know that?" Phoebe hit Daniel in the chest.

"I'm sure you can come, too," he said.

"I, literally, can't be around you right now," she said, walking off and leaving him and his stench behind.

The sidewalk abruptly ended. I launched the big suitcase off the curb, jumping it onto the asphalt. The plastic rollers making a racket over the rough surface. We entered the taxi pool through the exit that was guarded diligently by not one, not two, but four DO NOT ENTER signs.

"I don't think we're supposed to go this way," Daniel said, looking up at the signs.

"Seriously? Cause with what's gone on, going the *wrong way* is what we should be afraid of," Phoebe yelled without turning to look back at Daniel.

We were all a little edgy. We'd been up for twenty-four hours straight. And another day was just beginning.

This early on a Sunday morning the gigantic holding lot was less than a quarter full. Even then it was an impressive number of taxis.

I couldn't smell Daniel, which worried me. I glanced back to see he was lagging behind, his stride uncomfortable. I felt sorry for him, but we couldn't slow down.

We crossed the lot. Many of the drivers were standing outside their cars, smoking cigarettes and talking to each other. The cabbies coalesced into small groups. Even though America is a melting pot, the world of taxi drivers is segregated. There were drivers that looked Irish, another group that might be Polish. The Russians were talking to each other as were the guys wearing turbans.

Occasionally someone would breach the divide between the groups and bum a cigarette or a lighter.

We hadn't gotten within fifty feet of the taxis when one of the drivers began shouting at us. "No, no, no, no, no. You can't come in here with that," he said, pointing to our luggage.

"See," Daniel said. He was always a glass-half-empty kind of guy.

"We cannot take you. Go wait for the bus." The man wearing a blue turban had brownish skin and light eyes that were yellow around the pupils. Not a wrinkle on his face, even though he was at least fifty years old. A beard hung down six inches from his chin.

"I will pay two hundred dollars in cash to anyone who will take us to the international terminal. We need to make a flight and don't have time to wait for the shuttle bus."

"We can't do it," the blue-turbaned man said before anyone could bite at the offer.

"Are you too busy drinking your cigarette?" I said, commanding his attention by saying "drinking" instead of "smoking." In Pakistani English, *drinking* is the verb used to describe both vices.

I pulled out my Pakistani passport and waved it in front of him. His eyes widened. As if I had performed some sort of sorcery.

Suddenly, a dozen drivers were shouting that they would take us.

Without a word from me, the law of supply and demand took over with drivers offering to lower their price, a hundred and seventy-five, one-fifty, one-twenty-five, one-ten…until it got down to a hundred dollars.

They were bargaining themselves out of a windfall, and they knew it.

The blue turbaned man put up his hand and stopped the haggling, that, for the record, I wasn't engaging in at all. He stared at me suspiciously, then let out a sigh of resignation. "You have several offers for one hundred," he said, gesturing with his hand for me to choose one of the drivers.

I shook my head. "The price is two hundred dollars."

The man in the blue turban gazed at me. His vehicle was the first in line. This was his fare if he wanted it. He studied me for a long moment. It was a look of wonder and sadness and curiosity. I didn't understand the sadness until he pointed to an older driver among the group. "His family needs the money the most."

"Then I will make it three hundred. But he needs to be fast."

"Be careful what you wish for," the blue-turbaned man said.

Instantly, dozens of hands were grabbing our bags.

The older man tore out from his spot, which was ten cars from the front, tires chirping on the asphalt as he raced straight at us. The vehicle abruptly slid to a stop only a foot from where we were standing. As our bags were swiftly lifted into the trunk, an annoyed taxi control officer waddled toward the commotion. Raspberry from a jelly donut filled the creases around his mouth. He was about to scold the group for a violation of some rule, law, or international treaty when the man in the blue turban cut him off.

I couldn't hear what was said, but the dispatcher wore a dour grimace on his face. "Whatever. Just get him out of here. He's lost his place in line," was all I could make out.

We jumped into the back seat of the taxi, which squealed off before the doors could be closed. Luckily, the force of the acceleration slammed them shut.

The vehicle sped out of the lot, and immediately we were transported not to the international terminal, but to the middle of Islamabad.

The music playing in the car had a slightly whiny Eastern essence to it, but underlying the song was an ancient beat.

I've been to Pakistan and India over the centuries, no matter what name they had at the time or the political climate. I usually travel by myself but make sure to have a host in the area. A friend of someone I know, or the descendants of those I have visited long ago. The hospitality and kindness of the people is legendary. I enjoy the food and the families. That is perhaps the hardest thing for me. Being on my own so much of the time. I find it necessary, even refreshing, to submerge myself in the convoluted drama that comes with a multigenerational family residing under one roof. It's overwhelming at first, but I'm always terribly sad when I have to leave.

If your visit to Pakistan or India consists of getting on a plane and staying in a hotel, seeing sights and eating in restaurants featured in guidebooks, then you are missing the point. Even a tangential acquaintance will provide you with access to the warmth and kindness these places offer. Perhaps, it's like that everywhere to a degree. But there are certain cultures in the world, and this is one of them, where hospitality is a joyful burden. Pakistanis do not think of a visitor as a guest, but as a blessing from God. They don't even call you a guest. They call you "brother" or "sister."

Daniel began moving to the music with a sense of rhythm I didn't know he had. He caught me looking at him.

He yelled over the song. "I like it. Sounds like someone stuffed a goat into an oboe and then stepped on it."

"It's a *shehnai*," I said, shaking my head.

I wanted to forget about Europe. I wanted to take this old man home to his family. Visit his land. And lose myself in its richness and its loving craziness.

My eyes started to well up with tears.

Not from emotion, but from the incense burning in the wooden holder haphazardly stuck into the air vent mixing with Daniel's ripeness. I glanced out the window. The terminals seemed to be getting no closer.

Our driver tried to communicate with us. I know he was speaking English because, occasionally, words would reach into my mind and tickle recognition, but his thick accent and rapid delivery made it nearly impossible to understand him. This much I could decipher: He was very excited about the money. And wanted us to know how grateful he was, listing off the reasons for his gratitude, and all the people he would help with the money. You don't need to understand a word to understand gratitude. I wanted to give him more money just to stop him from speaking, but I feared it might have the opposite effect.

I did catch another ribbon of conversation, which luckily Phoebe didn't understand. "Your wife. She is very beautiful," he said. "I hope she bears you many, many children."

I smiled weakly, glancing in Phoebe's direction. She had a look of terror on her face, which was due to the man's driving rather than his words.

Driving in Pakistan and India is bedlam. Horns are the turn signals of Southeast Asia. That's what you hear, honking, at all hours of the day and night.

Making a right turn. Honk. Changing lanes. Honk. Passing you on the left. Honk-Honk. A car blocking your way even though there are five hundred cars blocking that car. Honk-Honk-Hooooonk.

The man weaved in and out and between vehicles as if they were traffic cones on a slalom course.

As the taxi came to a final, screeching halt and my stomach landed in the front seat, I offered the man the three one hundred-dollar bills with both hands. He took them, in the same manner, with both hands. This was not payment, this was a gift, and I was not vulgar or ill-mannered enough to treat it otherwise.

Both hands. That is the way one gives and receives.

I watched the way he held the cash.

A thought hit me.

Cash.

I turned to Phoebe and Daniel. "We may come under extra scrutiny, using cash to buy our tickets, which is less traceable. So, the ticketing agent might examine our IDs more closely. I want you to be prepared for it."

Phoebe motioned toward Daniel, whose jeans were stained. "Using cash is not our biggest problem."

As Daniel moved to get out, I was once again accosted by the stench.

I offered the man another hundred dollars for the air freshener hanging from the rearview mirror and the stick of incense he had yet to burn.

The man grasped my palms with his rough hands that were so smooth on the back. He would not let go. He thanked me profusely.

I nodded to him, and in Urdu, politely said, "A rich house makes its foolish inhabitants wise."

When he heard me say these words, he went silent and released my hand. He nodded to tell me he understood.

"Khuda Hafiz." I said.

"Khuda Hafiz," he repeated, softly.

May God Protect You.

We grabbed the suitcases from the back before the man could get out of the car to help us. Daniel slammed the trunk. Phoebe, the door. Just before it closed, I could hear the driver still yelling thanks and praises in his rapid Urdu-English. A second later, the taxi had already disappeared around the corner. Back to wait in line. Back to tell the story of three teenagers who gave him four hundred dollars for a two-minute trip.

Glaring at Daniel, Phoebe batted away the air under her nose. "What happened to you? You reek like—!"

"Shhhh," I said.

Daniel had a sheepish expression on his face. His cheeks flushed red. "I pissed in my pants. Then I took a dump in my pants." He shook his head, contemplating his terrible, terrible night. "Then I threw up."

Phoebe grimaced, then marched off, disappearing inside.

"I'm going to have to work with you on talking to…humans in general, but females in particular." I looked at him. "Open sesame," I said, waving my arms.

The glass doors parted before us, and we entered the international terminal.

"Will you stop that?"

"Magic," I said, sweeping my hand in front of his face.

A blast of hot air blew down on me, warming my body. I hadn't realized how cold I was.

Daniel and I stood there, a shared sense of relief. Which lasted only a few seconds before we noticed the intense police presence and beefed-up security. Port Authority cops in their blue uniforms. Dogs with handlers. Black-clad Boston police, wearing heavy gear and toting high-powered assault rifles.

I guess this was supposed to make people feel safer, but I didn't feel safe at the moment.

I never do.

We joined Phoebe who was staring at a monitor showing various live feeds from Beacon Hill and Wonderland Park. Most of the news coverage was focused on Beacon Hill. Crews had brought in emergency lighting; the kind you see on nighttime construction sites. Smoke was still rising from the rubble. The blast area was larger than I expected. The damage, astonishing. Under the bright lights, the aerial shots showed a landscape straight out of a war zone. The visuals were stunning, captivating, terrifying. It was hard to imagine that we had been standing right in the middle of what was now a forty-foot deep crater.

Anyone within the blast radius would not have survived.

"Do you think he got away?" Phoebe asked, thinking the same thing.

"You don't get to be nearly nine thousand years old without being a survivor."

I felt nauseous and had to turn away. It wasn't concern for Engel that had my stomach churning. I really believed what I said. That he'd gotten away. And it wasn't the tragic loss of the historic buildings and original cobblestones on that beautiful street. It was the sight of the rubble itself, the crumbled brick, the colors reduced to a gray-white, as if a dusting of snow had just fallen, all of it transporting me back to Europe and Japan during World War II. Neighborhood after neighborhood of homes and businesses destroyed by bombs that didn't care whether you were young or old, soldier or civilian, friend or foe. Places like Dresden, Hamburg, London, and Hiroshima. I've trudged through rubble in London, moments after a bombing, the smell of explosive still fresh. There was the smoke, of course. But it was the dust that follows a blast, thick and charged like the air after a lightning storm. It sticks to you. Aerosolized concrete and soil, metal and glass and brick, and…and the ashes of the dead.

Choking you, stinging your eyes.

"So, London?" Phoebe said.

I was startled by her words. As if she had reached into my mind. Then I realized she was speaking not about that terrible war, but about our travel plans.

"The Prime Meridian," she added.

Since Braeden relayed my father's words to me, I'd been going over them in my mind.

The key is at the beginning of time.

I fucking hate riddles.

"Doesn't that seem a bit vague?" Daniel asked. "Even assuming the Prime Meridian is what your father is talking about. The Meridian is more than Greenwich in London. I have a globe I got for my ninth birthday. The year before my parents got divorced. And whenever they would fight, I'd lock myself in my room and draw lines to all the places I wanted to go. Which was far away from them."

Daniel used to go between his mom and dad's, but a couple of years ago his mother moved a few towns away. During the school year, he spent more time at his dad's. His friends were in Great Barrington. He could take the bus to school, and his dad never asked him embarrassing questions about puberty or girls or masturbation like his mom did. When his father did talk to him about these things, it was straight to the point and over with quickly.

I liked Daniel's dad.

You could tell he wanted to talk to his son, be a presence in his life. Sitting around the table having dinner, I could almost hear his father starting a dozen conversations in his head that never made it to his mouth.

I've watched the interaction between parents and kids for a long time, and some adults are just better than others. The dilemma for adults is what are they supposed to tell us? What are they supposed to let us discover for ourselves? My father's had a hundred times the practice.

He still hasn't figured it out.

At least Daniel's dad tried. That's all you can really ask.

"The Meridian runs through England, France, Spain, and then down to Africa. And the last place it touches on the African continent..." He pulled out his passports and held up the red one. "Ghana."

I pushed his hands down so that he wasn't waving three different passports in public.

I pressed my fists into my face, rubbing my eyes. I was exhausted. Daniel reeked. Phoebe was the only one who looked halfway presentable, and she was wearing sweats that didn't match and didn't fit. "He wouldn't make it some random point."

"What if it's not the Meridian?" Phoebe asked.

"Then what is it? The beginning of civilization?" I asked. "The Indus Valley? Mesopotamia? Which are even more vague."

Daniel sighed. "Couldn't he have just given you the GPS coordinates?"

I shook my head. "No. It's a riddle. A word problem to unpack. My father would sit at the table with his head hanging over his soup, not saying a word, and then he'd look up and say something ridiculous like:

I am the beginning of eternity
And the end of time and space
The beginning of every end,
And the end of everyone.

"I would stare at him like an idiot. Because that's all he'd say."

Phoebe was trying to work it out. Daniel was wondering why I was reciting poetry while people were trying to kill us.

"So, no. He wouldn't just give it to me. Not his style. He would encode it. To make me think, but more importantly, to hide it from Elam Khai."

Phoebe was staring absently at the ceiling. "Oh, I get it!" Her face lit up as she realized the answer.

"It's easy once you see it, right?"

"So obvious."

"My father's message won't be that easy."

Daniel didn't want to admit he didn't know the answer. "What are we in kindergarten? So, what? Your father's going to be sitting there waiting for you at the Royal Observatory?"

"I—maybe—I don't know. But it's a starting point. There's always a second level with him. Something we haven't figured out that'll give us a more specific location. Every code has a key."

"The *key* is at the beginning of time," said Phoebe. "The letter T?"

"We already went through this!" Daniel said. "The subway from which I was kidnapped is called the T. 'Tea' is also something you drink. Tea is also what they dumped into the harbor."

"Yeah, I know, I was there."

It just slipped out.

Daniel turned and scowled at me. "You were *there*? At the Boston Tea Party?"

"We didn't call it that."

"I don't care what you called it. Your father knows this?"

I thought of the Scotsman. My father had probably known long before I ever told him.

"I may have mentioned it a few—" Hundred. "—times."

"Are you kidding me? Maybe we're supposed to be in Boston Harbor at the docks."

"The docks aren't in the same place. It's all filled in. It's buildings and office towers now."

"Well, maybe the clue is talking about one of those buildings or a street where the docks used to be. This is information you should've told us."

"Daniel, I can't tell you everything. You'd be dead long before I finished."

As soon as I said it, I regretted it.

"I'm sorry." I meant it, but the damage was done.

No one said anything for a while.

I didn't know where he was, but I knew one thing for certain. "My father isn't in Boston," I said. "I would know it."

Daniel lashed out. "You didn't know your father was Mark Antony. Or that your uncle used to be Alexander the Great."

Phoebe shook her head. "Wait. What?"

"Oh, right, you weren't there for that. Yeah. The guy back at the house, the one who kidnapped me. Alexander the Great."

"Alexander?" she said, confused.

"Not this Alexander, *the* Alexander. The Great! And he wants to destroy the world."

I looked at Phoebe. "Just technology," I added as if that made it okay. "You know, send us back a hundred years." I withered under her gaze.

"A hundred years?"

"Or so."

"Why?" Phoebe said, flatly. "Why would he do that?"

"Tell her why, Alexander the Pretty Good," Daniel said, sharply.

I took in a deep breath.

"Technology—it's making it hard for him and me and my father and the rest of us to do what we've done for thousands of years, go from being one person to the next without leaving behind fingerprints, photographs, DNA. Elam Khai is convinced it's going to catch up with us. That we will be discovered and destroyed. Even if we try to live so quietly and hidden as to not have a real life."

"So, he's planning to do, what?"

I shrugged. "I'm not sure."

"He was pretty clear," Daniel said. "Erase the twentieth century."

"Do you think he's capable of that?"

"You met him. I got the impression if he wants to do something, he probably can. He was Alexander. Augustus Caesar. I'm sure we won't be any happier when we find out who else he's been."

She wrapped herself in her arms, stroking her shoulders, trying to soothe herself. "But…he's afraid of your father."

"Not afraid of him. Afraid he'll stop him. Which tells me my father is already trying to do that."

∞

We stood in front of a bank of flat-screen monitors. Departures on top. Arrivals on the bottom. Only four overseas flights were leaving in the morning. Munich, Rome, London, and Montego Bay.

Daniel sighed. "I take it we're not going to stick our feet in the sand in Montego Bay."

I pretended not to hear him.

"C'mon, Jamaica, mon," he said, affecting his best—the world's worst—Rastafarian accent.

I shook imaginary dreadlocks. "No, mon."

"We've only got a couple of hours before the flight to London," Phoebe said, pointing at the British Airways counter.

"Actually," I began…

Daniel rolled his eyes. "This doesn't sound good."

"I want you to buy tickets to Germany and Rome."

"Not good at all." Daniel glowered at me. "We're not splitting up. The last time we did, things didn't go very well."

"No, they didn't."

"No, they didn't," Daniel repeated, mostly to himself as if reliving the nightmare.

"We *want* to go to London." Phoebe's body was still leaning in the direction of the British Airways counter, waiting for the go ahead.

"But we don't want anyone else to know that," I said.

"I'm assuming these 'anyone elses' are large, sword carrying several-thousand-year-olds," said Daniel.

"No, they're not."

"Are you just lying to make me feel better? Because, you know, your track record on telling me the truth is a little sketchy."

"I'm not lying. Not at this particular moment."

"Then who are these 'anyones?'"

I ignored the question. "We're going to buy three tickets each to three different cities."

"So, you have a plan?" asked Daniel, clearly relieved.

"What do you think?"

Phoebe looked at me. "I think Custer had a plan."

"Custer was an idiot. The man attacked anything and everything. All lion, no fox." I tapped my head. "And like most people who run straight into danger without thinking, he succeeded brilliantly until he failed spectacularly."

"So you *don't* have a plan."

"I have no plan," I admitted, shaking my head. I saw Daniel's expression fall. "But I'm working on one. And three sets of tickets is a start."

The corner of Phoebe's eyes crinkled as she pursed her lips and pushed her mouth towards one side of her face. "I'm worried about my family."

"I know. But the best thing you can do for them right now is to stay away."

She closed her eyes and shook her head, wondering how she'd gotten herself in the middle of this. "I've got to call my parents, Alexander. They'll have the police put a missing person's report out on me if I don't contact them soon."

I glanced at Daniel.

"My parents might wonder in a week or so why there was still food in the fridge."

I blew out a long sigh, imagining what Phoebe's parents must be going through. The fear. The worry. She hadn't shown up at the Homecoming Dance, hadn't come home, hadn't called.

"Okay. Contact your parents."

"And tell them what?" Daniel asked. "That we're okay? Cause I'm pretty sure we're not."

"Tell them whatever you have to in order to keep them from calling the police and drawing attention to themselves. If two kids from Great Barrington go missing, it's going to be easy for Elam Khai to figure out you're the two with me, who your families are, and where they live. Tell them anything. Anything but the truth."

We quickly went over cover stories. For Daniel, it was simple. His parents rarely spoke to each other. And when they did have something to say, they used Daniel as an intermediary. He'd always found this annoying, but now, he was beginning to realize the leverage he'd failed to take advantage of. He told his mother he was staying at his father's because he'd decided to go to Homecoming after all—which made her happy. He called his father and told him his mother was trying to reach him to discuss something. His father said to tell her that whatever it was to have her lawyer talk to his lawyer. The two calls took less than a minute combined.

Phoebe's single phone call was much longer and more complicated.

She stared at the contact page on her phone with her mom's photo for at least a minute, her finger hovering shakily over the screen as if touching the number could kill the person on the other end. She finally initiated the call.

Her legs twitched incessantly while she waited for the call to connect. I heard a woman's voice say, "Hello?"

"Mom? It's me." She listened for a moment, squeezing her eyes shut against the barrage of questions and recriminations. "Mom,

I'm okay. Honest. I know you were worried. I'm sorry. I didn't mean to upset you. I need you to do something for me. I'm not going to be home today. No, I'm not with Craig. I know. I'm sure he's upset about last night. No, he didn't do anything wrong. No, it's not because he clucked like a chicken. Honest. Mom? Do you trust me?" Phoebe seemed relieved by the answer. "Remember when I got lost in the mall when I was five? You were so scared. I'd never seen that look on your face. But remember what happened? Right. I did. Well, I need you to trust me right now. *Really* trust me. It's important. If anyone asks, even Craig, I'm visiting grandma, okay?" She waited, listening, her eyes filling with tears. "I don't care who asks. That's where I am. Okay? It's very important you do this for me. I know, Mom. I always find my way home, okay? I will. I love you, too."

Phoebe hung up the phone, visibly shaken. I held out my hand, but not to comfort her. She placed her phone in my palm.

"She okay?"

"She trusts me."

I nodded. I was touched by that. It made me want to meet her mom.

"I don't know what the hell she's going to tell my father."

With the calls out of the way, I went into the phone's settings and wiped the data.

"You know," Phoebe said, "Look at it like this…we're going to get to go to one of these three incredible cities."

"Where we will probably die," added Daniel.

A maintenance worker was talking to the young woman at the flower stand. As the two flirted awkwardly, I dropped our phones into his mop bucket of dirty gray-brown water, instantly frying their circuits.

We pooled our passports so that instead of having our own, we each had one set from a particular country.

"I think we should save the Pakistani passports."

Daniel opened the Pakistani passport and stared at his photo.

"I've never had a passport before, now I have four of them." He squinted. "It looks like little swords and fishing hooks and commas are fighting each other."

"That's Urdu, and this here is Arabic." I pointed to the different translations. Urdu, Arabic, English, and French. "We're going to burn one set of identities, which one I don't know yet. The Pakistani papers are very useful in some parts of the world." I glanced at Daniel. "Places where the words look like swords and fishing hooks and commas," I said sarcastically.

"Don't be too hard on him. His family's like hundredth generation Pilgrim or something."

Phoebe's coloring was darker. Mediterranean, maybe. Amara. It was one of those last names that could be from anywhere.

I pulled out eighteen thousand dollars from the stash in my backpack, trying to be as inconspicuous as possible. As inconspicuous as a teenager can be with stacks of cash.

"I keep thinking about how much money we left behind at your house," he said as I handed him a third of the money.

"I'll have access to more once we hit Europe."

He blew out a sigh staring at the bills. "I really wish we had eaten better meals."

"There's been times I've had to steal—just to eat."

Phoebe studied me. "Really?"

"Yeah."

It's easy to imagine what hunger does to the body. It's more difficult to explain to someone who's never experienced famine or malnourishment what it does to the brain. Long after I had enough to eat, I'd find myself obsessing over food. Hoarding it.

I handed Phoebe six thousand dollars, reminding myself that I had enough. Money. Food. Everything.

"But even when I was starving, the most frustrating part, and maybe the part that saved me, was that I had all the wealth I needed. I just had to survive long enough to get back to it. That's a motivation to survive that a lot of others didn't have."

I glanced at the rest of the money in the backpack as I zipped it up. The phantom pains in my stomach subsided. The need melted away.

"Still, all the money in the world won't stop a sword from lopping off your head."

"You are just a pocket full of sunshine," Daniel said.

Phoebe put her arms on our shoulders. "Well, I've always wanted to go to Rome. So, I may just fly there myself and leave you two behind." She playfully messed my hair before heading toward the ticket counter.

"And I've always wanted to be abused by East German border guards," said Daniel.

"You know, there's no such thing as East Germany anymore, right?" I said, not even bothering to mention that the flight was going to Munich, not Berlin.

His body slumped. "I know," he said, annoyed. "My entire life I wanted to go through one of those checkpoints, feel the fear, experience the tension, the adrenaline rush—"

"—the strip search."

"—and now I can't."

"You never could! The Berlin Wall came down before you were born!"

"It's not fair, is all I'm saying."

"Yes, I'm sure the Germans living in the GDR would've gladly endured another few decades of oppressive totalitarian government just so you could enjoy sampling their torment for a couple of hours."

"I suppose you got to cross?" he said.

"A few times," I said, remembering the first time in 1948, escaping Soviet-occupied Warsaw and Poland through East Germany. A time when it wasn't just an inconvenient, unnerving walk across the death strip between East and West Berlin, between freedom and oppression, but a dangerous run that at least a hundred people had been shot dead attempting. "It was always tense."

Daniel glared at me. "You suck, you know that?"

"What did I do?"

"Everything!" He glanced away as he spoke, as if the words hurt to say. "You've done literally everything. I'm so fucking envious. And it's not just because of the sports or that girls are always talking about you—" I started to ask him who was talking about me, but he put up his hand. "Don't even *ask* the question you're thinking of asking."

"I'm trying to live as low-key a life as possible. To not stick out."

"But you do!" He tried to find the words. "It's like, I'm happy for you, but then I'm not happy because I start thinking about myself. Being around you used to make me feel good. I had this great friend who I got along with who was fun and smart and interesting. Now, being around you makes my life seem insignificant and mundane and…" He paused. "…brief."

"So, you can't be my friend anymore because I'm different?"

"You're not different. You're better."

"I'm not better. I just have more practice."

"I like being your friend, Alexander. But I wonder how you look at us. What you said before, about it taking a lifetime to tell me everything. Is that how you see us? Something that comes into your life and leaves after a short time. Like a gerbil or a goldfish?"

"You're not a goldfish, Daniel."

Annoyed, he pursed his lips, sucking in his cheeks, which made him look a little like…a goldfish.

"I don't know if this will make you feel any better," I said, "but you're one of the nicest people I've ever met."

He stopped making his fish face, and the sides of his mouth curled down. "You couldn't have said 'coolest' or 'handsomest' or 'most awesome?'"

"Do you want me to lie? Or do you want me to be real?"

It took him a moment before answering. "I want you to lie." He glanced away, then back at me. "I want you to tell me I'm amazing. That I'm the best friend you ever had. I want you to tell me that everything is going to be okay."

"Everything's going to be okay," I said. Even though I'm not sure either one of us believed it. "I could have taken off. But I went to find you. Because you *are* my friend."

"I know." He swallowed as if something was stuck in his throat. "Thank you."

"That was hard to say, wasn't it?"

"So fucking hard."

"You know what the hard thing for me is?"

"You'll forgive me if I don't feel sorry for whatever this hard thing you have to deal with is."

"It's…always putting up walls. Not being able to tell the people closest to me who I really am. I don't think you can understand how alone that can make you feel. Being able to be honest with you and Phoebe, it reminds me just how much I hate that part. I haven't had many people in my life I could tell everything to. It means a lot to me. I really appreciate that."

"To be honest…" Daniel's face tightened. "I really appreciated not knowing."

∞

The young woman with the pleasant British accent wasn't surprised that I was at the airport trying to book three people on a flight only a couple of hours before departure using cash, which surprised me.

I checked the big suitcase.

A surreal moment took place as I showed her the three Ghanian passports at the same instant Phoebe was showing our American passports two stations over.

"Pretty girl," the woman said, looking at Phoebe's photo.

I could see that pretty girl in my peripheral vision less than ten feet away. "Yes, she is."

- THREE -
Sometimes...The Pencil Is Mightier Than The Sword

I meant it. About Daniel being one of the nicest people I've ever met.

He talked to everyone in school, no matter if they were from the cool set, the geeks, the stoners, the gearheads, the invisibles, always making people laugh. But ever since Engel's, Daniel had been sullen.

It was the knowing.

He thought everything came easy for me. And maybe that's the way it looked to the outside world, but he didn't see the years, the centuries of work I've put in.

It takes a lot of effort to appear effortless.

Telling him that, of course, would only make it worse.

Standing in the terminal, I appeared relaxed and under control, but I could feel the sweat dripping from my armpits. Nothing alerts security like a guy sweating through his shirt in the middle of winter. Phoebe, on the other hand, looked completely composed.

"You were steady up there," I said as we met outside security.

"I just kept thinking, what's the worse that could happen? We get caught and arrested for stealing a car, smashing through a house, driving without a license, get strip searched and thrown in jail? Seems a lot less dangerous than what we've dealt with so far."

"Still, you were like bank robber cool."

"I'm more a jewel thief."

I arched my eyebrow at her. "Really?"

She cringed a bit, the embarrassment hiding a morsel of pride. "Yeah. You're not the only one with secrets."

"I don't think secrets get any bigger than the one you know about me, so…" I motioned for her to spill it.

"Well, I—I used to be a klepto." She lowered her gaze. "I sort of was very good at it. Until I got caught."

I opened my mouth to say something when Daniel came skulking over. He was holding out what looked to be about seven dollars in change. He handed me the crumpled bills.

"What's the problem?"

"You mean, other than spending two thousand dollars apiece for our tickets?"

"That's what happens when you buy tickets on the day you're flying."

"Right, I forgot to put *Get kidnapped, tortured, and killed* on my calendar this week." He waved his arms in a grand gesture.

Every time Daniel moved, Phoebe covered her nose.

"There's nothing in the luggage he can change into?" she asked, her tone nasal. She grimaced as she held down whatever was threatening to evacuate her stomach.

I unzipped the edge of the bag and peered inside. "It's all ridiculously big."

"It can't look more ridiculous than he smells."

Just to prove her wrong, Daniel pulled out what looked like a packed canvas tent. He unfurled the tent, revealing it to be a pair of khaki pants. The legs unrolled on the smooth floor until they reached Phoebe's feet.

"Maybe with a belt?" she said.

"He needs to clean up before he puts anything on. There's a club with showers on the other side of security."

"We aren't going to get him *through* security smelling like that."

I held up the pine air freshener.

"What are you planning on doing with that?" Daniel asked.

"Sticking it down your pants," said Phoebe.

"I'm not putting that crap in my pants."

I gave him a look.

His face flushed with contempt. "Hhhhhaaaaaaaaa, I already have crap in my pants, I get it. Hysterical. So *funny*. Do you…have any idea how terrifying that was? They drugged me. Beat me. They nearly killed me. It's not funny."

"It's a little funny," I said, motioning to his pants. "*Now*. That, you know, you're okay."

"You should give him the incense, too," Phoebe said.

I shook my head. "People smuggling drugs use it to cover the scent. It's not worth the risk of getting marked for closer inspection." I held the air freshener out toward Daniel. "Rub this all over the outside of your clothes."

Daniel reluctantly took the tree-shaped piece of scented cardboard.

"And don't make that face. It does not smell worse than you do."

"Who came up with this?" Daniel asked while rubbing the cardboard against his jeans. "I mean, I can understand Spring Meadow or Summer Rain or Ice Cream Sundae, or even an air freshener that makes your car smells like burgers and fries. But a tree? Who wants a car that smells like a tree? What am I, a beaver?" He moved on to his shirt, transferring the intensely sweet, slightly synthetic scent to his sleeves and torso. The friction of his rubbing sounded like a DJ at a dance club scratching a record.

"I still don't understand why we have three sets of tickets in nine names to three cities," Phoebe said.

"Because…" I said as I reached out and preemptively pinched Daniel's earlobe. "We are being watched."

I could feel the tug on my fingers as Daniel tried to turn his head to look around.

Phoebe wanted to, but she restrained herself. "Here?"

I nodded.

She casually studied the architectural features of the terminal. The high ceiling, the floor patterns. But I knew what she was *seeing*.

Every corporate road warrior, every college student heading home for the holidays looked like an enemy.

I scanned the faces, narrowing the possibles to those wearing earbuds, since I didn't see any traditional com earpieces that would've been a dead giveaway.

Eye contact with one—two—three—four—five people. A girl, eighteen or nineteen. Rollerbag. A guy in his twenties wearing a small backpack over his right shoulder. A businesswoman, drinking coffee. Roller. Businessman. Small carryon, no wheels. Another man in a suit. No bag. Black gloves.

The girl. Hopefully, she just thought I was cute.

Twentysomething guy. Fit. A track star or private contractor.

Woman with the coffee. Not likely. PMCs don't like extraneous items in their hands.

Businessman. His bag without wheels made me nervous. It looked like something you'd grab if you hadn't planned ahead.

The other man in the suit. No bag. Gloves. Prime candidate.

My eyes swept the terminal again, but this time, instead of seeing targets, I saw weapons.

A fire extinguisher grabbed by the hose and swung around would make a deadly mace. The stanchions at security, a good quarterstaff or battering-ram.

At the newsstand:

Magazines, tape, belt: *Nunchucks.*

Umbrella, condoms, hair ties, tape: *Rudimentary crossbow.*

Umbrella, Q-tips: *Blowgun.*

Umbrella, nail file, tape: *Spear.*

Umbrella: *Club.*

You get the idea. Umbrellas are useful for a lot more than keeping dry.

Black Gloves greeted a traveler leaving the secured area of the terminal. He took the man's bags and they exited to the curb. Okay. Just a driver. One down.

That left Twentysomething with the backpack and Business Man.

We also needed to draw attention away from Daniel.

A handler led a dog casually through the crowd. I could tell by the collar tag it was a drug sniffer.

Drugs. Maybe it was that simple.

"Stay here. I'll be right back." I darted away so quickly Phoebe and Daniel didn't have a chance to respond.

I reached the newsstand and grabbed a half dozen packets of aspirin off the rack in front of the register.

"Bad headache?" the man working the kiosk asked.

I nodded. "The worst."

I didn't mention it would be someone else's headache.

"Anything else?"

I started to pay, then said, "Let me have one of those umbrellas and a box of Q-tips."

The man working the kiosk gave me a sideways glance. Now, I was someone with a headache and a lot of ear wax who expected a rainstorm on a clear November day.

I paid in cash and while he made change, I tore free two umbrella ribs and tied tufts of cotton from the Q-tips to the end of each. The clerk came back and saw the half-detached ribs. "Is that defective?" he asked.

"No, it's perfect." I pocketed the change, then began crushing the aspirin pills inside their little packets.

"Anything else I can get you," said a voice I hadn't heard before, exaggeratedly mimicking the languid speaking pattern of the clerk. All I could see of the speaker were the large black gloves resting on a tray of ridiculously oversized Boston-themed pencils. How could I be so stupid? Classic deception. They'd gone out and came back in behind me. "There is a gun aimed at the girl right now," Black Gloves said.

I glanced over at the man I thought Black Gloves was picking up. He was standing a few paces from Phoebe and Daniel, a coat over his forearm, probably hiding a gun. Our eyes met. The traveler appeared bored, which was more unnerving somehow. He lazily looked away.

"All we want is you."

"Yeah, so I keep hearing."

"Don't make this difficult and the others are free to leave."

I wondered if these guns-for-hire knew Elam Khai's plan would they still think their paychecks were worth it?

Phoebe and Daniel were having an animated conversation, oblivious to the danger three feet behind them. Part of me was jealous of their ignorance.

These people were hired to deliver a package. Me. There was a good chance if I went with them they'd leave Phoebe and Daniel alone.

I started walking toward the exit.

"Smart choice," Black Gloves said.

"Not for you."

Black Gloves didn't react. He was a professional. Still, it cost me nothing to try and rattle him.

"You have no idea what you're dealing with. Ask me how I know that?"

"I know what I need to know."

"No, you don't. Because you'd be a lot more worried if you knew what this was really about. You ever stop to think why they sent so many people to catch one teenager?"

I expected his reaction to betray that there were others in the terminal. But he gave nothing away.

I pressed on. "No matter how much money you've been promised, it won't be enough for what's coming."

Black Gloves smiled. "You have no idea what I've been promised."

He grabbed my arm. And that was when I stabbed him with one of the oversized Boston pencils from the Lucite case. The pencil went into his hand. So deep, I could feel the tip of the graphite pricking my skin. The gun dropped to the floor, and I instantly kicked it under a display before anyone could see it. The pain froze him. In that brief pause, I jabbed him in the Adam's apple. As he gasped for breath, I broke off the handle of the umbrella, ripped the main shaft free from the fabric top, slid one of the ribs I'd pulled off earlier into the shaft with the cotton side closest to my mouth, then lifted the tube to my lips.

I swung around and blew into the cylinder. As hard as I could.

The metal rib streaked toward the man training a gun on Phoebe and Daniel. I twisted the pencil as I watched the umbrella dart punch through the right side of the traveler's chest until only the tuft of cotton was visible. The traveler gasped for air, staggering away from my friends until he stumbled into a row of seats.

I collared Black Glove as he tried to staunch the flow of blood with his other hand. I spoke into his ear. "You tell him, if he wants me, he's going to have to come get me himself."

I gave the pencil one more turn and Black Glove finally surrendered to the pain with a guttural moan.

The twisting pencil wrenched the leather, revealing Black Glove's wrist. And the two triangles tattooed on his forearm. It was identical to the mark on Mrs. Dunn's wrist—point to point like an angular hourglass. I felt an unexpected rush of panic.

He pulled away, covering the symbol, fire in his eyes. He was about to say something when he touched his ear reflexively. I ripped out his earbuds, pulling the slender phone along with the cord. I glanced at the screen. It was running some custom app I'd never seen before.

He slammed his fist into my jaw, smearing my face with blood.

I slammed *my* fist into the pencil, sending another wave of pain through his body.

He didn't make a sound.

I stuffed the phone in my pocket. "I suggest you get you and your friend to a hospital. That's in your palmer artery. They like to bleed until you run dry. And your friend, I'm guessing his lung is about to collapse."

He stared at me, defiant. But he knew I was right. His look said, *until we meet again.* He headed toward his companion. I popped in the earbuds as I rushed to Phoebe and Daniel.

"We need to move now," I said, pushing them roughly toward the security line.

"What's going on?"

I heard chatter in my ear. "Targets located. Abandon all positions and converge on International Terminal. Communications compromised. Switch com set to Bravo Two. Bravo Two." And then the communication went dead.

"Just move."

Phoebe understood my rudeness meant danger.

Once in the security line, I pulled out the Ziploc bag containing the liquids that the owners of our purloined luggage had packed. I dumped the miniature bottles of shampoo, conditioner, hair gel, body spray, and mouthwash into a trash can. I emptied the packets of crushed aspirin into the baggie.

"What is that?" Phoebe said, pointing to the white powder.

Acetic acid is the dominant odor signature of heroin. It's what alerts a drug-sniffing dog to the possibility of illegal narcotics. It also happens to be a principal scent component of aspirin.

"Trouble," I said.

The trick was planting the baggie without getting caught. First, I had to decide who was going to get a few hours of TSA scrutiny.

That's when Twentysomething with the backpack quietly pushed his way closer to us in the security line.

"We've got just over an hour. That's including you getting cleaned up and Phoebe and I finding clothes for you." I checked the times of the three flights. The sequencing was good. "We use the Munich tickets." I leaned in and whispered to Daniel, "Just pretend these are East German border guards who will lock us up and imperil our lives if you screw up."

This…actually made Daniel happy.

Reaching the podium, Phoebe handed the TSA agent her boarding pass and passport. Her twitching leg betrayed her nervousness, but Engel's work was impeccable. Just an anxious traveler.

I thought of my old friend. I was sure he'd gotten away. You don't live nine thousand years without having a ridiculous number of back up plans. The other reason I believed he was alive was...I needed him to be. I didn't have anyone else in the world I trusted as much as him. Not even my father.

I had so many questions. Someone was *going* to answer them.

The agent shined a UV flashlight over Phoebe's passport, revealing a holographic seal. He glanced up from the photo to her face, then back down again, scribbled something indecipherable onto the boarding pass, and handed both back to her. "Have a good flight. Next."

Daniel stepped forward and the process was repeated. After marking his boarding pass, the man waived Daniel through, scrutinizing Daniel's clothing for a moment as he moved on. The agent smiled and shook his head. "Next."

I approached the podium.

I've done this hundreds of times since IDs were required to fly, but I was on guard, hyperaware, and anxious. I slowed my breathing. This man is not my enemy. His only job is to make sure that the name on the boarding pass matches the name on the identification and that the photo on the identification matches the person standing before him. He slid my boarding pass under the barcode reader. It beeped once. He checked my face against the photo, made his scribble, and returned the documents, motioning me toward the screening area.

"Have a good flight. Next."

Twentysomething with the backpack slowly, methodically moved up until he was only two people behind us.

With my focus on Twentysomething, I got to the stainless steel table sooner than I was expecting. Suddenly, I was peeling off clothes as fast as I could. Others around me were doing the same as if we were in some kind of strange race, shedding coats, hats, scarves, sweaters, mittens, belts, and shoes. I grabbed two gray bins, removed the grease-covered sneakers and placed them in one bin. I took off my belt and my coat. Put them in the other bin.

The drug-sniffing dog paced between our line and the one adjacent to it. Twentysomething was just reaching the table.

I emptied my pockets. Found the phone I'd taken off Black Gloves, the few dollars of cash Daniel had given back and—

—my butterfly knife.

I swore under my breath.

Phoebe and Daniel pushed their bags forward. My stuff was almost at the mouth of the x-ray machine. The dog tracked back and forth, its paws tick-tick-ticking on the smooth floor. A TSA agent waved the person in front of me into the millimeter wave scanner. I was next. That feeling of fire and ice again, fighting in my stomach. I had to stay calm. I went back for another empty bin. I wiped the handle of my butterfly knife clean using the inside of my pocket. Lifting the bin over several heads, I knocked the edge of the tray into Twentysomething's skull, and while apologizing, slid the knife into his back pocket. I didn't bother sneaking it in. I was deliberate. He knew he'd been made.

But he hadn't noticed me slip the aspirin baggie and the incense into his backpack.

The dog passed by Twentysomething's bag three or four times without getting a hit. I raced back and dropped the rest of my items into the third bin. Daniel was so transfixed by worry, Phoebe had to jab him in the arm to remind him to take off his shoes.

Twentysomething glared daggers as he pulled a brown lunch bag from his backpack. A hand went into his pocket. I barely saw it, but he secreted the knife into the bag, then handed it to a TSA agent, asking her to toss it out for him.

She threw it in the trash.

I felt my stomach sink. It looked like I would have to deal with him on the other side.

That's when the dog suddenly stopped pacing and sat down in front of Twentysomething's backpack. Instantly, I was seized with the feeling that I had made a terrible error. Even if everything played out as planned, TSA might lock down security and let no one through.

Movies give people the impression that a dog finding a bomb or drugs will start frantically barking to get its handler's attention. This makes the scene exciting as the dog's howling shatters the calmness.

Cue the dramatic music. And the audience wonders:

Where is the bomb?

Who has the drugs?

Reality is quite different.

The German Shepherd sat calmly, its tail swishing slowly, its right paw resting inches away from the backpack, eyes never leaving the bag.

Immediately, the handler asked Twentysomething, "Is this your bag?"

Twentysomething nodded, then said something I couldn't hear.

"Chemical check! E-three," the handler said into a mic clipped to his shirt. "Sir, please step away from the bag. Are you carrying any weapons or toxic material?" The handler's palm rested on the grip of the pistol holstered on his hip. Twentysomething glanced at me. "I—I'm not sure."

The crowd sensing danger quickly grew anxious.

"Yes or no. Are you carrying any weapons or toxic material?"

"I'm a private security consultant hired by a news organization testing airport security," Twentysomething said with his hands outstretched, making no quick movements. "I have ID in my wallet. I'm not sure what I'm carrying."

Smart cover story.

"Everyone, please step back," said the TSA agent who now had his gun drawn but down at his side. "Sir, stand where you are, and keep your hands where I can see them."

"No problem," Twentysomething said, his eyes looking off into nowhere, even though it felt he was staring at me in his peripheral vision.

The people closest to Twentysomething backed away, pushing against other travelers behind them.

Seeing the press of humans, the TSA agent directing the line cleared away the board blocking the metal detector normally used for crew and airport workers. We were waved through one at a time, bypassing the millimeter wave scanner that would have surely revealed remnants of an unknown substance in Daniel's pants.

Once we were at a safe distance, Daniel leaned over and whispered, "How did you know that would work?"

"I didn't."

Daniel stared blankly at me, chewing the inside of his cheek.

- FOUR -
Two Wrights Can Make A Wrong

There were three airport lounges in the international terminal. Only one had showers.

Phoebe and I stayed with Daniel until he got checked in.

"You're coming right back?"

"Right back," I said.

"Right right back?"

"Pretty much right back…if you let us go."

We were not right back.

There were way more clothing choices than I remembered. Shirts were easy. There were hundreds of options, t-shirts, sweat-shirts, polos, but finding pants that weren't Red Sox or Bruins or Patriots pajamas that was harder. The only place with real pants was a menswear shop.

"This is perfect," Phoebe said. "One store with everything."

And before I could say, "Help me pick out something," Phoebe had grabbed some cash and disappeared.

Fourteen minutes later, she returned, finding me two feet from where she'd left me. She'd exchanged the mismatched sweats for a pair of black leggings under a grey cashmere mini dress, riding boots with a scarf and a long sweater over the top.

"Wow," I said both to the change in her appearance and how quickly it had happened.

I hadn't picked out a shirt yet.

I tried not to seem like I was staring, which I totally was. She looked fresher, more awake. Had she bought make-up, too?

I caught my reflection in a mirror and realized I looked like Daniel smelled. Maybe worse.

Phoebe's arrival streamlined the process.

I put on the new shirt and shoes, dumping the greasy sneakers in the trash.

Daniel stared in the mirror as if he'd just woken up with amnesia and had no idea who he was, repackaged in a suit and leather shoes.

"I look like an idiot."

"You look great," Phoebe said when we rejoined her.

And he did. Like some young up and coming actor in the pages of GQ. Daniel's features took on a refined ruggedness when covered by day-old stubble.

"Perfect...I won't have to change for my funeral."

"Actually, you might look at little too good," Phoebe added. "You wanna go for spoiled private school kid. Here. Unbutton the collar. Undo your laces. And act like everyone's beneath you," she said.

"Easy. I'll just act like your boyfriend."

At the mention of Craig Coulter, Phoebe's cheeks reddened. Her compliment had been sincere. She had been loosening his tie to help him pull off the look, but now she tightened it until his face turned crimson. She stormed off, leaving him struggling to breathe.

"You know," I said, slackening the strangling necktie, "You can be tad bit unpleasant when you've been abducted and chained to a metal fence all night."

"Don't forget the drugging."

"I haven't forgot the drugging."

When I said I didn't have a plan, I meant to say, I didn't have a good plan. If this were the 1970s, I could've hijacked a plane, no problem. Hijacking a plane back then was like hailing a cab. I wouldn't even need a pilot. I could fly any of these jets—except the new superjumbos. I have a commercial fixed-wing pilot license with full instrument rating, and I've logged more than five thousand hours of flight time on multi-engine aircraft. Of course, the license is in a name I used six identities ago, faking my age so that I was the youngest-looking twenty-one-year-old in the world, but that's beside the point.

It was the one flashy, out-of-the-box thing I got my father to agree to. I started formal lessons in the 1960s, even though I'd been flying since, well, pretty much since people had been flying.

I was eating dinner at a friend's house in 1901 when his father began telling this story of a man who thought he was a bird.

My friend's father had sold the man—named Gustave Whitehead—some machining tools and installed them in the bottom floor apartment Whitehead was renting.

Gustave was a dreamer, an inventor, and he'd been bitten by a bug that had infected many before him. People have been dreaming of flight for thousands of years. I've been fascinated by it ever since I stumbled upon Leonardo da Vinci's drawings of his ornithopter—basically a wing-flapping device. Leonardo was one of the most brilliant people I've ever met. He was also one of the craziest. He would wake up in the middle of the night with fully formed ideas that he'd put to paper. Concepts and designs centuries ahead of their time, that had they been built while he was alive, would have accelerated the development of technology and changed the course of history.

I never told Leonardo about my true nature, not because I didn't think he'd believe me, but because I feared he would…then proceed to immediately cut into my skull to find out why I was the way I was.

I mentioned Leonardo's flying machine to my father, and he told me the story of Archytas, a Greek philosopher, mathematician, and general, who constructed a bird-shaped, steam-powered model he called "The Pigeon," which flew nearly two hundred yards on its own.

"Scared the hell out of the villagers," my father said, dryly. Which might be one of the reasons the Tarentines—this colony of Greeks on the heel of the boot of the Italian peninsula—elected him their leader seven years in a row, violating their rule against successive political appointments.

That was in 400 BC.

What I'm saying is, this flying thing has been around for a while.

It didn't take long for me to find Gustave Whitehead. I moved in down the street from his apartment/workshop in Bridgeport. He recruited boys from the neighborhood to help him, and I quickly slipped myself into the cadre of young men including Junius Harworth, Louis Lazay, and Bert and Andy Papp. We received no wages. He didn't even feed us. But the knowledge gained helped many of the boys get good paying jobs later on.

Whitehead was brilliant, disorganized, creative, methodical. He occasionally drew up plans. And almost never took real-time notes on his experiments. Most of his work stayed where it began: in his head.

I've always liked tinkerers and inventors. And over the centuries, I've gravitated toward them. Da Vinci, Revere, Ben Franklin, Marie Curie, Jerome Lemelson, Thomas Edison, Nikola Tesla.

I spent hours helping Whitehead. He never asked me why I didn't have to go home for supper. Why, unlike the other boys, I was never called home because it was time to sleep or do chores. All the things kids with families had to do.

Not once.

It's not that Whitehead didn't care, he just…didn't notice.

Sometimes late at night, he'd look up from his work and wonder where everyone else had gone.

Day after day, night after night, I watched him test his machines in his backyard. The planes were tethered to a stake in the ground that allowed it to spin around and around, gathering speed until it would rise a few feet off the grass. Whitehead numbered his designs. I still have a hardly noticeable scar under my brow from when I was clipped by the wing of No. 20.

It was not long after that I came to meet Orville and Wilbur Wright, the two brothers whose names would become synonymous with the advent of human flight. I knew Whitehead was expecting important visitors, so I made sure to be at the shop that day. The two brothers traveled from Ohio to see Whitehead under the guise of offering to help finance his inventions. They flattered Whitehead. They fawned over him, over his designs.

I stood outside his office, eavesdropping with my ear against the door, palm covering my other ear while the Wright Brothers asked questions and Whitehead answered every one.

"Why do they keep calling him Weisskoft?" Andy Papp asked me.

Startled, I nearly smashed my skull through the frosted glass.

"Jesus, Andy. You can't come up behind people like that," I said, trying to keep my voice down. "That's his name. It's German. Whitehead is Weisskoft."

Maybe Whitehead didn't notice it. But it felt to me like a not-so-subtle dig. He was a foreigner in the eyes of the Wright Brothers. Whitehead's command of English was extraordinary, especially his writing, which was impeccable. His accent, however, bordered on the comical, sounding like a vaudevillian performing an exaggerated Teutonic gargle for laughs.

Hours later, as Whitehead stood at the side gate watching the Wright Brothers drive away, he turned to me and said, "Now zat I hafe given to zem zee secrets of my invenchun, zey vill probably remember everything but zee fact zey promised to finance me."

Which turned out to be precisely what happened.

But Whitehead didn't care. He had a two-year head start on the Wright Brothers. He'd already flown a monoplane a considerable distance in 1899 with Louis Darvarich on board to fire the steam boiler used to turn the propellers. As for what happened after take off, well, that was mostly semi-controlled falling, which ended abruptly when Whitehead—unable to get the monoplane to rise high enough—crashed into a three-story building.

In the quest for manned flight, you've got to stick the landing for it to count.

One of my first tasks was to help repair and modify the steam engine Whitehead had used with Darvarich.

"Bringen zee engine."

We lugged the thing from two streets over. It was in shambles. Dented, twisted, and burned. Whitehead eyed it as if it was the most beautiful woman in the world.

"Maybe if we switched fuel," I said. "Maybe we could salvage it."

"Schteam is the power!"

I shrugged. "Maybe for a train. But I've been studying liquid propellants refined from petroleum. They're much more efficient, producing greater power at a drastically reduced weight." Knowing only enough to be dangerous, I stupidly suggested acetylene, which is inherently unstable and tends to explode under pressure. "There'd be no need to have someone aboard to fire the boiler."

The added weight of a second person was the main reason Whitehead and Darvarich had crashed two years earlier.

Whitehead rose to his feet, his eyes following an invisible something crawling along the ceiling. A look as far away as the clouds above. He finally blinked. "I haffit! I sink vee should be using *liquid* fuel!"

The other boys and I looked at each other.

"That sounds like a great idea," I said without a hint of sarcasm.

Retrofitting the engine for acetylene took time and patience. Testing and tweaking dragged on to the point we were all ready to kill him.

On a humid summer day where it had to be over a hundred degrees in the shop, Whitehead opened the door and screamed, "Za machine ist gohen!"

We would test the monoplane unmanned once more, and if successful, Whitehead would climb into the cockpit and make history.

On the morning of August 14, 1901, shortly after midnight,

Whitehead, Andrew Cellie, James Dickie and a few of us boys took the craft from the shed on Pine Street. Like his previous tests, Whitehead had chosen the hour to attract the least amount of attention. The wings were folded tight to the sides. In the dark, the craft looked like a sleeping bat being rolled down the road on wooden wheels.

At the corner of Fairfield Avenue and Ellsworth Street, just past the Protestant Orphanage, there was a field that ran along a stretch of road at the southern end of Bridgeport.

Whitehead spoke in whispers, causing the rest of us to do the same.

At a few minutes past two, we unfurled the wings. Even though I'd seen it countless times before, on this night, the craft looked like a ghost in the pale glow of the moon.

A wolf howled in the distance, and a shiver ran down my spine.

Two sacks of sand were placed in the cockpit and the now unneeded second seat. Four ropes were tied to the plane so it wouldn't get away from us. Then the giant white bat was wheeled into position.

Whitehead obsessively went over every detail, worried he was going to forget something.

"They're just sandbags," Harworth said.

"It iz not zee sandbags I am vorried about." Whitehead patted his machine gently. When even he realized he was stalling, he gestured for us to start the engines.

In the stillness of the night, the sudden sound was shocking.

The machine slowly rolled over the rough terrain. After less than a hundred yards, Whitehead tugged on a thin line leading to the cockpit, pulling open the throttle. Instantly the monoplane lifted at an angle of about six degrees. The wings rippled as air flowed over them. And the craft looked for all the world like a great white goose as it rose out of the early morning mist.

Those of us holding the ropes tripped over dirt mounds and grass tufts. I thought we might lose the thing, watch it fly off into forever, but Whitehead had set the power to shut off automatically, insuring the machine wouldn't repeat the May 6th test flight debacle where the plane smashed into a grove of chestnut trees at the end of the field. That had set us back three months.

The engines powered down and the air ship settled lightly to the earth, unharmed.

The machine, that is. We were scraped and bruised and cut and bleeding.

After removing the sandbags, we dragged the monoplane back to the other end of the field.

All of us were anxious. Now came the real test.

Two lines were removed, leaving only the ones held by Dickie and Cellie. Whitehead's two most trusted colleagues would make sure he stayed safe.

"You sure you don't vant to fly wiz me?" Gustave said to me as he climbed into No. 21.

You'd think that after hearing Darvarich's fate, after witnessing dozens of his machines slamming into the ground, crashing into trees, shattering into pieces that only a crazy person would want to get in the monoplane with Whitehead. You'd be wrong. I wanted to fly in the worst way. All of us did.

I shook my head. "I appreciate you wanting to reward my hard work, but—"

"You're za lightest one."

"Right," I said. I looked at him. "I'll get to see you do it."

"Not za same."

"No," I said.

Wolf howls transitioned to rooster crows as a blazing sliver of orange appeared in the east.

"You need to run as light as possible." I wanted to go. I wanted to climb in and soar into the clouds. "Less weight. More lift. Less mass, safer if you hit something," I said.

"I vas plannink on not hitting anysing," he said, slapping the side of the craft that looked like a boat or a coffin with butterfly wings.

"That's a good plan. This is your dream. It should be your glory."

"Glory, ha!" he laughed. "Glory ist for za fools."

He gazed into the sky as the sun peeked over the horizon. The light was good. He put out his hand to shake mine.

"We'll shake when you land," I said. "I'll be waiting."

A milkman on his early morning rounds stopped in the road alongside the field to see what was going on. His horse bucked and kicked and nearly ran away when the big white wings of the Condor rippled as Cellie and Dickie checked them.

"If it starts overheating, you put down immediately," I said. "I mean it. And no crashing. It's not like steam. It doesn't scald you. It explodes."

"No crashing." He flipped the starter switch, and I stepped down from the wooden ladder propped against the side of the plane. As two boys took the ladder away, I cranked the one-cylinder ten-horsepower engine while Dickie and Cellie started the two-cylinder twenty-horsepower engine. Whitehead finally let me know everything was good, saluting me by holding up an imaginary mug of beer. His fingers wrapped around the phantom handle, his thumb up. It was a gesture he would make before every flight from then on.

I returned the gesture.

My thumb up.

With a tremendous clunk, Whitehead engaged the wheels, and the monoplane rolled across the field as it had done with the sandbags inside. But this time, the craft held a human in its fragile grasp.

I could feel my esophagus constricting. It was one thing to watch Whitehead send his unmanned inventions tied to a stake round and round into the air. It was quite another to see my friend and mentor board an imitation bird and try to fly like a real one.

"Taking off ist easy," he once told me. "It'ist landing zat ist very, very hard." He chuckled to himself, laughing at his joke.

As the monoplane pulled away, the thing I remember most: the big smile underneath that ridiculous mustache.

The thought that he could die for his passion never crossed his mind. As he sat in that seat, he was the happiest man alive.

The field was close to the water. It was one of the reasons Whitehead chose this spot. Wind coming off Long Island Sound would help lift the plane. Flying into a five mile an hour breeze was the equivalent of adding another ten-horsepower engine. But the air was still and the wind wouldn't pick up until the afternoon. This seemed to me a serious flaw in Whitehead's planning. I understood his desire to keep his work as quiet as possible. Discretion was important, but so was having enough lift.

The plane picked up speed. Cellie and Dickie were running slightly behind the craft, holding the ropes. The rest of us lagged behind, our eyes fixed on Whitehead and his No. 21.

That's when I noticed fuel leaking from the left side. The cap hadn't been properly tightened, and forward momentum was pushing acetylene out the spout, dousing the fabric at the rear of the plane in the flammable liquid. A spark from one of the metal support rods striking a rock, heat from friction, static electricity in the fabric—any of these things could set the plane ablaze.

I gave chase, my feet pounding the uneven ground. I passed Cellie. Then Dickie.

I had to get between the stabilizing wing on the tail and the larger forward wing *and* maintain the same speed as the plane if I wanted to have any chance to cap the flow of acetylene.

Lose ground and I'd tear off the tail. Run too fast and I might stumble into the wing.

All of this was made more difficult by the air flowing over the top of the wing faster than it was below. This is what gives it lift. It also makes it nearly impossible to run without your legs sprinting ahead of you.

Somehow I made it past the tail section without damaging it. Inches separated my fingertips from the fuel cap that dangled from a chain. I stretched my arm, keeping it steady as I was buffeted with wing wash. Another inch.

Something touched my hand.

The cap.

I had it.

A last struggle of effort, and I popped it into place.

Just as the drizzle of fuel was staunched, I tripped, falling under the plane. I stared up to watch the belly of the monoplane pass over me and prepared myself for the pain of the tail whacking my crotch.

But as I lay on my back, waiting, the craft wasn't moving.

Then…sudden terror as I realized I was being dragged along with it! The sleeve of my work shirt had caught on one of the struts. I covered my head with my free hand to protect myself.

I heard Whitehead shout, "I'm gohen to speed za wings! Hold her now!"

Whitehead thrust the lever forward, disengaging power to the road wheels and adding ten horsepower to the propellers. The blades a few feet from my head spun even faster.

The craft rose off the ground. Cellie and Dickie couldn't keep up and released their lines before stumbling into the weeds.

As the ropes fell away, I could feel my body lift off the uneven terrain until only my heels dragged along the grass. A few seconds, and that sensation went away.

We were flying.

Flying.

Whitehead still had to land the plane safely to accomplish his dream. If he could touch down smoothly, he'd be the first person to achieve controlled motorized flight. Flying and then crashing, that had been done numerous times by many, including Whitehead himself. But no one had successfully landed a powered heavier-than-air craft.

And here I was, caught on the bottom, dragging the monoplane down with my weight, altering its balance, destroying the aerodynamics.

We were at least twenty-five feet in the air, which I knew because it was the *exact* height I did not want to fall from. I was facing the tail, watching the earth drift away from me. I twisted my body to get a better look at the new world ahead. That's when I saw: the stand of chestnut trees.

Whitehead had no idea the reason he wasn't rising as quickly as he'd calculated he would was because of the one hundred and twenty-pound counterweight hanging from the belly of his craft.

The milkman was shouting to him, frantically pointing at me, but Whitehead thought the man was cheering him on. He waved to the milkman.

I began screaming, but the engines drowned me out.

We were quickly closing on the same wall of trees that had caused the May 6th crash.

Chestnuts.

They look fluffy. Harmless. The sturdy trunk of an oak can smash open your skull, break your body, but the delicate branches of a chestnut can pierce your lungs, skewer your heart, kill you in a hundred different little ways.

I felt a gust of wind—a breeze!—blowing onshore from the Sound. It lifted the craft. I didn't know if this would be enough to clear the trees. My body tensed as I watched helplessly. Those ten seconds seemed like ten minutes as I tried to will the plane higher. Inch by inch. Until it finally looked like the monoplane might just make it over the treetops.

But...

There was no way I would. At the last second, I took a gamble. I pulled my legs to my chest, hoping my shirt would hold, and tried to make myself as small as possible.

I was stabbed in the thigh by a branch.

I screamed—first in joy, then in pain. We had made it.

That was...

Until I saw what lay ahead: Another clump of chestnuts.

I hate chestnut trees.

The plane was more than forty feet in the air now, which would've been high enough to clear this grove had they not been growing atop a steep knoll. Making matters worse, the breeze died away, and the plane dropped several feet. There would be no getting over these trees with me attached.

I glanced down. Even if I could get free…it was a four-story fall. It might as well be a hundred.

We were going to crash. Not into a building like Whitehead had done before, but into an unforgiving stand of trees that would tear us and No. 21 apart.

I started a mental countdown, adjusting the count as I reassessed distance and closing speed.

Thirty. Twenty-nine. Twenty-eight. Twenty-*nine*. Twenty-eight.

I heard shouts from below. Some of the boys were giving chase. But only Harworth and Bert and Andy Papp were able to keep up. And Harworth was losing ground.

Twenty-five.

"Let go!" Andy Papp yelled.

"I can't."

Harworth's legs finally gave out, and he disappeared from view.

Twenty-two. Twenty-one.

"It's not that far," yelled Bert Papp.

"Are you kidding me?"

"It's okay. I'll catch you."

Now, Bert wasn't a particularly stupid person, but I was fairly confident that even if he *could* catch me, it would turn out badly for both of us. "I would land on you and kill you, Bert. The only reason I *might* survive is because your broken body cushioned my fall."

Bert slowed, his feet thinking better than his brain.

"Even if I wanted to…" I motioned toward my sleeve.

The Papp brothers stared up at me.

Nineteen. Eighteen.

"He can't let go," Andy said. Drowned out by the engines, weakened by exertion and defeat, his voice was barely audible. And then, suddenly, he was screaming at his brother. Saying what, I couldn't tell.

Bert furiously reached for his waist. When his hand came into view, it held a knife. Just about all of the boys carried one.

The blade that Bert produced gleamed in the moonlight.

I stole a glance at the trees. Sixteen. Fifteen.

"Catch!" he said.

"Don't throw the—"

Before the word "knife" could leave my mouth, Bert had already flung it at me, the blade somersaulting in the air, its target somewhere roughly between my eyes. My first instinct was to catch it, but then my brain started working again and I realized that off-balance, hanging from a weaving experimental flying machine, I had little chance of snatching a spinning blade out of the air. I used what little energy I had left to tuck my knees to my chest again, hoping the fetal position might protect me as it had done getting over the trees.

I felt the blade sink into my flesh.

As the stab of pain spread, I pounded my fist into my leg and rolled out a string of profanity that made Bert and Andy—not the most saintly of the group—blush a deep crimson. The blade was sticking halfway to the hilt in the left cheek of my ass. I used my free hand to rip out the blade. Another shout of agony followed.

"I'm going to kill you, Bert Papp! Come under me so I *can* land on you!"

I took another quick peek at the line of trees.

Ten.

It wasn't about flight anymore, or history, or firsts.

Nine.

It was about survival. About saving Whitehead. And hopefully myself.

Eight.

I hesitated, the knife resting against the fabric of my sleeve, the steel tinted with my blood.

Seven.

I didn't want to fall. But If I didn't cut myself free, the monoplane would crash into the trees, dooming us both. Yet, knowing what you have to do and doing what you have to do are two different things.

Six.

The ground has one way to kill you. The chestnut tree, a hundred. I chose the ground.

Five.

I took a deep breath, then sliced through the sleeve of my shirt. For a moment, I hung in the air, the momentum pushing me forward faster than gravity was pulling me down. At least, that's how it felt.

Four.

Whitehead was feet away from the outer branches of the first row of trees. In seconds, they would slash through the wings, tearing them apart. But unburdened of my weight, the monoplane angled up, rising nearly ten feet.

Three.

Still, it wasn't enough to clear the tallest chestnut dead ahead. Whitehead was going to crash. His failure would be my fault.

Two.

And then…

He turned.

He *turned*.

Steering a plane might not seem like a big deal now. But even two years later when Orville Wright took off using a wooden ramp as a launcher, he flew their craft a grand total of one hundred and twenty feet…in a straight line. It would be nearly another year before Wilbur Wright would make what is erroneously considered aviation's first turn.

One turn.

Three years from now.

Whitehead leaned to the right, then the left, maneuvering his bird around the tallest tree.

As gravity began doing its job, I watched Whitehead disappear behind the branches.

Pain.

For some muttonheaded reason, my body crashing to earth came as a shock to me. The grass was high, thick, the ground marshy, and that's what saved me. My clothes were soaked, covered in mud and twigs, and I had stones sticking to my cheek. I found out later I'd broken my collarbone. Only the twenty-third time I'd done that. I probably fractured a few other bones as well, but doctors weren't as thorough in those days.

Bert and Andy were the first to reach me as I lay motionless in the grass.

"He dead?"

"He sure looks dead."

"You dead?" asked Bert, kicking at me with his boot.

"No," I said slowly. "But when I get up, you're going to be."

"He ain't dead!" Bert excitedly slapped me on the back.

"Owwwww!"

"Sorry."

The sound of the engines, which had been fading, grew louder now.

"What is that crazy fool doing?" said Andy.

Whitehead had executed a one hundred and eighty-degree turn and was heading back toward the field.

"Flying," I said.

I got to my feet with Bert and Andy's help. As the plane cleared the first line of trees, I forgot the pain and began sprinting toward the makeshift runway, my feet hardly touching the ground. No one, not the fastest man in the world could have beaten me in that moment. Because like Whitehead, I was flying.

More importantly, Whitehead was about to *land*.

As most people will tell you, the Wright Brothers were the first in flight. So, what went wrong that night in Connecticut?

Whitehead was in sight of the field. He had one more set of trees to traverse, and he'd be safely back to earth.

He'd landed dozens of times in his unmanned tests, controlling his machine by a wire from the ground, which seemed much more difficult than controlling it directly from within the cockpit.

I heard something.

It was a few seconds before I realized what it was—or rather, *wasn't*. The ten-horsepower engine had cut out. He still had the larger engine, but he was losing power. It was obvious from the way the first motor choked to a stop, the acetylene was running low. The loose cap had cost him precious fuel.

The last obstacle to a wide-open field lay just ahead of him.

The trees. Those stupid, stupid chestnut trees.

Since that day, I haven't eaten a chestnut, seen a chestnut, heard a holiday tune singing the praises of roasting chestnuts over an open fire—without thinking of that moment and cursing them.

The engine alternately roared and sputtered as Whitehead opened the throttle. He kicked at the machine, trying to dislodge the last bits of fuel. The plane rose six feet before the other engine cut out. The wooden wheels hit the upper branches, which scraped against the bottom of the ship, but somehow, did not damage the wings.

No. 21 glided past the stand, and a moment later, Whitehead set the monoplane down so gently on the grassy field that his head never bobbled.

Two years, four months, and three days before the Wright Brothers, Gustave Whitehead made the first free, controlled, and sustained flight in a power-driven, heavier-than-air machine. The first person to successfully fly and land a plane.

He climbed down from the cockpit, and I ran at him, throwing my arms around him. The others, Junius Harworth, Bert and Andy Papp, Louis Lazay, Andrew Cellie, and James Dickie were laughing and clapping him on the back, until all of us came together in a scrum, squeezing the breath out of poor Gustave.

On that day, over two demonstration flights, Whitehead traveled more than a mile, nearly five hundred yards of it with me dangling beneath him. In fact, I flew farther than Orville and Wilbur did on their first two flights combined. Six months later, Whitehead took a new version of his design, No. 22, and flew it for seven miles. Not a hundred twenty feet, or even a mile, but seven miles.

And yet, Whitehead has been mostly forgotten in the annals of flight. Part of it was his own fault. He barely ever wrote anything down until much later. But others did. Watching with amusement and awe that August morning was an editor from *The Bridgeport Herald* named Richard Howell.

Four days later, Howell published a detailed account of the midnight journey from the shed to the field and Whitehead's early morning flights. The piece included drawings Howell had made of the plane. Newspapers around the world picked up the story. The Wright Brothers would later use the delay as evidence the event never happened. How could such important news take so long to be reported? The answer was that Howell's account was so detailed, it took him more than two days to write and illustrate the article.

But the main reason for Whitehead's obscurity is the feud between Orville Wright and the Smithsonian Institution. The Smithsonian—showing favoritism to its former leader, Samuel P. Langley—displayed Langley's Aerodrome, calling it the *first heavier-than-air craft "capable" of manned powered flight*, relegating the Wright Brothers' to secondary status, even though both of Langley's manned tests a few weeks before the Wright Brothers' first flights were complete failures.

Orville was so enraged that he refused to donate the restored 1903 Kitty Hawk Flyer to the Smithsonian, and instead loaned it to the London Science Museum.

After more than a decade and a half of pressure from aviation experts including Charles Lindbergh, the Smithsonian finally admitted Langley's plane had never successfully achieved manned flight, and a deal was brokered to bring the Kitty Hawk Flyer back to the United States for display at the Smithsonian. The agreement contained strict conditions that if ever broken, would allow the Kitty Hawk to be reclaimed by the Wright Brothers' heirs in perpetuity. A portion of the agreement reads: *"Neither the Smithsonian Institution or its successors shall publish or permit to be displayed a statement or label in connection with any aircraft or design earlier than the 1903 Wright Aeroplane that claims such aircraft or design was capable of carrying a man under its own power in controlled flight."*

With the stroke of a pen, the Wrights and the Smithsonian made Gustave Whitehead and his monoplane disappear.

"Of course!" I yelled.

Phoebe was startled by my outburst. We were standing in an area equidistant from the three flights we had tickets for. "What is it? You okay?"

"Yeah. Yeah, I'm good. I'm very good." I glanced around the terminal. Thirty-three minutes left. "I know how we're going to get out of here without them seeing us."

"How?"

"I'm going to make a plane disappear."

- FIVE -
David Copperfield Aside, It's Not Easy To Make A Plane Disappear

"I knew it!" Daniel's exclamation started as a shout, then morphed into a whisper. "You're magical, like some wizard or something! You just—" He snapped his fingers. "And it's gone!"

"Enough with the—" I snapped my fingers in Daniel's face. He froze as if he was worried I was trying to make *him* disappear.

Phoebe leaned in. "You're going to make a plane...disappear?"

"Yes," I said. Then I qualified the statement. "For a few seconds."

"C'mon, admit it," Daniel said, poking me. "You got abilities. Supernatural, you know—"

I stared at him.

He faltered. "You know, superpowers."

I eyed him, something dark bubbling up inside me, until he finally stepped back and sat down. I immediately brightened. "Other than my gaze that can make you do whatever I want you to do... None."

He flipped me off.

The plan came together quickly. It wasn't particularly elegant, but it had the virtue of being bold and unexpected. Twenty-eight minutes. I could do this.

I found another one of those newsstand/bookstores/junk food emporiums. This one was bigger than the kiosk by ticketing. It had all the staples a traveler needed. Magazines, books, an assortment of gum, candy, cures for motion sickness and airborne germs, eye masks, neck pillows in various shapes and sizes, from bloated kidneys to pink chihuahuas.

I grabbed two tins of breath mints, two magazines, a miniature crystal Bunker Hill Monument—seriously, do they not realize these are basically medieval spike weapons?—a single-use instant cold pack, nasal spray, disposable razors, hair ties, nail polish, a nail clipper too small for a toddler—thankfully it had a nail file attachment—a Celtics pencil, a Bruins eraser, and a Patriots spyglass.

"Anything else?" asked the cute girl behind the counter with just a touch of sarcasm. She was maybe eighteen, wearing a cream sweater that clung in some places and was loose in others. It hung over a pair of fitted jeans. An oversized watch dangled from a slender wrist. She had an infectious smile and seemed to be enjoying her job.

Not that I noticed.

Now, if somebody had been paying close attention, they might've picked up on the fact that my items, used in a particular combination, could be extremely dangerous. To most people, my purchases would mark me as woefully unprepared for my trip.

But what I asked for next elicited a more curious response.

"How many disposable cameras do you have?"

"I'm not sure. A couple of dozen maybe."

"Can I get—" I hesitated. "All of them?"

"All…all of them?" she asked, her eyebrows disappearing beneath her bangs.

"Whatever you've got."

She didn't make any move toward the cameras, and instead, just stood there, looking at me. Still no sign of her eyebrows, which had retreated further under her hair.

"We're heading to a wedding overseas and—" I really don't have any idea what lie I told her, but it was apparently good enough because she gathered all the cameras hanging on the rack and several more stored in a drawer.

There were twenty-eight in all. Which…might barely be enough.

I paid cash. She started to count out the change.

"Can I get a bunch of pennies? I want to make some of those squished copper souvenirs."

Her cheeks flushed red, and a look of embarrassment washed over her. "I love those. I have a collection. I haven't been many places, but I'm hoping to get more."

"I have a few," I said. Actually, I had a shoebox full of them, but they were back at my place in Stockbridge. I didn't know if I'd ever see any of my stuff from there again. "My favorite is the one from Paris."

"I would *love* seeing Paris. My furthest is only from Washington D.C., but my favorite is the Statue of Liberty."

"Well, the Statue of Liberty was a gift from the French. There're smaller versions all over France, including one overlooking the Seine in a pretty little park at the tip of a manmade island. So, if you've visited the Statue of Liberty, you've walked on a piece of France."

"I never thought of it that way." She glanced down at the cash register. "How many pennies do you want?"

"Do you have an extra roll?"

She looked in the back of the cash drawer. "Sure."

I smiled at her. "Thanks."

I dumped several bills into the glass jar by the register as a tip.

"Thank *you*," she said, surprised. "More people like you, and I'll get to Paris."

"Maybe I'll see you there."

She blushed again. "Maybe."

I walked back to where Phoebe and Daniel were waiting. Phoebe eyed me as I handed her one of the bags. "That salesgirl seemed to be smiling a lot," she said, taking a quick glance in the bag.

I ignored the comment. "Daniel, I need you to take these apart." I pulled a camera from the bag, slipped off the paperboard wrapped around the body and cracked it open. "I only care about this piece," I said, holding up the circuit board that contained the camera's flash and its capacitor. "Keep the wires. And the battery. The rest is garbage."

Daniel broke one open and sent a AA flying. It hit Phoebe in the face. Luckily, she was able to close her eye in time.

"Sorry," he said.

Phoebe nodded as she rubbed her left eye. "I'm sorry I tried to choke you with your tie."

"It's okay. I kind of deserved it."

She reflexively adjusted his collar. "Maybe a little."

I watched them as they struggled through their clumsy effort at détente.

Daniel and I were friends. Me and Phoebe, we were…I don't know what we were, but it was something. But the dynamics we'd lived for almost a year and a half wouldn't work going forward. It couldn't be me and Daniel separate from Phoebe and me. It had to be Phoebe *and* Daniel *and* me.

I didn't want to interrupt this moment of bonding, so I took the items and laid them out on a chair. I ripped open the instant ice pack, careful not to pop the water pouch. After setting aside the water packet, I crushed the small white spheres of ammonium nitrate with the oversized pencil's eraser. I pinched in a few grams of table salt from a packet I had grabbed at the food court.

"This has been really stressful for all of us," Daniel said. "Every once in a while it hits me. My best friend is older than the Magna Carta. Older than Islam. Older than…matches."

"What?" Phoebe said.

"Matches were invented in five-seventy something."

"How do you know this kind of stuff, but don't know the capital of the state right next to yours?" I asked.

"It *should* be New York *City*," he said, emphatically. "And why do I need to know the capital of Wyoming? If I ever go to Wyoming, I'll just ask someone. 'Hey, what's the capital?' I know interesting things."

"Like…that I'm older than matches?"

"Like that it's illegal to hunt camels in Arizona."

I felt my face involuntarily scrunch up. "Empty one of those mint tins for me, will you?"

Daniel handed me the tin after pouring half the contents into his palm and the rest into his mouth.

I began filing pennies with the nail clipper, letting the shavings drop into the tin. I sanded through the thin layer of copper electroplating to get at what I really needed: the zinc core. Filing it into a coarse powder. The tin would separate the zinc from the other compounds for now.

"Hot! Burning hot!" Daniel mumbled through the chewed up mints. "Or burning cold! I can't tell. Owww! Owww!"

Phoebe shook her head. "Really? Are you two?" Their bonding moment was over. "That's what toddlers do. Put things in their mouth without thinking, then get surprised when, oh my God, it's too hot or too cold or they've just eaten sand or dirt or a handful of tacks and it's disgusting or painful and they have to— *Spit it out!*"

Daniel opened his mouth and let the half-dissolved mints fall into his other hand.

I found the pack of disposable razors and pulled the blue plastic head apart until I liberated one of the blades, which I used to cut the barcode from our London boarding passes, slicing the parallel lines so that each barcode was half its original height.

She looked over the items. "I don't get what we're doing."

"You see that guy right over there. And that woman. And that guy. And that guy?" I didn't look up from what I was doing, but subtly gestured with my hand. "They don't have bags. They're not paying attention to the boarding announcements. Not one of them has gone to the bathroom, gotten anything to eat, or played with their phones or even looked at their watches. They aren't flying anywhere."

Phoebe made her scan of the terminal seem natural. "Why haven't they moved on us?"

"They're watching to see which plane we get on so Elam Khai can follow it," said Daniel.

I nodded. "Which is why we have three sets of tickets."

Phoebe looked at me. "Three planes. Three airports. That's not that much harder than one."

"*If* all these planes go to where they're supposed to."

Daniel's head snapped back. "When you say, 'make a plane disappear,' do you mean we're going to hijack it?" He whispered the last part.

"We have to make absolutely sure," I said, "everyone knows *exactly* which plane we're on."

Phoebe's eyes narrowed. "You want to make it easier for him to know what plane we're on?"

"I want to make it impossible for him to not know what plane we're on." I extended the bag of cameras toward Daniel. "Take the rest of these apart."

"How much prison time do you get for hijacking?" he asked as I helped Phoebe to her feet. "What are you two doing?"

"Phoebe's going to help me steal something. Apparently, she's got a talent for this sort of thing."

"Sure. What's a little larceny when you're jacking a plane?"

∞

"Him," I said, nodding toward the man by the British Airways gate. He was at least six foot six, two hundred and eighty pounds.

"Wow. He's big." She tried regulating her breathing.

I put my hand on her back. "He's not one of the ones watching us. He's our mark." He was big. But his size might work in our favor. "So, jewel thief, huh?"

"Complete kleptomaniac."

"But you got caught?"

"Yeah. I got greedy. I used to only take the cheap stuff. But then I stole something of value and got *spanked*."

My expression showed bewilderment. Slang is often jarring for me. She meant *punished*.

"My *mother* gave me the spanking. It was her jewelry I stole."

"Ahhhh. You meant that *literally*."

"I'd sneak into her room every night and take something. I started out picking items from the bottom so she wouldn't notice. Then I got more daring. Finally, I took this piece she never wore. It was always on top, like she picked it up every day and held it. I found out later it was my great-grandmother's. She'd given it to my mom a couple of days before she died. My mom apologized later, but the truth is, I wanted her to catch me. I needed her to set boundaries. It must be hard...not having boundaries."

"I have boundaries," I said, thinking of all the restrictions put on me by my father. "But yeah, restraint is one of the tougher things to learn."

The large man kept touching the left side of his jacket. I'm not half bad at pickpocketing. It's something that over the years has been useful. You never know when your survival might depend on the property of others. Compared to the average person on the street, I might seem like a nimble-fingered con artist. But to a seasoned grifter, I'm more like a second grader who's been given his first book of magic tricks for his birthday.

The inside breast pocket of a sports coat is one of the harder places to pickpocket, especially for someone without a natural talent for thievery. And as I no longer have much need for it in my daily life, I don't get a lot of practice. I've been known to lift a wallet or cell phone off some of my classmates—people like Craig Coulter—and a few of the less pleasant teachers and administrators. I always return the items. Although, not where I took them from. Which makes my marks think they're losing their minds, not just their belongings. Craig cannot seem to figure out how his car keys keep falling out of his pocket and into the urinals at school. It's a mystery.

It's all for the sake of keeping my skills honed, of course.

Our mark was traveling with a daughter of about ten or eleven years of age and a boy perhaps a couple of years younger than that. No wife or mother or girlfriend in sight. Three passes. One pocket.

I was standing behind the man when Phoebe collided with him. As he was knocked back into me, I reached into his jacket. She apologized to him. He apologized to me. But the deed had been done before the first "I'm sorry."

This is why magicians have pretty assistants. Distraction.

Twenty minutes.

I sat in a section of mostly empty seats. Using nail polish, I affixed our barcodes onto the boarding passes I had just lifted, making sure to cover only half the code.

The hardest part was waiting for the polish to dry.

Eighteen minutes and thirty seconds.

Eighteen minutes and twenty seconds.

Eighteen minutes and ten seconds.

"Sir, I think you dropped these," I said moments later.

The man was surprised to see me holding his boarding passes. He instinctively patted his chest, finding his pocket empty.

"Thank you." He shuffled through the three sheets to make sure these were, in fact, his travel documents. "Thank you so much."

Daniel glowered at me from across the gate as he cracked open another camera.

"Can you go help him?" I asked Phoebe.

"Where are you going?"

"To set up the rest of the trick."

I saw a flight crew making their way through the terminal, laughing with each other, nodding to people saying hello, walking in sync, just generally looking like bad-asses in that way that lets you know being a pilot is the greatest job in the world. Pretty much every pilot I've ever known has an unwavering self-confidence. Same with surgeons. And elite Special Forces. And my father. And Elam Khai for that matter.

It's only overconfidence if you can't back it up.

I had to convince the Lufthansa pilots to fly their plane to anywhere but Germany. Not the likeliest of requests to be granted. But then, I can be very persuasive.

The most challenging thing about hypnosis is getting the subject into a state where they are receptive to suggestion. It's called induction. For a hypnotherapist, it's relatively easy, people are coming to them to be hypnotized. Stage hypnotists have a more difficult task. Generally, they're two types of people in the audience: the desperately willing, and the extremely skeptical.

A stage performer has to instantly discern which people to choose to have the best chance of success.

I wouldn't have the luxury of choice.

I'd be dealing with highly trained, extremely self-confident professionals with an embedded set of rigidly defined rituals reinforced by years of practice who had an absolute belief in their ability to remain in control.

My best option was to perform a snap induction, shock a person mentally and physically, opening a brief window of receptability that can be exploited. Enough time to implant a single, simple suggestion. Like go into the restroom. Where I could get them in the handicapped stall and take the time to lead them into a deeper state and install my complex instructions.

Then I got a look at the captain and her first officer.

That ruled out the restroom.

I breathed in, clearing my head as they approached. Okay, I could do this. In my pocket, I charged the capacitor from the disposable camera.

Face to face with the pilots, I set off the flash. The burst of light disoriented them.

There are goats with a hereditary genetic disorder called *myotonia congenita*. When startled, their muscles stiffen, and they fall over as if they'd been flash frozen. It's different in humans, but jolts of stimuli can put so much stress on our system, we overload.

For just an instant.

Like a deer caught in the headlights.

I hit them in the forehead hard with the palms of my hands and gently sat them into seats.

From the flash to the chairs took less than four seconds.

I rattled off instructions, encountering several points of resistance, especially from the pilot. After nearly a minute of trying every circumvention technique I knew, I had to bail out before I could lock them in. I got in barely half of what I needed.

"I'm so sorry," the captain said, popping into a fully conscious state on her own. Her small roller bag was tangled in my backpack. She was in her late thirties, tall, lean, with a bright smile made whiter by the kiss of sun on her cheeks. "I didn't even see you."

"Maybe *I* should be flying today," the first officer joked. He helped me to my feet. "You're a little old, but you've earned them anyway." He offered me a set of wings. Not the plastic versions crews hand out to kids. These were his actual pilot wings. This had been a suggestion of mine, so I'd know if any of my prompting had worked.

"Thanks," I said, holding the metal wings at eye level so both pilots could clearly see they were real. No reaction. "I think you dropped this." I held out the phone I'd taken from Black Gloves.

I had planted the idea that he'd been looking for his phone all morning.

"Thanks, I've been looking for my—"

The pilot cut in. "Your phone is in your pocket," she said.

"Oh," stammered the co-pilot, patting his pants. "I guess it is. Why'd I think I lost it?"

"Which is why'd *I'll* be flying the plane today," she said. This was obviously a part of their preflight banter.

He stared at the phone for another few seconds but didn't take it. I felt my stomach twist.

"You should turn that in to lost and found," advised the pilot.

"I will."

As they strolled away, I realized I'd have to take a much greater risk now.

My Wushu master once made me stand barefoot at attention atop a thirty-foot high tree stump that was less than six inches in diameter.

"You must learn patience," my diminutive master declared from the comfort of a chair on the ground.

"Boys hitting puberty don't have patience," I answered, my voice straining with the effort of trying to keep my balance. There was no net, no safety harness. Just a tiny circle unable to accommodate the full length and breadth of my feet coming between me and probable death.

"That is exactly why you must learn it."

"How many students have you killed this way?" My toes and heels hung over the edges.

He thought for a moment, sipping on a cool drink. "Let's just say that the type of people that fail this test…"

"You mean fall and die?"

"…they don't survive very long as warriors anyway."

He made me stay up there an extra two hours after I started cursing at him, insulting his ancestors, and explaining in detail in several dialects where I was going to stick this tree trunk once I got down.

Patience has never come naturally to me. It's mostly been beaten into me.

Staring out the window, waiting for someone, anyone on the ground crew to open a stupid door was testing mine.

I lifted the Patriots spyglass with its flimsy, far-from-clear plastic lens and focused on the external door at the end of the jetway that led down to the tarmac.

Somewhere out there, Elam Khai was sitting in his ONYX plane, waiting for me to make my move.

A few feet away, Phoebe and Daniel were combining the guts of the disposable cameras into something a mad scientist in a 1950s B-movie might make. They had the contraption inside the backpack to disguise their work. Daniel came up with the idea to daisy chain the boards so they would fire in sequence. Instead of one big burst, we'd have a cascading strobe lasting a second or two.

We had only a few minutes left before the first flight—the one to London—would begin boarding, and I didn't have our escape route nailed down.

Patience, I reminded myself.

I hate being patient.

Finally, a baggage handler stomped up the steps, pausing briefly to key in a code before pulling open the door. I tried to remember the pattern, at least the part I'd seen.

The sun hit the crystal Bunker Hill Monument laying on the ground, splashing little rainbows on the walls and ceiling. The distraction almost caused me to miss a woman climbing the jetway stairs. I raised the spyglass just in time. She unlocked the security door. Again, I couldn't see the full pattern.

An announcement came over the speakers. Boarding for the flight to London was starting. The man with the altered boarding passes gathered his kids.

I was running out of time.

The first baggage handler came out onto the landing and sent several bags down the metal slide running alongside the stairs. He kept the door propped open with his foot, so he didn't have to unlock it again. He disappeared back into the jetway. In another moment, he returned, sending more luggage skidding to the tarmac, his foot in the door again. A handler at the bottom loaded the bags onto a cart. The pulse at my temple was pounding. I'd only caught the first part of the pattern. Twice. I needed to see the rest of it. I also needed to be distracting the British Airways gate agent when the man and his kids boarded.

There were maybe a dozen people in front of him. I had thirty seconds tops.

I motioned for Daniel. "I need you to go bother the woman scanning boarding passes until that big guy and his kids get on."

"By doing what?"

"What you *always* do," I said.

∞

"Listen, can I ask you a question?" Daniel said to the woman. "I recently cut back from fifteen Cokes a day down to just two, and you'd think that, you know, cutting down, would make you less jittery, but it's made me more jittery, and also, a little confused, so my question is—"

"Sir—"

That was the British gate agent's first mistake, calling him "sir." Airport gate agents have always seemed oddly similar to Buckingham Palace guards—they must remain unflustered no matter what tourists do to bother them.

It was that imperturbable, Zen-like focus Daniel was attempting to disrupt so that our plan might have a chance. And honestly, there was no one better for the job. Daniel had a gift for getting under people's skin.

"So, my question is," he continued, "you announced that anyone who feels they need more time to board should come forward. Don't you think everyone on this flight feels that way? I mean, I want to have more time. I'm in zone—I don't know—fifteen, twenty-five, a hundred and seven, something like that. Basically, I'm getting on the plane seconds before we take off, which I—"

"Sir!" she said, again.

The man with the altered tickets shuttled his children forward, unaware he held the keys to our escape. Seeing he was next in line, Daniel kicked into a new gear.

"Am I a 'sir?' I think you have to do something important like defend the realm or show extreme bravery or, you know, be an aging rock star whose greatest achievement was not overdosing. When you think about it, the people being knighted nowadays couldn't defend the empire from anything except inane pop music. Do you still have an empire?"

The man reached out a massive hand that made the passes look like playing cards. The woman absently held them under the scanner as she tried to get Daniel to just…shut…up. "I was trying to be polite, *young man*." Her cut-glass English accent sliced through the air. "Is that better?"

"Now it sounds like I'm ten. How about, 'honored passenger.'"

"Sss…errr. Will you…please wait in line," she said, teeth grinding together. "I promise you *will* get on board." She said the last part as if it was a threat.

She hadn't noticed that each of the man's tickets beeped twice and flashed two seat locations.

It was done. We were heading to London.

Sort of.

∞

A moment later, First Class was called for our flight to Munich. If I didn't get the door code to the British Airways jetway, it didn't matter if everything else worked.

Out of the corner of my eye, I saw someone walking up the adjacent jetway. I took a chance and aimed the spyglass at the door. Punch. Punch. Punch. Punch. Punch. Door opens. It looked to me like the same pattern.

It was a five button pushbutton lock. I sketched five rectangles on the glass with the oils of my fingers, then pressed:

Top, middle, second from the bottom, second from the top, bottom.

Top, middle, second from the bottom, second from the top, bottom.

Top, middle, second from the bottom, second from the top, bottom.

I was confident I had the pattern.

I handed the spyglass to a girl, six or so, in one of the chairs facing the window. Her face lit up. "Wow. Thanks!" she yelled as I rushed toward Phoebe and Daniel who were already in line.

"You get it?"

I nodded.

Phoebe held the Rome boarding passes over a trash can. "Seems like such a waste."

"We don't need them," I said, my heart pounding. Top, middle, second from the bottom, second from the top, bottom.

I nudged Phoebe. She opened her hand, and the passes dropped into the trash.

"*Arrivederci, Roma.*"

I started teaching Phoebe and Daniel the pattern. Top, middle, second from the bottom, second from the top, bottom.

"Alexander."

The voice behind me was kind, tender.

I gripped the crystal Bunker Hill Monument in my hand, then turned.

The woman was graceful, long-limbed and luminous. Her stance, her presence, her features were soft. She was unpretentiously elegant with flawless skin and the turned-up nose of a child. Her blonde hair had shades of strawberry. Transparent eyes considered me with steely concentration, although, it was a benevolent gaze.

She looked on the younger side of thirty, but I instantly knew she was a hundred times that.

"I know you from somewhere," I said.

"I don't believe we've met, Alexander."

Her easy way of saying my name both disarmed me and made me uncomfortable.

Hers was a face one doesn't easily forget.

I quickly scanned the terminal.

"Don't worry. You're safe."

"For the moment," I said.

"Always." She put her hand on my arm. "I am Eleni. My friends call me Elle."

"I'm not your friend."

"My enemies have called me that as well." Her tone was warm.

And I realized she reminded me of my mother. Or at least the faded image I have of her. "Come with us. We have a plane. Your friends can join us. Or you can leave them here." She nodded toward Daniel and Phoebe who were nearing the front of the line. I motioned for them to keep going.

"I wouldn't go with him before, why would I go with you now?"

She tilted her head. "Because you need to come home."

The word hit me. "I don't have a home."

"Yes, you do," she said.

Where did I know her from? "Are we somehow related?"

"Not by blood, but I've known your father for almost half my life. He's like a brother to me." She put her hand on my shoulder. Her touch felt good. Maternal. Calming. "Elam Khai…is a great man. More importantly, he's a good man. And an even better father." Elle smiled again, but this time it had a sadness etched into it.

I tried to remember where I'd seen that face. A picture? A painting? A statue?

A painting.

"Gráinne Ní Mháille," I said, hesitantly. She rolled her lips in, trying to hide her amusement.

Redden up her hair and she could pass for Grainee O'Malley, the Pirate Queen of Ireland. Although, it was hard to imagine the placid woman before me commanding a fleet of ships that confounded the British in the late 1500s.

She could no longer suppress a smile. And with that grin, another portrait came into my head.

"Wait. Anne Bonny," I said. Also a pirate. Also Irish. Also roamed the seas annoying the British, just a century later.

"Does it matter who I was?"

"Actually, a little."

"What's important is who I am. Elam has been the father of all my children. He and Marcus—sometimes they are rivals. Sometimes they are allies. But always, they are brothers. Family. You should have been a part of our family. We didn't know about you, Alexander. My children…several have been great men and women. But none have been like you. You're the only Eternal of your generation in our family. Do you understand what that means? You're the only one we can walk through the ages with." She touched me again. I don't believe in magic, but the power of her presence was the closest thing to it. "If we'd known, we would have never left you out there, alone in the world."

My chest heaved and a wave of…I don't know how to describe it. An ache. Regret. Longing. It made me miss my mother. Brought back memories of the many—so many—devoted caregivers employed by my father during my centuries-long childhood that never quite replaced the nurturing I missed.

"A few kind words isn't going to melt a millennia and a half," I said.

"I suppose not."

"Tell my uncle, if he wants my father, he should find him himself. Leave me out of it."

"We don't know where he is, Alexander. And we *need* to be together for what's coming." She took my hand. "Help us find him. Help us bring him home."

I laughed. "You are very good," I said, sarcastically.

"I'm being sincere."

"You know what Elam Khai is planning," I said, flatly.

She did not break her gaze. "Just because I love him, doesn't mean I always agree with him. We are in danger. I would like to think there are different ways to solve this. I know Marcus feels the same. And I think, so do you. Be part of the solution, Alexander. Be part of your family."

She believed what she was saying. And I wanted to believe it, too. That I could be part of a family. That we could find a less destructive response to technology's threat than erasing it. But my father's absence, his sending Braeden, Elam Khai sending Elle to soft-sell his pitch, it told me things were past that point. A cold war had begun. A hot war would soon follow.

I pulled my hand away. "If you want me, you'll have to come get me," I said.

She reached in her pocket and produced a stack of boarding passes, shuffling through a dozen flights until she found the one for Munich.

She gave me that kindly smile again. "I'm not going to force you. But hopefully, I can convince you."

At least she couldn't board immediately. Her group number was after ours. Daniel and Phoebe entered the jetway.

As I turned toward the gate agent, a hand stopped me. Thick fingers dug into my shoulder.

The man was mostly torso. Spindly legs propped up an oil drum with a ten-gallon head topping it off.

I felt the tip of a blade through the fabric of my shirt.

"Is this your way of convincing me?" I asked Elle.

"Why don't you go with the nice woman?" The man's voice was deep. He pressed the edge of the glass-phenolic-resin knife against my abdomen.

He smiled. I smiled. I shoved the crystal Bunker Hill Monument into his undercarriage. Right side. I didn't want to kill the guy, didn't want him dropping to the floor, didn't want him causing a scene.

Elle blazed both of us with a look of disappointment. "I told you to stay back. He has to choose for himself," she said to the man. "Don't remove it. It'll keep the bleeding to a minimum."

She nodded to woman standing a few feet away who escorted the man toward the exit.

"I meant what I said, Alexander. You have to choose."

The gate agent scanned my boarding pass and I hurried down the ramp.

There was a logjam at the bottom of the jetway. A man with a broken leg had been brought to his seat in a wheelchair. The airline employee bringing the empty chair off the plane was blocking the bulkhead, fiddling with the brakes.

The seconds ticked away. I was about to drag the employee off the plane. We were running out of time. Elle would be in the jetway soon.

In 1981, illusionist David Copperfield made a plane vanish on live television. The hour-long TV special was filled with magic tricks and illusion. There were twists on old deceits—the often seen sawed-in-half-woman was, instead, the TV star sliced into eight pieces so small you couldn't figure out how the woman's smiling face could possibly fit, even if her head had been severed from her body. But the first fifty minutes were simply creative filler building toward the one thing everyone in America wanted to see:

A plane disappear.

I remember sitting in my living room—I was living outside St. Louis at the time—eyes glued to the screen.

No one had ever tried anything so audacious before, vanishing something so large.

He did it, of course. With a lot of dramatic music and theatrical hand gestures. Especially when he was tying ropes to the landing gears.

Magicians make a big show of tying knots. I mean, it's not like they're something unusual. People tie knots every day. They're called shoelaces.

Anyway, Copperfield blindfolded a group of men and women holding hands that were surrounding the aircraft. It's irrelevant whether or not these fifty people were in on the trick because we could see them, or at least, we could see their shadows as well as the shadow of the jet on the white canvas that was lifted in front of the plane. The shadows were visible the entire time, right up to the moment Copperfield switched off the lights for an instant before the canvas was lowered to reveal the people standing with their hands together, encircling—

Nothing.

I've watched that video hundreds of times since. Even with

assuming the shadows of the people and the plane were faked, I still have no clue how he moved/destroyed/hid a seven-ton Lear Jet quickly enough that it was completely out of view of even the widest camera angle in less than thirty seconds. That was the length of time from the moment the screen went up until it came back down.

I have a rule. If I can't puzzle it out myself, I don't want to know the secret.

Copperfield had hundreds of people and months of preparations to achieve a trick I've yet to figure out. I had Phoebe and Daniel and whatever I could gather from the airport travel shops. Copperfield worked in a tightly controlled area at night which made it easier to conceal the scheme. I had to pull this off in broad daylight in an environment I didn't control. His plane was seven tons. Mine weighed fifty times that.

And then there was Elle, the unexpected audience member.

I saw her enter the jetway. Since our seats were in First Class, which meant we'd be sitting in front of her, close to the exit, she'd wait until the last possible moment to board.

Finally! The wheelchair assistant made his way off the jet.

I glanced at Phoebe. She nodded. I looked over at Daniel. His hands were trembling. I glared at him, compelling him to get his shit together.

He nodded, then lifted the cover of the metal tin and very gently agitated the bag, mixing the dry ingredients of ammonium nitrate, salt, and zinc, making sure not to puncture the water bag.

Phoebe pulled the contraption from the backpack and closed her eyes.

Pop. Pop-pop-pop. Pop. Pop. Pop-pop. Pop. Pop. Pop. Pop. Pop. Pop. Pop-pop-pop. Pop. Pop. Pop-pop. Pop.

The flashes were uneven, unsynced, creating a strobing, disorientating burst.

When the blinding light subsided, the plane was gone.

There were screams of shock. A man nearly fell out of the

jetway that now led to nothing but open space. I bet even Elle was impressed.

"It's gone," Phoebe whispered. Her face was a strange mix of disbelief and curiosity. "No way a jet that size could get away that quickly." She looked to me for an answer.

But I was gone as well.

Daniel punctured the water pouch, then dropped the tin and the bag. Instantly a noxious, greenish-gray smoke filled the jetway.

And then... *they* disappeared.

SIX

We've Reached Our Cruising Altitude of Thirty-Nine Feet

I stared out the window, watching the soldiers methodically moving toward the plane, marveling at the pace at which things had changed. For tens of thousands of years, we traveled the same way. By foot, on the backs of animals or being pulled by them, by boat. Then in the span of less than a hundred years came trains and planes, automobiles and rockets. Ninety percent of the world's population was now less than a twenty-four-hour trip away from each other.

If Elam Khai had his way, that day-long trip would turn into months or years.

Trains were the first great advancement in transportation. I've always enjoyed trains, even from the beginning. Once, on my way from New York to Boston, I took a detour in Connecticut. I stepped off the train in Fairfield and walked two miles from the Southport station to a lovely tree-lined neighborhood. There were children playing in the street. Birds singing in the trees.

Noises and flashes came from one of the backyards, the brilliant light of a welder's torch flaring brightly even in the midday sun. A shed door swung open, and that's when I caught a glimpse of him. He moved with the same speed and agility, and his hair seemed just as black. Gustave Whitehead took a long pull from a cold drink, then wiped the sweat from his brow before picking up the torch and resuming his work. This was after World War I, after Whitehead had endured years of anti-German sentiment, after he'd watched others take credit for many of his discoveries and his feats. I didn't plan on talking to him. Too many years had passed to let him see me. But I wanted to see *him*. Something made Gustave glance up from his welding. A strange look of recognition washed over his face. That stupid mustache, that engaging expression, that too wide smile.

My instinct was to turn and walk away, get on the train and never again let curiosity lead me down this road, but I stood there, not moving as I watched him make his way around the side of the house to the street.

He was silent as he looked me over. "You are a man," he said, after a moment, even though my body had aged less than two months in the sixteen years since I'd seen him last, and I probably looked younger with my face not covered in grime. "You are a man now," he said again. This time with pride.

"You're not upset?"

"Seeing you. How could I be upset?"

"You know what I mean."

"Alexander…It doz not matter. History ist a story. A story zat gets written. What people write ist not alvays right."

I knew this, of course. I'd seen history up close, and there were times when what others said about an event was barely recognizable to what I had witnessed with my own eyes.

"You and me," he said. "Vee know zee truth. Ant az long az you ant I remember, zat ist all I need."

I glanced around at his modest house on the quiet little street. It was a nice home. A home to be proud of, but not the residence of an aviation pioneer. He made engines that others flew. That's what he became known for.

But *I* knew what he'd really done. And I would *remember*.

"I wish I could remember," Daniel said.

"Remember what?" I said harshly as I dug my fingers into my thighs. I was annoyed at everyone and everything at the moment. I wanted to get up, get out of here. My new shoes had dried, that was good. I was wearing the shirt and pants I'd stolen from a bag at the end of the jetway waiting to be gate-checked. The pants were tight, the shirt was too big, but they had the advantage of not smelling like the brackish water of the Bay.

"I wish I could remember all the stupid things I used to complain about. I mean, I complained a lot about things that seemed really important at the time, but in comparison to, you know, our current situation, seem…pointless and irrelevant. Which I guess is why I can't remember them. That U.S. History test we took? *Nada.* Total blank. Don't remember a thing. *'Nada?'* That's Spanish, right? What's *death* in Spanish? Three years. Can't remember a word. Except *nada.* They always say, 'Oh, you're going to need this later on.' How does knowing a quadratic equation help me in fighting an actual Emperor of Rome? Or how about diagramming a sentence properly? When they storm the plane and throw us to the ground, if I say, 'I ain't done nothing.' Are these soldiers toting machine guns going to correct me? 'You *haven't done anything,* young man.' I feel like I stupidly used up all my complaining. I should've been saving some of it for, you know, moments like right now."

Phoebe's gaze was fixed on the British anti-terrorist forces approaching the plane. "¿Hay alguna manera de callarlo?" *Is there anything that will shut him up?*

"Nada."

I glanced across the aisle. A man held a tablet displaying a live feed from a news app. Probably half the people on board were glued to the action being played out on their phones and tablets or those of people seated nearby. The rest were watching the scene truly live. Out the windows. The screens on the seat backs had been turned off, and the plane's wifi had been cut, but cell service was still active. I figured that would get scrambled soon.

The Special Forces teams were poised to storm the jet. Teargas canisters were set off around the air intake vents. Even before the toxic gas was sucked into the ventilation, my eyes involuntarily began to water. I've tasted teargas too many times for me not to have a Pavlovian response even if I didn't feel a thing. In the front of the plane, one of the flight attendants got out of her seat. Other crew members shouted at her to sit down.

On the tablet, there was a long shot of the plane. Far in the background, I saw it. It was hard to make out the letters, but I knew what it said. ONYX. Elam Khai had somehow followed the plane. Then the coverage switched to a close-up shot. The flight attendant's face appeared in the porthole, her hand covering her nose and mouth as she struggled to disarm the forward hatch. The aircraft door finally opened and white puffs spilled out from inside, looking like the gas Daniel had set off in the jetway.

Half a dozen heavily armed British soldiers rode atop airstairs rushing toward the jet. Before the portable stairs had fully stopped, one of the men grabbed the flight attendant, pulling her across the gap to the top landing, and quickly escorting her down the steps. The pilot and co-pilot emerged from the cockpit, their hands raised over their heads. The soldiers ascending the stairs screamed at the flight crew. I could see the pilots' lips moving. They were too far away to make out the words, but I knew what they were saying. They were my words after all. The pilots were pulled from the aircraft and dragged down the stairs, not protectively like the flight attendant, but harshly. Once on the tarmac, the pilot's were pushed to the asphalt and immediately handcuffed.

On screens large and small throughout the cabin, the live news feed zoomed in.

The co-pilot was still speaking, motioning with his head toward his front pocket. A cellphone was retrieved by one of the soldiers. It was compelling television.

What the co-pilot was trying to explain—and what he and the pilot would continue to repeat to anyone who'd listen—was that they were informed via a message on the phone that an explosive was on their plane. They were warned in further messages—actually calendar alarms I had set in advance—that if they didn't follow the directions given on the cell phone, an explosive would be detonated.

Each of these alarms triggered suggestions I had anchored in their minds.

It would later be determined that the device was a pre-paid smartphone purchased in the McLean, Virginia area. The phone was encrypted and was similar to ones used by U.S. private security contractors in places like Iraq and Afghanistan.

There was more shouting. This time from soldiers running under the fuselage. I could hear the boots on the concrete through the thick windows.

Phoebe jumped at the loud metallic clack as something contacted the plane's skin. She squeezed my hand even tighter, turning it white. She'd been grasping it for the last twenty minutes. Daniel had been doing the same to my other hand until I passed him the bag of candies I'd found in the stolen luggage. I lost count of how many wrappers were at my feet.

"I can't feel my fingers."

"Neither can I," Phoebe said. She didn't relax her grip.

With the pilots secured, the British troops swarmed the interior of the plane. They searched the cockpit, main cabin, service areas, galleys, baggage compartments, wardrobes, lavatories, and cargo bays.

But they didn't find us.

They didn't find anyone on board except for the cabin crew and one lone passenger. The man with the broken leg who'd been wheeled to his seat during pre-boarding.

They didn't find us because while the Lufthansa jet sat on the lone runway in the tiny two-point-three square mile British territory of Gibraltar at the mouth of the Mediterranean, we were a thousand miles away, parked at the end of Heathrow's runways, the furthest point from the populated terminals.

"Are they going to do that to us?" She nodded toward the man's tablet and the images of the pilots being dragged away.

"No."

Her grip relaxed the tiniest bit. "How can you be sure?"

"Because they're not looking for us?"

She wrinkled her forehead in confusion.

"They're looking for them," I said, nodding across the aisle at the man's tablet.

The news feed now displayed the faces of three people—looking nothing like us—who had, according to passport records, entered the jetway during the boarding process for the Lufthansa flight, but were not on the plane in Gibraltar or left behind at Logan.

A news reporter was interviewing a traveler who had seen the three "looking and acting suspicious." Never mind that they hadn't actually been in the terminal.

Why weren't our faces plastered on screens across the globe? Well, cruising somewhere around thirty-nine feet above Boston Harbor, I called the number Engel had given me, punched in the last four digits of each passport, triggering a sequence of encrypted, untraceable commands that deleted our data and our photos, and replaced them with the names and images being broadcast around the world. In the past dialing this number—and I mean *dialing* a rotary telephone—used to begin with a pleasant female voice asking for a passcode and end with someone breaking into the main passport office in the applicable country and physically stealing the files.

Elam Khai bitches about technology, but somethings are just easier now.

I wondered if these three somewhat threatening looking people were real or amalgamations of hundreds of faces combined by computer imaging software.

My thoughts were interrupted as the video froze on the man's screen and everyone else's in the cabin.

Cell service had just been cut.

I placed my right hand over Phoebe's, the one crushing my left hand. "Relax, everything's going to be all right."

Just then, with a clank and a boom, the bulkheads in the front and back of the plane flew open. Soldiers streamed onto our plane, guns ready, eyes staring down the barrel with us in their sights.

Like I said, I have no clue how David Copperfield made a LearJet disappear in 1981. So, you may be curious how I pulled off making an aircraft five times the size vanish without that key piece of knowledge.

It was the Statue of Liberty.

See, the year after disappearing a plane, Copperfield returned to television with an even bigger trick: He was going to make the Statue of Liberty in New York Harbor vanish.

Now, making a plane disappear is amazing. Making a football field high copper, steel and granite national treasure—something you can't roll away, collapse, destroy, or hide with a mirror—disappear is simply *unbelievable*.

No one was going to let David Copperfield or anyone else do *anything* to the Statue of Liberty.

And that's how I figured out the trick.

He could move a plane, but he couldn't move Liberty.

So, I realized:

He moved the *audience.*

Turned them, if you want to get nit-picky.

And that's exactly what I did.

I moved the audience…the people in the jetway.

In those precious seconds, while the flashes were strobing and everyone was confused and disoriented, I set the controls, then jumped into the plane as the electric motors slipped the jetway past the nose of the aircraft. From the jetway's repositioned angle, the aircraft was completely out of view.

When the zinc/ammonium nitrate/sodium chloride mixture ignited on contact with the water, fogging the jetway with smoke and noxious fumes, Phoebe and Daniel escaped down the external stairs to the tarmac. If anyone stopped them, they'd claim to be running away from what they believed was a hijacking or terrorist attack, which, given the situation, would be completely plausible.

It never came to that. Everyone was too distracted to notice them climbing the stairs several gates over using the spied door code to enter the British Airways jetway.

I was pretty proud of the plane trick.

But getting two veteran pilots to fly that plane to Gibraltar instead of Germany…that was a lot more difficult.

The work, the planning, the practice, the excruciating attention to each and every element. That's the *real* magic. The audience sees nothing but the elegant illusion.

My attempt at hypnosis had gotten me a pair of pilot's wings, a pat on the head, and not much else. I smiled, remembering Craig Coulter flapping his arms and clucking like a chicken. I missed his stupid, empty head.

Leaping onto the plane while the jetway rolled away, I came face to face with the First-Class flight attendant who stared at me mouth agape, nothing but blue sky behind me.

I stood in the bulkhead and waited until I could see Elle peeking out the end of the jetway, craning her neck to find the missing plane.

She caught a glimpse of me. The bait was set.

I turned and slapped my open palm on the flight attendant's forehead, sitting him down in the jump-seat. My only suggestion was that he make an emergency All-Call. He would close the aircraft door and inform the others flight attendants to arm and cross-check.

The cockpit door was open. The pilot and co-pilot were running through their pre-flight checklist. I stepped inside and locked the door behind me. As they turned, I said the word I had installed in the terminal. The pilots sat very still in their chairs.

I extended my hand toward the co-pilot. In it was the phone I'd taken from Black Gloves.

"Thanks, I've been looking for this," he said.

I don't know what triggered her. Maybe it was that stupid, stupid phone, but I saw movement. The menacing barrel of a gun was raised in my direction. I knocked the pistol from the captain's hand, just as she fired off a round. The bullet whooshed past me and lodged in the cockpit door. The crack of the gun blast in the confined space stunned me. But it woke the co-pilot and he got to his feet, grabbing a fire ax on the wall. I slammed him in the chest. Diaphragm shocked, his nose spurted blood as I cuffed him again. He fell back against the instrument panel, unconscious.

The captain pulled her hands away from her ringing ears and reached for the radio. I grabbed her hand and…

I shook it.

"So nice to meet you," I said as I squeezed her wrist gently with my left hand as we shook, then used that light touch to lift her hand toward her face, directing her to study the lines in her palm. "And…sleep." She went limp.

I caught my breath.

I took a moment to make sure I hadn't been hit.

I was fine.

I got to work.

The pilot's mental defenses were nearly impregnable. I needed her lucid enough to fly, but deep enough, so she didn't resist. Ritual. That was the way in. I methodically worked my instructions into the preflight checklist. I invited her into my dangerous game, playing on her need to lead, her tendency toward thrill-seeking, and her desire to control. I exploited her powerful instinct to protect her cockpit, her crew, her plane, and most of all, her passengers to guide her toward my plans.

After I disabled the plane's transponder, she radioed the ground crew, explaining that the plane needed to be taken to the maintenance hanger because, among other things, we had a malfunctioning transponder.

In a moment, the pushback tug was hooking up to the front gear.

I anchored every instruction to a piece of cockpit machinery. The heading to the radio frequency. The altitude to the trim. When I was confident she was won over completely, I asked her to get out of her chair and sit on the floor.

She did so without hesitation.

I jumped into the captain's seat.

And that's when I caught a glimpse of him.

Elam Khai was standing on the platform of a catering truck with its body raised. He was at eye level, just off to the right.

"Alexander!" he screamed, his deep, commanding tone piercing the thick glass. He didn't look angry. He looked threatening and dangerous and mildly amused.

And even though I was perfectly safe in a sealed aircraft, my body responded. My pulse quickened. My vision narrowed.

The good news was that from his vantage point, it was unlikely Elam Khai saw who had—and more importantly who hadn't—entered the plane. But if I didn't do something to draw his attention, he might see Daniel and Phoebe making their way to the other gate, which would reveal our deception.

The best way to do that was by doing something stupid.

And I was in the perfect place for it. Behind the controls of a huge commercial passenger jet.

I've kept my skills up-to-date by flying sims as often as I could. Still, the gauges swirled in a moment of vertigo. Squelching my body's stress response, I pulled myself together.

I clicked the mic button. "Ground, we are ready for pushback."

"Ground is ready," came the response from the person jacked into the plane's com system. "Release brakes."

"Releasing brakes," I said, trying to sound like I was old enough to legally be in command of this plane.

"Commencing pushback. All engines clear. Start at will."

The tug began pushing the plane away from the gate. I fired up engine one, then engine two.

Out of the corner of my eye, I saw the lift on the catering truck with Elam Khai lowering to the tarmac.

The engines were whining up and nearly ready.

How long does it take to push back from a gate? I wanted to tell the driver to speed up, but a pushback tug was geared to move an incredibly heavy object from a dead stop. It only had one speed. Excruciatingly slow.

Elam Khai jumped to the ground and started running toward the plane. He disappeared under the nose. What was his move? He could try to get in, the best bet would be through the gears. He could disable the craft. A few pieces of luggage tossed into the engine fans would do the trick.

I heard a clank as the tug slowed and the tow bar scraped the asphalt.

"Set brake," said the voice.

The man in a safety vest holding orange wands made an "X" to signal I couldn't move because someone was still under the plane.

I had no tolerance for proper procedures at the moment.

"Brakes set," I said, testily.

"Pin out. Towbar released."

"Thank you, Ground, you may disconnect the com. We have clearance to leave."

My hand was on the thrust lever, ready to go.

"What's the rush?"

The instant I heard Elam Khai's voice in my headset, I throttled up the engines. But even without it being connected, the tow bar prevented the plane from rolling forward. In fact, the tug was pushing us back.

"Alexander," Elam Khai said. "Stop. I admire your determination. I'd like to think you get that from me."

"I get it from my father." I was annoyed he had goaded me into responding.

"Marcus does plug away, doesn't he? I guess that could be called determination. He *did* have an older, wiser brother to guide him. Still...he is not quite as clever as you are."

I could hear the front gear creaking under the stress as the engines thrust forward.

"See, this situation is a perfect example of what I was telling you about. Technology's Achilles' heel. We have the tremendous

ANCIENT AMONG US | 113

power and innovation of this modern behemoth, this miracle, and it is rendered useless by a small, insignificant cart."

I still couldn't see him. He was limited in his movement by the comlink cable connecting him to the fuselage. This conversation was private. The tower couldn't hear. Neither could the pilot and co-pilot who were busy running the preflight check, flipping invisible switches. Their pantomiming made them look vaguely unstable.

"You know what the irony is? I'm not the greatest threat to you." Elam Khai laughed. "You don't fully comprehend how fragile our secret is. The forces that threaten us. How quickly things are changing. Eleni is right. We must come together. But believe me, I will become the greatest threat to you if you continue to defy me."

The shuddering front landing gear was reaching a breaking point as the tug pressed in the opposite direction.

I throttled the plane down.

"See, that is acting with intelligence, not just brute force," said Elam Khai. "You *are* different than my brother."

I didn't like his constant digs at my father. I had to be careful not to take his bait.

"We are not coming with you."

"I couldn't give a damn about the others. You, however, *are* coming with me."

"Phoebe! Daniel!" I yelled to sell the ruse. "Get those seat belts fastened. We're going to be hitting some turbulence."

"There is a limit to my patience, Alexander. And there is nowhere for you to go that I will not find you. No corner of the earth I cannot—"

Elam Khai's voice cut off as the headphone cable was yanked from the com jack when I thrust the plane into reverse. Jets don't actually have a reverse gear. They're meant to go in one direction: forward. But if you're willing to send some people and debris flying, you can engage the braking system used during landings.

I pulled up on the two toggles, then dragged the lever for both engines down past zero to full reverse.

Just a few seconds. Just long enough for the plane to pull away from the tug. Once I could see Elam Khai's menacing scowl—an expression that caused me to laugh and get a little queasy—I closed the reverse thrust vents, directing all the power out the back of the engines.

The plane lurched forward with enough speed to roll the front wheel over the tow bar. I didn't know how much damage I'd done to the gear, but the plane was still upright, so it wasn't catastrophic. I headed for the taxiway, throttling the engines back to maintain control.

I said pushback tugs only have one speed. In reality, they have four. Excruciatingly slow, very slow, rather slow and…slow. The most Elam Khai could achieve in that tug was maybe twenty miles per hour. I could get the plane moving significantly faster than that, depending on how much risk I wanted to take. And really, what was he going to do even if he could catch me? There weren't many ways to stop a jet loaded with fuel without endangering both our lives.

I *had* created a new problem. I was on a different plane than Daniel and Phoebe. The whole idea of my (amended) plan was for me to jump on this plane, get the pilots to fly it to the wrong location—Gibraltar—by hypnotizing them, then quickly get off the plane and join my friends.

My (amended) (amended) plan hadn't been amended (amended) yet.

I navigated the taxiway, keeping the red guideline directly under center.

Elam Khai felt no compunction to stay on the designated paths and had gotten out in front of me by cutting across the tarmac.

The maintenance hangers were off to the left. I turned right.

Little bells would be going off in the tower soon.

I counted two planes on the deck. Another on approach. Moving at sixty knots, I made a hard turn onto runway 4R two hundred feet in front of a 787 in a ground hold at the end, waiting for permission to take off. Without any passengers, we were light. I wouldn't need much take-off roll—maybe a third of 4R's length to get wheels up. After notching the flaps, I pushed the throttle levers as far forward as they would go. The acceleration pressed me into my seat as the plane surged ahead.

A lone figure was charging across the field. Elam Khai had ditched the tug and was on foot.

The plane picked up speed.

Every imperfection in the tarmac jolted the cabin.

I called out readings from the ground speed indicator, and the pilot countered with her check of the gauges.

Elam Khai sprinted onto the runway, then stopped in the middle of it.

Working the floor pedals and the nose gear tiller, I steered the plane, keeping it on track as it veered in the strong crosswind.

I was quickly closing on Elam Khai. He stood there, not moving. I could see his face. An instant later, I could make out his eyes staring at me.

Finally, we reached rotation velocity, and I felt the nose gear extend. I pulled back on the yoke, and the plane lifted off the asphalt as Elam Khai disappeared from view under the nose.

I kept the gear down and the flaps set as I made a slow, low, wide turn to the east, beginning a gradual loop. I had maybe eight minutes before fighter jets arrived and tried to force us—or shoot us—down. As we pulled around, I was strangely relieved to see Elam Khai unharmed and charging toward the general aviation terminal.

Heading for a plane with ONYX painted on the side. The jet from the photo.

Who the hell wanted to blow him up? I couldn't imagine another Eternal would be stupid enough to risk killing him.

Alarms were sounding, set off by the onboard collision avoidance system. I silenced them.

With the transponder off, air traffic control would only see us on radar if I let them. I hugged the water, hoping it might give me a few more minutes before fighters were scrambled.

"Take control," I said to the pilot, triggering her. "I can't handle her."

"I can," she said, climbing back into her seat.

I slid out and she settled in. Immediately, she was busy checking the switches and screens. I leaned in and spoke in her ear. "Keep turning until three-one-five. Line up for a pass. Then fly to safety. None of the other pilots have been able to keep their planes under fifty feet, so don't worry if you can't."

She smirked. "I didn't get here by being like the rest of the boys." She wasn't talking to me. I didn't exist, at least, not for her. I'm not sure who she was picturing, maybe it was no one, just her own cocky, defiant internal dialogue.

I jogged the co-pilot awake. It was easier to set triggers with him. My last instruction was, "Begin counting down from one hundred to zero." To the pilot, I said, "Climb sharply at zero."

"One hundred, ninety-nine, ninety-eight, ninety-seven, ninety-six..."

I took the co-pilot's phone and dialed the number Engel had given me. Once that was done, I slipped the device into my pocket and opened the hatch in the floor leading to the avionics bay. It was a tight squeeze to the maintenance door that accessed the nose gear.

Generally speaking, it's a very bad idea to exit a plane in flight. You can do it, of course, using a parachute, but even then jump planes are almost always prop engine aircraft, and you usually exit at an altitude of between five and eighteen thousand feet. It may seem strange but it's safer to jump from five thousand feet than it is from two thousand. And jumping from a few dozen, well, that's just crazy.

It took me longer than expected to get the access door open. Commercial airliners are, as you can imagine, engineered to keep people inside the plane and stowaways and more sinister folks out.

I finally got the maintenance door to budge. The co-pilot was below fifty and counting down. Air blasted me the moment I broke the seal. I wasn't prepared for the decibel level. The whine of the engines was a distant whisper. It was the screaming wind and clattering metal that deafened me. I could no longer hear the co-pilot.

I forced myself through the tiny opening, gripping the gear as the wind buffeted me. We were skimming less than fifty feet above the Bay, traveling at around a hundred knots. A terminal velocity into water of eighty-five miles per hour is fatal over ninety-five percent of the time. If I hit the water at our current speed, I—well, I didn't want to think about what would happen. This was not at all like hanging off the bottom of Whitehead's monoplane and dropping into a forgiving marsh.

I had to be patient and wait for the climb.

Have I mentioned that I hate being patient?

It couldn't be more than a few seconds now. It was impossible to keep my eyes open or closed. The lids just flapped in the turbulent air. My fingers ached. My failing grip was the only thing preventing me from being ripped away by the wind.

We were coming up on the runway.

Water bad. Tarmac much, much worse.

C'mon, c'mon. Zero. Say, *zero*!

The moment the plane launched upward, I let go and fired my muscles. I leapt toward the rear of the aircraft, against the forward momentum. The wind pressed me against the skin of the plane's belly, which slid across my body for what seemed like forever, and I worried I'd overlooked some quirk of aerodynamics, but the climb, the leap, the friction, all combined to slow my horizontal velocity relative to the water to a survivable speed. I spread out my arms and my legs, slowing my momentum further. At the last second, I folded my hands in over my head and pointed my toes toward the Massachusetts Bay, my body a pencil angled slightly to counter my horizontal momentum. I stabbed into the cold, murky, brackish water at the end of the runway like a bullet and disappeared into darkness.

I was disoriented.

It happened so fast. Piercing sound instantly turning to silence except for the plipping of bubbles passing my ears. It was dark and dirty. Claustrophobic. The shock of cold paralyzed my lungs. I was confident I'd landed feet first, persuaded mostly because I was still conscious and my feet and knees felt like I'd jumped onto burning coals. I found my right arm—not as easy as it sounds—and pointed it up like I'd been trained while scuba diving. *Follow the bubbles.* Then I kicked my legs. My lungs burned. My body craved oxygen, but I couldn't take a breath. I had to remain calm. Keep kicking. Shouldn't I be at the surface? How far down had I gone? Had I gotten turned around?

And then, I broke through, my head popping out of the bone-chilling water. I used my hands to spin until I found a reference point. I was less than twenty yards from the end of the runway.

Every frigid wave felt like a slap across my face. Already the temperature was sapping my strength. My muscles were failing. The cold robbed my ability to breathe. I swam automatically even as my body went into shock, my arms doing most of the work to conserve energy. The morning swells were mild, but water splashed into my mouth on every breath. It tasted like jet fuel. It burned my eyes, my lips. I reached the riprap that ringed the shore, but unlike when I leapt from Nikolay's boat, springing easily onto land, I struggled to pull myself out of the water, my shaking limbs grasping for anything. Algae-covered rock I usually had no trouble navigating slipped out of my hands. My shin cracked against the stone. I felt nothing. Muscles cramping, fingers numbed by the November waters, I dragged myself onto dry ground using the stanchion of a runway light as a handhold.

I rested.

But only for an instant. If I didn't make it to the plane where Phoebe and Daniel were waiting for me, I'd be stuck here.

Across the open divide, I could see the tail of the British Airways jet. The gate number signs were large and easily readable even from this distance. The vastness of an airport is deceiving. Distances are hard to judge. The sheer scale of terminal buildings and planes make everything seem closer.

My hands trembled from the cold, or maybe it was adrenaline.

I had a target.

I got to my feet. Wet fabric hung on me, and chaffed the skin under my arms, between my legs. I felt like the Tin Man, needing oil. As I moved, my muscles loosened. But the cold and the added weight of my water-logged clothes fatigued me. I didn't know if I would make it. I had maybe ten minutes to get to the plane before they closed the cabin door. No matter how long I ran, I didn't seem to be getting closer. There was a moment where I almost stopped, almost fell to my knees. I saw myself doing it in my head. Maybe it was better if I didn't make it. Better if I just laid down.

My mind had given up, but my body kept pushing on.

Training trumps instinct.

Nothing mattered but my destination, E6.

I caught a glimpse of Elam Khai's plane with the ONYX logo on the fuselage.

Even in my half-delirious state I could tell the craft was backing away from the private terminal. He was coming after me. I had saved his life, saved him from being downed by an RPG. And he was coming to get me.

At least, the plane he thought I was on.

After what seemed like an eternity, I found myself at the bottom of the jetway stairs. After running nearly a mile, those steps were the hardest, like the final strides to the summit of Everest.

I reached the top.

I punched in the *top, middle, second from the bottom, second from the top, bottom* pattern to gain access to the jetway. It didn't open. Had they locked down the airport. I took a breath. Tried again. This time my fingers got it right. A moment later, I was on board. With the help of the man who unknowingly presented the altered boarding passes, Phoebe, Daniel and I were where we were supposed to be. On this flight. In these seats. Under these names.

Not long after, we were in the air.

Adhering to my implanted suggestions, the Lufthansa pilots headed out to sea, keeping a low altitude to avoid detection. By the time fighter jets were scrambled, the craft was far enough over the Atlantic that it was out of range of ground radar and virtually invisible with its transponder disabled.

Which is how I duped Elam Khai into spending tremendous time and effort chasing a nearly untrackable plane he believed I had hijacked and flown to the southern tip of the Iberian Peninsula.

"He is not going to be happy when he figures out what you did," said Daniel, his mouth full of candy.

"You're going to choke if you keep shoving those into your mouth."

"Does it really make a difference at this point?"

The soldiers ordered everyone to remain seated and put our hands on top of the seat in front of us. Each passenger was frisked and led off the plane.

I could feel rumbling underneath my feet as the cargo holds beneath us were opened. I moved my head as slowly as possible to sneak a peek out the window. Soldiers were tossing bags onto the tarmac where dogs sniffed them.

"What happened when you were five?" I said to Phoebe.

She had been watching the action outside as well. "What?"

"The phone call with your mom. You said that she should trust you, like the time you got lost in the mall when you were five." I was hoping to distract her.

"I—" She struggled to find the words. "I got lost at the big mall outside Pittsfield. I wandered off somehow and my mom freaked out and security called the police. Actually, her trying to find me made it worse. I heard the sirens, saw the lights, the men with guns..." She stared at the soldiers with their rifles and close-combat machine guns. "And...I got scared. I hadn't been frightened until then. I had just misplaced my mom. But when I saw the police, I hid from them. I don't remember their faces. Just the weapons." She swallowed as if something was stuck in her throat. "I snuck out through a door at the back of one of the shops and hid in some bushes. I don't know how long I stayed there, but I remember seeing a group of people get on a bus. So I walked over to the bus stop and used the money I was going to buy candy with and got on the next bus. Then I got on a second bus, and a third, asking each driver how to get back to Great Barrington. Once I was in town, I somehow figured out the way to my house. The whole thing took maybe five hours. My neighbor had to call my parents because they were both up in Pittsfield looking for me. My father was so angry. I could hear the rage in his voice over the phone." She paused, remembering something. "But when he saw me, he just cried. And held me so tight, I almost couldn't breathe. My mother was...I remember her face. She wasn't mad. She wasn't tearful like my dad. She just stared at me. She brushed my hair back. I remember that. It was so gentle. She put me to bed. The normal nighttime routine. Except...when she turned off the light, she didn't whisper 'I love you' through the crack in the door before walking out. Instead, she just sat in the room and watched me, didn't take her eyes off me. You'd think that would be weird, but it wasn't. It was comforting. It was days before she finally started talking about it. She asked why I didn't ask anyone for help. And I told her, when I realized the men with guns were looking for me, I didn't want them to find me."

As the soldiers moved toward us, Phoebe's gaze focused on the barrels.

"They're not looking for you," I said as I stood up.

It was our row's turn to be searched.

Once in the terminal, once our IDs had been checked, our luggage had been searched—I had to explain the ginormous underwear by telling the soldiers my grandmother is extremely overweight and stores in Ghana don't carry items large enough as few people in Ghana are obese and since America has more fat people I bought clothes for her in the U.S.—you get the idea. Once we answered all their questions—had we seen anything suspicious at Logan or on the flight? Once all that was done, we were allowed to leave.

In all, we were detained about three hours.

I was worried that with this delay and the attention Heathrow was getting, Elam Khai might have people watching for us at the exits. So we amended our (amended) (amended) plan, taking a non-stop from Heathrow to Edinburgh using a different set of passports, and then immediately getting on another plane back to London, using our third set of passports, but this time landing at Gatwick. This inefficient do-si-do added five hours and shifted us thirty-eight miles south.

"Any more countries you'd like to visit for three seconds?" asked Daniel, nodding toward a departure screen in the Gatwick terminal.

"I feel bad for whoever those people are," Phoebe said, looking at a news report displaying the faces of our alter-egos.

Daniel shook his head. "I do *not* want to be them when a few dozen commandos bust down their doors."

"I doubt they even exist," I said, staring at the three faces. "And if they do, knowing Engel, they probably deserve whatever they get."

It wasn't the quality of Engel's work that made the difference. It was that he had seen *everything*, and because of that, he was always a hundred steps ahead.

It was raining. That late November rain that's heavy at times, that comes down in visible waves on the streets and sidewalks and parks and squares of London, and feels like you're stepping through a beaded curtain as it passes over you.

We bought three umbrellas, hearty ones, ones that would be good in a fight, and headed outside as dawn was breaking, gray and cold.

I hailed one of London's iconic black taxis, and we climbed inside.

We headed north on the M23 toward central London. About halfway there as we turned west on the A2, I could see a thin green ray of light firing north at a shallow angle. The steady beam stood out in the gray morning as a beacon, leading us toward our destination.

We arrived at Greenwich Park just past eight in the morning, the last chimes of Big Ben echoing in the distance as we stepped out of the taxi.

Phoebe glanced west, but the Clock Tower wasn't visible from our location. "I've always wanted to see Big Ben."

"You can't actually see Big Ben," I said.

"We're too far away, I guess."

"No, I mean, even if you could see the tower, you can't see Big Ben. Big Ben is the name of the hour bell inside the clock."

"So, what's the tower called?"

"The Clock Tower."

"That's real creative. 'What should we call the clock tower?' 'I don't know. How about Clock Tower?'" said Daniel in the worst pair of British accents.

"'What should we call the white house the president lives in?' 'How about The White House?' Same."

"You have an answer for everything, don't you?"

"I don't *alway*—"

"It's annoying."

Surrounded by the vast lawns of Greenwich Park, the Observatory buildings were a tangle of brick and mortar topped by scoops of ice cream—vanilla on one, dark chocolate on the other. These were the telescopes. A building off to the side looked like a gigantic piece of penne pasta pounded into the ground.

Except for the piece of pasta, the buildings were old, having the feel of a country estate in miniature.

A few people were mulling about in the courtyard. Given the early hour and inclement weather, I was surprised. But this was the zero point of the world, and people came to stand on it, straddle it, and hop back and forth between the eastern and western hemispheres.

The building which defined zero degrees longitude was the most unassuming of all the structures. If it hadn't been the origin of the emerald beam, you'd walk by it without a glance.

Just below the strand of light, about ten feet off the ground, a white sign with black letters read: Prime Meridian Of The World. The sign was metal but looked like it had been printed on a sheet of plain paper and fixed to the brick with red masking tape.

The sign, the building, the red line bisecting the door and running along the ground did little to convey the historical significance of this place.

In 1884, this spot corresponding to the square peephole in the main door was chosen over points in Paris and Washington, D.C. to become the universal starting point for time and navigation.

"I want one of those," Daniel said, his eyes following the laser from the building into the sky and then back.

"You want a powerful laser that makes it easier for Elam Khai to find you?"

"Okay, maybe I don't want one of these."

Phoebe crouched down and touched the metal line that traced away from the building. She let her fingertips linger on the names of the cities listed along the Meridian, each locale followed by numbers.

"Every timezone on Earth is measured as a plus or minus from this spot. The beginning of time," she said.

"Technically wouldn't the beginning of time be the International Dateline?" Daniel was standing next to the stainless steel sculpture in the middle of the courtyard. "Which is what? On the exact opposite side of the world from where we're standing."

"To avoid local paradoxes of time, the Dateline goes around land, countries, and islands," I said. "There is no 'place' the Dateline touches. Fiji used to have an island where the dates were different on either side, but not anymore."

"See, I would've voted for Fiji if I'd known that."

"Which is why we didn't have a vote."

"Which, honestly, wasn't very democratic of you."

Phoebe slid along the line. Havana, Dallas, Casablanca, Los Angeles, Chicago, Lima. She stopped when she came to New York,

73° 50' W. "Seventy-three degrees. That's about where home is, right?"

"Great Barrington? Yeah, seventy-three degrees, thirty minutes or so."

She screwed up her face, her eyes sorrowful. "I keep forgetting. My home is not your home." Her fingers trace the number 73. "I still wonder if he meant your home."

"I don't have a home."

"Where you were born, I mean."

"That place doesn't exist anymore."

I had held out a dim hope that I would find my father standing here, straddling the Prime Meridian. One foot in the Eastern Hemisphere, one foot in the Western Hemisphere. Which is kind of how I feel about myself. Half in the Old World, half in the New.

"We should look around," I said.

Daniel's eyebrows went up. "We flew across the Atlantic, then up to Scotland and back, and your plan is 'We should look around?'"

"We'll know it when we see it."

"Well, there you go. Phoebe, we're looking for something, and when we see it, we'll know."

Phoebe rolled her eyes. "I don't see you coming up with any brilliant ideas."

Daniel wagged his finger. "Hey, I told you this was stupid."

"Actually, you said it was 'vague.'"

"Well, this is about as vague as it gets."

Phoebe glared at him. "I've been taking it easy on you because you were nearly murdered a day ago. Why don't you stop complaining and start *thinking*."

"Really? What have you done besides cheerleading everyone of his crazy ideas? 'Goooooooooo Alexander!'"

Phoebe reflexively kicked Daniel in the groin. He doubled over.

"Give me an 'O!'" she said.

"Ooooohhhhhhh."

"There you go."

"Stop it!" I said.

For a moment, the only sounds were the heavy breaths of Phoebe and Daniel. Hers in anger. His in pain.

"I'm sorry," Phoebe said, finally.

"Me, too." Daniel's voice was a squeaky whisper followed by what I can only describe as the sound of a skate blade being dragged slowly across the ice.

When the Observatory opened, we scoured the inside. It was filled with thought-provoking tidbits and fascinating devices, but nothing remotely pointing to the whereabouts of my father.

After that, we searched the grounds, digging around in the mud at any sign of freshly turned dirt. We checked the graffiti etched on benches and trees. Most were proclamations that this person or that had been here, professions of love, and one simply said: *arbitrary*. It was this last inscription that flicked a switch in my brain.

I returned to the stainless steel line embedded in the stone courtyard. I measured my steps, making each one as close to the same distance as the one before. About a hundred paces due east, I stopped.

While the concept of having a universally defined point for time and distance is easy to grasp, in practice, it's a lot more complicated than that. Precise measurements of a particular point on earth are difficult to take, especially using the sun as a reference. It moves, it wavers, it wobbles, it expands and contracts. Then there's the earth itself. Tectonic plates shift and drift. Large earthquakes alter the rotation of the planet. It's a major hassle. Instead, the Prime Meridian—the zero longitude—is now calculated by observing distant quasars and celestial bodies, laser ranging the moon and artificial satellites to compute their distances from the surface, and then adding in data from GPS systems orbiting the planet.

All of which, more or less, pointed to right here. Where I was standing. Beside an unmarked, uncelebrated garbage can. Or as the English would call it: a dustbin.

Phoebe and Daniel arrived a moment later. I stared at the receptacle, trying to figure out how to open the thing.

"What is it?" Phoebe asked.

Daniel studied it, curiously. "A trashcan."

"This is the real Prime Meridian."

"This trashcan?"

I nodded, then motioned back toward the beam of light. "That's the historical Meridian. The actual Meridian, the one calculated with satellites, atomic clocks, and GPS is—" I motioned right in front of me.

"A trashcan."

"Yeah. 'Arbitrary.'"

I got down on my knees and looked underneath the bin, ran my hands along the edges. I looked under the lid, felt around inside, at least as far as I could get my arm in. When a maintenance worker asked what I was doing, I told him I'd lost my watch throwing away some trash. He opened the bin and let me dig through the contents while Daniel and Phoebe searched the now empty housing.

I delayed the worker as long as I could, stretching his patience until he informed us he couldn't wait any longer. He put the liner bin inside the housing and locked it.

It was ten o'clock in the morning when we—soaked and starving—finally gave up.

Phoebe put her hand on my shoulder, and I felt the weight of disappointment. I had no idea what else to do except get something to fill our empty bellies.

Thankfully, the rain stopped.

We were walking along a narrow street where small shops nestled themselves amongst the row houses, looking for a place to sit and eat.

I involuntarily stopped when I saw his face on the other side of the glass. I almost didn't recognize him.

It took three houses for Phoebe and Daniel to realize I was no longer beside them.

There are uncountable times a familiar face has passed me in a crowd. Each person is unique, but there are only so many noses, so many shapes and colors of eyes, cheekbones, lips, etcetera. These sightings trigger a sometimes hazy, sometimes sharp recollection. This one was a stab through my chest.

I entered the shop and was greeted by a tinkling bell and a well-practiced "'ave a seat. Be with you soon enough." I was too focused to notice who had said the words. I went straight for the magazines on the window sill.

"This is a hair salon," Daniel said, walking into the shop. "We need food, not euro hairstyles."

A beautiful actress in a stunning dress adorned the cover of Vanity Fair.

"She's pretty," Phoebe said, watching my reaction.

I grunted.

I searched for the table of contents, which was like looking for a needle in a haystack among all the ads. No, no, no, no, no, finally! I found the article page number and flipped to it.

There, splashed across page 46 and part of 47, was a blown-up version of the small photo on the cover. A bearded man holding his chin with his thumb and forefinger. The article said he was forty-seven years old, but he looked much, much younger than that.

Phoebe said. "Who is that?"

I pointed to the article's commanding title. "*Is Lance Crispin The Greatest Writer Ever?*" In smaller type underneath, it added: *(In Television)*.

"Lance Crispin?"

"Who's Lance Crispin?" Daniel asked.

I didn't answer. I was skimming the article. *Blah, blah, blah, blah, his latest television show is a monumental hit with both critics and audiences, another two seasons have been ordered, blah, blah, blah.* "Here it is. 'Crispin is preparing a new stage play in London, set to open in December.'" I read down further. "'He is personally over-seeing the production while filming of his hit series is on hiatus until January.'" I closed the magazine. "He's here."

"Your dad?"

"No." I pulled out a fifty-dollar bill.

"Not a lot that's gonna do you here, love," said a woman with towering pinkish hair who was holding a pair of scissors over the head of another woman.

"I was hoping to buy this magazine off you."

"Aye, that one? It's barmy worthless. You can 'ave it."

"Thanks."

I turned to leave.

"For that worthless *nifty* in your 'and."

I left the bill on the counter.

Phoebe took the magazine and flipped through the article as we hurried down Royal Hill Road. "He did all these shows? I love every one of these."

"Who is Lance Crispin?!" Daniel demanded.

"The greatest writer ever!" Phoebe and I said in unison.

"In television," she added.

I opened my mouth to correct her, froze like that for a moment, then decided against it.

SEVEN

2B Or Not 2B

"A TV writer?" Daniel was skeptical. "Maybe we could enlist a game show host, corral a family of reality stars. Build an army of artists and painters and B-list celebrities. You know how well *they* handle adversity. Worse than I do."

We were making our way west on the Queen's Walk along the meandering banks of the Thames.

"This play sounds amazing," said Phoebe, her nose in the article.

Daniel's arms were hanging at his side. "I'm hungry. I'm tired. How does a TV writer help us?"

"I used to work for him."

"Unless you used to work for him as a chef and you're going to cook him—"

"He knows my father."

"How do you even know he's going to be at the theatre?"

"He's always at work. Or at the pub closest to it."

"I vote for the pub."

I stopped abruptly, causing Daniel to slam into me. I gazed up at the theatre with its thatched roof and twenty-sided polygonal shape.

"Well, that was fast," Daniel said.

Phoebe looked up from the magazine. "This isn't it. Crispin's play is being performed at the *National* Theater."

"I know," I said. "This is the Globe. Not the original Globe. That was about a block east. This is a twentieth-century replica. A pretty fair copy, considering the lack of detail they had to work with. The stage is wrong, but not so much that anyone would quibble about it. I had to call in a lot of favors to get tickets to the opening. The Queen performed the dedication herself."

"Really? The Queen?" said Daniel, irritated.

I nodded, remembering the gala in June 1997. "The National is only a couple of blocks away."

For all the grandeur of its name, The National Theatre is rather ugly. Too old to benefit from the bold designs possible with the latest construction techniques and too new to be majestic or stately, the Nat was more or less a victim of its time. Its Brutalist architecture projected an atmosphere of totalitarianism.

The love child of a parking garage and a prison, the National was a great deal more pleasant once you passed through its doors.

It wasn't difficult to get through the almost nonexistent security. We told the guards we were actors. They pointed us to casting.

Once in the administration offices, I simply inquired, "Do you know where I can find Lance?"

The woman didn't immediately look up. "They've got a tech rehearsal scheduled today, so he's probably—" She lifted her eyes. We weren't what she was expecting. "Do you have an appointment with him?"

"I used to be his writing assistant."

She was silent for a moment as she tried to work out the math.

"What, when you were ten?"

Close, I thought.

"I'm older than I look. Lance is always saying, 'You should get on a series. You could play the role of a teenager for *years.*'"

"He's somewhere in the building. Either down by the stage or maybe his office." She unconsciously glanced at the ceiling.

"It's one floor up, right?" There were only three, and we were on the second.

"Yes. At the end of the hall on the left-hand side. In the corner."

Following her directions was not as simple as it sounded. The layout of the building was convoluted. I was about to start knocking on offices asking for help when I saw the suite number at the elbow of two hallways.

"You've got to be kidding me." I stood at the threshold, my eyes level with the brass symbols affixed to the door.

"What?" Phoebe said.

I knocked on the door marked 2B.

After a long moment, a man that looked to be in his mid to late thirties answered.

His was the face from the magazine.

"Seriously? Two-B?"

Crispin adjusted the hump side of the B, sliding the loose digit to the right. The door now read 213. "Or not Two-B."

I stared at him. Hard.

He shrugged. "You take your pleasures where you can." He motioned inside. "C'mon in. I'm going over script assignments for next season's episodes, and I'm late for a tech run-through down on the stage. You look good."

This was said as if he'd just seen me yesterday. It had been nearly a quarter century since the Globe opening.

"Thanks. I've got some friends with me."

"Oh, yes," he said as if just realizing two people were flanking me. "Come in. Come in."

The anterior room was adorned with posters and one-sheets from various productions performed over the years at the National. It was generic. Not at all personalized, except for a stack of scripts with Crispin's name on the cover pages.

He led us into another room. This space felt warmer. The furniture, the lighting, the posters were more in keeping with my former employer's tastes.

"You worked for me a couple of years back, right? I'm blanking on your name." He knew exactly who I was. He just wasn't sure who my friends knew me to be.

"They know."

"They do?"

"Yes."

"What do they know..." He paused. "*Alexander?*"

Daniel chimed in. "Everything."

"Reeeeally?" he said to me, his voice sounding grave and curious all at once.

I nodded.

"I true and surely doubt that." He took Phoebe's hand. "I'm Lance Crispin." He bowed and kissed the back of her knuckles.

I rolled my eyes.

"It's a pleasure to meet you, Mr. Crispin. I'm Phoebe."

"Phoibe. Goddess of the Moon. You wear your name well."

Daniel looked a little hesitant as he outstretched his hand, hoping, I'm sure, it wouldn't receive the same treatment. "I'm Daniel."

Crispin took Daniel's hand and shook it mightily. "Daniel. 'God is my Judge.' Good names." He finally let go of Daniel's hand. "Have a seat. Relax. I'm sure there's an interesting tale that brings us all together." He looked at me and waited.

"Can I tell them?" I said.

"Seems you've been in the telling mood." He stared at me, and I knew what the look was silently asking.

"I trust them." I said. "With my life."

"How about mine?"

"Sixty-forty. Maybe."

Daniel wobbled his palm. "Eh, fifty-five, forty-five."

Will pondered us for a moment. "A passable jest. In that case..."

I started to speak, but he put up his hand.

"Not that you aren't a tolerable storyteller, but please...let me." Crispin turned to Phoebe and Daniel. He opened his mouth, then stopped. I knew that feeling. That moment where everything is clear in your head, yet nothing comes out of your mouth. Telling is something we don't do. So, the doing of it is foreign. He took a moment to gather himself and find a way to convince his mouth it was okay to speak the words. "I have written under a few pen names during my career. Depending on how well read you are, you may have heard of a few of my *nom de plumes*—"

"You're Shakespeare," Phoebe said.

Crispin pressed his lips together. "That's one of them."

"You're…Shakespeare?" Daniel repeated. "William Shakespeare?"

"Yes."

"The man who nearly caused me to flunk freshman English?"

"I don't know if I can take credit for that achievement."

"Oh, I think you should get all the credit for me almost not getting credit. Can I ask you something?"

I saw the look on Will's face. It was the look of a man who'd heard the same questions over and over again. Questions he desperately wanted to answer through the centuries. He couldn't just say, "Hey, idiots, I'm Will Shakespeare and here's what you seventeenth, eighteenth, nineteenth, twentieth, twenty-first century halfwits are getting wrong." Not that he didn't do that subtly. Articles. Opinion pieces. He even tried suggesting corrections to planners and architects of the new Globe Theatre, but was overruled by so-called "experts" who said the at-the-time unknown TV writer didn't know what he was talking about.

And so, Will waited, expecting to be queried on one or more of the following things:

1. Did he actually write all those plays himself?

2. If so, how many other plays did he write since there are more than the thirty-seven in his official canon that bear his handwriting?

3. Were his sonnets really written to a man?

But this was Daniel. Not one of these questions occurred to him.

"What kind of stupid name is Shakespeare? I mean, you could've picked any name, right? *Any* name. And that's the ridiculous sounding one you pick?"

I've left out some of Daniel's tirade. He has a tendency to add generous amounts of profanity when confronted with people over a thousand.

"It was a joke," Crispin said. "Shake the spear. Rattle the status quo."

Daniel shrugged. "Oh. I figured you were talking about masturbating."

"That, too."

Phoebe blushed.

"Young beauty. Don't tell me you are offended."

"I—"

"I'm sure far more coarse words have been spoken and texted by you and your girlfriends on a daily basis."

The flush of red in her cheeks was now fueled by annoyance.

"Do you know what the problem with the state of society today is? Your profanity has no art. There's nothing wrong with discussing all manner of relationships, whether it be with yourself…" He motioned below his belt. "Or someone else. But try and use more than three words to describe it."

I had the feeling Crispin might get rolling and avalanche into one of his soliloquies. In his television writer persona, he was known for clever extended rants. Filmed in a walking and talking style, these quirky, intelligent diatribes could be about anything from personal hygiene to politics to the state of baseball. So, I figured it was prudent to rein him in before he built up any momentum.

I threw the magazine down on the coffee table.

Crispin's outrage over the modern lack of imaginative profanity receded. He stared at the two-page spread with his larger than life face. "Yeah, that was probably not very smart." He extended his hand in an attempt to start over. "My *old* friends call me Will."

Will had sandwiches brought up from the stage. We ate ravenously.

Will was supposedly talking to all of us, but his wit and attention were directed more toward Phoebe than Daniel or me.

"Every couple of hundred years I get so sick and tired of writing that I just give it up."

"What do you do instead?" she asked, her hand covering her mouth, which was full.

"Gamble usually. I mean, games of chance aren't much of a

stretch. A writer is a professional gambler. Every time I finish a script, a play, a book, I roll the dice."

She nibbled more slowly at her second sandwich—she had devoured the first. She was entranced. I would be too if I had just met the Bard himself for the first time. And not the man I knew in the late 1500s and early 1600s. He was certainly famous, lauded, and cheered back then. He was Shakespeare, of course. But he wasn't *Shakespeare*. Time magnifies the greatness of some and diminishes it of others. It tends to sift out, most of the time correctly, the truly great from the merely. Daniel was more interested in the food than basking in the aura of one of history's greatest writers. When Will was not in the depths of despair, agonizing over his work, struggling to find the words or incapacitated by doubt, he was an extraordinarily charming and fascinating companion. No amount of time, no literary critic could ever take that away from him.

"I do that for a while until I lose all my money, and then I know it's time to get back to the pen. Where I have to start all over again. The worst part is that the absolute manure I used to get away with publishing as a famous writer, turns out to be 'not good enough' when you're unknown. I flail around for a bit and usually fail at three or four lifetimes, then finally something will hit. And suddenly, I'm a 'genius' again." He gestured air quotes with his fingers.

It reminded me of what Elam Khai had ranted about. How he had remained the same—just as good, just as brilliant, cultured and enlightened, just as brutal as he'd always been—it was others who changed their opinion of him—good or evil—based on the circumstances of the time.

"Well, I love your plays," Phoebe said.

"*Romeo and Juliet*, right? Girls always seem to love that one. Or maybe *Twelfth Night*."

"Actually, I prefer *Midsummer Night's Dream*. Especially the play within the play. But my favorite is *King Lear*."

Will raised his right brow. "That's a little dark, isn't it?"

"So is *Romeo and Juliet*. And that's a good play."

"It's a great play," he said, glaring at me. "Though I'm fairly sick of it. 'Romeo, Romeo, wherefore art thou Romeo?' Blahhhhk. Makes me want to vomit my entrails. It's a *window*, by the way. Nowhere do I ever say balcony."

"Just because *you're* tired of it doesn't make it any less great. It touches people. Everyone has felt something like that. Two people wanting to be together but not being able to because of outside forces they can't control."

Even as she kept her eyes on Will, I could feel the pull from her, not like an anchor tied to my feet, but like the moon on the tides.

"I'll admit, I liked it for a couple of centuries. Most of it's excellent, but parts of it are a bit…swoony. Honestly, I cringe whenever I hear it. Actors can't even say the lines right. 'Where FORE art thou. Wherefore ART thou. Wherefore art THOU.' It's 'WHEREfore art thou.' Is that so difficult? I underline things now."

"You've always been strict about the words," I said.

"Even the biggest stars, I demand they say exactly what's on the page. None of this ad-libbing garbage. We might as well just walk around filming random people on the street."

"It's called reality television," I said.

"It's the rankest smell that ever offended nostril."

One of his assistants entered the room. "They're waiting for you downstairs. You're already fifteen minutes late."

"I know. I know." He got out of his chair and closed the door behind her. "I'm going to assume this visit isn't social, especially since you revealed information that tends to get people banished for centuries." He glanced at Phoebe and Daniel. "We can talk on the way down to the set."

Will stepped into the other room, giving instructions to his assistants.

Daniel leaned his shoulder into mine. "Why haven't you asked him about your father?"

"I'm not sure how much I should tell him."

Phoebe looked at me. "You trust us, but you don't trust him?"

"I trust him. Just…only to a certain point."

Daniel and Phoebe got up and followed Will into the hall. I pulled out the passports we'd used for the Lufthansa flight, then fed first Daniel's, then Phoebe's, then mine into the shredder. They made a satisfying grinding whine as they disappeared.

"You'll like this play," Will said to Phoebe as I caught up to them. "It's a story of love and betrayal. Genius versus sheer will. There's this incredible electricity between the characters."

"That's funny," said Phoebe.

"So you know what it's about," Will said as they laughed at the joke Daniel and I didn't get.

We passed a portrait of Shakespeare hanging in the hall. It had only a vague resemblance to Will, who looked younger and more handsome today than back then.

"Don't you think this is a little, I don't know, too close for comfort? The Globe a few blocks away? Images of you everywhere?"

"All these portraits were done after I was 'dead.' They hardly look anything like me." Which was more or less true. "And it's not like it's the *actual* Globe. Did you know, I wanted to stage a play there a few years ago. They wouldn't let me. Can you imagine that? Theatre's painstakingly recreated to perform *my* plays as originally intended. But apparently not *all* my plays. Do you remember how hard it was for you and me to even attend the opening?"

The hallway opened into a mezzanine.

"What about keeping a low profile?" I asked. "Nobody has said anything about the article?"

Will stopped, furtively glancing down at the cubicles on the floor below. "No. Why? Has anyone said anything to you?" He struck the most defensive pose he could manage, which is to say, not a very good one. I could've easily sent him tumbling over the rail to the floor below with one kick.

"Not to me," I said, laying a calming hand on his arm, causing him to flinch. "It's just…you're a little too well-known."

"I know. I know. Stupid. I need to start graying my hair. Maybe thinning it." He shook his head. "Vanity. It's difficult to overcome."

"Lance! Laaannce!"

We glanced up to see a heavyset tech in glasses and a thick beard charging our way. His sizable gut was swaying, necessitating the man to pull up on his belt every few steps. "This whole story is about power, right? The struggle for power. A power struggle over the struggle of power!"

"I guess you could say that."

"Well, I've got a power struggle on my hands, Lance. A big one."

"Louie, I don't have time to deal with this."

"Yeah, I heard you had guests." The tech eyed us, mistrustfully.

"You've got the power to make whatever decisions you have to."

"That's the problem. I don't have the *power*. We're gonna overload the circuits. You'd think a place that's got all the style of a nuclear power plant would have enough amps running through the system, but no! This is going to quickly go from being a spectacular artistic demonstration of power to a spectacular blackout!"

"Run lines from other circuits. Pull power from another building. I don't care. I'll pay the overrun. Just make it work."

"I already have, but you asked for hair-raising. This is hair-raising. I created the world's largest bug zapper, and we're the insects."

"Just do it, Louie."

Louie the tech peeled off as we reached a bank of elevators. Will was about to call for a car when he halted his fingers a few inches from the buttons.

"You don't like these, do you?"

"I prefer taking the stairs. It's healthier."

"So is kale and broccoli," he said, gesturing toward a stairwell a few feet away.

"You're *afraid* of elevators? You? The guy who takes on people brandishing swords and jumps off buildings. *Elevators?*" Daniel pushed open the door, his laugh filling the stairwell.

Will looked at me. "Never let people know your weaknesses. It invites others to exploit them."

"Blowing power circuits?" said Daniel. "I thought this play was about love and betrayal."

"It is. But it's set against the backdrop of the epic battle between two men over the greatest advancement in the history of mankind." He lowered his head and whispered, "Electricity."

"Tesla and Edison." Phoebe said, proudly.

"Tesla and Edison were in love?" Daniel asked.

"Nooooo," Will said, annoyed. "In the play, Edison's wife is an amalgamation of Edison's actual wife, the young, attractive, Mary Edison and the beautiful Catherine Johnson, wife of Tesla's best friend. She was in love with Tesla. And probably the only person he ever loved. I don't count the pigeon he fell in love with."

"Tesla fell in love with a pigeon?" said Phoebe.

"Genius is sometimes odd."

"Yes, it is," I agreed.

"If your comment is meant to suggest that my eccentricity indicates genius, I will gladly accept the compliment. Although, I fear my strangeness is merely an indication of strangeness." He stopped and turned to me. "Mark this, in a hundred years, I'm going to be doing a play pitting the peculiar Elon Musk against the even weirder Peter Krol. Two moneyed nutcases who think shooting regular people into space is a fine idea."

From the bottom of the staircase, an assistant wearing a headset yelled up. "Lance!"

Will cringed. "Sometimes I hate that name."

"Yes, Lance *Crispin*." I mocked.

"Doesn't Crispin mean red-haired?" Phoebe asked, motioning toward Will's not-red hair.

Will shook his head. "From the Latin. *Crispo*."

"Meaning *brandish*," I said. "Or flourish or wave or…shake." I let the words sink in.

Phoebe turned to Will. "Spear...shaker."

"I chuckle every time I see it splashed across a television screen."

"You're like a ten year old sometimes," I said.

"Forgive me if I toss out an ode to one of my former selves every few lifetimes. A lot better than the 'floppy timekeeper.'"

"Lance!" Another call from below.

"Although, at moments like these, I loathe my decision not to choose another 'H' name. Much harder to screech." He leaned over the railing and yelled, "What!"

"She won't come out of her dressing room." The assistant's words echoed off the concrete.

"Son of a motherless goat. What is it now?"

"She doesn't *feel* the script today."

Anger washed over Will and he suddenly lurched forward, descending the stairs without caution. Reaching the bottom, he grabbed the headset roughly from the assistant, tried to untangle it, finally gave up and just spoke into the boom mic, ignoring the earpiece altogether.

"Listen. I don't care if she doesn't feel it. I don't care if she doesn't like her hair. Or her make up. Or her wardrobe. Or doesn't understand the motivation behind a particular action or gesture or piece of dialogue. Or even why the world exists at all. You understand? I want her on that stage now, or I'm going to let everyone know what a nightmare she is to work with. That Hell is empty and all the demons are in her dressing room. You tell her all of that. Word. For. Word."

Like I said. He's a stickler for the words.

Will burst from the stairwell, swearing for a good minute before he finally had to take a breath. "No offense to your gender, young lady, but I liked it better when all the parts were played by men." He smoothed his hair at his temples. "Although, backstage didn't smell as good."

Will led us down a corridor that opened into the theatre. The enormity of the room was staggering. It had the feel of an ancient amphitheater with rows rising up and spreading out from the stage like a Japanese fan. The ceiling soared overhead, a labyrinth of catwalks and light banks.

I felt tiny.

I felt something else. Electricity. The slightly metallic taste on the tongue. The refreshing scent entering your nostrils. Like after a summer thunderstorm.

The set was impressive. A laboratory was on the left. The interior of a house, on the right. Dominating the center, accessible from stairs at the rear of the laboratory, was a towering structure. This was the source of the taste in the air and the power issues.

"Is that a Tesla coil?" whispered Phoebe.

I gawked at the device. "A very large one."

At the moment, the machine was dormant.

Daniel gazed at the massive space. "Wow."

"Yes," agreed Will. "It's going to swallow my actors, if I don't kill them first. I might as well have staged this at a football stadium."

Will's reluctant female lead emerged from the shadows, raising a delicate hand to shield her eyes from the harsh stage lights.

Will whispered, "Mary Edison liked her morphine. I did, too, before we found out it killed you. I'm concerned *my* Mary is taking her role literally."

His Mary was stunning. She was young. Maybe nineteen or twenty. A beautiful, bewildering wild child, known almost as much for her offscreen antics as her onscreen performances. She had that knowing look beautiful people often have, a veneer of strength that often conceals insecurity.

When Will greeted her, any animosity he was harboring drifted away. She was pliant, apologetic, and under the influence of something. She bounced nervously, biting her nails as she listened to Will give her directions. The fidgeting stopped only when she spoke in character, transforming into a self-assured woman of substance.

Phoebe was lifted onstage by a ridiculously handsome actor.

I swear I heard a *ting* and saw his teeth gleam when he smiled at her.

Phoebe and the actor stood in the wings next to the prop table.

I casually walked over and picked up one of the swords. I unsheathed it and touched my hand to the tip. It pricked several layers of skin, its razor sharpness surprising me. In seconds, a ribbon of crimson ran down my palm.

"A fight scene in a story about Tesla and Edison?" Phoebe asked her good-looking companion as the actors on stage were handed blades.

He shook his head. "A *love* scene. Mary is learning to fence. Her husband thinks it's a waste of time. She convinces Tesla to try it." He handed Phoebe a blade, then put his arm around her waist and guided her swing. "It's passionate. The swords become part of the dance of their flirtation."

He was mimicking each move in perfect synchronization with the Tesla actor on stage. He must be the understudy.

The actor playing Tesla was tall, dressed impeccably, and had a quirky, brooding handsomeness. The man portraying Thomas Alva Edison, his clothes were rumpled and covered in dirt and grime. His shock of white short hair stuck out at all angles. It wasn't the tamed look one saw in portraits of the man.

"I don't have time for these games. There's work to be done," grumbled Edison, tossing his sword on the couch.

"That is because you are as inefficient as a broom with a single stalk of hay!" Tesla yelled as his employer stormed off stage.

I could sense Will's frustration. Both Will and I had sat across from these men. It's difficult to watch historical portrayals of people you've actually met. I've found myself yelling at televisions and movie screens, "That's not how she acted! That's not the way he moved!"

There are many theaters I'm not allowed in anymore.

This only began bothering me since the advent of film. Books, plays, even paintings allow you to infuse your own imagination, fill in the blanks, recognize the artistic license, but watching a person in a realistic setting makes the pretense and imprecision more noticeable.

Don't get me wrong. I'm not a purist when it comes to historical accuracy in art. A work is more about the time in which it was created than the time it's portraying. And I've seen many performances where the affectations and mannerisms of a true-life person have been completely inaccurate. The voice, the look, all wrong, and still, the truth of the person I knew—their character—shines through. A good example is Mark Twain. The real Samuel L. Clemens didn't start wearing the now-iconic white three-piece suit until very late in life, after the death of his wife, and almost never while speaking in public. Twain's Missouri-flavored Southern drawl was slow and methodical. Much more leisurely than his imitators who talk way too fast and a little too brightly. These errors are compounded by imitators copying mannerisms from earlier imitators. Still, the warm, cutting wit of Twain emerges intact despite these flagrant mistakes, so that even the impersonators of the impersonators of Mark Twain bring him to life.

Tesla picked up Edison's sword. "Is the reason you took up fencing, madam, because it is the only way you might alter that incorrigible man's behavior?" He slashed at the air with his weapon in the direction Edison had exited.

Will grabbed the sword from the actor's hand. "No, no, no! Yes, there will be eleven hundred and sixty people sitting out there—a ridiculous number—but you don't have to scream like you're shouting to the very last one."

After calming down, Will repeated the last bit of dialogue in a fair—and much better—impression of the real Tesla. Will is a halfway decent actor, though not anywhere near as good as his words. Generation upon generation of performers have done his lines better than he could. The Tesla actor was not one of them.

"I took up fencing as a diversion," The actress wiped her brow as she parried with Will. It wasn't the heat of battle. It was the heat building between the characters.

"Your husband, my dear, has no hobby, cares for no sort of amusement of any kind including—I think—you!" Will thrust the sword toward her, the blade coming close to the woman's heaving chest. "He doesn't appreciate what he has."

"He is dedicated to his work," she said with an air of longing.

"His work! A little calculation would save him ninety percent of his labor." Another move. Faint, parry, faint. "His 'inventor's instinct' is the instinct of a toddler who stumbles inevitably upon the rattle by sheer blundering persistence. That, madam, is why your husband needs a hundred men to achieve as much as I can do with a handful. And why I am here, and he is back in the lab."

"Thomas says, 'Genius is one percent inspiration, ninety-nine percent perspiration.'"

"I am well aware that in your husband's world geniuses are uninspired pigs drenched in sweat."

"You are...perspiring at the moment."

"It is the swords."

"Not the nearness of me?"

A beat and then Will rushed the actress, taking her in his hands, his arms shaking with passion and emotion. "Electricity, Mary. Electricity." She gazed into his eyes. "Think of what it means."

"That everything will change," she said breathlessly.

"Not for us," Will said. Without letting go of Mary, he instantly fell out of character and turned to the actor playing Tesla. "You're frustrated. You *know* she loves you. And she is the only woman you've ever wanted."

Daniel came up behind me. "How much money do you have?"

"I don't know, there's probably sixteen, seventeen thousand still in the bag. Why? You need a snack from the vending machine?"

"I mean, *all* your money. Are we talking tens of millions?"

I glanced away without responding only to be smacked with the sight of Phoebe giggling at something the sandy-haired actor said.

"Hundreds of millions?"

I'd love to show off how cool I am and tell you I've got so much money I have no idea how much money I have, but I *do* know. Not to the penny, of course, considering much of it's in real estate, mines, precious metal deposits, stocks, and other, less liquid assets spread across continents. But as far as a general ballpark figure goes—

"I have enough, okay?" It was clear I didn't want to discuss the subject anymore.

"All right." He was quiet for about eight seconds. "So how much money do you think this Elam guy has?"

"I'm guessing a lot more than me."

"That's what I thought."

"What are you getting at?"

"If I had a lot more money than a person who left behind several million dollars without blinking an eye and has no idea how much cash he's carrying—it's fourteen thousand, eight hundred and change, by the way—and I wanted to find someone, I'd have everyone that person could possibly turn to under surveillance."

I was starting to see where Daniel was going.

"I get how he used the tracking device. But he had to find you to put it there. Maybe he was following Braeden. Maybe he has people following everyone like you." Daniel glanced in Will's direction.

"Electricity!" Will shouted, motioning toward the Tesla coil at the back of the stage. "It's the metaphor for what you feel for each other. She is only one you've ever let distract you. But you can't give in. You must finish your work. Otherwise none of this..." He motioned to the lights, the stage, the building. "...exists." He turned to the actress. "And *you*, you will not be abandoned by yet another man."

Daniel nodded toward Will. "If he knows your father, I bet Elam Khai knows him."

I was standing by the deputy stage manager, following the action in the prompt book, the master script marked up with all the actors' movements, all the music and sound cues.

Will and the blonde were coming to the climax of the scene. The script called for Tesla to tell Mary he had to focus on his work. This unleashes an explosion of anger in her.

Mary was holding the sharpened sword that had sliced through my skin.

"Men thrust their swords without any thought to consequence," the young actress said in character, her sword hovering inches from Will's neck. "It *has* consequence. I would plunge this world into darkness rather than let you go."

She edged the sword closer to his throat.

I grabbed the only remaining weapon from the prop table. I sprinted onto the stage, pushing Will to the ground, and raising my pitiful weapon in defense. One swipe and she could cut it in half.

The young actress stared at me, her eyes burning. She was in the moment. In character. Her pupils were saucers, large black orbs. She was definitely on something.

Out of the corner of my eye, I saw blood dripping from Will's neck. "Will? Are you okay?" Her blade had caught him in the confusion. A slice across the skin under his Adam's apple. "Help him!"

Daniel rushed over and clamped a hand over the gash, staunching the flow of blood. It was a bleeder, but not life-threatening.

Ignoring the actress's outstretched sword, I grabbed her by the shirt collar and knocked the blade out of her hand. Still in the moment, she defiantly lifted up her face to mine and kissed me on the mouth. It was much more than a stage kiss. It was passionate. After a dizzyingly long time, she pushed me away, but my hold on her blouse kept her close, unable to reach the weapon.

"I don't know you," I said. I did, of course. Her being a well-known actress everybody knew her. But I didn't know her personally. And she shouldn't know me.

"You're beautiful," she whispered. Her words and her tone froze me.

Then, suddenly, an earthquake. Before I could react, the air was ignited, forming a plasma along the Tesla coil. The corona expanded. Sparks shot out. There were rattles, clanks, screams, a winking out of the senses, all culminating in a great and powerful silence.

I didn't realize I was unconscious until I opened my eyes and saw the blonde actress lying motionless on the ground by my side. My body felt stiff, as if every muscle had been tensed all at once. I expected to find myself restrained by Elam Khai's goons, but there was nothing holding me in place except my fatigued muscles.

The set was in shambles.

The young star was just coming to. She looked up at me, fire still in her eyes.

"I don't understand," I said, unconsciously wiping at my lips, my fingers coming away red. Not with blood, but her lipstick.

"Because I wanted you."

"But why attack Will if you were after me?"

"Who?"

"Lance. Why hurt Lance?"

She reached for the blade, and I readied a counterattack, but when she touched the cutting edge, felt its sharpness, I could see the horror on her face.

I heard a voice spilling from the wings, a mix of anxiousness and excitement. I peered into the shadows and saw Louie the effects specialist. He stared at me as he hurriedly spoke into his cell phone.

I took the sharpened sword from the shaking hands of the actress. Louie didn't move. No one did. Daniel was only partially correct. Elam Khai may have people watching, but they weren't all highly trained PMCs like the ones we ran into at Logan.

I was halfway to my feet when Louie said, "Don't." He did a good job of keeping his voice strong.

I didn't buy it.

I took a step toward him.

"I'll turn it on again. I'll do it." His voice wavering this time.

"Go ahead. I'm betting I can reach you before the machine can knock me out again." Another step. "If it even works."

Louie flipped the switch on the controller. I heard the low buzz of the Tesla coil behind me.

"I've never turned this all the way up. I really don't know what it will do to the others."

"Anything happens to them, I hold you responsible."

"I can't let you leave."

"We are leaving."

"Do you have any idea how much money is being offered for you?" He held up a photo of me. It wasn't a very good one. Monument High yearbook, sophomore photo. "I get a call saying if this kid shows up looking for Lance, I'm supposed to call back, and I'd get a ridiculous amount of money."

"You never bothered to ask yourself, why such a big reward? Never stopped to think, the more ridiculous the amount is, the more likely they are to just kill you. And never worried it might have something to do with how dangerous I am?" I smiled an unnerving grin.

Louie's confidence faltered as he considered these questions that had not dawned on him. After calculating I might be more dangerous than I appeared, he increased the power to the Tesla coil.

I started my sprint, sword ready to strike. The machine zapped, the plasma rose, the hairs on the back of my neck went up, but before the machine could reach supercritical, Louie buckled and disappeared below the console just as I swung the sword where his body had been. Without him in the way, the blade clanged into the main curtain's counterweights, twisting the inferior metal.

Phoebe stood over Louie, having put him down with a kick to the back of the knee. She powered down the Tesla coil.

"You were going to slice him in half."

I held up the sword which looked like a giant fish hook. "This wouldn't have killed him. Most likely. And I figured you were too busy flirting." I nodded toward the young actor who was staring at the scene in disbelief.

"You just had your face devoured by a movie star, so I would shut your lipstick-covered mouth." She turned and passionately kissed the actor.

Okay. Maybe she does like me.

I went to Louie, who as writhing on the floor. Part of me wanted to smash my fist into his face, but I somehow restrained myself. I picked up his phone. The last text said: *5 mins away.*

"We have a couple of minutes, tops." I grabbed the backpack and pulled out a roll of silver duct tape.

Daniel looked at the roll as I knelt down. "That's what you pack? Some cash. A few personal items. And duct tape?"

Will glanced at Daniel. "Honestly, sometimes the duct tape is more important than the money." Blood was oozing out from under Daniel's hand and trickling down Will's shirt.

I ripped off three inches of tape, then cradled Will's head. "All right," I said to Daniel. "Take your hand away."

Will grumbled.

"Buck up. It's only going to really hurt when we take this off."

"Just do it right the first time."

Daniel removed his hand and I wiped away the blood. I quickly placed the tape along the wound, securing the edges with my fingers. "It doesn't look bad," I said. "The wound, I mean. The tape…that looks horrible. C'mon, time to exeunt." I helped him to his feet. "You have a car?"

"Yes," said Will. "Well, I have a driver. And he has a car. It's my car. But he drives—"

"Just…" I absently raised the mangled sword. "…where is it?"

"The garage."

Will led us toward the back of the theatre. I used the deformed blade to jam the exit closed after we passed through it.

Will called his driver. "He'll be there in a minute," he said after hanging up.

Reaching the garage, the three of us hid out of sight while Will remained visible.

"Roger," Will said as the driver stepped out of the stairwell, pretending to collapse to his knees because of his injury.

He really isn't that good of an actor.

"Mr. Crispin!"

Slipping behind the driver, I stretched a length of tape across his mouth, pulling him to the ground. Daniel and Phoebe held his hands behind his back as I wrapped his wrists. A last bit of tape fixed his ankles. When I finished, I removed a set of car keys from his front pocket. An ID badge was attached. The firm name: Xolaris.

"I'm sorry. I just don't know who to trust."

Of course, Will had no idea where the car was parked. None. And with his mouth taped shut, Roger The Driver wasn't much help, just a jumble of mumbled sounds.

"Again, I'm sorry about this." I ripped off the tape. Roger bit down, stifling an abbreviated yelp. He was big. The kind of guy you hire for personal protection. Not that any writer, even one as famous as Lance Crispin would be recognized in public.

Roger unclenched his jaw. "The car is in the third row. One floor up."

I unrolled another length of tape, tearing it with my teeth, pausing as I held it over his mouth. "I'll need to rip this off again if we can't find it."

Roger's shoulders sank as he let out a long sigh. "It's one floor down. Second row. And those are my keys. The key to his car is in my jacket."

I grabbed the key fob, then stretched the fresh length of tape over his mouth, slapping it with my hand to get it nice and tight.

"Thank you."

He mumbled something unintelligible, avoiding eye contact with me.

I stood and looked down at him. I'd watched men—bigger, stronger, scarier than my father—wither under his gaze. It was the force of his personality.

Feeling that kind of power, even for an instant, was intoxicating.

We found the car quickly. Daniel got in front with Will behind the wheel. Phoebe and I sat in the back.

I handed Will the key. He poked at the steering column with the fob, prodded it, whacked it, yelled at it.

"You just push *start* with the key inside." Daniel pointed at the button clearly marked: START.

Will pressed it and the engine turned over. "I was never a great horseman," he said. "I was just becoming adequate when these things came along. Took me a hundred years to get used to them."

He put the car in gear, glanced out the back window, and nearly plowed into the car in front of us. He hit the brakes in time only because the curb stop slowed him down.

We caught our breaths.

He shifted the car into reverse. "I don't normally drive," Will explained, backing out while continuing to stare forward. He slammed the brakes too late, so that when we tapped the vehicle behind us, its trunk popped open.

"I wouldn't have guessed that," Daniel said.

Will fumbled through several miscues before finally finding a gear. This was an automatic by the way. Approaching the exit at speed, RPM redlining because he'd put the car in first gear, I prepared myself for the impact of smashing through the gate arm.

Instead, Will brought the car to a full stop. A slow whine as he pushed the switch to roll down his window, the ticket machine imploring us to "please swipe card key." We sat there like idiots as he searched the interior.

"Where is that damn card?"

He ravaged the center console, the armrest, and finally found it in the side pocket of the door. He waved the card in front of the machine.

"Thank you," said the machine.

"You have sand for brains," replied Will.

The gate opened.

He'd felt smashing through the gate would be unwise, unsafe, perhaps impolite, but once he squealed onto the street, he was cutting off cars left and right.

"You might want to take it out of first," I said, pointing at the shifter.

When he nearly drove onto a sidewalk full of pedestrians trying to get the transmission to D, Daniel reached over and did it for him.

Although, we might have been better off keeping it in low gear.

In the next half mile, Will changed lanes forty-two times. Only a quarter of those did he bother employing his turn signal. And the majority of those, he flicked it on after he was already more than halfway into the adjacent lane.

"You witless knave!" Will screamed at a man aggressively honking his displeasure. "You have more hair than sense!"

The man was bald.

I was reminded of the time Richard Burbage and the other actors in Lord Chamberlain's Men took Will's horse. Made him walk the rest of the way to Avon on foot because he was such a danger to other travelers.

Will sideswiped a parked sedan.

"Those big things around us with four wheels are called cars. The object is to avoid them."

He glanced at me in the rearview mirror. "Oh, like you could do any better."

"He couldn't do any worse," Phoebe said.

He screeched to a halt in the middle of the road. "I want to know why Roger isn't driving me right now."

"Go!" all three of us said in unison as cars swerved to miss us.

"And I want to know why someone destroyed my set!"

"Will," I said with as much composure as I could muster. "I will tell you. If...you just drive the car."

Will hit the gas, veering around an accident he'd caused. "Well?" He looked at me in the rearview while continuing to drive in the oncoming lane. He veered out of the way seconds before having a head-on with a double-decker bus. "I'm waiting."

When my heart crawled back out of my throat, I said, "Did you hear about the plane in Gibraltar?"

He glared at me, his eyes filling the mirror. "The thing all over the news? You hijacked a plane?"

"Not exactly. Keep your eyes on the road."

"How does one 'not exactly' hijack a plane?"

"They *pretend* to hijack it." I pointed at the car he was about to rear end. "We needed to escape Boston without being followed. So, we created a diversion!"

He slowed just in time.

"You didn't have anything to do with that explosion, did you?"

"No. Well…not directly."

"Actually, *she* was directly responsible for the explosion at the dog track," Daniel motioned toward Phoebe, who slunk down in her seat.

"I thought a block of houses blew up. There was more than one explosion?"

Daniel held up two fingers. "And she stole a car. Just took it. A dad getting milk for his hungry kids."

Will glanced at Phoebe in the mirror.

"I've never done anything like that before," she said.

"You've all been very busy, hijacking and destroying things. Still haven't heard an explanation!"

"Someone tried to kidnap me," I said bluntly.

"And kill us," Daniel added, pointing to himself and Phoebe.

"So, you came to see *me*?" Will said. "What am I supposed to do? Write you a better ending? Have you seen me under pressure? I can only make matters worse." He had a point. "Why didn't you go to your father? He's the warrior."

"I don't know where he is."

"Well, *I* haven't seen him in decades. And to be honest, I could go a few centuries without seeing that *chiseled*…" he sounded annoyed by this adjective, "…face of his."

"I'm in trouble, Will. If there's anything helpful you can tell me—"

"I wouldn't have the vaguest idea where to look for him."

"You've gotten no notes? No visitors? No cryptic messages?"

"No."

"What about Elam Khai?"

Will's demeanor changed instantly, and he too quickly shook his head. "Never heard of him."

"Let's assume that's a lie."

Will looked around as if people might be listening to our conversation even though we were sealed inside a moving vehicle. His voice was barely audible. "I have never *known* anyone named Elam Khai."

"He was Alexander," I said. "He was Octavian."

"He was a hell of a lot more people than that."

I stared at him. "You were there, weren't you?" I thought about the great writers of those times. "Who were you? Virgil?" Then I remembered the 'floppy timekeeper' comment he made earlier. "Horace Flaccus."

Will smirked nervously. "I was there." His tone softened. "So, Marcus had the talk with you."

"I'm assuming you don't mean the Sex Talk."

"Sex talk? Nooooooo. *The* talk." He eyed me curiously. "You've got to be old enough. You're practically a man. What are you? Thirteen, fourteen hundred?"

"Fifteen."

"*Fifteen?* Really? Okay, so, he's definitely told you about your family. About him."

"He's told me many, many, things."

"'*Many* things?'" Will said, shaking his head. "Yeah, you haven't had the talk."

"We've had a lot of talks."

"You'd know this talk if you had it."

I shrugged, uncomfortable. "I haven't spoken to him in a while."

"What? In two hundred years?"

It still stung. My father confiding to Braeden the whole time I was in the dark. "A couple of months," I said, finally.

Will glanced in the mirror. There was something like pity in the look. "You haven't become stupid or unstable or clinically insane since you worked for me?"

"No."

Will was quiet a moment. When he spoke, it was like an actor on a stage. "Your father should be as a god to you, one that composed your face, your body, and to whom you are but wax to be imprinted by him, to be formed, to be made or to be disfigured."

I recognized the paraphrased sentiment. He was cribbing from his own work, probably envisioning a new play from all this drama.

"What's that supposed to mean?" Daniel asked.

"He means it's my father's right to influence who I am."

"More than influence," corrected Will. "Mold you."

My father tried to do that early on, but I think over the centuries he gave up. I asked too many questions, questioned too many answers, and was rarely swayed by absolute declarations. "That's not the kind of father he is."

"Maybe you're not that kind of son." Will's grin was dark. "So, then how do you know about—the other one?"

"Elam Khai?"

His jaw tensed.

"Elam Khai told me."

Will's eyebrows went up sharply. "*He* told you he was Alexander of Macedonia?"

I nodded. "And that my father was Mark Antony. That they're brothers. And that he'd been Octavian."

"You mean, Augustus, first *Emperor* of Rome? Not that the Republic wasn't mostly an empire before he grabbed it by the throat." Will scanned every direction, out the windows, the moonroof, in the mirrors, as if he expected Elam Khai to come hurtling through the next intersection or swoop down from the sky. "This is the sort of intercourse that gets people pregnant with trouble," he whispered.

"He's not going to kill you. Or me."

"Ohhhh, there are worse things than being killed. Just because we avoid murdering each other doesn't mean there aren't other ways of controlling a person. Have you ever been a prisoner for two centuries? Well, I have. Twelfth century, thirteenth century. No idea what they looked like."

"I can't imagine being in prison for two hundred years," Phoebe said, her nose wrinkling.

"I never said I was in a prison. Sometimes being held in an ornate room with tapestries and silk bedding and the finest meals served three times a day is just as horrendous if you're never allowed to leave. Especially when they give you no quill, no ink, no parchment, and have beautiful women dancing in the courtyard below your window. Every day. For two hundred years." Will flinched. "Wait. He doesn't know *they* know who he is."

When I nodded, his face showed disbelief.

"How are you two still alive?" He grabbed Daniel's wrist and turned it over, looking for…maybe the opposing triangles I'd seen on Mrs. Dunn, Mrs. Avery, and Black Gloves. "No. Seriously, how are you not dead?"

It wasn't as if Phoebe and Daniel hadn't realized knowing the truth put them in danger, but hearing Will Shakespeare personally pronounce their death sentence added a dramatic flair that sliced through the abdomen.

Phoebe took in several deep breaths.

"Forgive my insensitivity," Will said.

"Just call us the Running Dead," Daniel grumbled.

I wanted to allay their concern, but what could I tell them? The way to ensure their safety was to solve the problem. "We need to find and exploit Elam Khai's weaknesses."

"He doesn't have any."

"Everyone has a weakness. Usually, a lot more than one."

"Have you met him?"

"This isn't just about me. Or them. *Your* future depends on it. That 'power' your play is about. He's planning on doing away with it."

Will dropped his shoulders.

"You know, don't you?"

He didn't answer for a moment. "Rumors. Stories of people stockpiling food and supplies." He tossed his wallet on the center console. I didn't have to open it to see what was inside. The shape was molded into the leather.

Daniel flipped open the wallet to reveal the X inside a box inside a circle. Displayed in this way, it looked like a detective's badge.

"You've seen that symbol?"

"Yes," I said.

Will looked at me. "You don't have one of those, do you?"

"No."

"Until you've been given one of these by, in your case, your father, you need to keep out of their little wars. I do something, you're not responsible for it. But anything you do, your father can be held accountable. Anyone who plots with you, helps you, becomes accountable for your actions. Against anyone with this, you're not afforded the same respect. Not in battle. Not on the street. Elam Khai could put you over his knee and spank you like a misbehaving little boy." He nodded toward the symbol, "*With* it, he'd have to treat you like a man."

Daniel's eyebrows went up. "Wait. You don't kill each other, but you're okay with abusing each other's children?"

"This is meant for his protection. And everyone else's. There've been adolescents who didn't appreciate the consequences of their actions. You know what happened at Halifax. Nine thousand injured. Two thousand dead. Twenty-five thousand basically homeless in the middle of winter. A dozen of us killed. I'm not saying you'd cause something like that, but if your own father doesn't trust you enough, no one's going to come to your rescue if you take on your uncle. Even if you had one of these, you'd have a hard time. You are part of a family most would rather avoid aggravating." Will wore a sad expression that instantly aged his youthful features. "This is no way for you to find out who you really are. Marcus should have told you."

"I already know who I am. Some piece of metal isn't going to change that. Yes, he should have told me. But it doesn't matter who my father was. I know who he *is*. I've seen the sides he chooses to fight for. He *did* mold me, but he wasn't the only one." I stared at Will.

"I appreciate you thinking I had some beneficial effect on you."

"You…and a lot of others. I am not my father."

"No, but you're more like him than you think. And even more like your uncle than I'd like. That's not a bad thing. Necessarily. But it's the truth. It's why I let you hang around so long. I'm a different breed than you are. I hoped I might…soften your edges." He gripped the steering wheel harder. "I'm sorry I couldn't tell you."

I nodded as I peered out the window, a thousand years of London passing by. "I need you to tell me anything you can about Elam Khai. Because if he isn't stopped, it'll be exponentially worse than Halifax."

Will sighed. "He's what you'd expect of a warrior and a king."

"Awesome, a warrior king," said Daniel.

"Only a lot more brilliant. Smarter than you or me or any of us."

Daniel ticked off two fingers. "Warrior king. Evil genius. Got it."

"He's not evil. I've known him a long time. Not by that name. Never by that name, but I know him as much as anyone, except maybe your father, and a few others no longer alive. He's done great things for the world. In Rome, he kept the peace, maintained order."

"I could keep order, too, if I killed everyone."

Will ignored Daniel. "He was tutored by Aristotle. He spread culture throughout the Middle East and deep into India. He modernized warfare. He created libraries across his empire so the people he conquered could expand their understanding. He didn't destroy cultures, he added to them and learned from them."

"Warrior king. Semi-evil genius. Fanatical librarian." Daniel was just self-stimulating now.

"But he has to beat you first." Will wagged his index finger. "That's the catch. Then he brings culture, stability. He has to win for that to happen. And he doesn't stop until he wins. Ever." Will's hands trembled ever-so-slightly as he gripped the steering wheel. "Of course, he's incredibly kind and very, very handsome."

"He's not here, Will."

He let out a long breath. "I was fourteen when I started hearing about them. Your father, your uncle. There were others. Not like us. Other warriors, leaders, but without our curse."

"You think living forever is a curse?" Daniel said.

"We don't live forever," he said sharply. "Those of us who are truly brave may revel in the centuries. But for others like me who worry and question…it weighs on the psyche. It *is* a curse. Which do you think is more tragic? Dying young if you only have a hundred years to live. Or dying young if you might have ten thousand more? Thoughts like that can be overwhelming. Maybe that's why I find people like Marcus and Augustus fascinating. Soldiers who dine with their enemies the night before a battle, exchange gifts with them. How can someone do that? Be so brave, so cordial, so honorable, so callous."

"Augustus lived two thousand years ago. Elam Khai must have lived a lot of other influential lives since then," Phoebe said. "Someone like that doesn't give up power easily."

"No, not easily. Or at all."

"So, who has he been?" she demanded.

I shot a withering glance at Phoebe.

"If he's going to kill me, Alexander…I want to know who the hell is doing it." She prodded Will to continue. "Who has he *been*?"

Will was quiet for a moment. The road noise whispered to us through the closed windows.

"Twenty contemporaries recorded the deeds of Alexander during his reign. Not one of those texts survives. Why do you think that is? Bad luck? Carelessness? Poor record keeping? From the man who built libraries? No. I believe he worked to eradicate those texts in the ensuing centuries. What's in the history books is hearsay from those who heard from those who heard from those who read the originals. But I remember. Your uncle was looked upon as a protector and a destroyer. As a God. And a monster. He is all of those things. After Rome, there were other places in the world that became beacons. But he was careful to avoid having people write too much about him. Maybe that's why no one rose up and stood so tall as Augustus and Alexander." Will chuckled. "'Pater Europae.'"

Whatever was said next, I didn't hear. I wasn't in the car. I was drowning. At the time, I didn't realize I was dying as my lungs filled with water. I was calm. At peace.

It wasn't until I was ripped from the warm embrace of the clear water and thrust naked into the chill air, coughing, choking, sputtering, the cries of women, the shouts of men filling the air that I was filled with fear.

"What are you doing, little Andros," the man said, his voice an excited growl.

At the time, that was the name my father told me to answer to.

The man's eyes were intense, but warm and blue like the water I'd just been pulled from. I was young, almost three hundred. That peaceful moment underwater, eyes wide open, sun piercing the clear liquid is my first fully formed memory.

Everything prior is simply flashes, including my mother.

Pater Europae. The Father of Europe.

Charlemagne.

The Emperor of the Holy Roman Empire—and if what Will just let slip is true, Elam Khai—saved me from drowning.

The year was 810.

It's strange that immediately after being dragged from the bottom of the gigantic thermal pool, people were more concerned with the king's well-being than mine.

"They think I am weak." He yelled for someone to get me dry clothes. His beard and hair were long and streaked with gray. But he did not appear weak. "My doctors advise me to give up roasted meat. I'm not a boiled meat kind of man. Unless it's the doctors

I'm boiling." He smiled broadly. The cadre of healers hovering over him seemed less amused.

His grin was not the one I've seen since in paintings of Charlemagne, which have a beatific, religious feel to them. His was mischievous.

I was called mischievous then. Devilish, spirited and many other things. I was in the very late stages of the terrible two hundreds. A "handful," my father would say.

It's hard to tell if my memory is fully my own or if retelling by my father has colored my recollection.

"You were saved by Charles the Great," he'd say when I was older. He'd go into detail about how the King of the Franks—an excellent athlete—had taken me under his wing, taught me to swim, and let me have the run of his estate.

There was never any mention of Charlemagne being my father's brother, never any discussion that he was like us. He was merely one of the thousands of powerful men and women I've met over the centuries.

Sometime after the incident in the pool, I got in trouble for picking up a sword and taking a swing.

In my memory, the bearded man with the sardonic grin looks down at me, his hand mussing my hair. "I see a great deal of you in me, Andros of Nowhere." Then the smile disappears. "My time here is soon coming to an end. I would like to leave my realm in the hands of someone worthy."

"What concerned me," my father told me centuries later, "was that he wanted you to remain in Aachen. To be raised and groomed to be his heir. If you stayed, he'd soon realize the truth about you."

Refusing Charlemagne had been made more difficult by the story we had told. That my father was not my father. That I was merely his ward. Son of a man he'd killed in battle. No matter how many times my father told me differently, for decades, I was never quite sure if that was true or not.

"You seem to have a habit for collecting other men's children," Charlemagne said as he patted another boy on the head.

The child was maybe nine or ten. Only now escaping London in a car driven poorly by Will Shakespeare do I remember this boy had been traveling with us. Images come flooding back, of us playing together, acting out epic battles—which he never let me win. "Victory must be earned," he'd say. Something my father always said. His hair was dark, and he had the eyes of a predator.

Braeden's eyes.

I saw the Scotsman's blade cut into my stepbrother's side and I gasped.

"What is it?" asked Phoebe.

"I was at Aachen."

Will shrugged. "A lot of us were at Aachen. The accommodations were good. There was food. Very little plague. There was even a heated swimming pool. I mean who has a heated pool in the Middle Ages?"

"Elam Khai…"

"Well, right, he did."

"…was Charlemagne."

"Yeah." He winced. "I have a tongue looser than a whore."

"What about my father?"

"He never had a pool like that."

"That's not what I'm asking."

"Your father is more of a blunt instrument."

I was getting frustrated. "Where is he? I need to find him."

"I told you, I don't know where Marcus is. Don't get me wrong, I like your father, but I think he'd run a sword through me if he had the chance. *Antony and Cleopatra*—let's say, he's not a fan."

He grabbed a tablet from behind the seat, causing the sedan to swerve. He unlocked the device with his fingerprint, opened a reading app.

"Doing that while driving," Daniel said, ready to grab the wheel. "Is more dangerous than driving drunk."

"I already drive worse than someone who's intoxicated. So, this isn't…" He trailed off as he found the works by Shakespeare in the app, then swiped to *Antony and Cleopatra*. "There are things he needs to tell you himself." He passed the tablet back to me. "But everything you need to know is in there. I lie, I've altered things, but you're smart enough to see past the distraction to the truth."

I knew the play. Anger issues, vengeful, loyal friend, strong, accomplished general, heavy gambler, user of public funds for his own benefit, husband of one of the most desired women in history. This was my father from Will's perspective.

I handed the tablet to Phoebe. "I told you, I already know who he is."

"I guarantee there's a lot you don't know."

I thought of Braeden.

"How about a woman named Elle? Like us. Maybe a thousand years younger than you. Blondish, fair-skin, pretty. Might've had red hair in the past."

"Well, that narrows it down. I've known a lot of women over the years matching that description. But frankly, as a rule, I don't date actresses *or* women like us. And for the same reason. You never know who you're talking to. The part or the person." He glanced at me in the mirror. "Are we just driving? Where are we going?"

I relayed the cryptic message Braeden had delivered.

"'The key is at the beginning of time?' The man is not a poet. And how do you get London out of that?"

"He's always been fascinated with navigation. I figured the spot where global time and navigation originates made sense in this context."

"But Marcus hates London. He hates all of Britain. Ever since it was the backwaters of the Roman Empire. Caesar wasted a lot of blood and treasure on *Provincia Britannia*."

The truth is, I thought London was right for exactly the same reason Will thought I was wrong. My father hated this place.

Where better to meet in secret than someplace everyone knew he couldn't stand.

"Marcus is clever when it comes to battles and politics and women," said Will. "But not so clever when it comes to words. I think you have to take this message at the most basic, straightforward meaning possible."

Unlike Julius Caesar or Alexander The Great, no great displays of oratory are attributed to Mark Antony. There is only one speech I know of, Caesar's eulogy, where he worked the crowd into a fury, first methodically listing Caesar's great deeds, then his generous gifts to the people, and ending it by tearing the blood-stained toga from the assassinated leader's body and holding it up for the throngs to see. Frenzied by the bloody spectacle, the people rioted, burning the conspirators' homes, causing Caesar's killers and their supporters to flee Rome. It was not an eloquent speech, but it was politically effective.

I knew my father as a soldier. He mentioned battles but never claimed to be at the head of them.

I am only a soldier, Elam Khai said.

Why do people who have held such incredible power think of themselves simply as soldiers? Is it false modesty? Or is it something else? Arrogance can lead to mistakes. My father taught me that. I was trained to approach each situation as if I was the least knowledgeable participant. My father believed that was the only way to assure you were never surprised, never underestimated an opponent, an obstacle, a situation.

Will had been turning the phrase over in his mind. "This 'beginning of time' thing. If it was a meridian, Greenwich would be too obvious."

Daniel turned. "You just said it would be straightforward."

"Yes, but not stupid. This is the first place someone would look. What about the one in Paris? I'm not supposed to say this, you have to act surprised if your father ever tells you himself. And I mean, real surprise. From what I remember, you're not the best actor."

"I'm not that bad."

"You're not the worst, but you're pretty close."

"What is it?" I said, irritated.

"Your father was very influential in the French military in the late eighteen hundreds."

"This is me acting surprised." I did my worst impression. "I already know that."

"Well, the French used the Paris Meridian for three decades after the rest of the world agreed to use Greenwich."

"We considered that, but…"

"*Very* influential," Will stressed. "He personally lobbied for it to be adopted as *the* meridian at the eighteen-eighty-four conference in D.C."

Phoebe switched over to the map application on the tablet, then she searched "Paris Meridian." I zoomed in closer. Like Greenwich, the meridian was centered on an observatory.

I dragged the map, following the imaginary line of the Paris Meridian south from the observatory. Nothing. Except the entrance a block away to the catacombs where the bones of six million Parisians were stacked in creepily artistic displays. I moved north where the line crossed the Seine and went through the Louvre Museum and toward the whitewashed glass roof of the Gallery Lafayette.

"I'd be thinking history," continued Will. "First calendars. The origins of civilization, that kind of thing."

"The Louvre," Phoebe said.

She scrolled back down until she came to the museum.

I laughed at my stupidity for not seeing it earlier. "The Louvre," I said agreeing. I zoomed in on the southwest corner of the Sully Wing. "My father and I lived for a while in the Chateau du Louvre, which is the foundation for this corner of the modern Louvre. It was at the end of the middle part of The Hundred Year War."

Daniel shrugged. "'End of the middle part.' I don't even know what that means."

"Thirteen eighty-one."

Daniel started scratching his chest. "Seriously, history is now starting to give me hives."

Phoebe leaned over and worked the map. She pointed to where the meridian line passed through the northern wing of the museum. "Here are the Etruscan and Mesopotamian exhibits."

"You've been to Paris?"

"I was supposed to go two summers ago until I broke my leg in gymnastics. Spent the week torturing myself, learning about all the places my friends were posting photos from. *That's* art from the beginning of civilization."

"I think Paris is a very good idea," said Will.

"Why's that?" I asked.

Will held up a hand. "I'd really like to avoid spending another two centuries locked up inside a castle, so, let me just say Marcus has spent a llllllllllot of time droning on and on and on about French castles."

"That's all you're going to tell me? French castles?"

"I can't stress enough how long two hundred years stuck in a single suite of ornate rooms really is."

It could be Paris. My father and I had a strong connection to the Louvre and the City. I had my first crush there when I was about eight hundred. And it's where I made my greatest mistake.

"Okay. Let's go to Paris," I said, hoping I could avoid running into that mistake.

DESCENT

"The descent to hell is the same from every place."

—Anaxagoras c. 450 B.C.

- EIGHT -
The Light At The End Of The Chunnel

The wild scramble to Paris began slowly. It took us thirty minutes to get to the next exit, where the word 'scramble' took root as Will circumvented bottlenecks, dodged pedestrians, and ignored thousands of pages of traffic laws to finally get out of the city.

By the time we hit the M20, the urban density of London gave way to pastoral landscapes and roads lined with wooden fences weathered to a uniform gray.

"Aren't the airports that way?" said Daniel.

"We're not going to the airport," I said.

Daniel's face registered confusion.

"I'm driving you there," Will said.

Daniel's bewilderment was punctuated by several abortive attempts to form what I can only imagine were the words "English Channel" or "We're on an island."

I turned to Phoebe. "You want to explain it to him?"

She grinned. "This is one of those cars that can turn into a boat."

Will eyed her in the rearview mirror.

"Really?" Daniel said.

"Ah huh."

Daniel swiveled his head around, studying the car, searching for evidence of James Bondian seaworthiness.

"Don't touch that!" Will shouted as Daniel opened the glove compartment and went to press a yellow button inside.

Daniel jumped, realizing he almost had just launched a missile from under the hood.

It was, of course, the trunk release.

This occupied my friend for a good hour.

At some point during the drive—okay, I know exactly when and where, the outskirts of Ashford as we passed over the Great Stour River, which isn't really all that great—Phoebe took my hand. Her skin was warm. I glanced at her. She smiled, then lowered her eyes, her fingers curling around my palm. She held my hand against her side where her black leggings met the hem of her cashmere mini dress.

It was the simplest gesture. And it calmed me.

Ten minutes later, we passed a road sign for Shakespeare's Cliffs.

Daniel glowered at Will. "I hate everything about you."

"You aren't the first," said Will, wistfully.

Cresting the rise, the extent of Folkestone Terminal came into view. Columns of trucks filled with goods waiting to be transported to the continental mainland threaded past lines of cars.

Daniel's shoulders dropped. "The car's not turning into a boat, is it?"

I shook my head. "No."

He sighed heavily. "You know, there *are* cars that can turn into boats."

"I know."

"And considering the fact that you're *fifteen hundred years old*, thinking *William Shakespeare's* luxury sedan can turn into a channel-crossing watercraft doesn't seem all that strange to me."

Shakespeare's car.

"Is this car registered to Lance Crispin?"

"Yes," said Will.

I knocked my forehead against the window.

"Is that a problem?"

No matter what mode of transportation we took to Paris—plane, train, automobile, ferry—we'd be exposed. It came down to this:

Shuttling the car via the tunnel, we would be in a confined space for the shortest period of time. Thirty-five minutes.

"So far everything else has," I said. "But maybe we can use it to our advantage."

There was space on the next shuttle.

Will read over the printed receipt which had a list of instructions on it. "We've got to stop at the concession area."

"Good. I'm hungry," said Daniel, opening the door.

"Stay in the car!" I shouted, stopping him.

Will waved the receipt. "We have to pick up a breathalyzer. Every vehicle in France has to carry one. Border control takes place at departure. We risk getting pulled out of line."

The thought of waiting for the next shuttle made the hairs on the back of my neck stand up. "Fine. I'll get it."

Phoebe rested her hand on my leg. "Let me and Daniel go. He's like a toddler when he hasn't had his snackies."

She grabbed some bills from the backpack.

"You want anything?" she asked.

"No."

"Will?"

"A nice strong Port. Taylor Fladgate, sixty-three."

"Which will pair perfectly with the breathalyzer. Just the breathalyzer," I said.

I watched Phoebe and Daniel until they disappeared into the cluster of shops.

"I've seen that look before," said Will.

"What look?"

"Alexander, how many times do you think I've had to describe two people and how they feel about each other? Lovers, enemies, friends, family?"

I was silent.

"The answer is quite a few."

"They're my friends."

"I'm referring specifically to the charming and winsome Phoebe.

It's a fool's errand, Alexander. It can only end in misery, suffering, and pain."

"That pain is the only thing worth living for," I said.

In the rearview mirror, I saw Will raise an eyebrow.

Daniel and Phoebe were back in less than five minutes.

"The place to get your last-minute motoring accessories and all the travel equipment to comply with European regulations," he said, holding up a yellow AA Travelshop bag. "Catchy slogan."

"So what are we doing about the problem of Lance Crispin's car?" asked Phoebe.

"We use it. I think the three of us find another way to get to Paris. There'll be a hundred other cars on board. A few dozen trucks. Somebody's going to be heading to Paris. Will should drive on to Brussels. There aren't any controls on the border, but if you can get a speeding ticket or run a red light near the airport, it might draw some attention."

"I can do that," he said.

Pulling up to the control checkpoint, Will jumped the curb, left a streak of auto paint on a safety barrier, and nearly took out the guard checking paperwork in our feeder line.

"Probably without even trying," Phoebe added, dryly.

We showed our passports. Were asked the usual questions. Were we transporting any hazardous materials? What was the purpose of our trip? Did we know about the breathalyzer law? Did we have one in the car?

Will's bad driving earned us slightly more scrutiny which included a peek in the trunk, but after an extra moment we were cleared to continue.

"Have a safe trip," the guard said, more a stern warning than a pleasantry.

Vehicles flowed down a dozen ramps toward the platform. Lorries loaded at the back. Their uniformity made the trucks look like linked together metal sausages.

For cars, there was an upper level and a lower level. We were directed onto the top deck. We passed through several carriages, the transition noted by a slight clank as we drove over the plate between each compartment. Red brake lights cascaded toward us. Will was stopped by an attendant as the car in front of us slipped into the next train. Two aluminum framed doors with vertical windows folded in from each side.

"Please keep moon roofs open and windows at least halfway down," a recorded voice announced. Apparently, it helped equalize pressure in the train as we raced through the tunnel.

Seeing other passengers milling about, we decided to stretch our legs and scope out who might be able to give us a ride.

Other than a near lack of windows, the interior looked like a subway car stripped of its seats.

Will stood by the hood. Daniel sat on the steel floor, his feet against the tires. Phoebe stared through the glass door between the train cars.

"I've always wanted to see the Mona Lisa," Phoebe said.

I gripped a yellow rail running along the side and let myself be entranced by the lights of the tunnel flashing by the small square windows set every ten feet. "We're not going to the Louvre to appreciate the art."

Will chimed in. "You can check out Delacroix's 'Romeo and Juliet at the tomb of the Capulets' so you can douse it with gasoline and set it on fire."

Phoebe turned toward me and scrunched up her face. I put up a hand, indicating 'don't bother.' "I'm not that bad of an actor," I said, hoping to derail him.

"Are you as awful at interpreting my work as Delacroix?" Will gave an exaggerated shrug. "Is Juliet dead in the crypt? It looks like she's dead, but there's Romeo dancing with her perky corpse! Are you as terrible as the idle-headed fools who want to make it 'easier' for everyone to understand my words by reciting them using modern pronunciation? If you don't pronounce 'whore' and 'hour' the same, you don't get the jokes! 'And so, from hour to hour, we ripe and ripe, And then, from hour to hour, we rot and rot…" Will said 'hour' like O.R. and 'rot' like rut. "'And thereby hangs a tale!'"

He gesticulated between his legs below his crotch to demonstrate the tired state of his character's manhood after a long night of debauchery.

"*Those* are the professional productions, a few of which are *tolerable*. I'm not even talking about high school productions, summer stock, small town local theatre. Even *you* could do better. I want to pierce my eardrums so I don't have to hear my words butchered so. You know the best thing about doing film and television? The words are set."

"We go up to a small theater in the Berkshires once a year with our English class," said Phoebe. "It's actually very good."

"Yes. Yes. The ones who perform my plays in the woods. As if they've somehow mistaken me for Robin Hood. I've never once performed a single scene in a forest. I send my *characters* into forests, out to sea, into nature, but me, I want a nice soft, feathery bed. I saw one of these companies do a Star Wars-inspired version of Macbeth, complete with lightsabers. I don't know who should be more mortified, me or George Lucas."

"If it's so painful, why go to these performances at all?"

"Writer's curse. The hope that you'll hear someone speak your words, and bring something to them that you never could have imagined. It's rare. But when it happens, it's beautiful."

"He's lying."

"I am not lying," Will said. "Not completely."

"The truth is, Will doesn't think he's any good. The applause soothes him, and for a while, he thinks maybe he's not a complete hack."

Will looked away. "Self-doubt is a curse stupid people do not suffer. Sometimes, I can't stand the things I write."

"If it makes you feel any better," Daniel said, "I can't stand the things you write, either."

The floor angled down as we began our descent beneath the

English Channel. Thirty minutes and we would be on the other side.

"You know, when you first came by the theatre, I was hoping maybe you wanted your old job back. The assistants I have now, smart as they are, have maybe three minutes of experience between them. He was one of my best." He said this last part to Phoebe.

"One of?" I said indignantly.

"One of, yes. He was a savant of the not funny. I'd write something wickedly clever, comically riotous. He'd read it and ask, 'Is this supposed to be humorous?'" Will mimicked a toddler voice.

"I was barely a thousand years old. I didn't get half the jokes."

"More like ninety percent of the jokes."

"I have a sense of humor."

"Yes. Just not a very good one. Don't get me wrong, it's not like you don't have *any*. Not like your father. Now, that's a man whose humor has been neutered."

Daniel wiped his hand across his forehead. "Can't wait to meet him."

"Oh, you're going to *love* Marcus," said Will.

"I'm the *best* assistant you ever had."

"Except for that minor incident where you ruined *Romeo and Juliet*."

"What?" Phoebe said, involuntarily.

"You know the play?"

"Of course."

"You know how it ends?"

"*Everyone* knows how it ends."

"Not the way I wrote it. Night before the play was to open, I had this epiphany—"

"Mental breakdown," I corrected.

"*A moment of sudden revelation.* It was beautiful. I spent all night rewriting the last scene. It was dramatic. There was tension and pathos. It was funny, soaring. A triumph of love. And this one… he ruined it."

"He?" she said, pointing at me. "Ruined *Romeo and Juliet*?"

"I didn't give the actors his last-minute freakout changes. Yes, Will, the writing was fabulous. It was inspired. Truly, some of your best work. In *comedy*. There are comedic moments in the play, but *Romeo and Juliet* is a *tragedy*. You tell the audience in the first thirty seconds. 'A pair of star-cross'd lovers take their life!' By the way, 'lives' would've been more grammatically correct. But that was your brilliance. Setting up the ending and leading us there step by step, knowing what was to come. Unable to stop it. That is, until twenty-four hours before the curtain went up." I stabbed his chest with my finger. "You got scared."

"Wait. Wait. Romeo and Juliet were supposed to *live*?"

"Happily ever after," Will said.

"Oh—I—I—" Phoebe was so happy/shocked she couldn't speak.

"See, *that's* the reaction," Will said, glaring at me.

I shook my head. "That's only because the real ending haunts people. It makes us desperate to envision ways we could have saved these two lovers. If the friar hadn't been jailed. If his messenger hadn't been quarantined. If Romeo had only known of Juliet's plan. If he had just mourned her death a few moments longer."

"I had to write a whole 'nother play to work in that ending."

"*Much Ado About Nothing*," I said. "Tell me again...which play is more acclaimed and remembered?"

Will sneered at me. "'My only love sprung from my only hate.'" He poked my chest this time.

Daniel rolled his head to look at Will. "By the way, in answer to your earlier question...I think it's more tragic if something were to happen to us." He motioned to himself and Phoebe. "You've already lived fifty times longer than you're supposed to."

"We are never satisfied with what we already have," Will said.

"You see how I might find that greedy, unsympathetic?"

Will nodded. "None of us want to die. And when it comes, no matter how early or how late, it's always too soon."

"We should start looking for a ride," I said.

There was a moment where only the soothing repetitive sounds of the train filled the silence between us.

Then I heard a noise. A clatter. Felt a shudder.

The train was tilting. It was steel against steel, the wheels trying desperately to hold the tracks, metal against concrete, the side walls scraping the tunnel. There was a tremendous jolt, and the noise suddenly changed. The screeching ceased. We were thrown roughly, the train bouncing. It felt, it sounded like we were riding atop a rocket, blasting into space.

It seemed to last forever. It was only a few seconds.

And then...

Silence enveloped the train. A quiet quickly filled with the cries of agony, pleas for help, and the occasional shifting of debris.

"Phoebe!"

"Yeahhhh."

"Daniel! Are you all right?"

He grunted.

"Will? Will?"

The injured were scattered among the cars tossed about like dice. We finally found Will on his back, his hand to is head. He'd landed in the space between two cars that smashed into the wall. A man a few feet away wasn't as fortunate. He was being crushed by one of the cars. A half-dozen of us struggled to shift the sedan. More people came and we finally got him free. He had visibly broken bones, and it was painful for him to breathe, but it could've been worse. For some, it had been.

Wails came from both directions. But most emanated from the rear.

Will and Phoebe began helping other passengers.

I grabbed Daniel and pulled him toward the back of the train.

"I don't know what we're going to come across, but I need you to stay strong."

He nodded.

"You okay?"

"Just trying to comprehend all this," he said as he scanned the wounded.

The compartment doors had been torn away in many of the carriages. And we moved through the tangle of cars.

The design of the tunnel had lessened the impact. Maintenance walkways on either side of the tracks kept the train from buckling after a derailment. Had this occurred on an open stretch of track, the accident would've been catastrophic, train cars piling up like a logjam of fallen trees after a flood.

Which is why when we reached the back of the train, the damage was far, far worse.

Daniel and I stood in a vault two football fields long carved out of chalk. Two of these crossovers, each a third of the way through the underwater passage, allowed trains to bypass disabled trains or sections of track being maintained.

At about half a football field wide, the safety features that constrained the train inside the tunnel did not exist in the crossover.

The rear cars had been ripped apart, savaged by G-forces, sheering, and the weight of the rear engine.

The debris field was littered with train and truck parts, random scraps and patches of branded cargo. In one area, it looked like a bomb had gone off in a teddy-bear factory.

To the left, a dozen massive sliding doors divided the tunnels. Crossover tracks disappeared beneath the doors.

Blood smeared the ground. I saw flesh and bone. Daniel gagged. I wanted to close my eyes, but I had to keep searching. My heart slowed only after I realized it wasn't human remains. A meat truck had spilled its guts.

Again, good design saved lives. Unlike regular passengers who stayed with their vehicles, drivers of commercial trucks had their own club car well in front of the devastation.

At the far end of the cavern, I found the first door partially slid open.

I took in the scene, then envisioned the crumpled and scattered debris rewinding, coming together rather than blowing apart. Forward and back again. Forward and back. Almost immediately, my attention was drawn to the pattern of the debris field. I backtracked until I found what I was looking for.

"What is it?" asked Daniel.

"This switch isn't fully closed."

"Which caused the train to derail," he said.

"But if it had been that way the whole time, the lead locomotive would have smashed into these doors."

Daniel thought a moment. "Maybe it happened because of the crash."

I replayed the scene in my mind again. "Damage to the forward cars is less severe. They were pulled from behind instead of jamming into each other."

A power line buzzed overhead. Stress fractures ran along the ceiling. Water trickled onto the floor. I suddenly felt very cut off from the world.

The ventilation system was operational. There was no lack of oxygen. No feeling of claustrophobia. Still, I was very aware the English Channel was weighing down on that ceiling.

Daniel picked up one of the mangled teddy-bears, its grinning head half torn off, one arm missing, an exit wound through its chest.

"I assume we're the cause of this somehow." He put his finger through the hole in the bear, wiggling it toward my face and screeching like the infant creature in *Alien*. "Aaaaaaaggggrrrrhhhh!"

"Let's get back to the others," I said.

"I'll take that as a yes."

Phoebe was helping calm an injured woman while Will tied a tourniquet just above her knee.

"We need to go," I said.

"Help is coming," she told the woman as Will checked the tourniquet one more time.

"You found something?" Will asked.

I started to answer, but Daniel spoke first. "A half-opened switch that had to be activated *after* we passed over it."

"So, not a coincidence," said Phoebe.

"Someone wanted to stop the train, but minimize killing anyone," I said.

"That was nice of them."

EuroTunnel workers were arriving. A small army of blue jumpsuits and lime green safety vests flooded the cavern. We climbed down the twisted metal to the tracks. The scene was crawling with workers and passengers. I didn't know who we could trust. I decided we couldn't trust any of them.

A woman on a bullhorn announced we'd be picked up by another train and taken back to Folkestone.

Back to England.

The wounded were treated in place. Those able to walk were directed toward the service tunnel.

That's when I noticed one of the workers.

"Head to the emergency tube," he said to the people passing by. "Head to the emergency tube."

The others were calling it the "service tunnel." *Take the cross passage to the service tunnel.* That was the mantra recited over and over. Anyone half-listening could've repeated it. Two other men coalesced around the first. While everyone else in uniform was in motion, these three remained static.

I ducked behind a group of people. "Eleven o'clock. I don't think they've recognized us yet."

Phoebe located the three men. "How are we going to get by them to get to the rescue train?"

"We aren't going back to England," I said before climbing back into the last intact carriage.

The others found me standing over several motorcycles crumpled on the floor. I was waving cash from the backpack, hoping it was enough. "Who's bikes are these?" I shouted.

A quartet of men came forward. I handed them the bills—fourteen thousand, eight hundred and change, according to Daniel. They told me in German to take whatever we wanted, their helmets, their luggage.

I wrenched one of the bikes upright and turned the key, the roar magnified by the confines of the train, jangling the nerves of already anxious passengers. I shoved the bags off the luggage rack. They tumbled onto the floor. I'd ridden dirt bikes with Daniel in the woods behind his house. He could handle a bike. "Will with me. Phoebe, go with Daniel."

From her expression, it looked like I just ordered her to have sex with him.

"Phoebe, Daniel rides better than I do."

"I can handle myself," she said. "Besides," she pointed at his crotch, "I don't want a repeat of—"

"It was the adrenaline!" shouted Daniel.

The Germans helped her right one of the remaining motorcycles. She strapped on a helmet, adjusted the mirrors, started the engine, and kicked up the stand, ready to roll.

Okay, maybe I'm the worst rider of the three of us.

Revving the engine, I felt the back wheel skid across the metal. I led, weaving through the cars, debris, and the injured.

I stopped at the torn open edge of the rear carriage.

Will slipped off the back.

"What are you doing?" I said.

"They're after *you*." He picked up a strip of metal that had come loose, probably a door threshold. It was jagged at one end. He tore fabric from his shirt and wrapped it around his hand, strapping the weapon to him. "And instead of slowing you down, maybe I can slow them down."

"You're a terrible fighter," I said.

"They don't know that. And remember, I'm a *very* good actor."

"Will, don't be foolish. You're an *okay* actor."

He grabbed me by the shoulders, a proud look on his face. "*That's* comic timing."

"Come with us, please," implored Phoebe.

He shook his head. "He's searching for his father. *They*," he nodded toward the three men who still hadn't seen us, "scare me a thousand times less than Marcus."

"You don't have to do this," I said.

"Yes, I do. The pen is mightier than the sword. But sometimes you still have to use the sword." He swung his makeshift weapon. "Go. I'll be all right."

I had a pang in my stomach. He put his hand on my arm.

"You were right," he said, squeezing. "I *was* scared. Scared they would hate the ending, hate *me* for letting two beautiful lovers die. I lost my nerve. I was so angry with you. I wanted to strangle you. Until I heard the applause." I saw in his gaze that he was thinking back to that opening performance, the accolades just as potent across four centuries. "I was wrong, and you were right. Sometimes important characters must die."

I gave him a stern look as I revved the bike. "Don't die."

"Really? Those are your parting words? Twenty years in my employ and that's what you come up with? 'Don't *die*!' Nothing poetic or dramatic? Nothing to tug at the hearts of the audience?"

I had no answer. He shook his head, disappointed.

"Something like—"

> *Take thy sword, and through*
> *Their heartless hearts give them their due.*
> *Which does allow our friendship be remained,*
> *Your reputation and your robes unstained,*
> *Until we meet again, us two,*
> *I bid thee fare thee well, adieu.*

"When you write about this, say I said that."

He jumped down from the back of the train.

"That's the kind of horrible shit you would write trying to sound like me. I'll come up with something far better." He turned and moved briskly toward the cluster of passengers and was out of view.

I gunned the engine and flew out the back of the carriage. Daniel and Phoebe navigated their bikes more cautiously.

EuroTunnel workers screamed at us as we squeezed between the canted rear locomotive and the wall, shouting first in English, then in French, then in German, then in frustration.

The three men, realizing what was happening, started running toward us.

I pointed at the gap in the crossover doors. Controlling the bikes over the debris and switch tracks was a challenge.

Daniel reached the half-open door first, wondering which direction to go.

"Left," I shouted, motioning in the direction our train had been traveling.

Daniel flipped down his visor, then disappeared into the darkness. Phoebe followed him through the gap. I skidded to a stop, glaring back at the three men who halted, understanding our plan now. They sprinted toward the carriages. There were more motorcycles to be found there.

Will stepped out of the shadows and took a fighting pose between the men and the back of the train. As they approached, he swung his makeshift weapon, displaying a technique more artful than warrior-like. I revved the engine, my bike bucking underneath me, urging me to flee. Will was surrounded. He stood his ground, the metal strip keeping the three men at bay. I'm not sure if they sensed that this man, this genius of words, was not a killer, or if it was that they outnumbered him, but they swarmed him, hit him, knocked him to the ground. I wanted to defend him, but from the scrum I heard his voice echoing in the cavernous expanse. It told me, no, it *ordered* me to leave.

"'Stand not amazed, Romeo, away, be gone!'"

I gunned the bike, wheeling past the crumpled metal, the teddybears, the scattered meat, into the darkness, the faint cries of my friend fading until there was nothing but the lonely whine of my bike echoing in the tube.

Once my eyes got used to the ambient lighting, the tunnel was surprisingly well lit, like a city street at night. It took concentration to keep the bike under control as I pushed the machine to the limits of safety. I was surprised by the evenness of the concrete track bed, offering a smooth drivable narrow between the rails.

After less than a minute, I was on the back wheel of Phoebe. I motioned for her to go faster. She accelerated, causing Daniel to speed up as well.

Our headlights bounced and jumped, the jangling, strobing, crisscrossing beams brought me an odd sense of calm.

There were miles of track to traverse before we reached the French terminal where a series of fences and security systems built to keep animals and people from crossing into England awaited us.

I focused on the wheel in front of me. The zen of the cyclist drafting in the peloton. My concentration was broken when, in the acoustical chaos of the tunnel, I heard a sound beyond our three engines. At first, I worried it might be an oncoming train, but quickly realized it was two approaching motorcycles, maybe a mile behind us.

Will's stand had given us a three-minute head start.

We had twenty miles of tunnel to go.

If you think it's hard to do math problems at a desk in a classroom, try doing it while racing under the English Channel with people after you.

They were gaining on us, meaning they were taking risks. We were going about twenty, which doesn't sound fast, but felt uncomfortably quick on the narrow between the tracks. Could they push it five or ten miles an hour faster?

I guessed we had four minutes before they'd overtake us.

I had only one weapon. And I was riding on it.

I got ready to dump my bike, hoping in the dim light, moving at dangerous speeds, the chasers wouldn't see it and start a chain reaction of exploding gears and flipping bodies.

It was worth giving up one of our bikes.

Without warning, Daniel slammed on the brakes. It was all Phoebe and I could do to keep from pitching over him in the same manner as my violent scheme.

I could clearly hear the bikes now. I opened my mouth to tell Phoebe and Daniel we were about to get caught, that we had to move, that I was going to use my bike as a tripwire, but Daniel held a finger to his lips, "Shhhh." He turned off his bike. Phoebe and I did the same. Daniel glanced in the direction of the chasing bikes, then quickly returned his attention forward. He repeated the motion. He wasn't looking but listening. And that's when I heard it. A noise different from the growls of the approaching motorcycles. A high-pitched squeal mixed with a rumbling that teased the lowest range of human hearing.

"Train," Daniel said so calmly and quietly that it frightened me more than if he had screamed the word.

A Eurostar passenger train is capable of traveling at over three hundred kilometers an hour, but in the tunnel, its speed is restricted to a hundred and sixty. Le Shuttle travels only slightly slower, still fast enough to cover a mile in about forty seconds.

Daniel wrenched his bike, trying to turn it around.

"We can't go back," I said. "We're being chased."

"We can't go forward!" said Phoebe.

"We need to get to one of the emergency exits." I started my bike. Emergency doors placed every three hundred and seventy-five meters—roughly every quarter mile—connected to a service tunnel. "The closest one is that way." I pointed ahead.

"A train is coming from that way!" Phoebe screamed.

"At the train's speed, the difference between the two doors is eight seconds. We're wasting more time discussing it." I reached over and started Phoebe's bike. "We go forward."

Daniel flipped the ignition and popped a wheelie, allowing him to quickly realign his bike. His back tire spun has he raced ahead. Phoebe followed, driven by fear and determination. I took off, all of us pushing our speed to a dangerous pace.

Fifteen seconds never dragged on so long. Was it even possible to hear the train with our engines revving? All I can tell you is I heard it bearing down on us.

When we reached the access door, Daniel jumped off his bike, popped his front wheel up and gunned the throttle. The rear tire grabbed the deck, and the bike launched itself onto the landing. Daniel lost his grip and the cycle skidded off before coming to rest on its side.

The men chasing us were about half a mile away. They'd never get to us before the train did. They'd have to duck inside the exit three-hundred and seventy-five meters from ours, which meant we'd have to deal with them again in the service tunnel. With only a quarter mile between us.

Daniel motioned for us to pop our bikes onto the landing, but neither Phoebe or I could handle a bike as well as he could. Dropping my machine, we concentrated on getting her bike onto the platform. I hummed the harmonics of the approaching train. The slow upward shift in frequency as the train grew nearer gave me a sense of its relative distance. It took both of us standing on either side, pushing the machine, twisting the throttle. The thing nearly landed on me twice, but we forced the bike onto the walkway. Daniel was fumbling with the bulkhead, searching for a way to open it without a handle.

My humming grew higher in pitch. The train was closing in. A mile every thirty-six seconds. I couldn't see the lights. But they were coming.

Fast.

I jumped onto the platform. I felt a push of air. A train in a tunnel is a piston in a cylinder. Periodic relief ducts connecting the two tunnels helped equalize pressure, but the heavy thickness of the yellow bulkhead told me the forces created by the trains were intense. We might be able to hang on to pipes in the alcove, but if we lost our grip after the pressure wave at the front, we'd be pulled under the train and crushed to death.

"We have to get inside," I yelled.

You would think emergency doors were meant to be opened so people could get quickly to safety, but the words stenciled on the bright yellow steel told me I was wrong.

DO NOT OPEN. NE PAS OUVRIR.

Without Authorisation From Command Centre.

"Well, we certainly aren't waiting for that!"

A wheel like the helm of a ship stood off to the left. The door's manual override. Daniel's face contorted as he struggled to turn it.

I could make out the faint lights of the approaching train. It's hard to judge distance in a tunnel. Uniformity can play tricks on the eye.

I figured we had maybe forty-five seconds.

I joined him, my hands pulling on the felloes, as he pushed on the spokes. Slowly, the wheel turned. The pressure continued to build in the tunnel, making our task more difficult. When we cracked the seal, there was a momentary change in the pressure as it released into the cross passage.

The gap was wide enough for us to fit through without the motorcycles.

Phoebe was still fiddling with my bike on the track. I screamed at Daniel and gestured for him to run through the gap. He shook his head and said something I couldn't hear. I ran back to him.

"What are you doing? Get in there!" I yelled into his ear.

"Are we walking?"

He had a point. I rejoined the effort and together we turned the wheel two more revolutions. He grabbed his bike and steered it toward the bulkhead, sending it into the service tunnel, the bike wobbling until it tipped and slammed to the ground. He grabbed our helmets and bowled them one by one through the door. Then he disappeared.

I ran to the edge, yelling at Phoebe to forget about my bike. Again my words were drowned out by the clatter. I seized her by the fabric of her top, dragging her onto the platform. The wind was building ahead of the speeding train. It was three doors away.

A thousand yards. I took several steps deeper into the alcove as I picked up her bike and rolled it through the gap to Daniel. Phoebe let go of the rail and immediately was pushed past the door by the increasing wind pressure. Her feet slid, and she tumbled to the concrete, hitting her head on the handrail. I grabbed for her, my fingers clutching at nothing until I stepped from the safety of the alcove and caught her hand. I felt the push of air, the pull of her body. Her fingers were being ripped from my grasp. She was staring into the lights of the oncoming train, I could see them reflected in her eyes. Behind her, a pair of helmetless men on motorcycles were racing toward us. They needed to get off the track immediately. They needed to dump their bikes and duck into the closest alcove, which they were now approaching. They were twenty seconds away from reaching us.

"Stop!" I screamed futilely into the din. "Stop," I said, this time begging.

The advancing hurricane nudged us further from the alcove and I wrapped my arms around Phoebe. Our combined weight stopped our slide across the smooth concrete floor. I pulled at her and we scrambled to the edge of the alcove, grasping at pipes and conduit to regain our footing.

She shot through the door and motioned for me, her hands pleading me to hurry.

Ten seconds.

I glanced back. The men were just now understanding their predicament. The closest man, the one I had first noticed, went full throttle, taking incredible risks with his bike. I tried to will this person who would think nothing of turning me over to Elam Khai, will him to move faster.

But he was too far away. From us. From the exit. From escape.

Both of them were.

I could see the expression on his face.

I turned away.

The train was closing.

Six seconds.

I dove through the gap. I pulled on the door as Phoebe and Daniel wrenched the interior wheel. The bulkhead crept toward its destination, then finally slammed shut. There was a metallic CLANG as the train shot my abandoned motorcycle into the door. A sickening feeling came over me. I pounded on the metal. And screamed, "No, no, no, no!" Phoebe slid her hand on my shoulder.

Thankfully, she had not seen the look on the man's face.

She squeezed me tight, her body trembling.

"We should keep moving," I said. My voice was weak. Like someone had shoved a fist down my throat.

I stared blankly at the two remaining bikes.

Phoebe climbed on hers, started the engine, and I listlessly got onto the back. I wrapped my arms around her, felt her warmth, rested my head against her shoulder and closed my eyes. She revved the engine and I felt us accelerate.

I don't know how long it was before I opened my eyes again. The world seemed too bright when I did. The service tunnel was more friendly to people, but it was narrow in parts and the ceiling was low.

I expected to see more vehicles on our trip to Calais, but with the location of the accident on the English side it was likely the evacuation and medical response was being handled from Folkestone.

The security system in the tunnel seemed more concerned with keeping people out than keeping anyone in, and when we finally reached the end, I was able to open the two massive barn doors without trouble.

Emerging into sudden brightness blinded us briefly. We continued on the maintenance road until we slipped through a gate and cut across a grassy median, veering into the sea of passenger cars.

Calais Terminal was in chaos, vehicles were being turned away, the lines of trucks were growing longer. A derailment in one tunnel and a fatal accident in the other had shut everything down. There was a lot of honking and yelling, and frustrated attempts to turn around, to change lanes, which only made the gridlock worse. Other motorcycles were slipping through the mess, weaving between the stranded cars.

We fell in behind a pack of riders and followed them out of the terminal into the French countryside.

The surroundings were beautiful, but the bucolic view couldn't erase from my mind the horrified face of the man in the tunnel.

NINE

I Put "My Foot On The Ground" In My Mouth

It was late afternoon as we approached Paris from the north, the setting sun casting the buildings in a golden brilliance. As with everyone who visits this place, Daniel and Phoebe were instantly captivated by *La Ville-Lumière*, the City of Lights.

Phoebe gave away her excitement by pressing her chin sharply into my shoulder, her hands wrapped around my waist as she snuggled up on the seat.

We had taken turns driving the moped.

Yes, *mopeds*. I know, last time I mentioned our mode of transportation, we were screaming away from the Calais Terminal on two high-performance motorcycles.

The only thing these whining, woggling machines had in common with those bikes is they each had exactly two wheels.

Let me back up a bit.

As pretty as the farmland around the Calais Terminal is, the city proper to the north has been a major port between the continent and England for centuries, and like any port town, Calais has its seedier edges. We traded the bikes to three teenagers—two guys and a girl—for two Peugeot mopeds. I didn't feel at all guilty we'd given them motorbikes that people, including Elam Khai, might eventually start searching for, mostly because I was pretty sure I'd just bartered for two boosted mopeds. I can't pinpoint exactly why I felt that way—maybe it was that when I told them it wouldn't be smart to get caught with our bikes, they nodded knowingly, unconcerned, a twinkle in their eyes.

Phoebe found a little over two hundred dollars change in her pocket from the ticket purchases. We gave them cash to ride the motorcycles at least as far as Belgium, about an hour due east. I didn't expect them to drive them as far as Brussels, but by the joy on their faces, as they sped off, engines roaring, wheels squealing, I thought they might ride these bikes all the way to Berlin.

And so we rolled toward Paris on our fifty-cc engines, pumping out six point two horsepower. It might seem laughable, but that pitiful power plant was enough to get the mopeds up to forty-five miles per hour. As long as you were going downhill. With a tail-wind. And two riders. Where our combined weight was an advantage. Most of the time, Phoebe and I couldn't keep up with Daniel. He had to stop every few kilometers and wait for us.

We cruised into Paris a little after five.

Daniel's helmeted head swiveled left, right, up, down as he tried to consume the passing sights along the Rue Royale. He was speaking excitedly, but I couldn't hear a word.

"It's beautiful," was all Phoebe could say, street after street.

The limestone buildings, the black wrought iron fences topped with gold leaf, the cobblestone streets, the people sipping wine at sidewalk cafés. At every corner, another delight. Sometimes when you see a place so often, you forget how beautiful it is. It takes being in the presence of someone who's never experienced that place to once again appreciate it. It was like that with Paris. It's been like that with every city I've ever lived in. On some days I'm able to look at the world with a fresh point of view. It's in these moments I most appreciate the gift of time I've been given. As for Paris, what makes it so special is that—for me, at least—it somehow remains on the cutting edge while maintaining its character and charm.

If you're familiar with Paris today, you could've found your way around it two hundred years ago, and will probably still be able to two hundred years from now.

We passed the eastern end of the Champs-Élysées, engines whining, wheels wobbling, frames shuddering, and glided past the Egyptian obelisk in the center of the Place de Concorde, then dipped into the short tunnel, coming out along the bank of the Seine.

The sun, now at our backs, was stretching for the horizon behind the Eiffel Tower. The fireball hung like the weight of a pendulum stopped mid-tock between the sturdy legs of what was once the tallest structure in the world. For three thousand years, the Great Pyramid rising from the Giza desert had been man's highest achievement until Maurice Koechlin and Emile Nouguier's eighty-one story tower—whose design rights were bought by Mr. Eiffel—climbed to the top of the Paris skyline. This instantly recognizable combination of steel and bolts and human sweat built as a ridiculously oversized gateway to the 1889 World's Fair had been called a scar on the face of Paris.

Actually, I called it that in the pages of *Le Figaro*. I was working for the newspaper as a cub reporter. I'd been sent out to get reactions from prominent artists. In my defense, they said far worse things about the structure, several noting it looked like the city was sporting a permanent erection. I skipped their quotes. Instead, I gave my own opinion on the tower. The owners of the paper were big fans of Mr. Eiffel's gigantic "temporary" installation (the only way the city would approve the tower was if it was bolted together so it could be easily taken down at a later date). The paper even set up a printing shop on the second floor.

My opinion didn't go over well.

I was fired the next day.

I've embraced technology all my life. Yet, part of me longs for things to stay the same. It's the pang I feel as a treasure of the old world is lost, whether it's a building, or an empty plot of land, or a way of life.

I guess it's the reason why people like me are rarely the engines of progress in creative endeavors, scientific pursuits, or society.

Those like me are too often weighed down by the comfort of the past.

I aimed the moped for the arches cut in the side of the Louvre's southern wing. Daniel followed me through the short passage, and we arrived on the Place du Carrousel at the center of the museum's horseshoe-shaped complex, looking *very* imposing on our mopeds.

Someone once told me, "a happy life is a well-lit life." It's a simple maxim I've tried to achieve wherever I land.

The courtyard, the buildings, the grounds were illuminated in an appealing, understated manner. Even the glass pyramid looked spectacular, its interior glowing at the center of the plaza.

I'll admit, like the Eiffel Tower, I was not originally a fan of the see-through pyramid. I also called it "a scar on Paris"—I don't have a lot of range when it comes to my architectural critiques—but I've been slowly warming up to the thing over the last few decades, as I did a century earlier when one day I realized the Paris skyline wouldn't be the same if the Eiffel Tower were taken down.

In fact, I fought against its removal. Giving my own money to the cause in much the same way—but to a smaller extent—as I'd done with Paul Revere's house.

"All those photos my friends sent me," Phoebe said, gazing out at the glowing grounds and buildings. "None of them do it justice." I could see that she was starting to tear up.

Daniel said, "Are you okay?"

She nodded, wiping her eyes. "It's just so beautiful."

And for a moment, I thought about my home in Constantinople that isn't there anymore, and all the other beautiful things that have been consumed by the centuries. I mourned them but tried to be grateful for the beauty that remained.

"In there is the answer," I said.

"Then let's go in," urged Daniel.

I could just make out the clock face on the west wall. Almost quarter past five. "It's too late. They begin cutting off access to rooms half an hour before closing. We're going to need a lot more time than that. We're not exactly sure what we're looking for."

Daniel noticed me scanning the roof and the windows. "So, we're going to break into the most famous museum in the world? Which I'm sure has absolutely no security measures whatsoever."

"No, that would be idiotic. We're going to wait until morning, buy tickets and walk in."

"Oh," he said. "That's…probably a better idea."

"You think?" Phoebe said, hitting Daniel on the helmet.

The orange rim at the sky's western edge was a line of fire as the dark blue above was deepening to black. We rode along the Seine, crossing the river at Pont Neuf—the New Bridge—which is ironic since it's now the oldest bridge in Paris. Pont Neuf poured us onto the larger of the two islands in the middle of the river. At eight blocks by four blocks, home to the Notre-Dame Cathedral, Le Cité is, as its name hints, the patch of land that was once the entirety of the City.

We slowed our tired steeds as we approached the cathedral, its bell towers reaching for the emerging stars. We found a cluster of mopeds, motorcycles, and bicycles on the narrow street behind Notre-Dame and added our Peugeots to the pack.

I removed my helmet, resting it on the seat. "We can walk the rest of the way."

My legs were stiff. I could feel my feet buzzing, a side effect of the vibrations of the overworked engine. The others were suffering as well. We looked like a trio just released from a drunk tank, still not completely sober. After a block, our muscles loosened. So did our tongues. We talked about the buildings, the Notre-Dame, the river, the fire. The conversation was comforting after the forced stretches of screaming and no talking from Calais to Paris.

We reached the eastern tip of La Cité and crossed the bridge to Ile Saint-Louis. Three blocks down, after the street curved around to the southern edge, we stopped in front of a slender building sandwiched in the middle of the block.

"Whose place is this?" Daniel asked.

"Mine."

"Yours?"

I stared up toward the top floor. "Well, part of it."

Daniel's expression reminded me that the things I too often see as commonplace are, in reality, extraordinary.

We arrived out of breath at the top landing.

A narrow door awaited us. The knob had a standard keyhole with a digital keypad beneath it.

I squeezed my eyes shut, trying to remember the code, cursing Engel's warning against using the same passcode for everything.

I glanced up and to the left. Non-dominant hemisphere visualization. It's how we tend to access remembered imagery, which for me being right-handed means up and to the left. It took a moment, but the code came to me. And something else. I noticed a hair at the top of the door. White blonde. The woman who currently cleaned the apartment every few days, and kept the fridge and pantry stocked, I was pretty sure she had dark hair. I searched the edges of the door, the floor, the walls, but nothing stood out besides that one strand of hair.

I put a finger to my lips to quiet the others, then I slowly checked the gap under the door. No lights inside.

I listened, waiting to hear something. Nothing but muffled street noise. I got up on one knee and punched in the six-digit code.

The lock whined, and I pushed open the door, scanning the room from my crouched position.

The apartment was warm and the fading light filtered in through a wall of windows looking south onto the Seine.

I flicked on the lights and stepped inside my rooftop *pied-à-terre*, which literally means *foot on the ground*. A small place to sleep if you work in the city but live outside it. Or like me, live somewhere else and visit from time to time.

The place smelled fresh. The surfaces were dust-free.

My apartment was bigger than the traditional *pied-à-terre*, more like an artist studio than a home. The majority of the space was open with room for me to train. In a locked cabinet, I kept a few swords, bokken, and my usual array of martial arts equipment. There were no televisions. No phone. Bookshelves crammed with titles from obscure history texts to mainstream bestsellers lined the walls. A collection of original vinyl LPs shared space on a shelf with a turntable and a 1960s vacuum tube Mcintosh sound system. There were two bedrooms, each with a bed, one on this floor, the other a few steps up that opened onto the rooftop patio. That was it. No dining table. No coffee table. No side tables. No night tables. And no place to sit other than the couch.

Paris is not a city you stay in. It's a city you live in. It's a city where it doesn't matter how small your *foot on the ground* is. Only that you have a place to go at the end of the night. To live in Paris is to walk in Paris. To be on the streets, in the cafés, in the restaurants, and in the parks and theaters and clubs, bars and museums.

From a wall safe that sat behind a striking Picasso forgery, I pulled out the one piece of twenty-first-century technology in the apartment. A laptop computer, a couple of years old. The lithium-ion battery had expanded, deforming the bottom of the case. There wasn't much cash in the safe. Maybe five thousand in euros, and a couple of thousand in dollars. I closed the safe and hinged the Picasso back into place, then stared at the painting I got for next-to-nothing after informing Sotheby's they were auctioning a fake. They didn't believe me at first, but eventually, a thorough examination convinced them. Especially after the sellers made a hasty disappearance.

I removed the swollen battery and plugged in the power adapter. The machine started up. There was no password—there was no need, it contained no personal information. The lone accessible application was an encrypted web browser anyone could download from the Internet.

Only two people alive knew I had this place. My father wasn't one of them.

So far our diversions had barely delayed Elam Khai. But I couldn't shake centuries of covering my tracks. The IP address would appear to be from somewhere else in the world, randomized each time I logged in.

There were fifteen WiFi networks in range. Five of them close enough for reliable high-speed access. I had broken the passwords of two.

Even if Elam Khai knew what to look for, I was one query in a billion.

I wrote my father a brief message and placed it into a BBS folder my father and I had been using for almost thirty years. There was nothing new from him. His last message was from three months ago, checking in and telling me he'd be coming to visit the next day. The parent-teacher conference with Mrs. Avery.

Daniel was reading a book he'd found on the shelf. "Son of an owl!"

"What?" asked Phoebe.

"Hindi swear. They think owls are stupid and lazy." He flipped through *Curse Words From Around The World*. "'I would dry my dirty underwear on your mother's crucifix!' Ohhh-kay. Romanians are weird."

He flopped on the couch and moaned with pleasure at finally being horizontal.

Phoebe found the bathroom. "There's a drawer full of tooth-brushes that haven't been opened. Is it okay to use one?"

"Of course. That's what they're for."

Daniel ran his tongue over his teeth and moaned again. "Feels like I just licked asphalt. I'm next. If I can get up."

Phoebe emerged from the bathroom, brushing her teeth. "Wha ow yao oowing," she asked me.

"Checking the news."

"Ah-out wha?"

"What is she babbling?" Daniel barked.

"Um ushin I eet, oh eh?"

I didn't want to tell them that I was worried about their families, looking for any hint of trouble, so I just ignored the question.

I flashed through a couple of news portals. The Eurotunnel was big news. So was the hijacking incident. There was a lot about Boston. The explosions were being covered prominently by American media. Images, video, opinions. The story was popping up on international outlets as well, mostly as it tied into the hijacking. Reports were sprinkled with mentions of past attacks that had occurred in each news organization's prime market. London, Paris, etcetera. I found very little about the light tower collapse at the football game. Stations in Springfield and Hartford were the only ones to pick it up.

Near tragedy at a high school homecoming game in Western Massachusetts. A portion of stadium lighting crashed into stands filled with students and parents watching Monument High's Homecoming football game against Housatonic in Great Barrington Saturday afternoon. Spectators were able to get to safety before the structure collapsed. There were no reports of fatalities or life-threatening injuries. However, at least two dozen people visited local hospitals, most with cuts, bruises, and broken bones.

"It was a miracle," said Police Chief...

The shugga shugga shugga of the brush against Phoebe's teeth continued as she read over my shoulder. The local newspaper in Great Barrington told the same story with a few added details.

In the initial confusion, several people contacted police concerned they couldn't locate family members. State Police search and rescue dogs were brought in and found evidence of blood in the woods only a few hundred yards from the football field. One witness reported seeing a

202 | EDWARD SAVIO

female possibly wearing a cheerleader uniform heading toward the woods accompanied by a male. Police said there are no open reports of missing persons, and that all members of the cheerleading squads from both schools are safe and accounted for.

"Nice work, GBPD," said Daniel. Only his feet were visible as they dangled over the arm of the couch. "Remind me never to get kidnapped in Great Barrington."

"Ee-uz I gall em."

"What?"

"She called her parents, they're covering for her."

"Airs uh-ing ah-out aiden," Phoebe said.

"No. Braeden doesn't have a family to miss him."

"I een, ay-ee, eez ah-ive."

Maybe Braeden could have survived if he'd been rushed to a hospital immediately. But his loss of blood was extensive. He had only minutes to live when we left him. Alone. He might be at the bottom of the Housatonic. More likely his body had been removed by the Scotsman and the others to keep anyone from doing an autopsy. That would bring too many questions without answers.

I thought about the two caretakers, the husband and wife that ran the farm I owned in Great Barrington. There was nothing in the news about them. But that didn't necessarily mean they were safe.

The mention of a cheerleader concerned me. Even though the report said everyone was accounted for. If Elam Khai's people followed up with the two schools on Monday, checking on students who were absent, it might lead them to Phoebe's family. There'd be more kids out than normal. People shook up by the incident at the stadium. Families taking advantage of the short week to extend their Thanksgiving holiday travel. Still, it'd be easy to narrow it down by ignoring anyone not on the cheerleading squad. Daniel's identity would be harder, but they'd only focus on him if the cheerleader angle didn't pan out.

I tapped out a note to the lawyer again. And this time, I sent it.

Phoebe returned to the bathroom and rinsed her mouth out. "It's all yours," she said to Daniel's dangling feet. "Maybe he's alive," she said, this time without a mouth full of toothpaste.

Phoebe and Daniel grew up watching so many television shows and movies where a character dies only to turn out not to be dead. I knew Braeden was gone, just like I knew Engel was not. My oldest friend had survived, once again, while the stepbrother I never knew had his life cut short. What confirmed Braeden's death for me was when Elam Khai sent the flaming pipe through the Scotsman's chest.

Still, it cost me nothing to give them hope of a Hollywood ending. "He could be," I said.

And maybe that's why I was trying so hard to protect Phoebe and Daniel. Because I hadn't protected Braeden. He knew they were there to capture me, not kill me. He traded his life, not for my life, but simply for my freedom.

No, not exactly. He died so my father—*our* father—would not have to bargain for my freedom.

I watched Daniel's feet bouncing, watched Phoebe browsing the books on the shelves. I knew I should leave them here, leave them behind. I was reminded of my father's words when I first told him I was buying Paul Revere's house to save it from demolition. "What are you going to do? Buy every house with historical importance and try to save it?"

Maybe that was my greatest weakness. My ineradicable desire to save things, protect things that can't save themselves.

Daniel never got up to brush his teeth. The last thing I heard from the couch was, "'You're as ugly as a salad.' Bloody Bulgarians." Soon his feet stopped moving and his breathing slowed.

I showed Phoebe to the upstairs bedroom, then I got back on the computer and searched for ONYX. The name was generic enough that I couldn't sift through all the possibilities. Xolaris was easier. The private security company Will's driver worked for was a joint

South African-British firm registered in the British Virgin Islands and headquartered in Dubai.

Nothing opaque about that.

I switched over to the Louvre website. My father and I had lived for several years in the ancient fortress now buried under six centuries of construction. Part of me was hoping I'd see something in the virtual tour and we could avoid the museum altogether. Beyond our personal attachment, there was no shortage of art with a tangential connection to my father and my uncle—Mark Antony, Augustus, Octavian, and Alexander the Great. But nothing obvious stood out. I hoped seeing it for myself would reveal a clue if there was one.

I closed the computer, then checked the lock on the door.

I went to the bedroom on the first floor and fell onto the bed.

After several hours of tossing and turning, staring at the ceiling and getting annoyed by the imperfections in the beams, I went upstairs to get some air.

I found Phoebe out on the patio.

"Why don't you live in this luxury all the time?" she asked without taking her eyes off the City. She seemed unfazed by my sudden appearance.

"I don't know if I'd call this place luxurious. It's small. It's got no furniture."

"It's Paris."

"Yes, it is."

"It's charming and warm. If you took five minutes to decorate it, it'd be lovely. And this patio…" She spread her arms out, motioning to the small trees and manicured plants that ringed the roof, and the weathered table and chairs. "Who has a place like this and doesn't live here?"

Once again, I saw the city and my *foot on the ground* through her eyes. Like I said, you can see something so often, you don't realize how beautiful it is.

"I'd never leave," she added.

I searched for a way to explain it to her.

"I love it here. It is one of my favorite places. But there're a lot of beautiful places in the world. And it's...more difficult to stay sharp in a place like this. Life hasn't always been this easy. Walk down the street to a store, get food. Turn on the faucet, get water. Even a hundred years ago, life was so much harder. Even when you had enough, there were others more desperate trying to take it from you."

Phoebe watched me with a mix of surprise and sadness.

"That doesn't seem like a very pleasant way to live."

"For portions of my life that was the only way to live."

"But it's different now."

I smiled, bittersweetly. "I've lived through many times of surplus and abundance that everyone thought would never end. They always do. Golden Ages followed by the Dark."

"But you have money. You could survive a crisis, right?"

"Money can buy a lot of things. Sometimes what it buys is too much attention."

She looked downcast, her gaze fixed on her hands.

"I'm upsetting you."

She shook her head. "It just makes me sad thinking you've had to live your life preparing for the worst."

"I don't always," I said. She raised a disbelieving eyebrow. "Okay, mostly I do. But I have fun. Sometimes."

She laughed. It was good to see her smile. It made me smile.

She leaned against me. It was a moment before she spoke. "Do you remember your mom?"

"Not really. Just flashes. Warmth. I remember that. She was pretty. My father had a sculpture of her made right after I was born. For years after she died, I would hug that thing. Sometimes when the sun hit it, I could feel that warmth again." I played with the handrail. "But usually it was cold."

"Do you still have the statue?"

"The home we had in Constantinople was looted in—" I had to translate the date, "—eleven eighty-two. Her statue, everything I knew...was gone. My father never set foot in that house again."

"What about your father? Is he nice?"

I laughed out loud. The sound echoed off the buildings on the other side of the Seine. "I don't know if I'd call my father nice. He loves me. He can even bring himself to say it at times. But 'nice' is just a bit too bland a word to describe him. He's not the toughest teacher I've ever had or the most demanding, but he *is* the most exacting. I think he wants to make sure I'm prepared." I heard the last of my laugh-echoes die away. It was quiet, the late night noise of the city melting into the background. "I'm not sure about anything anymore."

Phoebe stared down at the water. "That picture. Back at your house. You were on the *Titanic*, weren't you?"

I nodded. "I got on in Southampton."

She shook her head. "I...can't imagine how horrible that must've been. How did you survive?"

I rubbed the knuckle on the index finger of my left hand. I'd sliced it getting off the ship. There wasn't a scar, at least none I could see. I have nightmares sometimes about being on *Titanic*. "I wish I had some heroic tale to tell you. How brave I was." I touched the knuckle again, feeling some of the guilt come back. "I wasn't on board when the ship went down. My father wanted me to join him here in Paris. I'd heard about this great ship. 'Biggest ever built.' And I wanted to see it for myself. So, I booked passage from England to France where it was picking up more passengers before heading on to America. Seventy-seven nautical miles. That was my whole trip. I don't believe in curses, but if I did...that ship would be proof. I wasn't on it ten minutes when the thing nearly sank leaving port. You've got to understand, *Titanic* dwarfed anything else on the water. Our wake caused these two huge transatlantic ocean liners in dock to be tossed around like toys in a bathtub. One ship had several crew members go overboard.

The other one, the mooring lines snapped. I heard it. Sounded like cannon fire. Cannon fire tends to get my attention. I'm standing on deck. Everyone's waving, shouting, horns are blasting, and I see the *City of New York* heading straight for us. That was the ship's name. I remember that because it was coming at us stern first. Accidents between ships aren't like car crashes. Everything happens in slow motion. This tugboat crew springs into action and somehow gets a line hooked onto the *City of New York* and with its engine maxed out, black smoke pouring from its stack, the tug is able to slow the ship just enough to avoid it colliding with us by less than three feet. Three feet! The length of my arm. That ship would've ripped a hole in *Titanic* and ended its journey right there." I stopped, waited for the ache in my stomach to pass. "Sometimes I think about that tugboat. Think about its captain. And wonder if he blamed himself."

Phoebe pulled in a gasp of air as she imagined the weight of what that man must've felt.

I was quiet for a moment, the sounds of the city filling the silence.

"Once we got to France, the port couldn't handle a ship that large, so we had to transfer to shore on a tender. I watched almost three hundred passengers including John Jacob Astor and the Unsinkable Molly Brown come aboard. I was the last of twenty-four that got off. I cut my hand on a bad weld as I stepped off *Titanic*." I rubbed my finger again. "I was so pissed at my father for making me get off in France. Its maiden voyage was going to be a huge party. When news reached Paris five days later, I felt such a terrible sense of guilt."

Phoebe put her hand over mine. "You didn't do anything."

"That's just it. I didn't. Do anything. I know it's normal, survivors guilt. But part of me wonders, if I had been there, could I have helped? I've been aboard more than one doomed ship and lived to tell about it."

"There were a couple of thousand people on board, Alexander. Not a couple dozen."

I glanced up. "I know. If I had been on board, I'd probably feel even worse. Because I would've made sure I survived."

"I'm glad you didn't have to go through that. Those poor people. I would've been so scared." She was quiet, her eyes studying me. "You never seem scared."

I blew out a snort. "Phoebe, I'm scared all the time. I'm just good at hiding it."

"Now you're trying to make me feel better."

"You're stronger than you think."

"I'm...starting to understand that...a little." She pulled her hand back and warmed it in her pocket. "All the stuff I used to worry about. Am I skinny enough? Am I wearing the right clothes? Who's dating who? It doesn't seem important anymore." She stared out into the night, at the lights of Paris. "It's beautiful."

"Yes." I wasn't looking at the city.

She turned and caught me staring at her.

As the lights flickered in her eyes, I let her in. All the feelings I'd been keeping locked up. I wanted to tell her that ever since I'd met her, there'd been something drawing me to her, something I didn't understand. That I had dreamed of a moment like this. Us. Alone. In the perfect place.

Her hands were back on the railing, so close to mine, and all I wanted to do was reach out and take them. I wanted to know everything she was thinking.

Unfortunately, she told me.

"I know how many girls would want to be here right now, in this place. With you," she said.

I knew where this was going. Nobody says a sentence like that without following it up by dropping an anvil on your head. I didn't want to give her the chance. I wanted to savor this moment on the roof with her and not have it spoiled by her telling me she could never be with me because she couldn't handle me watching her grow old.

I turned. Her body unconsciously pivoting toward mine. I

grabbed her, held her in my arms, something raging in me, my arms shaking, hers trembling. I kissed her. Her soft, moist lips pressing against mine. It was hotter and deeper than our kiss on Boston Harbor. I felt the warmth of her thrust against me. I pulled her tighter. I don't know how long our kiss lasted. Minutes, an hour. But when it was done, we were breathless. My heart was racing, and I could see her chest rising and falling.

"That's not fair. Not fair." She wiped her mouth, then folded her arms, then self-consciously dropped them to her side. "There's nothing more I want than to feel this…" She fumbled for the words. "*This*," she said. "But it isn't how it should happen."

"You're right. Paris. Overlooking the Seine. Starry night." I pretended to shudder. "Just dreadful."

She laughed. "That's not what I mean. We've been running for our lives. I can't be held responsible for my actions under duress." Her coyness turned serious.

I reached for her hand, held it. "I get it."

"Do you? I don't know if you can. You, the way you are. You've seen too much. Things I'll never see."

As if on cue, the Eiffel Tower lit up for its hourly show. Her eyes sparkled as she watched the light show, biting her lip, shaking her head in awe. The tower's beacon sent a sweep of xenon white light across the city. Since it was one AM, the last show of the night, it went on twice as long and was more dramatic with the tower's orangey illumination turned off for the night. Ten minutes later, it was over, and the skyline went back to simply being beautiful.

"You got to see *that*," I said.

She nodded, her mouth turning down at the sides. "Makes me think of Homecoming. Craig must be so angry at me."

An image of Craig putting his fist through a wall popped into my head. No, that wasn't right. He wouldn't hit the wall, he'd hit one of the guys *hugging* the wall, struggling to build up the courage to ask a girl to dance. Craig wouldn't recognize the irony that he was just as dateless as the wallflowers he was terrorizing.

"Before I started dating Craig," she began, "guys were always on me. You can't understand what it's like being a girl who's not with someone. Guys think you're fair game to hit on, hit on, hit on. They think you want a guy. That you need a guy. Even when you tell them you don't. *Especially* when you tell them you don't. And if you refuse, they call you a slut, like *not* dating them makes me easy somehow. The nice guys were afraid of me. The ones who weren't afraid, who didn't see me as some fragile thing that couldn't be touched…they were just assholes."

"*Craig* is an asshole."

"But he's my asshole. And he's not like that when we're alone. He's kind and vulnerable and he listens."

"You should be with someone who always treats you well. Not just when you're alone."

"I don't think I'm as nice as you think I am."

"I know you're more complicated than you appear." I ran my hand along her cheek. "You asked me why I never asked you out."

"You said it was because I was dating someone. Someone *you* think is an asshole. Which makes that an even more lame excuse. Have the balls to let me say, 'no.'"

"You're right. But that lame excuse was only part of it."

She stared up at me. "Then what was the reason?" She wanted desperately to know.

I breathed in. "Because every time I talked to you, every time I saw how you were with people, every one of our interactions made me realize—"

"How hot I am? How much you *want* me?" She lowered her voice and leaned against me. Her tone exuded an exaggerated passion that concealed a touch of pain.

"How I wouldn't be able to lie to you." I was quiet a moment.

She lowered her eyes. "I don't want you to think I don't feel this… thing between us." She raised her gaze to meet mine. "Because I do." She had a finger hooked through one of my belt loops. Something I wasn't aware of until she tugged at it. "I *do*. But we're from different worlds, Alexander."

"Not so different."

"So very, very different," she insisted.

I pushed her hair back over her ear. My fingers lingered as I slipped them down the back of her neck. "Can I tell you something?"

"You can tell me anything," she said, her natural warmth returning.

I tried to gather my thoughts. I knew what I wanted to say, but I didn't know if the words would make it worse. "You're right. I've been in this situation. Not as many times as you would think, but..."

"But more than I would like," she whispered.

I stared into her eyes. The next bit was brutal and honest. "Yes. The perfect night. The perfect moment. Alone with a beautiful girl. Free from rules, parents." The words landed hard. She started to respond. I stopped her, putting my hand up. "But I've never felt like this. You can believe that or not, it doesn't matter. I know it's true. I just haven't."

She studied me a moment, her eyes never leaving mine. That is, until her gaze lowered to my mouth. She kissed me. Softly. Tenderly. Her hand on my face. Not the reckless passion of our earlier kiss, but filled with something much harder to describe.

She pulled away, her fingers still on my cheek.

Before it could all be ruined by the truth of who we were and what was going on, she said, "Let's get some sleep."

We did sleep. The first real rest in two days.

In fact, we overslept.

We slept through the noise of the cars on the street, the people heading for work. We slept through the grating din of the major restoration project being done to the building next door, nail guns, power saws, pallets being dropped.

We slept through the sun shining in the windows.

We slept through all of that until, finally, at 9:21 AM, a fly that had found its way into my *pied-à-terre* landed on my nose. Deep in slumber, I instinctively batted the annoying insect, thus punching myself in the face.

I rolled out of bed and onto the floor, one hand pinching my nose, the other catching the blood before it could drip onto the bedding.

With a wad of toilet paper sticking out of both nostrils, I roused Daniel.

"What *is* that!?" Daniel said, waking up to the sight of a tissue-breathing dragon standing over him.

"We're late. We overslept," I said, nasally. "C'mon."

Phoebe looked up at me as I stood by her bed. "Wow. What's the other guy look like?"

"Dead. I think. I can't find him." Off her suddenly concerned look, I added, "It was a fly."

"Ah."

We grabbed our IDs and enough cash for the day. We each tore off a piece of the freshly delivered baguette, shoved the bread layered with a few slices of cheese in our mouths before charging out the door.

We were leaving the safety of my apartment and going out into the open. Where anyone could see us.

We took the stairs and burst into the street.

We crossed the bridge from Ile St. Louis to the Left Bank even though we would need to cross back over the Seine. The pedestrian path along the south side of the river was a straight shot, no streets to cross or traffic to wait for. Passing the tip of Île de la Cité, the Louvre became visible across the water. Seeing it made us quicken our pace.

Up the steps, jogging now. Crossing the Pont du Carrousel and under the same arches we took last night. Once in the courtyard, we sprinted toward the glass Pyramid, anxious to get inside.

I got there first but stopped a few feet from the door.

Daniel rushed by me, his outstretched hands ready to push through the revolving doors.

He slammed hard into the glass, bounced off, and fell to the ground, dazed. "What the—"

"It's closed! See. *Fermé.*"

"I can't read French."

"Can you understand a rope across a door?"

"Not in French! How can it be closed?

Phoebe pointed to the sign. "It's closed every Tuesday."

"Tuesday? Why Tuesday? What did Tuesday ever do?"

There, in the middle of the open courtyard, we were not more than a hundred yards from whatever clue would lead us to my father. We might as well have been a thousand miles away.

I suddenly felt vulnerable, exposed. I found a garbage can and started rooting through the trash, finding a soiled map of the museum.

We sat at the back of Angelina. The door to the kitchen that led to a back door was a few feet away. I had a good view of the café, including the front entrance.

I unfolded the map and spread it out. The stained glossy paper contrasted with the pristine white tablecloth.

With exaggerated theatrics and precision that tripled the time it took, a waiter poured the first cup for each of us, then, annoyed because he was required to put on this show and because he—mostly correctly—took us for Americans and—mostly correctly—teenagers, put the pitcher down directly on the map.

I lifted the bone china cup to my lips, taking a warm, velvety sip.

Betrayal. That's the hardest thing for me to understand. It's not like I haven't been betrayed before. I've been betrayed too many times to count. In a way, I've betrayed just about everyone I've ever met. But my treachery and bad faith was done to protect myself. And my father. And my friends. I didn't do it to harm anyone. At least, not deliberately.

My father and Elam Khai fought against each other as Mark Antony and Octavian, and then were friendly during the reign of Charlemagne. How many times in between those moments and since had they oscillated back and forth between friend and foe?

How many times had they stabbed each other in the back only to risk their lives for one another?

"Oh, my God, this is incredible," said Phoebe as the thick chocolate mixture slipped over her tongue.

"I am never leaving this place," Daniel said, pouring a second serving of the African hot chocolate. "If this was a woman, I'd want to marry her."

"If this was a woman," said Phoebe, "she'd be out of your league."

"Sadly, true."

"There are five levels in the Louvre. Two underground and three above." I marked a line across each of the levels roughly where the meridian passed through the galleries, courtyard, and underground lobby.

Phoebe licked some errant chocolate from her lips as she studied the map, making me briefly lose my focus.

"The Mesopotamian exhibits. I'd start there. Like Will said, beginning of history."

I marked the area with the number one.

Daniel leaned in. "I was thinking, Elam Khai ruled Rome when B.C. became A.D. I know that change over didn't mean anything back then. But, you know, 'beginning of time?'"

The line also passed through *Greek and Roman Antiquities*. I marked that exhibit hall with a number two.

We annotated the map in this way, not limiting ourselves to the exact coordinates of the meridian, assuming it was possible that what we were looking for could be anywhere in the building.

"I don't know if your father could've made this more difficult if he was doing it on purpose," said Daniel as I folded the map and put it away.

"It's only hard because we don't understand the riddle."

Exasperated, Daniel said, "Do not say a word about the dwarf."

I shrugged. "If he'd only seen the sawdust, he'd be alive today."

Hoping to defuse the situation before Daniel took a swing at me, Phoebe put up her hand. "I was thinking…since we have to wait until tomorrow morning for the Louvre to open, maybe we could check out some of the amazing sights Paris has to offer. The Tuileries. The Champs-Élysées. The food. Maybe have a nice dinner."

"I was thinking we should head back to the apartment. Get inside. And stay out of sight."

Daniel nodded. "So we've got 'risk being kidnapped and possibly killed,' or 'risk being completely bored to death.'"

"Pretty much. Kinda like we saw London. *Zoom.* There's the Globe Theatre."

"You really know how to show a girl a good time."

I waved at the pitcher and the cups that had been licked clean. "But…the hot chocolate."

"It's incredible, Alexander. It's *not* the Eiffel Tower."

We slipped out the back.

I suggested we split up—we'd be less obvious—but was overruled. We compromised. I walked ten paces behind them.

The stroll back to my flat was short. But in Paris, there is a feast on every block. Phoebe and Daniel were smiling and laughing, pointing at the sights along the way. The gilded statue of Joan of Arc, Claude Perrault's Colonnade on the eastern face of the Louvre, the glass-covered tourist boats like fattened up gondolas slipping under the bridges.

I found myself enjoying them enjoying this little slice of Paris. But it was a joy dampened by a cloud of danger and uncertainty.

Back at the apartment, I put in an intense aerobic workout while Phoebe and Daniel occupied themselves with my books.

"I've heard about this," she said, showing me a picture of a spot a few hundred yards away. "The bridge with all the locks."

"It's gone," I said, concentrating on my feet as I increased the speed of the rope.

"Gone? But it's some sort of French tradition. Lovers come and set the locks on the bridge, showing their love can't be broken."

"It's not a tradition. It's not even French. The locks started invading Paris around two thousand-seven. Some—" I tried to catch my breath. "Some Italian writer put the idea in a love story. It spread here and took hold on the Pont d'Arts. Eight years later, they had seven hundred thousand locks. And seven hundred thousand keys tossed into the river." I sped up, the rope just a blur now. "This is why we can't have nice things. We don't stop to think about what we're doing. A few locks is cute. Forty-five tons of locks, part of the bridge collapses. It doesn't even fit how the French view love. They don't believe in love that's confining and permanent."

Winded, I stopped jumping rope.

"Well, I thought it was sweet." Phoebe's expression registered sadness as she got up and went upstairs.

Daniel punched me in the arm. "Nice going, you hopeless no-mantic. 'Yes, Phoebe, that's the sweetest thing I've ever heard. A padlock on my heart. Tell me more.'"

He joined Phoebe on the rooftop.

I didn't go after them. Instead, I wound up the rope and punished my body for another ten excruciating minutes. Lacrosse kept me in shape, but I could feel the effects of taking a couple of days off. As much training as I've had over the centuries, I was not fully prepared for the Scotsman, and not at all for Elam Khai. It's the difference between practice and a game. Preparation helps, but in that moment when everything's on the line, there's no substitute for irreversible consequence.

I made dinner with Phoebe's help. It was fun and it took our mind off everything. We removed the cushions from the couch and ate sitting on the floor.

"I miss school," said Phoebe breaking a quiet moment. "Isn't that stupid?"

"I don't miss it at all." At least that's what I think Daniel said. He had a mouth full of steak.

"I miss the comfort of knowing what's going to happen next. This class, then this class, then this class, then practice after school.

I miss my friends." Phoebe played with the food on her plate. "I miss my family."

"I know," I said.

Daniel sighed. "Listen, I miss my parents, too. Sort of. And all of my friends are right there." He pointed at me. "But we're here because being there would put our families in danger. And as much as my parents annoy me, I'm not okay with something happening to them."

"I don't—" I pushed my plate away. "I don't know if they're safe even if you don't go home."

"Why? What changed between yesterday and today?" said Phoebe, concerned.

"The news report last night, mentioning a cheerleader. That makes figuring out who you are a lot easier."

"We should warn them." Which seemed like a good idea to Phoebe until she heard in her mind what that might sound like.

"I have a lawyer in Connecticut who could get your parents enough money to leave everything behind and get someplace safe."

Daniel laughed. "My parents aren't going to just leave and go live on some island or in a cabin in the woods. First of all, they can't stand each other, so even if you got one of them to go, the other wouldn't go simply because the other one was."

"As much as I want them to get away, I can't imagine my parents leaving without a very persuasive reason."

"How about the truth?" I said.

Again Daniel laughed. "What? That my best friend is older than-than-than—"

"Matches. Islam."

He nodded. "*Matches. Islam.*"

"Toilet paper. Windmills. I'm…older than windmills."

"Mom, Dad, you remember my friend, Alexander, who is older than *windmills*. Funny thing, his nutty uncle, Alexander the Great, wants to drop us in the middle of 'Lord of the Flies.' Yeah, my folks'll buy that. Right after they put me in rehab."

"At some point, Elam Khai's going to figure out who you two

are. I don't believe he'd harm your parents. But he'd absolutely use them as bargaining chips."

Daniel turned to Phoebe. "Maybe we should go back home. Try to convince them. Make up some lie that's more believable than the truth."

Phoebe shook her head. "Don't you get it? It doesn't matter. We know who he is. He's never going to leave us alone. Ever. Isn't that right?" She stared at me for an uncomfortable moment, then climbed the stairs to the upper bedroom and slammed the door.

∞

I couldn't fall asleep. None of us could.

My mind was screaming. I was obsessing over everything that could go wrong at the museum. Wracking my brain, wondering what could my father want me to see or know. Hoping I could find a way to protect Phoebe and Daniel's families.

"I can't sleep," Daniel yelled from the couch.

"Try," I said.

"I can't."

"Try anyway."

Silence. The sound of people laughing and talking drifted up from the street.

"Don't they know…people are trying to sleep?"

It was a little after ten. "It's Paris. They probably haven't had dinner yet."

"I'm hungry."

"Then eat. There's food leftover."

"I'm tired."

"Then sleep."

"I can't because I'm hungry."

"Then eat."

There was a long pause.

"They're going to be waiting for us, aren't they?" Daniel said.

I could hear Phoebe moving upstairs. But so far, she'd been silent.

"We went the whole day without seeing anyone," I said.

"We stayed inside most of the day."

"Maybe the bike switch threw them off," Phoebe called down.

"It might have bought us some time," I said. I doubted the ruse would work for long.

All of us remained quiet. Not sleeping. Just pretending to.

"Alexander…?" Daniel said.

"Yes."

"So, were you in diapers for like three hundred years?"

"Nooooo," I shouted. I could hear Phoebe stifling a laugh. "We— we didn't *have* diapers."

Now both of them were snorting.

"Right. You're older than diapers."

I sighed. It was going to be a long, long night.

~ TEN ~
All is Fair in Love and Warsaw

Phoebe slipped her fingers along the side of my head, pushing my hair over my ears. Like I did last night on the roof. Like I've wanted to do countless times since meeting her.

Her touch was tender, soothing, and I woke to find her gazing down at me, the light from the street lamps illuminating half her face.

"You okay?" I asked sleepily.

"I woke up and didn't know where I was." Her voice was a whisper.

"That can be disorienting." I reached for her and slid my hand down her arm. I felt the need to grab her.

"I miss my bed," she said.

"I never get attached to a particular sleeping arrangement."

She let out a breathy, silent laugh. "Sounds awful."

"It's not so bad. Comes in handy. I can sleep anywhere." I yawned. "Anywhere."

"Yes." She tried to bounce on my bed achieving zero lift. "A park bench is more comfortable than this."

I shrugged. "I've spent decades sleeping on the ground. I still wake up sometimes on the floor. This—" I hit the bed with my fist. "—makes me feel like I've gotten soft."

She punched me through the covers, catching me in the stomach. "Ow!"

"That's not soft. My brother, *he's* soft."

"You have a brother?"

"He's a senior."

I shook my head. "Why didn't I know that?"

She went quiet. "He and I don't hang out. He says I embarrass him. The cheerleading, the socializing."

"That's what people say when they're not good at something. They make fun of it. Denigrate it."

She nodded. "He's kind of a complete failure of evolution on the social side. But he's brilliant. I tried to help him in the beginning. It just made us angry and frustrated with each other. So, I gave up."

"I've never had a brother or sister. Not really."

"Your dad's had other children."

"Lots of them. I'm not even sure how many. I've known a bunch of them. But only briefly. It's difficult to explain a kid that never grows up. It scares people. They start believing I'm cursed by God. Diseased. Possessed. Better just to avoid it all. My father's gotten to enjoy family life occasionally. Wife, kids. A few decades, forty years at most. The longest I've lived in one place—except when I was with my mother—is four years."

"All I've ever wanted was to get as far from Great Barrington as possible." She played with the edge of the bed covers. "Do you miss her?"

I tried to picture my mother's face. "I miss the thought of her." The image in my mind, was it really her or just my memory of her sculpture brought to life? "It was harder for her than me."

"Taking care of a baby for so many years?"

"That…and leaving a baby behind. Knowing as she was growing old that she wouldn't be there to protect me. I've tried to imagine what my father feels. That moment when he makes the decision to walk away. When he has to leave his family. His flesh. His blood. The woman he loves. The children who are part of him. Never to see them again. How does that happen? Does he wake up one day, and think…that's it? My life here as this person is through. Or does he deliberate on it and plan it years or even decades in advance? Knowing every single moment when he is going to leave."

Phoebe lifted the covers and slid under them. I could feel the warmth of her body as she snuggled next to me, her hand on my chest.

"I don't know if I could do it," she said as her breathing slowed and she closed her eyes. "Walk away."

"You'd have to," I said.

But she was already asleep.

I woke up some time later with Phoebe's head resting on my shoulder, the gentle breeze of her breath on my neck. Night still had a stranglehold on the city, but the distant sounds of wrens and robins and blackbirds filtered into the room. I extricated myself from the bed without waking her and crept into the main room.

Daniel was asleep, his feet hanging over the arm of the couch.

I brewed some tea, poured the hot water over the leaves in a strainer held above the cup. Let the aroma drift up into my nostrils. I warmed my hands, wrapping them around the ceramic mug before bringing the cup to my lips.

I stretched.

I worked each muscle before moving on to the next.

Typically, this takes forty-five minutes.

I glanced at the clock to find an hour and twenty minutes had passed, the consequence of being unable to stretch since Saturday.

Some days I meditate next. I'm not very good at it. And I don't mean in comparison to the monks I've trained with over the centuries. I mean, I'm terrible. In the orders that allow their ranks limited speech, these monks have used this precious privilege to express how very terrible I am. I can, with a great deal of effort achieve some modest level of quietude in my mind. Not often. And not all that quiet. Today, I didn't bother trying.

Instead, I moved directly into my physical training.

It began, as always, with a simple set of movements.

A muscle can be tensed for as long as you can hold it, but the strongest it can ever be, hardened into a shell, is for a heartbeat.

Since my third place finish in the World Chess Championship in 1948, my father has forbidden me to enter any tournament of any kind so practicing the pure disciplines is useless to me.

For centuries, he taught me every weapon and manner of warfare. But in recent years, he's forced me to begin weaponless. What is called "open hands."

"The purpose is not to train you to defeat an armed attacker when you are unarmed. The goal is to survive until you can obtain their weapon or a better one," my father said.

Which, when you think about it, makes sense. For centuries, I walked around carrying a variety of deadly weapons. Now, that sort of thing is frowned upon.

"Force equals mass times acceleration. That's what you learn in those physics class," he continued. "But a punch is not one force traveling in a single direction but a combination of forces twisting and turning and pushing. The rotation of the hips, core tension to increase body mass, hand speed, impact tension, angle of attack.

"You do not train to have a referee raise your arm in victory. You must master staying alive. Survival depends on the avoidance of force, the redirection of force, and when those are not enough, the projection of force."

His speech usually ended with me on my ass.

Daniel woke up about forty minutes into my session. He rubbed his eyes, grunted, and shuffled across the room, making no effort to avoid my jutting hands and kicking feet. I came within inches of knocking him senseless. I paused to let him pass unharmed. He trudged into the kitchenette and absently opened cupboards, drawers, the fridge and freezer, genuinely surprised to find each of them well-stocked.

"This refrigerator is full," said Daniel through a mouthful of banana. "You've got chicken. Salads. Fresh vegetables. More steaks. The milk is good."

"A woman comes in every few days, dusts, vacuums, brings fresh food."

"When was the last time you were here?"

"Couple of years ago."

"Doesn't that seem a little wasteful to you?"

"She takes the food brought the last time home to her family."

That earned several grunts and a hmph.

He shoveled food into his mouth as he watched me perform a rapid succession of forearm blocks, roundhouse kicks, palm-heel strikes, side roll kicks, ear claps, ending with a butterfly kick.

"That looks hard," he said, chomping cereal.

I glared at him, my chest heaving.

I resumed my work out.

I heard a clank, followed by a tinkle.

"Put down the knife," I said.

I didn't have to look to know Daniel had grabbed the weapon off the counter. It was similar to the blade Elle's bodyguard had threatened me with. A glass resin knife can slip past metal detectors.

"This feels weird."

"It's glass."

He dropped it, testing if it would break, I guess. It didn't.

Phoebe emerged sleepily from my room. "Hey," she said to me, her hair tousled and ringed with emerging curls at the fringes.

"Hey," I answered, not realizing until it started to hurt that I was biting my lip.

Daniel glanced from me to Phoebe and back at me. "Hey," he said. There was an uncomfortably long pause. "You slept downstairs?"

"Hey," I said to Daniel, harshly. "Put on your shoes. We're going for a run."

"We are?"

"Yes." I walked over to Phoebe. "You sleep okay?"

"I did. Thanks. I just needed..." She touched my chest.

I stared into her eyes. She didn't smile. Her look was almost melancholy. I turned to Daniel who was staring at us. "C'mon. Lace-up."

Daniel waited until we were halfway across the bridge that connected Ile Saint Louis to the Left Bank until he quizzed me.

"Did you two, you know..." He jumbled his hands in another of his undecipherable gestures as we jogged.

"Did we what?"

He glowered at me. "Did you sleep with her?"

"She couldn't sleep. Strange surroundings. She didn't want to be alone."

"So you didn't sleep with her?"

"I did. I slept in a bed in which she was *also* sleeping."

He peered over at me. "*I* was uncomfortable. *I* felt alone. You didn't let me sleep in your bed."

"No, I didn't."

I sprinted off. It took a minute for Daniel to catch up. He was in pretty good shape for not playing a sport.

Braeden's pendant bounced out of his shirt as our footfalls synced up.

"Have you been wearing that this whole time?"

"Yeah." He was self-conscious. "It seemed like the thing to do after what he did. Stupid."

"It's not stupid."

He was quiet. "I'm so angry," he said after a moment. "Here's this person I don't even know and he dies for me. I mean, I know he did it for you, but if it wasn't for him, I'd be probably be dead. And I can't even thank him or—"

Thinking about Braeden brought everything back. He should have been an important part of my life. But he wasn't because my father kept him from me. He was someone I didn't even know. It only made it worse that he had been there when I was young and that he was now tied loosely but permanently to that child that had played with me. I felt confused, guilty his death didn't affect me more. I should be mourning him. But feelings are like water, the more tightly you try to hold on to them, the more they slip through your fingers.

Daniel held the pendant, turning the smooth surface in his hand. "When we were getting away from Wonderland Park and I was freaking out and my heart was pounding, I put my hand on my chest because it hurt so much, and I felt this. It calmed me." He glanced over at me. "You're not even breathing heavy," he said, annoyed.

"Lacrosse. All we do is run. And I do about five miles every morning."

"On purpose?" he asked, skeptically. "With no one chasing you?"

"I pretend people are, if that makes you feel any better."

Looping back, we found ourselves at the Jardin du Luxembourg. Despite the November chill, Parisians of all ages were jogging in the park. Passing *La Liberté Éclairant le Monde*, I was reminded of the cute salesgirl at Logan airport. This wasn't the Statue of Liberty I had told her about, the one overlooking the Seine. This replica was less than ten feet tall. The salesgirl dreamed of someday visiting Paris. Elam Khai wanted to make that dream a nearly impossible one.

I wondered how dearly I would pay for making him chase a phantom to Gibraltar. I can't imagine Charlemagne, Augustus Caesar, Alexander of Macedon would be too pleased with me showing him up like that.

Fuck him.

Daniel and I were rounding the Grand Basin—the fleet of toy boats sailing on the breeze—when I caught a glimpse of a most stunning woman standing at the water's edge. She was slender, lithe. At some angles she looked in her thirties. But I knew she was older than anyone would guess. Not old in the way that I am, but old in the way that most people are.

Her hair was a platinum shade impossible in nature. I must have been staring too long because she sensed someone was watching and turned her head in my direction. I felt the shock of recognition.

We can calculate the position of a star or a galaxy backwards and forwards and know its position at any point in the past or future. It was like that with this face. Seeing the way it looked now and calculating—given its features and subtracting the weight of time— what it looked like years before.

"What is it?" Daniel followed my sidelong gaze and saw the woman.

In her eyes, I saw a glint of joy and the fire of rage. She was in her eighties, but most people would estimate her age at least fifteen or twenty years younger.

I grabbed Daniel, altering our course back toward the river.

We burst through the apartment door, frightening Phoebe.

"What's wrong?" she choked out, her heart in her throat.

Daniel threw up his arms. "All I know is, after jogging for miles and miles, we sprinted back here to get away from a fairly tall... *little old lady.*"

I paced the room, gathering items, the exhibit map for the Louvre, my scribbled notes, anything that might give away our plans, and stuffed them into the backpack. We had come with little, and it took less than a minute to pack.

"It was a mistake to come here," I said.

"To Paris?"

"To this apartment. It was *foolish.*"

I peered through the slits in the shutters, seeing no one.

"Grab everything. We're not coming back."

I surveyed the apartment. Unlike the homes I've lived in and left, I've periodically come back to my foot on the ground over the last hundred years.

I would never set foot in this flat again.

Not until she was dead.

If I didn't care about hurting innocent people, I would've burned the building to the ground so nothing could be found. No finger-prints. No strands of hair. No bedding with our scents. Nothing.

I understood why Engel destroyed Acorn Street.

It was safer.

Phoebe stepped onto the landing at the top of the stairs. Daniel waited in the doorway for me.

I went to the window again. A taxi was making its way across the bridge. It turned onto my street and stopped outside my building. I saw the shock of white hair for an instant and then, it disappeared out of view.

I pointed upstairs. "The roof."

Daniel let out a long, exasperated sigh. "It's an old lady! I don't want to be rude or anything, but I think we could take her."

"You don't know this old lady," I said. "She's dangerous."

I sprinted upstairs and out onto the terrace.

I motioned for Phoebe to climb the trellis that was attached to my neighbor's wall. I scaled the wood lattice covered in purple wisteria.

I reached down to Daniel.

"C'mon, c'mon."

He grasp my hand, and I hauled him up. His other hand latched onto the top edge, and he scrambled onto the roof.

We moved quickly across the copper sheeting that had long ago turned blue-green. I remember the color of these roofs when they were new, a comforting warm hue that is more pleasing to me than even gold.

The sun had not yet burned away the night's condensation and my foot slipped on the moist surface. I nearly slid off the roof, dragging Phoebe with me. It was the oxidized patina that allowed me to regain my balance and save us both. We would have slid off a new roof. I suddenly liked the blue-green tinge a lot more.

Catching my breath, I glanced over the eaves. The woman was standing in the middle of the street. The taxi was gone. A black SUV crawled to a stop in front of my building, and a man with a thick mustache got out. He and the platinum blonde spoke. She glanced toward the roof. I snapped back so I was not visible from the street.

"You mind telling me why the hell we are running away from this woman?" Phoebe asked in an angry whisper.

"Her name is Katrina D'Lor. She was…" I watched the anticipation in Phoebe's eyes, "She was my first real girlfriend."

∞

My father tried to keep me out of harm's way during World War II. Out of Europe, out of Africa, out of Russia, out of Southeast Asia. But I didn't want to hide in America. It would've been safer, less complicated to remain in some quiet town in the middle of Iowa or Kansas or even, it turned out, New York or San Francisco or D.C., go to school, collect scrap metal for the war effort, listen to the radio programs that tried to take people's minds off the fact their loved ones were fighting and dying on, in, and above foreign beaches and forests and deserts and islands and seas.

That would have been the sensible thing to do, but that was like sitting at home on Saturday night while all your friends are at the biggest dance of the year.

In defiance of my father, I spent the war traveling around the world. I didn't intentionally go looking for trouble, but I stumbled into more than a few dangerous situations. When he finally tracked me down and sent me back to America, it nearly backfired. Civilians returning from overseas were scrutinized more closely and so, arriving on U.S. soil in late January of 1944, I thought it wise to present the same documents I had used to leave the country. Since according to my papers I was born October 4, 1925, now eighteen, my name and address were checked against Selective Service records. It was determined that Alexander Banks of Highgroves, Missouri had been drafted into the United States Marines while I was overseas.

I was ordered to report immediately to Fort Benning, Georgia for basic combat training or face a General Court Marshall.

In past wars, I could show off my skills to get assigned duty that fit my strengths, which enhanced my chances for survival. But in the months before the invasion of Normandy, the military was only interested in putting boots on the ground. Any boots. It was a game of numbers. This doesn't diminish the bravery of the men who stormed the beaches on D-Day, but it wasn't skill with a rifle or knowledge of tactics or one's ability in hand-to-hand combat that helped those soldiers survive that day. The men who made it through—at least, the ones who made it through the first waves, especially at Juno and Omaha—were simply lucky. There was nothing those men could study, no training they could be given, no tactic they could practice to increase their likelihood of getting off the beach alive. Once the Allies took the high ground and marched deeper into France, their training took over. But on that first day, in those first hours, survival depended mostly on whether or not the Germans holed up in their fortified pillboxes were aiming at someone *else* the instant you hit the beach.

I got a message to my father, telling him I had been drafted.

He didn't come and rescue me. Didn't show up with forged papers like he had after the Battle of Gettysburg. Didn't use a well-trained extraction team to free me as he did in Verdun in 1916. No, he let me rot in Georgia for *three weeks*, suffering through bad meals, insects the size of small airplanes, a shaved head, and woefully inadequate, but nevertheless demanding physical training. Two days before I was to be shipped out to England, a colonel found me in my barracks. I was the only one sleeping comfortably, judging my cot a little soft, to be honest.

"Do you have something to tell me, Private?"

I opened my eyes to see the officer leaning over me, grimly staring down, hands behind his back.

"No, sir. I have nothing to reveal. Loose lips sink ships, sir!"

His eyes narrowed, then just as suddenly, they softened. "Son. You are a credit to your community and your country." A hand shot out, holding a small piece of paper. "But you are ordered to go home."

I sat up, took the sheet from the colonel's hand, and read the words.

"Falsifying documents is a court-martial offense, son. But you're not the first boy to want to serve his country and kill Japs and Krauts." His other hand appeared. In it was an envelope containing cash and a bus ticket. "I would tell you that you'll get your chance to fight once you're old enough, but God willing, this war to end all wars, will be over before then." He gazed at me with paternal eyes. "You're a brave young man. Go be with your family. They miss you."

Then, without warning, he saluted me. I was so stunned by

this—an officer saluting a private—I didn't stand or salute back until after he was halfway out of the barracks.

Three weeks earlier I would have been overjoyed to receive this missive, but now, I was disappointed. I wanted to fight. I had made friends. I wanted to protect them. Most wars I've been in were fought for idiotic reasons. But this was to stop a madman with an insane vision of world domination. It was a fight for ideals that however imperfectly applied were worth fighting for. Because Hitler didn't just want to control the world, he wanted to Germanize it. He wanted to erase different thoughts, different beliefs, different peoples. He proved that in Poland.

The destruction of Warsaw was never in doubt. Even before World War II, the Nazis' had drawn up a plan to redesign the city, the first step in their dream to Germanize Eastern Europe. After the Warsaw Uprising, those plans changed. Heinrich Himmler told his staff that Warsaw must completely disappear from the surface of the earth. By the end of the war, ninety percent of the buildings in Warsaw were destroyed. The cultural heritage of the Polish people had been systematically and deliberately eradicated.

It's hard today to grasp the gravity of seventy countries at war at the same time, tens of millions of soldiers deployed on ever-changing fronts, and perhaps hardest to imagine, millions and millions and millions killed. We tend to homogenize war, focusing on a few famous, very understandable events. But World War II wasn't D-Day or the Battle of the Bulge or Midway, or the Bombing of Dresden, Hiroshima or Nagasaki, or the Attack on Pearl Harbor. It wasn't a war that took place only in Europe and on some islands in the Pacific. Most people know that six million Jews were killed. A startling number, rendered more devastating when you consider eighty percent of all Jews in German-occupied territory were exterminated.

That was Hitler's most egregious act.

But World War II was not particular in who it killed.

It wasn't until later that I realized how foolish I had been. How

232 | EDWARD SAVIO

easily I could have been in the wrong place at the wrong time and joined the uncounted dead that piled up during that terrible war.

Two years after the war, my father handed me a single sheet of paper. At the time, it was a secret document compiled by a then-unknown-to-the-public intelligence agency. The title was direct and to the point: *Total Civilian and Military Deaths by Country, Direct and Indirect (including war-related famine and disease).*

Soviet Union—**24,000,000**
China—**20,000,000+**
Germany—**8,800,000**
Poland—**5,600,000**
Dutch East Indies—**4,000,000**
Japan—**3,100,000**
India—**2,500,000**
French Indochina —**1,500,000**
Philippines—**1,050,000**
Yugoslavia—**1,020,000**
Romania—**833,000**
Greece—**800,000**
Hungary—**580,000**
France—**567,600**
Korea—**473,000**
Italy—**457,000**
United States—**418,500**
United Kingdom—**50,700**

The page continued, listing the fatalities of another twenty countries. A total of roughly eighty million lives lost. A staggering 3.5% of the earth's population at the time.

It was a dark age.

I've lived through desperate and austere periods, but never in a time where people could do such unimaginable damage to each other at so impersonal a distance.

Victory in Europe came in May of 1945. Japan surrendered four months later on September 2, 1945. A day after that, I left America, making my way slowly through Asia, the Middle East to Northern Africa, up into Europe and Russia. I'm not fascinated by death and destruction. I do not take pleasure in seeing them. But I have learned to question history told by others. I wanted, I needed, to see for myself the effects of that war.

Words cannot fully tell the story. Even photos, black and white, stark, don't complete the picture.

When I visited Warsaw, I was struck by the completeness of its destruction.

Poland lost disproportionally more people than any other country, nearly twenty percent of its population.

I remember the empty streets. The red-gray piles of debris. The incomprehensible street lamp that somehow remained upright and intact. The windowless façades of homes and buildings, empty, their guts removed.

Old Town Market had been at the center of Warsaw since the 1300s. It was now a barren rectangle surrounded by piles of crumbling bricks that spilled into the streets. It was in this desolate square, in 1948, that I met the younger, unspoiled version of the woman chasing us.

I had detoured to Warsaw on my way to Moscow for the start of the World Chess Championship. Standing atop the rubble of the *Strona Dekerta*, I noticed a small crowd gathered at the edge of the square. I climbed down to investigate.

What I found at the center was a young woman dressed in a draped-shoulder full-length gown, white opera gloves, and heels. A photographer was shouting directions in Italian, teasing out of her the look, the attitude he wanted.

Some idiot fashion editor without any sense of decency or appropriateness had come up with the marvelous idea to send a young model and a craggy photographer to Warsaw for a fashion photoshoot. You know, the juxtaposition of innocent beauty and horrific destruction. Just the kind of insensitive thematic an editor who spent WWII doling out wartime fashion advice to American women from the safety of midtown Manhattan would think was *"absolutely brilliant."*

I know I just ranted how stupid and insensitive this idea was, and it was stupid and insensitive, but watching her pose for the camera with the skeleton of Warsaw as a backdrop, I was profoundly touched. It wasn't her beauty, and it wasn't the dramatic effect the idiotic editor was hoping for either. It was the look on the Polish faces standing in a semi-circle behind the photographer, gazing at her in awe.

It was hope.

The recognition that beauty and life and goodness had somehow survived.

During one of the many breaks the photographer took to change film, I went up and introduced myself to Katrina D'Lor.

"You're American," she said.

"I am," I lied.

She giggled for some reason. "What are you doing here?"

"I should be asking you the same question."

"I know. It's *awful*. It is, isn't it? It *is*. I'm not sure if these photos will shed light on what happened here or minimize it. 'Look a fashion shoot. It can't be that bad over there. What is everyone crying about?' I must look ridiculous."

She did look ridiculous. She also looked stunning. She was young, just fifteen, but she had the air of someone older. I learned that she'd grown up in Manhattan. After the war, her modeling agency sent her to Paris and Milan. She would grace the cover of Vogue Magazine in less than a year from now.

"You still haven't told me what you're doing here. You know the absurd reason I'm here."

"My father's a diplomat," I said, effortlessly.

I've come to realize that every relationship I've ever had has begun with a lie. Every single one.

"Diplomats bring their children with them to war-torn areas now? Isn't that unusual?"

"I come from an unusual family."

"I like unusual families." Her eyes sparkled in the late afternoon sun. "They're much more interesting."

"Mine is very interesting."

"Then I should meet them."

The photographer called her back to work, saving me. Rule number one when lying: Never tell a lie so interesting that a person wants to know more about it.

"*Stellina!* We're losing the light."

"I have to go now," she said. "Maybe we could talk later."

"I'd like that, '*Little Star*,'" I said, mocking what the photographer had called her.

She stepped in front of the camera. Instantly, the relaxed, easy-going girl aged ten years. Her look, her expression, her pose more mature.

It wasn't difficult to sneak her out of her hotel later that night. Her Italian photographer was drunk by sundown.

They were forced by lack of accommodations to share a room. The unconscious photographer was draped on his twin bed, hanging over the edges like a human comforter.

We walked to a small restaurant a few blocks away that had been pieced together from the rubble. Most of the roof was gone, allowing a view of the stars.

No longer in the gown, Katrina looked younger, less glamorous. I found her warmer and much prettier.

We enjoyed a rather dismal meal and some surprisingly good wine.

She talked. She talked a lot. She spoke fast and had opinions about everything, people, politics, the world. She was independent and unafraid. She was one of the few girls I'd met up to that point that could speak her mind and meet my eye.

I'd met women like that before, but girls my own age, almost never. The only young females with confidence rivaling Katrina's were Mohawk girls. They may not have played *tewaarathon* for days, but they were strong and forthright. *Very* forthright. I, unfortunately, didn't have the same level of interest in girls in the 1620s as I did in the 1940s.

Katrina D'Lor reminded me nothing of a Mohawk girl. She was pale and tall. The upper part of her face was larger in proportion to the lower. Her chin and jaw delicate. Her cheeks and eyes prominent. Back then her hair was a natural dark blonde.

Her parents were Hungarian and Italian immigrants. She spoke a little Hungarian—more than she admitted—but was fluent in Italian and French. These are the languages of fashion. Only Milan and Paris matter.

People mostly correctly have the impression that models hardly eat anything, but Katrina devoured food like she hadn't been fed in a week. Maybe she hadn't. Maybe she prepared for a photo shoot by starving herself, then consuming everything in sight once it was over.

Over the past two hundred years or so, I've been introduced to girls my age at court, at dances, at community gatherings. I've taken a fair number of them out on the time period's equivalent of a "date." But this was different. *She* was different.

Maybe—I was different.

While we were tolerating dinner and enjoying each other's company, a trio of Russian soldiers zigzagged down the broken boulevard, knocking on doors, hassling people caught on the streets. They were supposedly searching for conspirators, rooting out anyone helping the "Home Army." The Armia Krajowa, or AK, had been the largest resistance force against the Nazi's in Europe, greater than the French Resistance. The AK fought alongside the Russians and were instrumental in driving the Nazis from Warsaw. Their bravery and sacrifice were rewarded with betrayal. Immediately after the Germans withdrew, thousands of Polish men were rounded up by the Soviets and sent off to Russian gulags.

The soldiers were checking the papers of a middle-aged woman when one of the three-pointed toward the cafe. It wasn't the food they were interested in. They entered, yelling at the owner as they swaggered through the tables. The place was mostly empty. A few diners were scattered around the place. There weren't many people who could afford to eat out. Which was fine with the owner. He didn't have enough food to feed a full house if he'd had one.

The soldiers made a show of checking documents, but their examinations were cursory at best. Their attention was focused on our table.

"Don't tell them you're American," I whispered, my lips hidden by the glass of wine.

Now, you might figure that us having been allies in the war and all, it would make sense to let these fine Russians know we were Americans. Comrades in arms. But this was 1948. The war was over and the world had flipped upside down. We were getting along better with the Germans—at least the West Germans—and the Japanese than we were with the Russians.

"Speak Italian," I said.

"*Perché?*"

"Because they will wonder what a very attractive American woman is doing here. And the answer they'll immediately come up with is that you are a spy."

"You think I'm very attractive," she whispered, trying to flirt even as her hand shook with fear.

They finally made it to our table, the destination they'd been meandering toward since arriving. Back then, I could understand Russian, but speak it? I was worse than I am now. I greeted the soldiers in Polish. I pretended not to understand as they spoke to each other in their native tongue. It was apparent they were more interested in the pretty girl than catching conspirators.

"*Documenty,*" asked the soldier in the middle, the leader or, at least, the alpha of the three. The other two flanked him, a half step behind. A wing formation. He hadn't said *papiere*, a good sign. He didn't think we were Germans. He'd spoken Russian, but the word for documents is pronounced nearly the same in Polish and Italian as well.

I produced a set of Polish papers. Two other sets of forged papers were hidden under the soles of my shoes. These bogus documents, as always, were delivered to me in pristine condition by Engel. Great forgers are proud artists. They sweat over the details. In reality, nothing says fake papers like clean papers. As soon as I got them I made sure to scuff them up, tear them, get them dirty, stain them with my blood so they looked ragged and pitiful and ready to fall apart, so that anyone checking my documents would believe I had gone through hell and back to survive.

Seeing I was Polish, he studied me. "Did you fight?"

I shook my head. "Too young."

"You don't seem too young to fight."

"I'm fourteen."

He glanced at the wine, frowning.

"—and a half," I said.

If I had not been sitting across from a striking female, he'd have pressed the issue.

"*Documenty*," he said to Katrina.

She answered with a passionate torrent of Italian.

"What is she saying?" he asked me.

"She's Italian."

"Do you speak it?"

"Not very much."

He laughed, leering at me. The message: there wasn't a need for much talking between a man and a beautiful woman.

Prick.

One of the wingmen put his hand on her shoulder.

I pushed down the instinct to respond with force. "She has left her papers in her room," I said.

This was not a lie. Katrina didn't have Italian papers, of course, but as it turned out, she didn't have any papers on her. We'd forgotten them in our hurried escape from her snoring chaperone. Her hands and body shook, the tremors traveling through the wooden table to my forearms.

"She'll have to come with us," he said.

The hand on her shoulder was slipping under her arm.

It was clear from their Russian banter, they weren't planning to bring her to their post. They'd get her into one of the nearby deserted shells and assault her, probably rape her. That meant getting rid of me. I waited for one of them to make a move.

"You are free to go and get her papers." The man never mentioned a location to deliver them. He was offering me a way to save myself. He rested his hand on the pistol strapped to his hip.

I had to play this just right.

I nodded.

The two soldiers at his side lifted Katrina from her chair.

I heard a guttural scream. A battle cry. I glanced up to see the owner standing in front of the bar, aiming a shotgun at the soldiers, shouting at them to leave the girl alone. Others in the restaurant scattered for cover. Shotguns aren't choosy about who they hit, spraying pellets in an ever-widening path.

The owner was risking his life for a stranger. Maybe he was tired of being pushed around. Maybe it was the violation of one more girl he couldn't take.

The leader drew his weapon and without hesitation shot the man. One bullet in the upper right of the owner's chest.

With their attention diverted, I attacked. Quick hands to the throat, the head, the solar plexus, a kick to the groin, a knee to the face, and two of the men were incapacitated. Although the leader had been closest to me, he survived my initial flurry, ducking many of the blows and absorbing the rest. I *was* able to kick the TT pistol from his hand, sending it across the room. He reached for the Nagant resting in the limp grasp of one of his unconscious men. I stomped my foot in the path of his hand, blocking the revolver. He rolled, snatching his forearm back before my other heel could stomp his outstretched limb and break it.

Katrina slumped into her seat. She was in shock, frozen in place.

I shoved her off the chair, the shock of hitting the ground brought her to her senses. She scurried toward the diners taking cover on the far side of the cafe. The soldier glanced around for a weapon. He kept the table between us as I feinted one way, then the other. He looked less intimidating now that I was standing. Tiring of the game, I removed the obstacle, flipping the table out of the way, sending plates crashing to the floor.

"Three against one. That seems fair. You like to force yourself on defenseless girls?" My Russian was nowhere near that coherent, but I think he understood. What surprised him was not my horrific grammar, but that I spoke so ignorantly with an *aristocratic* accent. Only the oldest Russian families spoke with my inflection. A style of speech that became a liability after the Czar was overthrown. "I guess that's because they don't hit back." Which, to give an idea of how bad my Russian was, I said, literally, "Hit you back, she don't, I think."

Anyway, the message got clearer when I smashed him in the jaw.

A sharp pain shot up my arm. He reeled, stumbling backwards, his chin slightly askew. My right hand was broken. Seeing I was momentarily distracted, he rushed me. He thrashed about, arms, fists, legs, and feet flashing. In movies, people take turns throwing punches. He jabs. I jab. He punches. I counterpunch. It's choreographed, practiced. It just looks better. In real life, fist fights are rarely cinematic. They're an angry, confused jumble of limbs. They progress slower and are shorter in duration than their movie incarnations. People don't conveniently stay unconscious once you've hit them, and they don't suddenly spring back to life, either. I had to kick the other two soldiers a couple of times whenever I noticed them coming to. The lead soldier and I threw punch after punch simultaneously, several of the blows cracking knuckle to knuckle. Adrenaline kept the agony from fully registering. A few more of these direct collisions and my bones would be permanently, irreparably damaged. Funny thing, though…you realize the prospect of living thousands of years with a gnarled hand isn't all that important if you're not alive to endure it. And so, in close, I narrowly directed my strength to achieve maximum thrust. My left hand crushed his chest. My right stunned his diaphragm. My vision blurred, tears filled my eyes, pain trumping the adrenaline. Gasping for air, he lifted his hands to his throat. Which was stupid because it wasn't his throat that was the problem. I did not let up, and took him down with a rampage of blows.

He fell hard to the floor, semiconscious, mumbling feeble excuses. Enraged, I kept kicking him in the chest, in the face, between his legs, until Katrina wrapped her arms around me.

"It's okay," she said. "It's okay."

I stood there, my chest heaving, my heart pounding. After several seconds, I was finally able to speak. "We have to go. Others will be drawn by the sound of gunfire."

I pulled her toward the exit.

She didn't budge.

"No. We have to help him." She ran to the owner.

The thing to do was leave, get out of town, out of Poland. Take her with me if I could. Leave her if she wouldn't go.

Instead, I joined her.

She checked the man's pulse. "He's alive, but he's bleeding so much, we have to stop it."

"Don't!" I said, stopping her from touching the wound.

I listened closely to the barely audible noises rising from the man's chest. I tapped the left side of his rib cage with my finger. The sound was hollow, the vibrations spread out over a wide area. I did the same to the right side, the side of the bullet wound. It felt like I'd tapped his thigh.

"His lungs are filling with blood. He could suffocate before he bleeds out." I stuck my finger into the wound. Felt my fingertip touch the bullet. There was a sickening gurgle as I pulled the slug toward the surface. Blood oozed more quickly once the bullet was free. I stuck my finger back into the wound, plugging it temporarily.

We were in a restaurant with a bar, which meant it was nearly as well-equipped as a Civil War hospital.

"I'm going to remove my finger. When I do, I need you to put your finger in the wound." I looked at her slender hands. "You're going to have to use your thumb."

"I don't know if I can do this," she said.

"You wanted to save him. The only chance we have to do that is if you stick your thumb in his chest. If you can't, we should walk out the door right now because we're putting ourselves in danger by staying."

She tipped her head. She would try. As I backed my finger out, she slid her thumb into the wound. Her face was colorless. Not the beautiful pale glowing skin she normally had, but almost translucent. I thought she might get sick.

"This is no different than touching raw steak."

"This is sooooo much different."

"The only difference is in your mind."

Katrina made a disgusted moan as I've vaulted over the bar and went to work figuring out what I could use. I grabbed a liter of vodka. Cloth napkins that were soiled. They would have to do. I needed tape. I've said it before, I'll say it a million times over, tape, any kind of tape, but especially duct tape, is perhaps the most versatile tool you can carry. There was no tape.

Plugging the wound was the priority. I spied a box of wine corks under the bar and grabbed several. A straw. I needed a straw. There were swizzle sticks, but they weren't hollow. There was a beer keg along the back wall. I could rip out the tap and use that, but the diameter was too large. It would do even more damage.

From the other side of the bar I heard, "He's dying." "They're coming." A muddle of words.

I rifled through the tools, tossing one after another to the floor. A Shaker, a jigger, a strainer, a long bar spoon.

The spoon hit the tile floor.

The ping was high pitched.

I picked up the silver spoon and flicked my fingernail against the stem. It rang out. Bending the metal back and forth, I remove the top handle, then the spoon end, leaving a narrow tube.

I came around the bar.

"He's dying," she said.

"I know."

"They're coming."

"Yes."

I opened the bottle of vodka and took a long gulp, the liquid burning my throat on the way down. I needed the alcohol more than the owner did. He was in shock and feeling little pain. I was about to plunge a metal spike into his chest.

I poured vodka on the wine corks, then my hands. "Pull your finger out."

As she removed her thumb from the man's chest, I doused the wound with alcohol. His body hardly flinched. I plugged the bullet hole with one of the wine corks, stopping the flow of blood.

I drenched the hollow stem in alcohol and poured more on the man's rib cage.

The two ends of the stainless steel tube were jagged, one slightly less so. I took a deep breath, then jabbed the sharper edge into his chest. Immediately blood squirted out, spraying my face and my clothes.

Katrina screamed as a river of blood formed on the floor. Immediately, the man's breathing became less labored. His head cleared as oxygen reached his brain. He was more conscious of what was happening. More conscious of the pain. The flow of blood didn't stop. And for a moment, I regretted trying to save him. Soon he'd be aware enough to know he was dying.

Suddenly, he reached out and snatched my wrist. His eyes opened. "My daughter," he said. "My daughter. Please save my daughter." And then he fainted away.

The tables and chairs were empty. The other patrons had fled. I could hear the march of boots cutting through the night. The blood spread out, the river becoming a lake. I got to my feet and burst through the door that was at the back of the establishment looking for his daughter. It led to stairs, and I climbed them as fast as I could manage in the dark.

I nearly fell two stories to the rubble below as the stairs abruptly ended. Whatever had once been there had been bombed out of existence.

I stood for a moment. Feeling the weight of tremendous loss. For the man. The city. The country. Every corner of the world the war had touched.

The echoing steps dragged me back from my thoughts. From my vantage point, I could see four dark shadows heading our way. Another three shadows approached from the other end of the street. The two groups were converging on us.

I stomped down the steps and into the cafe. Katrina was stroking the man's forehead, talking to him gently. He wasn't responding, but he wasn't dead, either. The pool of blood on the floor had grown no larger, a single drop trickled from the end of the stainless steel tube. His chest was rising and falling, his breathing was no longer labored.

"I'm sorry," I said, "We've done all we can. We must leave."

I took her hand.

But it was too late.

One of the coteries of shadows reached the cafe. It was the cluster of three dark figures. They were armed. Two of the weapons were Russian. One was German. All of the shadows were Polish. The one brandishing the *Sturmgewehr* spoke. "Is he alive?" He pointed the barrel of the assault rifle at the owner. The man's face was familiar.

"Yes," Katrina said, nervously anticipating the pop of the gun that never came.

"Leave him to us. You must go. Soldiers are coming. Go to this address." He handed me a scrap of cloth with three rows of numbers on it.

290

2 3 1

5 0 9

There was no street name.

"What is this?"

"The middle number is the house address. The top is the pass-code you will give to be let in. The bottom are the directions from here. Five blocks. A zero means turn left. Then nine blocks." He tapped the numbers. "You will be safe there."

He took a tablecloth, spread it on the ground. We slid it under the owner's back. The other men were stripping the unconscious soldiers of guns, ammunition, and uniforms.

"He mentioned a daughter. He asked us to protect her."

"His daughter is dead," the man said. He turned to Katrina. "She looked a little like you."

The man glanced down at the metal spoon handle jutting out of the side of the owner's chest, not sure what to make of it.

"He's bleeding internally. He needs a doctor," I said.

"They've killed most of our doctors. We will help him as best we can. I don't understand why *you* helped him."

I realized why he looked familiar. He'd been one of the other diners. He'd run out of here and come back. He was young, frail. So were his companions. Were these men the last of the AK, or had the struggle been passed on to them because they were the only ones left?

"Why wouldn't we?" Katrina said.

The man snorted a tiny laugh. He'd seen the worst of humanity. It was hard for him not to be jaded.

"It's time for all of us to go," he said.

We slipped out a side door. He and his two buddies carrying the owner and their looted weapons. Me gripping Katrina's hand.

"Thank you," he said before disappearing into the darkness.

We turned to the right, padding quietly on the dirt. But we didn't go all five blocks. I jerked Katrina around the corner after two streets. We leaned against the remnants of a house.

"Five blocks, turn left, then nine blocks," she said.

"We're not going to that house."

"You don't trust them?"

"I do, but if you don't show up back at your hotel, your photographer's going to go looking for you. He's got rolls and rolls of your pretty face. They'll have your photo at every checkpoint in Poland."

"You're not the son of a diplomat, are you?"

"I'm the son of a soldier."

We doubled back, skirting the square. We found the photographer in the same position as when we'd left.

She pulled me close, her body shaking, shivering. But hot, not cold. Then the trembling stopped. She looked into my eyes. And suddenly, what had happened during the evening melted away. I kissed her in the dark. Tears streamed down her cheeks and I could taste the saltiness on her lips.

I devoured her. The night, the fear making us need each other.

"You should sleep," I said sometime later.

"You're leaving?"

"A young man and a young woman beat up three Russian soldiers. They'll be looking for us. They won't be looking for an old man and a girl."

She squeezed me as I went to the door.

"Don't worry. I'll be watching."

"Promise?"

"Promise."

She kissed me, her lips soft. "Next time I see you, you better be able to tell me what I wear tomorrow."

I smiled.

I made sure she and the photographer got out of Poland safely. If you're wondering, she wore a beige riding-wear-inspired ensemble, wool tweed jacket, wool pants, silk blouse, handkerchief, and leather gloves.

Getting myself out of Soviet-controlled territory was rather more difficult.

I finally made it into East Germany and to Berlin. It took another week to devise a plan to cross the death zone between East Berlin and West Berlin. Once in the free zone, I caught a ride to Hanover, where I then—not kidding—hopped a plane to Soviet Moscow to play chess.

For the next two and a half years, Katrina and I continued to see each other. Sometimes in New York. Sometimes in Paris or Milan or Rome or London or Jerusalem. It was an ideal young-love relationship. She traveled the world for modeling assignments. I traveled the world because I could. We met in crazy, beautiful places. And with the exception of that first meeting, we never saw each other in less than perfect settings.

Over those thirty months, Katrina continued to age. It was barely noticeable at first, but she was becoming more fully a woman. I remained the same. Not a boy, but not a man, either. One night, she revealed that she'd gone on a few dates with a photographer who was twenty-eight—she wasn't even eighteen at the time.

"It was odd," she said. "He wasn't as sophisticated as you, Alexander. Couldn't talk about art or fashion with as much depth. Couldn't talk about anything as well as you can. But the way he treated me…like a woman."

I was so jealous, I nearly blurted out the truth to her right then. You want older? I'll give you *older*.

I resisted. And for a while, she seemed to forget about other men.

But there was a sense that something was brewing under the surface. I felt her pulling away. As if she found my "youngness" no longer attractive. And so it was in 1950 in the very apartment we were escaping from that I committed the worst mistake of my life. Telling Katrina D'Lor the truth about myself.

One of the few times I've told anyone my secret.

Well, that's not exactly true. I'd blabbed it a thousand times while I was growing up. People would ask me, "How old are you?" and I'd answer in my toddler voice, "Three hundred and two years old." "Four hundred-eleven and a half."

Everyone always thought it was cute.

The glow of your first time, young love. It can make you feel things that seem real but aren't always. It felt to me like Katrina was the first person—other than another Eternal—who understood me. And I was losing her. In a desperate attempt to save our relationship, I revealed in a quiet moment, a moment of beauty as we sat on the roof under the stars, who I was.

I didn't know anything other than I wanted to spend every day I could with her. I didn't realize what telling her would do. At first, she couldn't handle it. She withdrew, thinking I was insane. But as I showed her in a thousand ways, she began to believe me. Her interest in other men ceased. She was fascinated in the beginning and wanted to know everything about me, the lives I had lived. Then it changed. As time passed, as she realized she would become old and I would be forever young, she asked me to teach her how to stop aging. I tried to explain that I didn't have that power, but she didn't believe me. I finally had to leave her, change my name, and disappear after she began to tell others about me.

I have seen her uncountable times in the years since. Not in person. Never that. But on magazine covers. In ads. She became a famous model, wealthy. She married well, and continued to work. She tried to contact me in the beginning, using places we had been, my *pied de terre* in Paris being one. For more than a decade in the '50s and '60s, I sublet the apartment to a series of people.

I've been to Paris a number of times over the years, but never to that apartment unless I knew for certain Katrina D'Lor was at least a continent away. Until now.

∞

"*Girl*friend?" Phoebe asked, her face frozen in a grimace.

Crouching on the peak of the roof, Daniel nearly fell off, his legs giving out unexpectedly. He got himself under control, staring anxiously over the back edge of the building. "That is…just…I don't even know what to call it," he stammered. "*Wrong* doesn't begin to cover it. She's like a hundred years old!" He cocked his head. "Although she is younger than you, so you gotta factor that into the stomach-churning nature of this."

"She was fifteen at the time," I said.

Daniel opened his mouth to respond, but I hushed him with an outstretched palm in front of his face. The voices filtering up from the street had fallen silent.

"We can't just sit here and wait for them to figure out there's only two ways out of that place," he whispered.

I peeked over the edge.

"No, we can't."

We heard a distant crash, the sound of splintering wood as my apartment door was kicked in.

I got to my feet. The rooftops ahead were steeply angled, uneven, and varied in material and form. I'd walk with Deganawa in the Adirondacks across perilously thin ridges of shale. A rock so fractured and fragile that it often cleaved and fell away underfoot, but it took me months of practice before I could follow him the entire way. And even then, it took me twice as long.

It was weight distribution, balance, and most of all, confidence.

Phoebe frowned. "By the way, I hate heights."

"Pretend it's a balance beam," I said.

The man from the black car appeared on my neighbor's roof several houses away and cried, "*Arrêt!*"

When has anyone trying to escape ever stopped because someone screamed, "Stop?"

The big man was hesitant, uneasy as he navigated the rooftops. We stretched the distance between us. An ear-piercing explosion cracked from the barrel of a gun and we all hit the deck. It took a moment to realize the man wasn't shooting at us. He was hugging the rooftop for protection as well. A second volley fired, then a third. It was a ceremonial salute at a funeral at Notre Dame.

I felt my heart racing in my chest. We got back up. The man shouted at us, but his eyes were fixed on his feet and his next step.

We went the entire length of my block until we came to the turn in the road. We could continue—the homes wrapped around—but right here was the narrowest point from building to water. I peered over the edge. It was about eleven meters—thirty-five feet—to the water.

"What are you doing?"

It was another seven or eight feet to clear the shallows. Fifteen meters minimum. More like eighteen. So, sixty feet. I could do it. Probably.

"I think I can make it," I said.

"You *think*?" said Phoebe.

"I can make it."

"Oh, yes, this is good. Us drowning won't draw any attention," Daniel said. "I can't jump a street!"

"He wants me." I nodded toward the man, who had stopped, ready to turn back if I jumped. "Just meet me at the pyramid."

"We're going to Egypt?" cried Daniel.

"No, you idiot, the Louvre," said Phoebe.

This roof was not as steep as the others. At this height, if I sprinted, I'd make it. I couldn't slip or trip or misjudge the edge. I'd be dead. I slowly paced toward the rear of the building, counting my steps. Seventeen.

I gathered myself. Focused. My front foot was bouncing. My back foot twisted to get a better grip on the metal. I was a panther ready to spring.

Phoebe crouched nervously near the edge. "Alexander..." She didn't finish. Or maybe she did and I didn't hear. I was concentrating.

I pushed off.

Daniel grabbed my shirt. "Hey!"

My feet ran out from under me, and I landed on my back like a cartoon character.

"Why don't we just take the stairs?" he said.

"What?"

He pointed to a staircase at the rear of the next building, leading from the roof to the ground.

"Oh," I said, staring at the steps, my heart racing. "Right. That's probably a better idea."

ELEVEN

Daniel Stabs An Old Woman

We took the cement stairs two at a time. At the bottom, Daniel suddenly stopped.

I slammed into him. "What is it?"

"There's an Apple Store and a McDonald's in the Louvre," he said out of the corner of his mouth.

"We're not *in* the Louvre. We're in the underground shopping mall *surrounded* by the Louvre."

Phoebe surveyed the modern underground complex. "Our mall is surrounded by a dairy farm."

"Which is why I like Paris slightly more than Great Barrington."

We had covered our tracks, taking a circuitous route to the museum, going at least a dozen blocks out of our way. We'd seen no sign of Katrina or the man after climbing down from the roof.

At the main entrance, we found a line of visitors two hours long that serpentined through a maze of roped-together stanchions.

"Why are we in a shopping mall," asked Daniel.

"There's another entrance down here. Which is usually less crowded. Everybody wants to enter through the glass pyramid. Not as many want to enter by the McDonald's."

We bought day passes at one of the automatic ticket machines and headed toward the mall's museum entrance.

The line was still daunting.

A plaque perched on a stanchion about a dozen people ahead of us announced ONE HOUR FROM THIS POINT in four languages.

"We could take turns waiting," Phoebe said. "I wouldn't mind checking out some of these shops."

Daniel's response was instantaneous. "No, no, no. The last time we split up, I ended up crucified on a fence in an abandoned dog track. So, no."

"Actually, the last time we split up you took a shower," I said. "And I thank you for that."

"Most of Boston and Northern Europe thanks you," Phoebe added.

"Hhhhaha. You two are hilaaaaarious." His fake smile disappeared. "No. No shopping. No splitting up. No."

Phoebe folded her arms. "Fine."

A small group passed to the right of us and was immediately let through.

"How come those people don't have to wait?"

"That is a very good question."

I slipped under the lane line and approached a kiosk offering guided tours, which allowed visitors to bypass the general admissions line.

There was just one problem.

"I'm sorry, but zere are no tours available until ziss afternoon," said the young French woman behind the counter. "And we only have room on our private tours. Zose are three hundred and fifty euros for five or less people."

"We'll pay the fee, plus a thousand American dollars to someone who can take us in *right now*."

The woman stared at the stack of bills I produced. Her training was telling her brain to tell her mouth to tell me no one could do that because of some inflexible museum rule, but she couldn't make her lips comply.

"I'll do it," offered the young man behind her.

The woman let out a relieved gasp as if she'd been holding her breath underwater.

The man in his mid-twenties slipped on a badge, then whispered into the woman's ear. "Cover for me. I'll split the money with you."

He put his hand out, I thought to take the money, but he was offering a greeting. I awkwardly thrust my hand toward him. He shook it.

"My name is Jens," he said.

"Alexander," I stammered as if this were my first time out in public. Ever.

"Ah. Olympus belongs to the Gods, but the Earth is Alexander's," he said. "We will definitely have to stop and see *Alexander with the Spear*." His voice rose on the last word, as did his fist.

Jens wore a dark jacket with a light rose, almost white oxford shirt. His black curly hair was groomed short on the sides and fuller on top. A trace of stubble on his porcelain face and the slightly wrinkled fabric of his shirt gave the tiniest bit of edge to his other-wise clean-cut appearance. He stood at least two inches taller than me. His posture was finishing school perfect. And he had a subtle, pleasant accent that sounded like Dutch to me.

"Leiden?" I asked.

Astonishment flashed on his face. "I'm from outside Leiden, but I went to University there." He started to ask me something but stopped after drawing in a breath. The paranoid part of my brain wondered if he had been told to lookout for three out-of-the-ordinary teenagers.

With Jens escorting us, it took only a moment to get past security even with a backpack full of assorted odd items and stacks of cash. The guards knew him by name, and he greeted each one in a casual, affable manner.

I put the backpack in one of the self-serve lockers as Daniel read through an info sheet he'd grabbed on the way in. "It says here that if you spent four seconds gazing at each object in the Louvre, it would take three months to get through the whole museum." He glanced up from the sheet.

"I'm hoping to get out of here in under an hour," I said.

"Soooo, we know what we're looking for?" Daniel's eyes darted about.

"I'll know it when I see it."

"Great," he said. "I'll start planning to winter here."

Once inside, the modern feel of the lobby faded away. We entered a long room lined with statues guarding the path to a broad, majestic staircase.

"Why haven't you gotten in touch with your father to figure out what we're supposed to be doing here?" Daniel asked. "Or if we're even supposed to be here."

"I've tried him a couple of times. He hasn't responded. What am I supposed to do?"

"Oh, I don't know," he whispered aggressively, "Try *harder*. Have you bombarded him with messages?" He pantomimed talking into a phone. "'Hey Dad, it's me, your son. Just wanna say thanks for leaving me with a big pile of your bullshit to deal with. Could use some help. Get back to me as soon as you get this.' 'Hey, it's me, still haven't heard from you. You know your brother, Alexander the Great? Yeah, well, he stopped by to say hi and kidnap me. Oh, and murder my friends. Call me back.' 'Dad, me again. Hey, love the riddle, but I still don't have any clue what the hell's going on. And anybody who could possibly offer me help is either being watched or can't help because being extremely fucking cryptic is apparently *our way*. Call me.'" He had whipped himself into such a fervor that he was out of breath by the end of it. He dramatically fake pressed End Call on the fake phone.

"When we find my father...I want you to be sure to use that tone with him."

Daniel turned skeptical. "Why?"

"No reason."

As we approached the end of the hall, more of the Daru staircase became visible until finally, there at the top, the figure of a headless woman was revealed. Standing on the prow of a ship, angel-like wings outstretched behind her, she was the focal point of the space.

Phoebe ran up the stairs. "She is amazing."

Jens voice echoed in the expanse. "High classical Greek sculpture is what most people are used to seeing. Poised. Serene. Unruffled. But here, the detachment and placidity are gone, replaced by a voluptuousness and urgency. There's emotion and energy."

Phoebe viewed the statue from various angles. "She's moving in several directions at once. She's stepping into the wind, but her stomach is twisting, and the wings are back like she just landed."

"Yes, yes. Look at how her clothes drape her body. They are wet from the spray of the ocean. They cling to her. You can feel the wind against her."

Phoebe nodded. "I feel it." Her voice an impassioned whisper.

"Where is her head?" Daniel asked.

"Lost," said Jens. "Scholars have done digital recreations, but I prefer her this way. What the rest of her looks like is left to each person's imagination."

"Or nightmares," said Daniel.

"I see her throwing back her head in joy," Phoebe said.

"So joyful she snapped her head right off."

"*Joy* and exultation," said Jens, ignoring Daniel. "She is 'Winged Victory of Samothrace.' The goddess Nike."

"The goddess of sneakers?"

I shook my head.

Phoebe inhaled slowly, then turned to Daniel. "Please, stop talking. Forever."

"I know who Nike is," he sneered. "She's the goddess of victory. I'm not as stupid as you think I am."

"It would be nearly impossible for anyone to be as stupid as I think you are." She turned to Jens. "Is there a god of stupidity?"

"Koalemos. No statues of him, unfortunately."

Hoping to speed things up, I showed the marked-up map to Jens. "We'd like to start here."

"You have a plan of attack. Excellent." Jen's noticed the X's through most of the galleries. Parts of the museum I felt were unlikely to hold the answer to my father's riddle. "You can't seriously want to skip the Mona Lisa."

"It's not an imperative. I've seen it a number of times."

"I see it every day, and I'm surprised by it every time."

"And not *all* of us have seen it." Phoebe dug her nails into my arms.

"If we have time," I said, firmly.

"Then we should get started. Where does your map tell us to go first?" asked Jens.

"The oldest artifacts you have."

"Wonderful." Jens led us toward the Richelieu Wing. "I'll introduce you to the museum's oldest piece, our nine-thousand-year-old man."

Daniel forced a laugh. "That's funny, I was just introduced to a nine-thousand-year-old man just the other day."

Phoebe kidney punched Daniel. He doubled over like a slinky.

The statue's asphalt eyes stared at me.

Jens was explaining its importance, plaster smeared over woven fibers, blah, blah, blah.

"Nope. Nothing," I said, turning away and scanning the room.

Large stone carvings from the ruins of ancient temples dominated the gallery. Museums like the Louvre are a powerful draw because they have artifacts from every part of the world. Archaeology has changed drastically in the last half-century. Countries want to maintain control over their heritage. International agreements have made it illegal to move historic treasures like these across borders without permission. It would be difficult for a museum, even one as powerful as the Louvre to create a collection of antiquities like this today. Artifacts found in the future will not be divided and doled out to the world's great museums. They will be kept together in their country of origin. It's the right thing to do, of course, but there is something powerful about having a taste of every part of the world in one place, under one roof. It creates a sense of connection to other cultures and other times.

Jens stood in a doorway flanked by two massive winged bulls sporting human heads. "These are really fascinating," he began. "They are an Assyrian protective deity that—"

"Jens," I said, gently cutting him off. "You're obviously very knowledgeable about the art and the museum, but we really just wanted to avoid the line."

"Oh," he said deflated. "I see."

"The extra thousand is still yours…"

"No. I mean, thank you. I just thought—" He didn't finish. "The tour you paid for is normally four hours. I can hang back, let you browse, and still be available to answer any questions you might have."

"We want to move quickly."

"I'd like to be out of here right now," said Daniel, glancing around, paranoid.

Phoebe smiled at me. "He's so good at knowing details. Which might be useful to us." She raised an eyebrow. Then she turned to Jens. "How are you able to remember everything?"

Was she flirting with him?

I felt stupid for the thought. I hate testosterone sometimes.

Then she touched his arm. *Was* she flirting?

Jens' gaze went from Phoebe to me. "Rather than rush by everything and see nothing—is there something *specific* you're looking for?"

Suddenly an idea knocked the jealousy from my mind. "We *are* looking for something specific," I said. Phoebe and Daniel were just as curious as Jens to hear what I was going to say next. I was rather curious myself. "We're…" Here's the bit where I hit a speed bump and went blank for eight excruciating seconds of dead silence. "We're part of this private contest," I eventually blurted out. "It's been set up by…let's just say, someone very wealthy…" I nodded to my friends for support, a lifeline, something to grab onto, but they were absolutely no help. "*Royally* wealthy." Why did I say *that*? Nobody knows who the Dutch royals are, yet they still somehow cost their citizens more than any other monarchy in Europe. Jens probably hated them. "*American* royalty. You know, too much, too soon, too young. Doesn't know what to do with it. This...individual...found out there was this thing called 'culture' as if they'd discovered it themselves, and now wants everyone to appreciate it. Anyway, the," I whispered the next part, "prize is...well...big."

"How big *is* the prize?" Daniel asked, darkly curious.

I eyed Daniel with a stare capable of burning *Why are you acting so stupid, Koalemos?* into his forehead. "Very. Big. Don't you remember?"

Late, but better than not at all, Phoebe came to my rescue. She made up for her tardiness with total commitment. "Fifty thousand dollars," she whispered to Jens. "Each. But more importantly, whoever wins gets big bragging rights. We lost last year by one minute. One minute! It was crazy. The clue leads us to the Prime Meridian. We scramble to get a flight. It would have been easier to just hijack a plane to London." She laughed.

We all laughed.

"We search the Royal Observatory, the grounds, nothing. Until we see this door that has Two-B on it and we think, Two-B? Or not to be. We rush to a theatre nearby putting on Shakespeare's latest play—"

"You mean his *last* play?"

"You would think. Seems there may be others we don't know about. It quickly becomes clear Shakespeare is limited in his ability to help us. And then—"

I waited. Interested.

"Then we realize *Royal* Observatory, *Royal* Family, Buckingham Palace. That's where the item is. Of course, we can't just stroll into Buckingham Palace and start snooping around, right? So, by the time we get in touch with someone who can get us inside, another group has gotten invited in by the *Queen*. We haven't heard the end of it ever since. Blah, blah, blah, 'you only know the sixth in line to the throne'—the entire year." She finished with a flourish, nailing her impression of a spoiled daughter of high society by rolling her eyes and resting her hand jauntily on her hip.

"Yes," I said, slowly, concerned that Phoebe had downed a bit too much of the Kool-Aid. "As you can see, we're still not over it."

"So, exactly what are you searching for *this* year?" asked Jens.

"Somewhere in the museum, there is…something."

"Something?"

"Yes. Something unique. Perhaps out of place."

He thought about this for a moment. "I know the museum pretty well. Can you describe some parameters of what this something out of place might be?"

"No."

He stared at me blankly. "No?"

"No."

"But he'll know it when he sees it," said Daniel.

I cast a dark look at Daniel. "I will."

I figured Jens would politely excuse himself and head back to his kiosk with some easily earned cash in his pocket, mumbling "Crazy Americans." Instead, he became animated. "I've got to tell you, giving tours is great. But a treasure hunt! I've spent years coming to this place. I studied art history at the Sorbonne. I know the Louvre backwards and forwards. This is exciting. I feel like, I feel like, like—"

"Like you could just shit your pants," said Daniel.

"Exactly!" Jens said, smiling. Americans were always so wonderfully colorful with their sayings.

Phoebe patted Jens on the arm. "He means that, literally."

After enlisting our Norwegian guide in our quest, we moved through room after room with a kind of determined purpose that compelled other patrons to clear out of our path.

I brushed aside millennia of art and culture with a few glances and a shake of my head. Mesopotamia. Ancient Iran. The Near East. Ancient Egypt. No, no, no, and…no.

Jens valiantly attempted to get us to contemplate a piece here and there. A small statue of the Pharaoh Akhenaton and his queen Nefertiti walking hand-in-hand. The Seated Scribe. Ramses' towering stone figure. The painted gravestone of Nefertiabet, a sister (or maybe daughter) of the Pharaoh Khufu. I felt bad for Jens, but I forced our group to pass these artifacts and all the rest as if they were nothing more than mile markers on the open highway.

We weren't here to appreciate art. We were here to find my father.

As we approached the vestibule where the Egyptian collection led into the Greek, Etruscan and Roman Antiquities, I felt a tightening in my chest. I had no idea who else my uncle had been, but in these rooms, I would be staring into the eyes of Alexander the Great and Augustus Caesar. Gazing upon the face of Elam Khai.

I halted at the doorway as if some invisible force field had been put in place. I've been shot at, battled warriors, lived through plagues and famines and Nature's fury, endured deprivations that most people in the world today thankfully don't have to experience, and yet, the hesitancy I felt at walking through a *doorway* astonished me. I filled my lungs with the cool, dry, highly filtered museum air, prepared myself, both mind and body, and stepped through the archway.

"Alexander," Jens said to me, excitedly, "meet *Alexander with the Spear.*"

I stepped closer to the small statuette, less than a foot tall.

"It's believed to be a copy of a work created by Lysippos who was the personal sculptor to Alexander the Great. The only artist he allowed to portray him while he was alive."

I recalled that *three* artists were allowed to portray Alexander the Great. One could paint him. One could etch his image in gemstones. And one, Lysippos, could sculpt him in metal.

Daniel tilted his head as he studied the figure. "He doesn't *have*...the spear." The obviousness of this didn't prevent him from sounding unsure.

"It was torn off. Along with his arm. Like Victory's head and Venus de Milo's arms." Jens pointed to the armless beauty just a few feet away.

"This place is a *verdomme* house of horrors."

I regretted Daniel finding that book of foreign curse words.

"Did he have his pants ripped off, too?"

"It's heroic nudity!" I yelled, then lowered my voice. "The mortal as divine being."

"Alexander was worshiped as a god even while he was alive," Jens said. "Clothes are a construct of humans. Gods do not need them."

Stories abound about Alexander's strength and stamina in battle, but depictions of him have always been more slender than the modern image of the rippling, hard-bodied warrior. Elam Khai was more muscular than this or any other representation of Alexander the Great. Or for that matter Octavian or Augustus, whose portrayals were more slight than Alexander's. It was understandable that Elam Khai was in better shape now than in the past. Better training. Better food. Better medicine. But why was Octavian portrayed as less muscular than Alexander?

Phoebe pressed her shoulder against mine. "It's him," she whispered. "I don't know why it makes a difference. But seeing this. Knowing it's *him*," she motioned to the statue, "who's after us... it's..."

"It's scary as hell." Daniel said as he stepped back, his eyes scanning the crowd.

Daniel tripped over the barrier and fell to the ground. He jumped to his feet. I saw the flash of gray as he whipped out the glass-resin knife, whirled around and stabbed Venus de Milo in the abdomen.

The knife bounced off of the marble and skidded across the floor. I stepped on the blade, hiding it under my foot. Retying my laces, I palmed it and slipped it into my pocket.

"No-no. You can't go past the cordon," said Jens, panicked. "Please. You must get out from behind the cordon."

Daniel hopped back over the rail and threw his hands into the air like he'd been caught in the middle of a bank heist. On either side of him, Phoebe and I pulled down his arms.

The fact that Jens was with us saved Daniel from a trip to the security office. I dragged Daniel out of the room while Jens assured the staff that everything was under control.

"What happened back there?"

Daniel's complexion was ashen. "I don't know. I guess what Phoebe said hit me. The guy who's after us…it's Alexander the *Fucking* Great." Apparently, *Curse Words From Around The World* failed him at that moment. He shook his head. "How do you fight someone like that?"

I had no answer.

It was as we entered the next gallery that I saw him.

My father.

He was facing away from me, looking toward the main entrance. The one we should have come in. When I realized it was him, it hit me just how much not being able to see him or talk to him had affected me. I had come here, hoping we would find a clue. I never thought I'd find him here.

He wasn't supposed to be here.

I walked up to him. A pit in my stomach. His gaze was cold. A thousand miles away. His face a dark tan. I'd never seen this piece in the Louvre in all the times I've visited. I glanced at the museum label and gave a little laugh. It was a mold of the marble original on display at the Vatican Museum in Rome.

"Whoa," said Daniel. "Your father."

Phoebe rested her chin against my arm. "That's him?"

"Yeah."

"He looks…powerful."

"Yes, yes," said Jens joining us. "This is fascinating. It was part of a special exhibit on how these marble statues and busts originally looked. Most of us think the monochromatic tone was an artistic intent. Reinforced when Renaissance artists inspired by unearthed ancient sculptures created white marble works of their own. But modern art historians began finding traces of pigment on the originals that had been lost to the elements or centuries of cleaning. Surface treatment—painted on skin tone, clothing, eyes, hair—is now recognized as integral to the overall realistic effect ancient artists were trying to achieve."

I was surprised how much this full-color bust of Mark Antony looked like my father. There were things not quite right about it, and I wasn't sure if it was artistic interpretation or my father's attempt to disguise his face and age or the art scholars overly vivid paint job. How could I have not seen it before? The nose. The chin. The thick head of hair.

"This is what we're looking for," I said. "This and anything else in the museum having to do with Alexander the Great or Octavian or Mark Antony."

∞

We spent a considerable amount of time searching the bust of Mark Antony for anything that could be a clue. We did the same with a bust of Augustus, which wasn't lavished in vivid colors, just the monochromatic gray-white we're more used to. I guess it sort of looked like Elam Khai.

The drawback of vague clues is that you can easily career down paths that lead in the wrong direction. I saw nothing that might lead me to my father.

If he'd only seen the sawdust, he'd be alive today.

The truth is, that riddle, instead of revealing the story of the shortest man in the kingdom being tricked by the second shortest man into thinking he was growing taller, could have just as easily been about the man who didn't realize termites were eating away at the railing of his third story balcony.

If he'd only seen the sawdust, he'd be alive today.

My father's cryptic message was beginning to feel like a

Rorschach test. Every time you looked at it, you saw something different.

Jens tapped me on the shoulder. "You said you were interested in Alexander, Octavian, and Antony. You seem focused on ancient works. But there's a *painting* by Hubert Robert of Alexander that might mean something to you. And if we're heading that way, there's another item I think Phoebe would like."

The room was large, rectangular, and well-protected. Slender entrances choked the flow of patrons, a security feature that would be considered a fire hazard in an American museum. The walls were mottled, like coffee with a bit too much cream. A sea of people moved in a circular pattern. Flashes constantly lit up the room as people raised their phones to take pictures, getting mostly images of other people's phones taking pictures of other people's phones taking pictures of other people's phones. The digital clicking created a constant clatter.

I smiled when I saw her.

La Gioconda, as the French call it, is not a large painting. It could easily be covered by a movie poster. Compared to the massive works lining the other walls in the gallery, the Mona Lisa seemed minuscule.

The painting hung without distraction on a free-standing wall that bisected the room.

Hung might not be the right word. Bunkered, is more appropriate. It sat behind a thick plate of bulletproof glass in a temperature controlled enclosure.

The only other artwork visible when directly viewing the Mona Lisa were signs depicting one stick figure reaching into the purse of another stick figure, with the warning "Beware of Pickpockets" in several languages.

"You are looking at the most famous piece of art in the world," said Jens. "Mona Lisa is the world's first superstar. Its first celebrity."

"It's smaller than I expected," said Phoebe.

Jens nodded. "Just because someone screams doesn't make what they're saying more important than someone who whispers. Usually, it's the opposite." He gestured for us to move closer, the cordon pressing against our legs as we leaned in. "She's painted to scale. Life-size. Hung at eye level. Everyone has seen an image of her. That familiarity makes it easy to forget why she's so special."

"And why's that?" asked Daniel, clearly underwhelmed.

Jens didn't know where to start. "There are many reasons. Da Vinci's stature as an artist. The hands. The sfumato technique, no clear lines or edges. The perspective and the background, which changed art forever."

Jens went on listing the academic reasons for the painting's greatness. All of which were valid. But he left out one crucial detail. The single most important reason the Mona Lisa is the most famous painting in the world:

"She was kidnapped," I said.

In 1911, the greatest art theft in history was pulled off by a five-foot-two journeyman who walked out of the Louvre with the Mona Lisa hidden under his coat. It took twenty-six hours before the theft was discovered.

Newspapers around the world went crazy. A massive blundering, bumbling investigation commenced. Everyone from wealthy American collectors to Pablo Picasso were considered suspects. Suddenly, everyone knew Mona Lisa's name. When the Louvre reopened a week later, thousands came to stare at the small, blank, faded space where she had hung.

Which, I guess, proves you never appreciate something until you lose it.

"The theft drew the world's attention to La Gioconda, but I believe what's kept its attention is her curious smile."

"That's a smile?" Daniel said.

"Is it?" asked Jens. "I don't know. Could be she's mocking us. Or seducing us. Maybe she has a secret. Or indigestion."

"She was nice," I whispered to Daniel.

He kept his voice low. "Who?"

I motioned toward the painting. "My job was to keep her from getting bored while she was sitting for the portrait."

"I literally get nauseous when you say these things, you know that?"

I smiled at Daniel's reaction. And then I noticed her smiling back at me. And she *is* smiling.

It's hard to describe what I feel whenever I look at the Mona Lisa. I've seen it numerous times, mostly before it was sealed up and kept at a distance from the crowds.

I've met a great many people over the centuries, but none could come close to Leonardo and his ability to astonish me. There've been geniuses throughout history. But they're focused geniuses. A Mozart, an Einstein. An Alexander. Leonardo was different. He was brilliant at everything he touched. Art, engineering, architecture, mathematics, dynamics, thought, science, humanity. Everything but love. He sucked at love. He truly did.

He was never satisfied. More than once he complained to me that he felt he was a failure because he'd never finished a work of art. Not one. He continued to tweak the Mona Lisa well into old age. I met him again on the street once, years after I stopped serving as his assistant.

"Do I know you," he asked, his artist's eyes, old as they were, seeing a pattern he'd seen before.

"No, master," I lied. "But I know your work. An extraordinary body of work it is."

He grunted. "Hardly. Unfinished inferior imitations of what could have been."

One of the greatest minds in history and his self-assessment was: loser.

It's not impossible to understand why Leonardo was disappointed with himself. He flitted from one project to the next. Never focusing on any one thing. He had too many ideas. Too many things he wanted to explore. For him, there was never enough time. There've been a number of people I've wished could have my quirk, mostly for selfish reasons so I could spend more time with them. But if there was anyone in all of history I could somehow make like me, it would be da Vinci. He was the one person I've met that needed much, much, much, much, much more time.

The painting seemed dull. The colors muted by varnish and the centuries. Not as vivid as they were when I first saw it.

Leaving the gallery, I took one last look at her. The world in the background was very much like Leonardo's mind, a place of mystery, possibility, and dreams.

"Here's what I wanted to show you." Jens gestured toward a large painting entitled, *Alexander the Great Before The Tomb Of Achilles*. It depicted Alexander having Achilles' burial chamber opened so he could pay homage to the Trojan War hero. "I studied Robert. What's always struck me about this painting is how it highlights Alexander's confidence of his place in history. He saw himself as heir to Achilles. A great warrior. Formidable. Invincible. But it was, perhaps, in grief that their connection was sealed. Achilles, the unconquerable warrior, openly wept at the death of his friend— perhaps lover—Patroclus. He held his body for hours, smeared himself with his blood. Alexander had a similar experience."

"Hephaestion," I said.

"Yes. When Hephaestion died, Alexander—like Achilles—flung himself on the body and lay there in tears, refusing to leave until he was dragged away by force the next day. He had Hephaestion's doctor executed. He ordered his men to raze the Temple of Asclepius, the god of healing, because the god had not done his job."

I studied the painting, the steeply angled pyramid at its center, the clothing that was all wrong for Alexander's time.

For Elam Khai to have such an emotional reaction to Hephaestion's death, there had to be something more to it. Some believe Hephaestion was his lover. But I think there was a more extraordinary explanation. The story of their lifelong friendship had literally been true.

"Thank you, Jens." I handed him the thousand we'd agreed to.

He said we had more time and I handed him another thousand to get him to leave.

I turned to Daniel. "You asked me how do you fight someone like Elam Khai. You find their weakness and exploit it."

"What weakness is that?"

"I think Hephaestion was an Eternal."

We walked toward the main exit.

"He's been dead for over two thousand years. How does that help us?" Phoebe asked.

"He is using me against my father. Because he believes that will draw my father out. Because that's what Elam Khai would do. Risk everything. My father is more calculating than that."

Phoebe glanced at me. "You don't think your father would come for you?"

"I don't know. Maybe. Probably. That's not the point. It's what *Elam Khai* thinks. I'm betting someone is as important to him as Hephaestion was. Elle. Children. Someone. We have to figure out who. And use that."

Maybe Will was right that I was more like Elam Khai than I wanted to admit.

We took the stairs to the lobby in silence.

I searched the sky through the glass pyramid. A grid of shadows marked the floor. I had once called this "a zit on the face of the Louvre." That is a direct quote from a letter I wrote to French President François Mitterrand, which I derisively called *Le Pharaon* because of his megalomaniacal penchant for building grand monuments and edifices.

But now, I was charmed by the Grand Pyramid.

Climbing the spiraling steps toward the plaza, I felt foolish for criticizing this modernization. It was no different than the centuries of demolition and construction that created what everyone thinks of now as the traditional Louvre from the original stone fortress where my father and I—

I stopped, causing a human pile up as several exiting visitors crashed into me.

I cursed in seven different languages, two of them dead as I reversed direction forcing my way down the stairs against the flow.

"What is it?" Phoebe called out after me.

The Louvre began as a bunker that turned into a castle that turned into a palace that turned into a museum. Beneath the lobby, a maze of passages opened into the subterranean ruins of the medieval Louvre. A squat, round stack of ashlar blocks at the intersection of two walls were all that remained of the original fortress. Everything here had been underwater.

Phoebe and Daniel found me on the walkway that followed the path of the original moat.

"There," I said.

I climbed over the cable roping off the restricted area. It was just inside an opening in the wall. Three symbols carved in the rock of a small passage. The etching was faint, nearly invisible unless you knew it was there. It had been buried for centuries before being uncovered during excavations for the new lobby.

"PTA?" said Daniel, squinting.

Phoebe read from a plaque. "These marks spread throughout the ruins were made by stonecutters who were paid by the jobs they accomplished."

The plaque was wrong, of course. I can't blame the museum or the experts. How would they know? "The masons did mark their work. But this isn't one of theirs."

I don't know why—it was so long ago—but I was too embarrassed to come out and say it. The sickening feeling was just as strong now as when my father caught me carving this. Not hate, not love...*embarrassment* is the one emotion that doesn't fade over time.

Believe me, I know.

"I etched that. Late fourteenth century. I looked eight or nine." I searched for a sign something had been hidden or buried. "There was a girl. Like me. Except five hundred years older. She was—" I caught Phoebe's gaze. "I had a crush on her."

Daniel laughed, his face contorting. "You were eight."

"You can have crushes when you're eight," said Phoebe. "I wanted to marry Bobby Felter in kindergarten. I was six."

"You *liked* Felterup Felter?"

"He was not—" She hesitated, thinking about it. "You know, he *was* kinda handsy even back then. All I'm saying is, you can have crushes as a kid." She gestured for me to continue.

The ground seemed undisturbed.

"The Louvre was built to defend the city."

Phoebe rolled her hand for me to speed it up.

"Anyway, they had to drain the moat to repair it. I'd come down here and explore. I saw men marking the stones. Figured it would be okay if I did it. I used a leather punch to carve the rock. It's not 'PTA.' It's 'P *plus* A.'"

Phoebe came closer. "Her initial plus yours?"

I nodded.

"Awwww, that's so cute." Daniel slapped my shoulder. Then after a moment: "Those're your initials, too." He pointed at Phoebe and me.

I blushed. "Actually, what you think of as an 'R' sound is symbolized by a 'P' in Greek. My first language. Her name is Renika."

Daniel studied the small corridor we were standing in. "What was this? Some secret passage to smuggle in goods or allow people to escape the castle without being seen?"

"It's where the toilet shafts emptied into the moat."

Phoebe gagged and Daniel wore a look of disgust as if they were at this moment crawling in raw sewage.

I stared at them. "Seriously? It's been six hundred years." I went back to the marks in the stone. "I didn't see my father. He was standing right over there." My face flushed again. "He thought it was funny." The color of my cheeks grew darker. I didn't tell them what he said to me.

"You're not the first to fall for her. And she's barely hit womanhood. Do yourself a favor, son, and let that one go. I don't think I've met the man who could tame her." *Never mind a boy.* He didn't say that last part, but the specter of his insinuation hung in the air. "I don't think you could control her even if you had her under lock and key."

"The key!" I said, suddenly. "She's the *qui*." My grin turned into a laugh. My friends looked on as if I'd gone mad. "My father was saying *qui.* Not key."

"You're saying the same thing," said Daniel.

"No. *Qui* in French."

"What is key in French?"

"*Who* is *qui* in French."

"Who is key in French?!"

"Exactly."

Phoebe put her hand on my chest. "Hold on there Abbott before Costello here has a brain hemorrhage." She turned to Daniel and explained that in French *qui*, Q-U-I, meant who.

As I stood there staring at my six-hundred-year-old handiwork, my gut told me things were about to get complicated. With Renika around, things always did.

– TWELVE –
Femme Fatales

"So, where is this Renika?" Phoebe asked.

The truth was Renika could be anywhere. She rarely stayed in one place for very long. But she had a house in Paris.

I was pacing at the entrance to the footbridge linking the Tuileries to the Musée d'Orsay as if a force field was keeping me from crossing.

"You're walking back and forth. You're not sure which way to go. Which way she is," narrated Daniel. "Still pacing. No forward movement in any direction. Is she that way? Nope. Oh, but she's not that way, either."

"I know the way."

"I take it you don't want to see Renika," said Phoebe. She grinned. "You still like her."

"No. No, no-no-no-no-no."

"That's a lot of no's," she said.

I felt the rush of blood to my face. I marched onto the bridge. Delaying this was not going to make it any easier.

The sixty-story Tour Montparnasse looked like a black dagger plunged through the heart of the neighborhood of low buildings.

Renika's place wasn't far now.

Settling down for a decade or two is more manageable for adults, where I can squeak out four years tops in a place. But Renika didn't buy into the making-yourself-look-older, gradual-aging-thing that helped Eternals like my father remain in one location for extended periods, sometimes forty years or more. She'd rather pick up and move every couple of years than start dabbing dark circles under her eyes and wearing frumpy outfits.

She once told me if I ever saw her wearing something that made her look old, I was to immediately quote, "stab her in the fucking chest," unquote.

Renika was like that.

Hard to explain. Harder to ignore.

On Avenue du Maine, we crossed to a triangle of sidewalk dotted with trees at the end of Rue Daguerre.

"Over there." I indicated a house three in from the intersection.

"Rue Da Guerre?" Daniel remarked, somewhat irritated. "She lives on the *War* Street? Of course, she does."

I slipped the backpack off my shoulders as I watched the house.

"*Guerre* is war," I said, calmly. "*Daguerre* is the name of an artist."

"Art of war," he said under his breath. "Great."

"You think she's here?" Phoebe asked.

"I don't know." I regretted giving the toy Patriots spyglass to that kid at the airport. "I guess I should see if she's home."

Daniel grabbed my shirt, stopping me. "Dude, this is what I've been ranting about. Your homicidal uncle is probably watching. Who's to say if we go up there and knock on that door that they aren't already waiting inside for us, *Empire Strikes Back*-style. Maybe they're that flower vendor there. Or that guy sipping his coffee suspiciously over *there*." He pointed at an innocent old woman selling carnations and then an even older man enjoying an espresso and a croissant.

"You're right."

This scared Daniel even more. "I am?"

"We have to assume people are watching. But there's been a lag before the heavies show up. We get in, talk to her, get out. That's it. No chit-chat, no reminiscing, no asking her about me, no getting all goofy and drooling over her."

"Why would I drool?"

"He's saying, she's hot."

I took a breath and unconsciously smoothed the front of my shirt. "Here I go."

Daniel grabbed me again. "You can't just walk up and knock on the door."

"We don't have time to mess around. We've already lost a day because the museum was—"

Phoebe gave an annoyed sigh. She was already in the street before I could stop her. Daniel was about to yell something to her when I pressed my hand over his mouth.

"Shhhh."

Phoebe waited to let a Renault two-seater the size of an arm chair drive past. Then the world grew quiet. At least, that's how it seemed—except for her footsteps, which echoed off the surrounding buildings.

Step step step step. Step step step step. Like music in 4/4 time. Was it just my imagination, hearing the heavier accent on the first beat? *Left* right left right, *left* right left right. How many steps was she taking? Had to be double the amount necessary.

I was overwhelmed by hyper-acuity.

My breathing.

Daniel's fidgeting.

But mostly Phoebe's footfalls.

She reached the curb, and step step step, she was at the door. The knock on the wood rung out like a church bell.

Knock-knock-knock.

Knock. Knock. Knock.

Knock-knock-knock.

Three short. Three long. Three short. S-O-S. I was hearing Morse code now. Did she have any idea she was doing that?

"She's gonna be home, she's gotta be home, she's home," Daniel kept repeating in various order.

Phoebe persisted. Each time I heard her knuckles rap against the door, my heart skipped a beat. I almost couldn't take it any longer, when finally, thankfully, Phoebe stopped knocking. She stood there, waiting for the door to open. Waiting. Waiting. Still waiting.

Then the waiting was over.

She turned and skipped across the street.

"Doesn't seem like anybody's home," she said.

"I knew it!" Daniel shouted. "Maybe it's the wrong house."

"It's the right house."

"Maybe you didn't knock hard enough."

"My knuckles are bleeding."

"She's probably in Milan or Rome."

Daniel was agitated. "No! I'm not going to Italy or whatever people-trying-to-kill-us place you want to go to next."

"You'll like Milan and Rome"

"No, I won't."

"Yes, you will. They're very nice cities. Hardly anyone there who'll want to kill us."

Phoebe shifted impatiently. "There was mail in the mailbox."

"More proof she's not here."

"*Outgoing* mail."

I crouched over the lock.

"You're breaking in." Daniel turned to Phoebe. "He's picking the lock."

"My eyes *are* working."

"He's breaking in."

"I'm trying to concentrate," I said. "She'll have a security system. If she's anywhere near Paris, she'll rush here once she's alerted." I thought about it. "Although, there's a chance she might cut and run." I briefly paused what I was doing. "No, she'll want to confront whoever's stupid enough to mess with her stuff."

"What about the police?" said Daniel.

"I can guarantee her system will not alert the police. The last thing she wants is people snooping around her house."

I had the nail file and two of the bobby pins from the million-count package we bought at the market two streets over slipped into the cylinder. I was making progress. It was a good lock. Bump key resistant. The lock pins were sturdy. I had torqued a few bobby pins already. Which wasn't a problem. I had roughly a million left to work with.

"What's taking so long?" Daniel had gone from indignant to impatient in under a minute.

"It's not like the movies. It takes..." I slowly bent the nail file, turning it into a torsion wrench. "...a lot of skill and practice. And most of all, patience." The first pin clicked. "I break into my own place..." I got the second pin, then the third. "...all the time. Doors. Windows." The fourth gave me trouble, but it finally went. I closed my eyes and focused. I had to jigger the back pin without knocking the other four out of place. I felt the last one give. "Got it. You might want to step back. No telling what kind of security she has." Phoebe and Daniel retreated. "And..." I turned the nail file, then pushed open the door. "Voilà."

"Don't move! Put your hands on your heads!" came the voice from inside.

I looked up to see the barrel of a Beretta pointed at my chest. The pistol didn't have a laser sight, but there was a bright red dot on my shirt.

"Which is it? Put our hands on our heads or don't move?" asked Daniel.

When Renika saw it was me, she lowered the gun and threw it on the counter. The laser dot disappeared a second later. "What the hell are you doing?"

"I thought you guys didn't use guns?" Daniel said, probably thinking he was saying it in his head.

"Who gave you that stupid idea?" Renika scowled at me. "Don't you know how to knock?"

"We *did* knock."

"No, some girl I don't know knocked."

"That would be me." Phoebe waved her hand, a little defiantly. "Some girl."

Renika waved back, blankly. "Hi." She grabbed my shirt. "Get inside." She surveyed the rooftops, the yard, then she looked Phoebe over. "Nice outfit." She pointed to Phoebe's boots. "Jeffery Campbell?"

"Uh…I think."

Daniel's response was pretty much what I expected, a dazed stare, mouth slightly hung open, just minus the saliva. To be honest, Phoebe's reaction wasn't all that different.

Renika was difficult to describe. Whenever anyone tried, it always came off as superficial or patronizing or both. Renika had studied at Bologna, Oxford, the Sorbonne, Harvard. Unfortunately, most people judged her before she ever opened her mouth. Because Renika was stunning. Painfully so. Like a jolt of electricity. She was tough, brutal at times, but her bluish-green eyes and her flawless bronze complexion, lightly colored lips, and long lashes softened even the harshest words or action or look.

Listen, I get it—probably better than most. Beauty is fleeting and not only because it fades with time—something that effected Renika more slowly—but it also fades with familiarity. We get used to someone's beauty until it becomes muted, less obvious.

Renika defied this phenomenon. Each time you saw her, whether it was the first time or the thousandth, whether it had been decades or minutes, the shock was the same. Like getting slapped in the face with a train.

When I first met Renika, it wasn't her beauty that attracted me. It was her fearlessness. She railed against anyone telling her what she could and couldn't do. Fight with swords, hunt with the boys, go into the forbidden parts of a castle. I'm not sure how many suitors were spurned with the line, "I will kill him in his sleep if you force me into marrying him or bearing his children." And that was when she was about my age.

She's one of the most intelligent people I've ever known. Okay, not Einstein, Marie Curie, or Hawkins level, but smart. *Really* smart.

A room tipped when Renika entered it. Unmistakably pulling everything and everyone toward the gravity she created.

Renika wagged a finger at me. "Whatever you do, do not go to your apartment. Your *old* girlfriend," she emphasized the word old, "hasn't given up her teenage crush." She stared at me with those light oceany eyes, the color of the water at the edge of a white sand beach. The glare devolved into a glancing over. "You've grown up since the last time I saw you."

"It's only been fifteen years."

"Well, it was an important fifteen years." She ran her hand over my shoulder and down my arm. Realization hit her. Her hand stopped. Her tone changed. "*Seems* like fifteen years. That was me calling you a baby, because you would've been a baby," she said, laughing the kind of laugh I can honestly say I've never heard from Renika.

"They know."

The laughing ceased. Renika flung a string of physically impossible to achieve profanity at me. "I take it all back, you haven't changed one bit. You are still an idiot." She stomped the floor. "Idiot!" She scrutinized me for a moment. "You already went to your place, didn't you?" My face twitched. "You are an *idiot*."

"I—"

"Don't even." She pointed at two sheets taped on the back of the front door. A page torn out of a magazine with Katrina's face under the title, *The World's Oldest Fashion Model*. And printed in black letters on plain paper: DO NOT ANSWER THE DOOR FOR THIS WOMAN. UNDER ANY CIRCUMSTANCES. "Actually, I'd amend that to 'put a bullet in her if she comes by again,' but I like my housekeeper. I don't want to make her uncomfortable."

Phoebe glared at Renika. "'Some girl' is going to keep a watch for the 'old' girlfriend." She went into the front room and leaned one shoulder against the narrow slice of wall between the windows, which made it difficult for her to be seen from the street below.

Renika raised an eyebrow in reference to Phoebe. "I can see why you like her."

"Why do you think I like her?" I whispered.

"Because you have a penis and you're an idiot." Renika impatiently gestured with her hand. "Owing to your idiocy and your penis, we don't have a lot of time. What do you have for me?"

"I thought you'd have something for me."

"Nooooooo." She pulled open a drawer and retrieved a memory card. She tossed it onto the desk. "I have this useless piece of tech from your father and you're supposed to give me the key to unlock it."

Daniel shot me a look.

It seemed ridiculous, way too literal, but I told her about the message from my father that had led us here, skipping the missteps and multiple felonies we'd committed along the way.

Renika pulled out a laptop. "That is brilliant," she said, lifting the lid.

"I don't know if it's all that brilliant. Will was like, 'Guy's not a poet.'"

"Will is a pompous ass."

Daniel hovered over Renika. "You know Will?"

"Everyone knows Will. Which seems to be how Will likes it. But he's been allowed to get away with it." She said the last part with more than a hint of scorn.

"Why's that?"

"Because no one notices writers."

She logged in, then checked the surveillance around her house. Nothing out of the ordinary.

"You're not worried about someone hacking into your system?" Daniel asked.

"No, other-person-I-don't-know, I'm not worried. This has..."

"My name's Daniel. Alexander and I are best friends."

She didn't miss a syllable. "…military grade encryption."

"Looks like the computer I have."

"Yes, but I actually clicked on the little checkbox in the System Preferences that turns on the hardware-based military grade encryption any moron can use."

I picked up the memory card. "One gigabyte? How old is this?"

"Marcus gave that to me about a decade ago. Saying you'd come if you needed the info on it."

It always startled me when she called my father Marcus. The familiarity in the way she said it.

"*Ten* years ago," I said.

"Yeah. It's encrypted. I spent a lot of time running attacks on that and got nowhere."

"You…hack?"

"Yes, Donald—"

"Daniel."

She rolled her eyes as if to say, whatever. "This is a four thousand ninety-six-character RSA key." She slid the memory card into an adapter. "That's NSA, CIA-level encryption. And a decade ago, it was almost unheard of."

She plugged the adapter into the computer. A password window opened.

"'The key is at the beginning of time.' I don't care what Will says, that's pretty clever." She typed in *atthebeginningoftime*. All one word. As soon as she hit enter—

Nothing happened.

She tried it with spaces. No good.

Then the whole phrase. Nope.

A lot of swearing followed. I thought she might smash her laptop.

I replayed my conversations with Braeden. "Try *Festina lente*," I said. No effect. "How about 'Make haste slowly.'" That didn't work either. I let out a heavy sigh. "Try *filiolum*."

Her left brow raised a quarter inch.

"Just do it."

"Okay, *my little son*." Until now her fingers had been dancing across the keyboard, but she entered my father's endearment for me, pecking at each key with her index finger like a two year old. One. Letter. At. A. Time.

Sometimes she really pisses me off.

She finally hit Enter. *This drive is encrypted. The password you entered is incorrect.*

The joy she felt from ribbing me dissipated. Three more attempts. Three more failures.

I told her how I thought Braeden had mixed in *qui*—who in French—for key. When I mentioned Braeden's death, her fingers froze, hovering above the keyboard.

"Did you know him?"

"I did." Her hands remained in midair.

"You okay?"

"Yeah. It's just...one of us dying. He wasn't much older than me."

She squeezed her eyes shut, breathing slowly. After nearly a minute, her eyes shot open. She punched in *atthebeginningofthyme*. The instant she hit return, the drive became available.

Seeing my curious frown: "*Qui*, key. Homonyms. Marcus likes to use a lot of oregano and thyme when he cooks."

That familiarity again. My father cooks?

"An herb reference. The great dramatist didn't see that one coming. *'I know a bank where the wild thyme blows, Where oxlips and the nodding violet grows.'*" she said, quoting *A Midsummer Night's Dream*. "Pompous *ass*." Renika shook her head, a broad smile across her face. "I love you, Marcus."

I felt the stab of envy again. Women love my father. He speaks just enough to have them feel he understands them and little enough that women can project on him anything they want to. That's probably the jealousy talking. I love my father, too. Admire him. I understand that draw. He doesn't demand attention, he commands it. For most of my life, young women got married as early as fourteen years old. There have been wives of kings of France and England who were not yet fifteen. It wasn't unusual for someone my father's age, who looks about forty, to take a bride Renika's age, a woman who is physiologically twenty years old. The most dominant male pairing with the most fertile and desirable woman. This is how we survived for tens of thousands of years. It may seem strange to those who've only known a world where our survival is not threatened by too few people. Where science gives offspring to those that nature would not. A world where the rights of women have evolved.

This world is not the world as I have known it. This new world, this modern society, is barely a blip on the radar. One I fear could easily disappear.

I guess all of this is a long way of saying that when Renika says, "I love you, Marcus," she could very well mean she feels for him the way I have felt for her for nearly seven hundred years.

She opened the drive. There was a single file on it. She dragged it over to her computer, then clicked it. An image filled the screen. It was a photo taken of a photograph. A room or passage cut into stone. The lighting was harsh. There were symbols on the walls. And words and symbols scribbled on the photo itself. Definitely my father's handwriting. At first, I thought it was a scan of a photograph he'd written on, but I realized these notes had been added digitally. The thought of my father using a computer or tablet or digital pen and annotation software made my head spin. Like the idea of him cooking. Who was this man?

The symbols on the walls were unintelligible. My father's notes in ancient Greek didn't make much more sense. Disconnected phrases, each more odd than the one before it.

Destroy the Old Man's trees before he finds them?

Black and white and gray and green and brown?

"These seem more like notes to himself than to me."

I told Renika everything that had happened over the past few days. About Elam Khai and his plan. She made no comment. Asked no questions. I wasn't sure she was even listening until she pointed at the screen. "He's afraid of this."

She meant the computer, not the image.

284 | EDWARD SAVIO

"That in the end, this is what will out us, maybe even destroy us."

I nodded. "That seems to be a big concern of his. Never being able to be famous or even known again."

"It's a thing. He's not the only one."

"So you agree with him?"

"I'm saying there is a lot of uneasiness. He will have allies."

"Which is why we need people we can trust."

"And who would that be? These two?" Renika pointed at Phoebe and Daniel. "We need Genghis Khans, Queen Boudiccas, Caesars. Not the Hardy Boys and Nancy Drew."

"Who are the Hardy Boys and Nancy Drew?" Daniel said, confused.

"Never mind," Renika and I said in unison.

Renika turned her attention back to the screen. Daniel studied it as well. The symbols painted in red on the stone had a vague pattern. I don't know *every* language, but even the ones I don't know I can usually identify. This wasn't anything I'd ever seen before. There was something primitive about it.

We deal with written language every day, and have for thousands of years, but the symbols that make up words—and the words themselves for that matter—are arbitrary. The fact that the letter B looks like it does and isn't Ω is simply because along the way somebody, or a group of somebodies, somewhere, made a choice. I mean, the word *spatula* could just as easily describe the things you wear on your feet.

"These symbols don't mean anything to me."

Renika zoomed in on one of the characters, focused on it for a moment and made a noise. "But they might mean something to some—" She was interrupted by a notification on the laptop. "Dammit."

She grabbed my backpack, unzipped it.

"What are you doing?" I asked.

"We no longer have time to sit around and figure this out. Elam Khai is not our most immediate problem."

A still image popped up on the laptop screen. "Um, there's a picture of that sweet old lady," Daniel announced.

"That not-so-sweet old lady has blown through every cent she's made, the fortunes of two dead husbands, and is working through the third corpse's money…trying to find him."

"Staaaaaalker," sang Daniel.

"She's a block away. *You* led her here."

"We made sure we weren't followed."

"Six years ago."

Daniel looked up from the laptop. "I thought you haven't seen him in fifteen years."

"She wasn't home," I said.

"I happened to be in Monaco, enjoying myself. After you stopped by, after she lost you, she decided to loop back to my place."

Renika went to her desktop computer and opened an archived file. Footage played in vivid detail on a 5K monitor of Katrina screaming at the surveillance camera above the front door. There was no sound, which somehow made it much more terrifying. Renika unmuted the video, and the audio kicked in. "…whatever you do. He is a user. A liar. A scoundrel. A louse!" This went on for an uncomfortably long time. Insults. Threats. Demands to know where I was. Professions of undying love. Pleading. Swearing. A potted plant smashing against the door. Renika mercifully cut the video short.

"There are eight more just like it. I'll make you a mix tape. '*Louse*,' that's my favorite, by the way."

Renika brought up an encrypted messaging app, typed in a few sentences that were turned into a series of hexadecimal pairs, and hit send.

She waited. Once the text was confirmed as delivered, she pressed a white programmable button affixed to the wall and instantly her desktop computer and its storage were fried. A white cloud billowed out of the machine.

Renika was always prepared for a quick exit.

She mocked a swoon. "'I am just so in love with him.' Nauseating."

She slid open the top half of the bookshelf, revealing a small weapons cache.

"What is it with you people and secret bookshelves?"

Renika tossed a dozen of what always reminded me of the ornaments people hang on their trees during the holidays into the backpack.

"Just in case," she said.

Daniel was studying the unlocked file. Not the image, but the metadata of the file itself when Renika closed the laptop.

"Hey! Privacy."

"Wait, wait, wait! There's something weird about that image file."

"There's a lot of things weird about it." Renika slipped the computer into the backpack.

"You got that memory card a decade ago?"

"Yes."

"That file is dated five *weeks* ago."

"That's not possible."

"No, it's not," he said.

"I copied it over to the computer."

"If it had changed the date, it would be today's date."

Phoebe yelled from the living room. "She's here!"

I went to the window and peered over Phoebe's shoulder while Daniel peered over mine. Katrina was talking to the old man sipping espresso.

"I knew it! The old guy drinking coffee!" Daniel punched me on the shoulder.

I shoved the backpack into his chest. "I have to talk to her."

I made it to the top of the stairs before Renika blocked my path. "I swore if she ever came back here, I'd kill the *futatrix*. What I can't figure out...with all her popping off to anyone who'd listen about some kid claiming to be over a thousand years old, is why anyone *else* hasn't killed her."

I didn't appreciate the "kid" reference, but the question was valid. Bad things tended to happen to people who were indiscrete about our secret.

"Let me try to talk some sense into her."

Renika put a pistol in my hand. "Make this your opening statement."

I refused the gun, then took the stairs down to the street.

When Katrina saw me, her face flickered through a half-dozen expressions. Satisfaction, excitement, relief, anger, hurt, sadness.

I stopped a few feet from her. "Katrina."

She moved closer until we were almost touching. "Alexander."

I had spent six decades avoiding her. This is unkind, but I'd been waiting for the problem to pass along with Katrina.

I had to do what I should have done all those years ago. My gaze went from her right iris to her left. Back and forth. And in her hazel eyes, I could see a flicker of the girl I knew. "I...I'm sorry," I said.

She slapped me across the face. Hard.

"He's a liar. Don't believe a word he says," she shouted toward Renika and Phoebe who were watching from the doorway. Katrina's gaze returned to me and the girl was gone. Everything I once cared about had vanished. It wasn't her looks but *her*. "Your entire life is a lie," she said.

I wanted to tell her that lying to people is not the same as living a lie, but the distinction would be lost on her. Besides, this was my fault. What I did had been unfair. Selfish.

"You were my first love, Alexander. And you broke my heart. Do you have any idea what you put me through?"

"You pulled away first, Katrina. You wanted to be with a 'man.' Remember? I was a boy. I wasn't old enough for you. Don't you see the irony? I told you my secret because I didn't want to lose you."

"And I stayed. But *you* left when it got hard," she said. "Did it mean anything? Or do the names and faces fly by, blur together, hard to keep straight."

My chest ached. "I meant everything I said to you."

She laughed. "Do you know what I've sacrificed to find you? The years, the money. *That's* everything." She grinned. "But now, I've found you."

The look of satisfaction on her face grew as the ground beneath my feet began to shake. A black vehicle screeched to a halt behind Katrina. Two men climbed out dressed in suits and ties, which clashed with the assault weapons they were brandishing. A third stayed in the car, speaking into a radio.

Without hesitating, I ran at them. I could hear Renika shouting, "Idiot!" and the sound of her boots on the sidewalk. I put the first man down with a punch to the ribcage, up and under. His body stiffened from the shock, then he fell to the ground. The next man came at me, his gun aimed in my direction. I broke his arm. Mid radius, mid ulna, both bones, clean break. The gun went off, the bullet passing through the fabric at the edge of my jacket. I twisted his snapped arm down. He screamed, his reflexes squeezing the trigger again and this time he shot himself in the leg. He dropped the gun, and I kicked it into the sewer. I smashed my foot into his face. Renika came up behind me and finished off the man coming out of the passenger side. He was down on the ground.

She kept kicking him over and over and over.

"Nika!"

"Sorry." She kicked him once more. Then still unsatisfied, one last time.

I marched toward Katrina, the smell of cordite wafting up from my jacket.

I could feel the rage on my face, the blood in my cheeks. "You come after me with hired guns? Do you want to die right now?" My voice was on the verge of cracking. My fists were clenched so tightly I felt I might break my own fingers.

"It's not like I have all that much longer to live if this doesn't work."

I felt the smallest pang of sadness for her. I steeled myself against it. "I didn't do anything wrong but trust you."

Despite my fury, she touched my face. "You haven't changed."

She glanced at the unconscious man at my feet. "Still my brave Alexander. You saved my life in Warsaw." She smiled. A grin that disappeared. "Only to ruin it. I loved you. I still love you."

I heard Daniel let out an involuntary groan. "Oh, good *God!*"

"I felt the joy and the pain. Same as you, Katrina. But any feelings I had for you, you've obliterated with this obsession."

"I'm sorry I'm an inconvenience for you."

"Don't," I said firmly. "You act like I have some choice in this. I have no more control over how I am than you have over your fingerprints. I didn't mean to hurt you. And I'm sorry I didn't know better then."

"We were young and foolish. But you are still young."

"We need to get back in the house," barked Renika. "We're gathering attention."

I held up my palm for her to give me a moment, then turned back to Katrina. I could still see glimpses of the girl I knew in her eyes. "You put me in danger," I said. "You put yourself in danger. This isn't about your feelings for me. You think I'm holding back on you. That I can make you young again. I can't."

Katrina stared at me. "You have no idea what it's like, do you? Feeling time race. Knowing it crawls for you."

My throat tightened. "Ever since you've known, you've put me at risk. I thought telling you would bring us closer. It tore us apart. My father warned me."

"I warned you," Renika yelled, making a looping finger motion around her ears.

Katrina shot Renika a contemptuous look. "You think you will be any different?" This, she said to Phoebe.

Phoebe's expression betrayed no emotion.

But in Katrina's eyes, I saw something dangerous. She was stalling.

Renika forced a fake smile. "He may have a problem killing you, but I don't. Take your hired goons and leave before someone really gets hurt."

Three more vehicles charged around the corner.

When Renika saw them, she raised the pistol, aiming it at Katrina. I put my hand up in front of the barrel.

"Alexander, I will shoot her through your fucking hand!"

I took Katrina by the arm. Her always slender frame was thin and bony now. Frail. "I don't think you understand. The only reason you're alive is you think you made some kind of deal."

"A deal to live forever."

"That's not how it works. Even if she doesn't kill you, *they* will."

"We'll see," she said. And I immediately felt a stabbing pain in my side. My hand came away with blood. Just a spot. Katrina held something in her hand. The tiniest vial filled with a few precious drops of crimson. I tried to snatch it out of her palm, but she stepped out of reach as the first wave of men poured from the three combat-modified armored vehicles.

Unlike the suits lying unconscious on the ground, these dozen hired guns were straight out of a PMC promo video dressed in black/gray urban camo and body armor.

The closest man barked instructions to the others. As soon as I heard the accent, I knew we were in greater danger than I thought. These weren't American contractors. Or German or Austrian. Not even Russian. These were Chechens, some of the most ferocious and ruthless warriors in the world. Collateral damage was not an issue for them.

Twelve Uzis. Two each were aimed at Phoebe and Renika. Three at Daniel. Four at me.

"You don't know who you're dealing with, Katrina. These men will kill you."

"These men…" she tilted her head, "…work for me." She couldn't see the twelfth Uzi aimed at her head.

"You only think they do. They used you to find me."

You know how in movies the villains are always shown firing thousands of rounds of ammunition at the heroes. It produces thundering noise. It creates a lot of kinetic action. It makes for great visuals. It never happens. First of all, indiscriminate gunfire tends to harm people. Innocent people. Non-innocent people. People doing the shooting. Just people in general. Second, next time you see a movie where more than ten or fifteen shots are fired—okay, thirty-two for the Uzis—ask yourself where are they carrying all that extra ammunition? Do they have another bad guy tagging along behind them with a red wagon full of preloaded magazines? A fully automatic Uzi empties its clip in three point two seconds. One one thousand, two one thousand, three one thousand, aaaand…scene's over. Even shooters with extensive training miss their targets. The real world hit rate during a gunfight is about fifteen to twenty percent. When the target can't shoot back, it's about thirty percent. Stray bullets are in the majority.

A second wave, the men in the rear seats, pulled out two heavy machine guns, each with a belt loader that disappeared into the back of the two flanking vehicles.

Which meant, ironically, that here was one instance of bad guys actually having enough readily available ammo to lay down several minutes of continuous, gratuitous, indiscriminate fire at twenty rounds a second without so much as a change of clip. And they were aiming this firepower directly at my friends and me.

Patrons began pouring out of the restaurant located on the ground floor of Renika's home.

I wasn't sure if these men worked for Elam Khai or whoever sent those two clowns to shoot down his plane in Boston. Whichever, I hoped they hadn't brought this much manpower just to kill me. It takes a lot more people to capture someone alive than it does to assassinate them. A single sniper can take care of that.

I stepped in front of the line of fire.

The Chechen glared at me. "Get in the vehicle."

A crowd had gathered, keeping their distance, but still too close for their own safety.

"I would put those guns away, gentlemen." Renika was back on the sidewalk by her front door.

The Chechen smiled at her. Men always underestimate Renika.

292 | EDWARD SAVIO

It's the pretty package. He quit smiling when he saw the red pinpoint of a laser sight aim ed at his chest. He put his hand out, and the others halted their advance. One of the other men had a laser sight pointed directly at him as well.

Renika's tone became even less friendly. "I said put the guns away."

It took a few seconds, and a lot of squinting, until the Chechen was laughing. "Nice try, Beautiful," he said, once he realized the dots were not from a gunsight, but a laser pointer, actually two laser pointers, one in each of Renika's hands.

He barked out an order in Chechen I didn't understand, and the barrels were raised again. I was pissed at myself for never having the patience to learn the language. I mean, it's got *forty-four* vowels. Who has the time for that?

"I wouldn't do that," said Renika.

Another order of vowel soup, and suddenly, gunfire was directed at the second floor, cutting through the windows, splintering wood, chipping away the limestone. The crowd across the street scattered. Katrina collapsed to the asphalt, her face filled with fear. The men weren't firing directly at Renika or Phoebe or Daniel, partly because I was in the line of fire—a bullet would have to go through me before it hit my friends—and partly because this was meant to send a message. A strong one.

The interior of Renika's home was being shredded. She cursed at them. She was pissed.

Something whooshed a few feet over my head. In an instant, the Chechen leader was knocked back. An instant after that, he was blown to pieces by a terrible explosion. I was shocked by the violence of it. Another sound of something slipping through the air and one of the vehicles went up in flames.

I was moving solely by instinct. Compulsion. I sprinted for Phoebe and Daniel, using my body to defend them. But the Chechens didn't care about their orders any longer. A bullet passed my ear, then another one hit me in the back. I felt it go through my side. A clean exit.

Gunfire and small rockets were raining down from the roof line of Renika's building from auto-tracking turrets.

The last onlookers finally scrambled to get to safety.

I pushed Phoebe and Daniel inside the doorway, forcing them up the steps. An explosion knocked us to the ground, sending us sliding across the floor. "The back! The way we came in!" I screamed.

Nothing, not the walls, not the art, not the fireplace, not the furniture, not a thing in her house was recognizable after being riddled with bullets. I stumbled over rubble and smashed into remnants of a staircase before landing on my face. Bullets ripped into a painting above me. I was eating twisted debris and dust. Several canisters came through the window, one landing at Daniel's feet. I screamed at him a second before they went off, one after another. But instead of exploding, they spewed out a sickeningly sweet gas. It felt wet and sticky.

Phoebe reached out her hand to pull herself up. I managed to slap her down before the next necklace of bullets came.

Renika's weapons cache had been destroyed by a direct hit.

We scrambled toward the back. The floor was slippery from a combination of milk, sodas, cooking oil, the sticky gas, water from smashed toilets. It could've been anything, it could've been everything. Phoebe lost her footing. I caught her inches before her head struck a jagged piece of molding. We hit the wall hard. The splintered wood dug into my arm. She was dazed.

Daniel was the first to the back door. Showing courage, he waited for us. I dragged Phoebe, practically flung her toward him. He grabbed her hand and lead her away as a string of bullets knocked a set of pans off their hangers.

Where the hell was Renika? Fragments of exploding walls, shattering glass, debris being kicked up, the thick fog, I couldn't see.

I wanted to stand, to run, but another thread of gunfire tore into the back wall and through the open door. I crawled the last twenty feet on my belly.

An RPG whooshed through the house and out the back door into the courtyard.

I heard Daniel scream to Phoebe seconds before the ordinance exploded.

The fireball didn't reach the house, but the concussion blast did, sending another round of debris my way. I covered my face just in time. The shockwave cleared the fog. The gunfire stopped. The scene was eerily quiet, just the sounds of settling rubble.

I glanced back through the gaping hole in the front of the house and saw Katrina on the ground, holding her ears. She was splattered in blood, in shock. The others were dead.

Renika appeared from out of nowhere. "Don't even think about it, Alexander. She brought this on herself."

I nodded. Whatever was going to happen, I couldn't save her.

We made it out into the courtyard just as the ceiling collapsed.

The RPG had taken out a shed in the back.

"That was an interesting security system," I said.

"Effective," she said. "Originally for laser-guided bombs, but I modified it. Minimizes collateral casualties. I told my neighbors it was pigeon abatement."

My pulse was pounding crazily in my ears. We sprinted through the yard, leaping over hedges, climbing on the rooftops of sheds and backyard studios.

There was a passage to the street under one of the buildings on the block. Once we got around the corner, Renika pushed me up against the wall, her hands sliding over my face, then hungrily down my chest and over my hips. Her body was so close to me. I felt her. Then I felt something else.

"I don't think this is the time for—" Searing pain. "Yeowwww."

"You're hit," she said.

I pressed my eyes together, tears forming, and held my breath, my head nodding without my permission. "I'm okay," I said, my voice at least a full octave higher than normal.

She lifted my shirt, the softness of her hands on my skin, warm, comforting. I heard a sickening squish, like the sound of raw chicken, and felt her finger poke into my perforated body.

I saw blazing white spots behind my eyelids.

"No. You're not."

"I felt it go clean through."

"A gunshot is never clean, you idiot. You're hemorrhaging."

"I have tape. In the backpack. Where is the backpack?"

I was yelling. I knew I was. My ears were ringing.

She left me there. My eyes squeezed shut as I tried to push away the pain. I don't know how long it took her to reach Daniel and retrieve the roll of duct tape—it seemed like forever. I sensed movement. I tried to ready my body to defend itself, but couldn't.

I was pushed hard against the wall.

I opened my eyes to find Renika swabbing something into my wounds with a cloth napkin.

"Honey?"

"Yes, darling?" she cooed.

I laughed. Which hurt. Honey is an effective antibiotic. She tore the napkin in half and poured more of the nectar onto the strips. After covering the entry and exit with the honey-infused fabric, she staunched the hemorrhaging in the same way I had controlled Will's bleeding. Two strips of tape making an "X" over each hole.

Will.

I hoped he was safe.

"I'm sorry," she said. At first, I thought she was apologizing for stretching the tape across my bare skin or blowing up a man right in front of me, but then I realized she was apologizing for making me run again. Rifle fire. It was coming from behind us. Single shots in sequence.

One, two, three. One. One. One, two.

I heard sirens. Even if we could trust the police, they wouldn't get here in time or be equipped to handle what was coming after us.

We moved as quickly as I could, stopping whenever I needed to let the pain subside. I was on the edge of going into shock. I hadn't lost much blood, Renika had stopped the hemorrhaging, but the body doesn't like being punctured. It reacts poorly. Capillaries constrict. The heart and lungs and brain become a priority. Muscles in the limbs get less oxygen, which causes lactic acidosis, which causes hyperventilating, which causes me to be pressed into this alcove.

I heard a helicopter approaching. I couldn't see it directly without revealing myself. It hovered over the building where Daniel and Phoebe were. Then its shadow moved directly above our location.

"They're trying to pin us down until ground forces can reach us." Renika made it sound like a military operation. Which, I guess, it was. "I've got transport out of here," she added. "But it's that way." She pointed in the direction we'd come.

"I don't think going west is an option right now. North, south, and east aren't looking so good either," I said, whirling my index finger around indicating the helicopter.

She curled her hand into a tube and put it up to her eye, warning me to look out for snipers.

We advanced toward Daniel and Phoebe's position. The shadow of the helicopter slowly tracked east, its concussive blade noise buffeting the street.

A tiny Citroen screeched to a halt. Renika and I prepared to fight the driver as he jumped out. But he sprinted to a small shop to buy a baguette.

Daniel darted into the street and climbed in the driver's seat. "C'mon," he yelled to us.

I guess he figured, Phoebe stole a car, why can't he.

I got in and pushed him into the passenger seat.

"Why can't I drive?" he said as Phoebe and Renika jumped in the back.

"Because you stabbed Venus de Milo."

I went to pop the car into first but ended up grinding the gears, which drew the attention of the car's owner.

"And why can't *you* drive?"

"I can drive."

"A chariot, maybe," Renika said.

"I was a toddler when they stopped racing chariots."

"Yes, *explaining* a joke makes it so much funnier."

I finally shoved the stick shift into first, and hit the accelerator, launching the tiny car forward.

Renika screamed, "Stop!"

I slammed on the brakes. I had been staring down at the shifter, not looking ahead.

Renika pointed out the windshield. The helicopter had dropped out of the sky and was hovering a few feet off the ground, blocking our path. It had the same menacing, weaponized look and stylized "A.i." logo as the vehicles outside Renika's home.

The helicopter slowly inched toward our position. It was still a hundred yards down the road.

The owner of the Citroen caught up to us and slammed his fist against the roof, then slapped the windshield several times with the baguette, shouting in French.

The noise was making me crazy. The blades of the helicopter. The baguette spanking the glass.

Renika opened the back window making it worse. "I've got an idea," she shouted over the din. She reached out and dragged the owner through the window. "Let's 'castle' him. Go!"

"Oh, I love castling!" I said as I accelerated straight at the helicopter. I had no intention of slowing down or giving ground in this game of chicken. Phoebe screamed, tried to put her foot through the floor as if she was hitting the brakes. The pilot realizing I would not yield lifted his craft slightly. Then just as I was about to pass under the helicopter, I whipped the wheel around and sped down a small alley.

"Turn right," Renika said. "Now, left."

"I see it."

The helicopter recovered and was in pursuit. There was a driveway that passed under an office building. I jammed the stick into second, then dropped the clutch. The tachometer redlined and the tires smoked as I squealed into the driveway, disappearing from view. The passage wasn't long and wouldn't provide us much protection. It was obvious where we'd gone and where we were going. As the Citroen sped out the other side, I waited for the helicopter to follow, but it didn't. It remained over the building. An identical helicopter approached from the north. It paid no attention as the car passed beneath it. Now, there were two of them. Both circling the building. Both ignoring the Citroen speeding away.

Of course, we weren't in the car. We were in the passage. We'd jumped out, returning control of the car to its owner. He was currently attempting to get away from us as quickly as his one-liter engine would let him.

Unfortunately, the chess move didn't seem to work.

Renika scowled. "They're tracking us."

"Heat signature?"

"No. Too many people on the street and in these buildings. It's got to be something else."

"Do you think we're tagged like in Boston?" Phoebe asked.

We quickly checked the backpack, our clothes. If there was a homing device, we couldn't find it.

I peered out from the edge of the passageway. "Those things on the bottom of the choppers. Could be radio frequency equipment, heat or radar imaging."

"I think they're radiation detectors."

Phoebe glanced over at Renika. "Radiation?"

"The gas they shot into the house barely made my eyes water. It wasn't tear gas. My guess is it's similar to the stuff they use for radiological marking during medical tests. It's probably all over our clothes, our skin."

Daniel was trying to figure out a way to remove his epidermis. "You're telling me we've been irradiated?"

"The equivalent of five or six X-rays."

"Oh, just five or six."

Renika headed toward the front of the alley. We were under an entire building of wood and stone and metal and furniture filled with people. But instantly, one of the two helicopters turned and followed her progress.

I ran after her.

"What are you doing?" Daniel whisper shouted.

"If they can detect us through buildings, we might as well keep moving."

Renika glanced back at him. "Or maybe you'd like to wait for them to come."

"No," Daniel sighed.

We moved out from the shadows and into the bright sunlight. The two helicopters matched our pace whether we were visible or not.

"We've got to wash this stuff off us," Renika said.

"How about that fountain?" Phoebe suggested, pointing across the street.

Renika shook her head. "That might get it off our skin, but not our clothes. And we'd be a little easy to spot running around naked. I've got a better plan. We go underground."

THIRTEEN

Stumbling In The Dark In The City of Lights

The tree-lined avenue led toward the cobblestoned nightmare at the heart of the Place Denfert-Rochereau, a convergence of six streets where cars move like schools of fish being chased by hungry predators, swirling, cutting, turning with such quickness and precision that the bent fenders and broken taillights you'd expect rarely occurred.

Renika motioned toward the edge of the plaza. A Metro station entrance less than fifty yards away.

The helicopters closed in, one ahead, one behind. Black-clad PMCs on foot weaved through traffic in pursuit from the rear, openly brandishing assault weapons. These were not the mercs at Renika's. Her "security" system had obliterated them. The gory scene flashed over and over in my head like a sadistic GIF. Several ominous-looking vehicles with the same "A.i." markings converged on our position. The charming streets of Paris had become a combat zone.

Daniel and I made a break for the Metro stairs.

"No, no, no! Not there! There!" Renika wasn't pointing at the subway entrance, but at a small, black building beyond it and across the street.

I cocked my head, wondering if Renika's plan was brilliant or boneheaded. I laughed to myself at the unintentional pun.

I glanced at Daniel as we ran into the street. "You wanted a little more action. How do you feel now?"

"Like I regret ever speaking to you first day of sophomore year!"

A car honked, and I glanced back to see the hood of a Peugeot come to a halt inches from hitting Phoebe. She never slowed down.

The ground ahead of us was strafed by bullets from one of the helicopters in an attempt to keep us from reaching the building. The only effect the warning shots had was to clear tourists waiting in line out of our way.

"What is this?" Daniel asked as we entered.

Phoebe pointed to a plaque honoring the six million Parisians buried in the catacombs below.

"Uh-ah." Daniel tried to retreat.

Phoebe shoved him forward. "Stop being a pussy."

"There are at least thirty of them heading this way," Renika said as she ran inside.

It's not the first time I've been outnumbered with Renika at my side, but thirty was a bit much. And if she *saw* thirty, you can bet there were at least thirty more she hadn't seen.

I threw cash in the direction of the ticket taker, and we made for the stairs, ignoring the shouts of the people who'd been waiting. Broad steps quickly devolved into a narrow spiral staircase that plunged toward the center of the earth.

I couldn't see more than ten feet up or down, which concerned me tactically. I had no idea how close our enemies were.

"Where's Renika?" Daniel said.

We stopped at a landing connecting to another set of stairs and waited.

Phoebe peered up toward the surface. "Do you trust her?"

I shrugged. "She cooks with my father."

"And calls him *Marcus*." She mimicked Renika's easy, seductive tone.

"You noticed that."

"Yeah. Get a room."

My father and Renika. Not an image I wanted in my head at the moment. Or any moment, really.

"Maybe she's in trouble," Daniel said.

I appreciated his sudden bravery even if it was primarily fueled by hormones.

"She can handle herself. I'm the one they're after."

Daniel eyed me as we moved toward the next set of stairs. "So you're saying, don't get lost cause you won't be coming to save us."

"I didn't leave you at Wonderland. Or the airport. Or in the tunnel. I told you at the airport, I'm tired of the people close to me never knowing who I really am. You two knowing the truth, it…"

"It makes me feel all warm and squishy inside," gushed Renika. She checked me into the wall as she hurried past. "I could hear your sap twenty feet up. Look, it's dripping off the walls." She dragged her fingers through the moisture clinging to the stairwell.

"What were you doing?"

"Getting this," she waved a sheet of white paper. "We're not going on the guided tour."

We corkscrewed toward a bottom that never seemed to get closer. We forced our way past several slower moving parties. The catacombs were only six or seven stories below street level, but the low rise and long run of the steps, the gradual angle of the descent, made it feel much deeper than that.

A final stairway dumped us at the start of a narrow tunnel. We rushed past more tourists, sending cameras, phones, and bottled water tumbling through the air.

"This is a bit of a letdown," wheezed Daniel. "Where are all of the dead bodies?"

"Don't worry. There'll be plenty of them," I said.

"Yeah, maybe even ours," said Phoebe.

We finally wound our way to the ossuary. One step inside and the air felt colder, the lighting, more dramatic.

Dense stacks of bones lined the walls, all that remained of what had been thousands of people.

"I see dead people," Daniel whispered.

These bones didn't start out down here.

The dead nearly overran Paris like some zombie apocalypse. By the late 1700s, the central burial ground, *Les Innocents*, was overflowing with bodies. Heavy rains caused remains to spill into the streets. Collapses thrust skeletons into the basements of adjacent buildings. A foul odor choked the area. Disease spread.

I was in Paris at the time, and believe me, the place had a putrid, rancid stench. Before modern waste disposal, cities always smelled, but this was something much worse.

I came to France to join Ben Franklin as his personal valet. Others helped the American Minister dress and run his household. My talents extended beyond the suit closet. Mostly, I observed. There may have been a little light spying. Definitely a lot of sneaking about delivering secret missives. To politicians, diplomats, the King, and more than a few French ladies.

When Thomas Jefferson arrived in Paris to take over as Minister to France, I stayed on. Jefferson quipped, "I come to *relieve* Mr. Franklin. Because surely no one can *replace* him."

My errands for Franklin and Jefferson often took me to central Paris and face to face with the work being done to empty *Les Innocents*.

Daniel stared at a pinstripe of skulls running through the stacked bones. Perhaps that was the most disconcerting thing. These weren't haphazard mass graves, these were intricately patterned works.

The dead as art.

"This is like a serial killer's dream home basement," Daniel said, the hollow eye sockets staring back at him. A Dutch family snapped a group selfie in front of a stack of bones. Daniel motioned to the couple's children. "Seriously, this is your idea of a family vacation?"

I dragged Daniel away from a hail of Dutch obscenities.

The catacombs lined with bones are the most famous, but they're only a tiny fraction of the tunnels and caverns beneath Paris. Heavy iron gates forced us to follow the public path with its one way in and one way out. If we couldn't get into the labyrinth of off-limit carrières before our pursuers caught up with us, this was going to turn out to be a simple squeeze play.

Renika waited at an intersection of tunnels, looking over the sheet titled, *Carrières de Paris*. It was a complex map inked by hand with names and notations in French. "They confiscate these when they catch cataphiles in restricted areas. This was the most detailed they had."

Daniel scanned the map. "There's hundreds of tunnels."

"Hundreds of miles of tunnels," she corrected. "Hopefully, we can get to one of the more remote exits before they find us."

There was a commotion. Screams, shouts, the pounding of feet. No gunshots, but I had no illusions, there would be guns.

It happened so quickly, I didn't have time to think. Foolishly, the first three to reach the intersection came at us without waiting for backup. I guess they figured they'd catch us off guard, which they did, but centuries of battle experience is tough to overcome.

Without thinking, Renika collared the first man and rammed him into a column of bones.

I snatched a DSLR camera with a heavy zoom from a tourist taking a photo and smashed one of the attackers in the face, then I wrapped the camera strap around the last one's throat and choked him until his legs stopped kicking.

The tourists scrambled to get as far away as they could.

Daniel stared at the bodies. "There really is no end to your ability to make even the most innocuous items into a weapon, is there?"

"Is he...dead?" The man I had hit with the camera was at Phoebe's feet.

Blood spread onto the dirt, looking dark like heavy crude in the low light. It oozed from a gash on his scalp.

I checked his pulse. It was strong. The blood was already coagulating. "No."

Renika rushed over with a leg bone and was about to crush in the man's skull to finish the job.

"No, no, no!" I shouted, grabbing her arm, her face flushed with rage.

Renika gripped the femur tightly, squeezing the blood out of her hands, her fingers turning white. "You're getting soft, Alexander." She grabbed Daniel and spun him around, opening the backpack.

Phoebe's eyes were wide. "Yes, Alexander, I can see why you had a crush on her. Totally."

"Listen, I didn't choose to go after these people. They came after us. You and *you*," Renika jostled Daniel as she reached into the backpack. "...would be dead if it weren't for me."

Daniel turned to get a glimpse of her. "Hey, I'm not complaining about the not being dead part. I think what Phoebe's saying is, we're trying to acclimate ourselves to this whole 'eye for an eye' way of thinking."

Renika growled in his ear. "It's not an eye for an eye. You cut off my finger, I cut off your arm. You take out my eye, I take off your head."

Daniel snapped a single nod. "Got it. I'm going to pretty much stay away from every one of your body parts."

"You wouldn't know what to do with them." She took out one of the green spheres and tossed it to me, then studied the map. "I was hoping to make it to here." She pointed to an intersection further ahead. "This offshoot's not as direct, but I don't think we have time."

I ran my hand over the rough iron bars, staring into the dank void, then set the device for concussion.

Phoebe came behind me. "Shouldn't we take their guns?"

Renika laughed. "You think there's enough bullets here to kill all the people coming for us? If we get caught in a shootout, we're done for."

"Fight or flight. This is a time for flight," I said.

Daniel bobbled his head eagerly. "I am very good at flighting."

Renika stepped around a corner, pressing herself into a small alcove. I ordered Phoebe and Daniel behind the thick column of skulls and bones.

"I would cover your ears."

"Cover my ears?" asked Daniel.

"Yes." I pulled the pin on the grenade and set it into the gate near the hinge, then joined them, sticking my index fingers into my ear canals.

An explosion rocked the cavern, dirt fell from the ceiling, and the wrought iron gate flew into the opposite wall.

As the dust and debris settled, Renika admired the destruction. "I *have* missed you, Alexander."

"I've missed you too, Nika."

"Good times," said Phoebe, dryly.

The man I choked stirred, the dust in the air gagging him. Renika settled him down with a kick to the face. She climbed the pile of rubble. "Clear!" She disappeared.

Phoebe followed, glowering at me.

What can I say? I've always liked strong women.

Daniel shouted over the ringing in his ears. "You used a grenade to open a door?"

"It was locked."

"I thought you were the master lock picker!?"

"You need to stop shouting," I screamed.

I heard a steady drumbeat of boots pounding dirt. The others were closing in. Shouted orders in at least three different languages, German, French, English, became more desperate. I saw shadows on the walls, saw the bottleneck of tourists fall like pins in a bowling alley. Daniel clambered over the chunks of blasted rocks. I had just enough time to grab a flashlight off the bleeding man's belt before disappearing into the dark passage.

In the jangling beam of the flashlight, I saw Renika a dozen yards ahead, dragging her fingers along the wall to guide her way.

These tunnels hadn't been dressed up for the public like the others. Debris littered the ground, chunks of limestone, abandoned chisels, wood timbres, but that wasn't the worst of it. We had to wade through a sea of bones, most of them broken, imperfect, not worthy for placement in the artistic displays. Daniel didn't say a word, didn't voice a complaint. Neither did Phoebe. But there's no getting around it, trampling over the bones of others to save your own skin is an irony you can't ignore. As the femurs and tibias and clavicles, scapulae, ulnas, and ribs thinned out, we were able to move more quickly.

Paris rests upon a layer of Swiss cheese. Imagine the buildings, the cathedrals, palaces, seats of government, homes, offices, monuments, and realize that everything built in stone above came from below. Portions of the city, especially here on the Left Bank, were precariously perched atop cavernous voids held up by the occasional pillar of rock.

I oscillated the flashlight. Still, it was difficult to see. Phoebe lost her footing. I instinctively reached for her, but in doing so, I tripped, my face scraping hard against the dirt. The flashlight flew out of my hand and smashed into the rock wall. The LEDs flickered, then winked out.

We were in complete darkness.

"Are you okay?"

"I'm fine," I said. "You?"

"I have rubber-band tendons."

I gave an unseen nod as we got moving again.

It's hard to comprehend true darkness. If you've spent time in the woods on a moonless night, you have some idea. But even then, the stars give you perspective, up and down, left and right. Here, in the blackness, I felt my body swaying as I stood. So much of our balance is tied to our vision. When there is nothing to see, our other senses become overly acute. They betray us. Our equilibrium overcorrects.

Our ears, our feet, the tips of our fingers became our eyes.

Flashes appeared in the corner of my vision, phantoms of light that weren't really there. When the lights came for real, would I know the difference?

Without warning, a sharp pain shot through my body. I must have cried out.

"What is it?" Renika asked.

"Nothing." My voice was tight as I pressed the duct tape covering my wound.

Renika sighed. Even when we used to play in the dungeons and drained moats of Louvre Castle, she always thought of me as the weak one. I wondered if she still thought of me that way. I was never weak. Sure, I wasn't as strong as her when I was only eight hundred, but I wasn't that little boy anymore.

I'd need to get this wound cleaned and checked soon.

More immediately, the issue was that one direct punch might put me down. Being incapacitated for even a few seconds could prove deadly.

I saw faint flickers of light again. This time they were not hallucinations. Someone was blundering their way toward us.

The passage forked numerous times. Daniel whispered "left" or "right" to himself each change of direction. The flashes faded. For the moment, we seemed to be outrunning the teams chasing us. Our extreme response at Renika's and blowing the iron gate with an explosive would make them cautious. They'd be methodical, sweeping an area before advancing. To keep us from backtracking or outflanking them, they'd have to divide their forces at each branch. The police patrolling the catacombs utilized TTE, but I doubted even well-equipped contractors would be carrying the kind of ultra-low frequency radios used in mines. That evened the odds a bit. They wouldn't be able to call for backup or radio their positions. The more we split them up, the better our chances to find an unguarded exit.

Renika stopped, and we stumbled into her. I saw the intensity in her gaze. She was striking even in this—

Light.

There was light up ahead. Not the glimmer of candles, or the flickering of a jostled flashlight, but a steady glow. I crept forward, Renika off my shoulder. The passageway narrowed until it was so tight, we had to squirm through like worms.

Peering through the small opening, I saw a line of tiny bulbs strung up on the wall, the electricity powering them pirated from a utility cable somewhere. The tiny lights burned like the sun after ten minutes in pure darkness. What I could see of the room was empty. I listened but heard nothing. I emerged into the chamber, the others squeezing through after me.

The light strings appeared hastily put up and easy to take down. Part of the game of cat and mouse between the cataphiles who explored the tunnels and the police charged with keeping them out.

A half-dozen skulls sat on ledges carved in the rock. There were tables and chairs cut from stone. Beer cans, liquor bottles, half-melted candles, and spent cigarettes were sprinkled about.

"What is this place?" asked Phoebe.

A mural of ocean surf, an interpretation of Hokusai's "Great Wave off Kanagawa," wrapped around three walls and extended to the dirt floor.

"La Plage," I said. "The Beach."

"There are spaces like this all over the catacombs," said Renika. "It's totally illegal, but people still come down to roam around, chill out, put on raves. Friday and Saturday, this place becomes a party."

Daniel shook his head. "Sad that a creepy, oxygen-deprived cave has better nightlife than Great Barrington."

Phoebe stared at Daniel. "Yes, you are so the 'raving' type." She twirled her finger around her ear.

There was the sound of footsteps in the distance.

"Well, this was fun," said Daniel, glancing at the art dotting the walls.

"We should go." Renika pointed toward the black void at the far end of the room.

None of us wanted to leave the safety of the light. I led the way, the illumination slowly receding. Then without warning, we were plunged into darkness.

I heard the rustling of something being shoved into the backpack.

"What are you doing?" complained Daniel.

"I stole the lights," Renika said. "I figured they might be good for something. Tripwire, garrote."

Daniel faked a laugh. "You are *never* coming over to my house for the holidays."

"I'm fairly certain there is zero divided by zero chance of that happening," said Phoebe.

As we pressed on, the ceiling dipped, the walls became lumpy and uneven. At times, we had to crawl on our knees.

There is no adjusting to a complete lack of light. It never gets better. The challenge is ignoring what you think you feel. What you think you hear. I waved away thousands of spiderwebs that may or may not have been there. I heard creatures scurrying in the dark. Rats. Or maybe bats. Or maybe my imagination.

The brain doesn't care what's real. It reacts to what it *thinks* is real.

Renika took the lead. I brought up the rear. We didn't speak for a long time.

The ones searching for us tried to travel in silence, too, but the sheer number of them made it impossible. A low rumble pervaded the tunnels. Stomping boots, murmuring voices, the clang of weapons. The volume should've been decreasing as they split off at each fork, but the level remained constant.

At least, I heard no noise coming from ahead of us.

That was, until Daniel let out an agonized yelp. A second later, I made the same sound when my head hit a loop of metal.

Both of us were spinning, swearing, crashing into each other.

My hand found the culprit, a huge eye bolt larger than my palm. Then I heard a clamor as Daniel fell. I tripped on the edge of something but managed to somehow keep my balance.

Fumbling in the dirt, I found a fissure four feet across. I whispered Daniel's name. No answer. I extended my arm as far as I could, searching for him, my hand getting nothing but cooler air. Stretching farther, I finally felt rubber soles. He was on his side, about seven feet down.

The majority of the carrières were located on a single level roughly six stories beneath the surface, but a few stacked chambers existed where the limestone layer was deepest. The eye bolt could be the remnant of a pulley system to raise stone from below. Without light, I couldn't tell if this was a ditch or a shaft to another cavern blocked by infill.

I blindly checked his head for blood. A deep creak resonated as I tried to move him. The sound was hollow. I grew panicked, and I grabbed at his waistband as the wood under him groaned. My shoes bit into the rock. Crumbling limestone fell on Daniel. He spit and swore. A good sign. He was awake.

I couldn't lift him without getting into the hole and I didn't think whatever debris was blocking the shaft could hold our combined weight.

It took Renika and Phoebe more than a minute to find their way back to us in the pitch black.

"Daniel fell into a shaft."

There was a loud CRACK! and the debris beneath Daniel fell away. I instantly felt the full weight of him. He threw out his arms and legs, catching the wall, relieving some of the load. My grip held, but I couldn't last long in this awkward position.

"Help me," I said in a strained whisper. "I can't hold him."

Phoebe grabbed onto me.

Renika dropped to the ground. "If it comes to it, you drop him," she said to me in a low voice.

She reached for Daniel, and from the assorted wails, whimpers, and groans, caught him in the balls before finally getting hold of his waist.

After pulling him out of the hole, the four of us collapsed, panting in the dark. Phoebe pressed against me, and for a brief moment, we both found comfort.

I had been forced by my father to remain in the purgatory that is high school well beyond its ability to teach me. I could have skipped out, endured his wrath, and I had done that, here and there, but what kept me in those hard, unforgiving, one-size-fits-all seats were the Daniels, the Phoebes, even the Craig Coulters. There is always the smart, intelligent, popular girl. The funny, slightly caustic wingman. The ancient teacher. And the asshole jock. There are the class clowns, the ditzy sweet kids, the awkward, the shy, the kid with the pimples. Always. Everywhere. It doesn't mean any of us are less special. It just means we aren't alone.

"We aren't alone," Renika said. "They're closing. A dozen at least."

I listened. A dozen seemed like a lot. "How many people are after us if they can keep that many on any one path?"

Renika slid toward the hole. "If we draw them in, this could be an opportunity."

"Yeah, an opportunity to die." As long as Daniel was bitching, he was fine.

"They have lights. We need lights."

"And they have guns," Daniel said.

"I told you, we don't need guns."

I knew Daniel was probably shaking his head. "That's not what he means," I said.

"I know what he means, Alexander. What I don't know is are you ready to fight?"

"You know I am."

"Good. Because I wasn't so sure. You don't bring a knife to a gunfight."

"I thought you just said we didn't need guns."

"She's saying I shouldn't have brought you two. You're the knives in this scenario."

Renika reached for my hand. Not tenderly. Not like Phoebe had. It was then we all realized Phoebe and I were holding hands. "I need to borrow your boyfriend for a moment," she said.

"He's not my—" Phoebe released my hand without finishing the sentence.

Renika snatched my wrist. She spelled large capital letters into my palm like we'd done as children sneaking around the castle at night to avoid alerting the guards. I concentrated, hoping I could make out her furiously delivered message. I didn't get every letter, but I got enough to get every word.

We couldn't risk talking. I communicated with Phoebe and Daniel via gentle tugs and nudges as we braced ourselves against the steep, pitted walls at various depths.

The footsteps stopped. An eerie quiet spread as the voices became wispy slivers of sound. A slip of a toehold, a deep breath could reveal our location.

I watched through a crack between stones rimming the lip of the shaft as the lights grew brighter. A woman paused at the doorway. She was slight. Her rolled up sleeves revealed sinewy arms. She scanned the room with her flashlight.

A man with an assault rifle stepped past the woman. The red dot from a laser sight traveled the uneven walls.

A second pass of the woman's flashlight and the beam slashed the wall over my head.

The last thing Renika traced on my palm was, *L-I-G-H-T*.

A third figure appeared in the door holding a device at waist level. He surveyed the floor in front of him in a sweeping motion, then he raised the device, checking the wall. I heard a jumble of pops and clicks. I understood now why there were so many footsteps. It wasn't an abundance of manpower.

They weren't splitting up.

They knew exactly the path we'd taken.

Renika and Phoebe had gone further before doubling back. The radiation sloughing off us continued at least into the next chamber. The trail they were tracking would soon end, but they'd have to pass us before they figured that out.

More stomping as others arrived.

We were vastly outnumbered.

I pressed my forehead against the rock. I wanted to sigh to let out the tension, release it from my body. I swear, half of fighting is breathing. I had to make do with shallow sips of air.

Their numerical advantage was mitigated slightly. This wasn't open ground or an urban grid. They couldn't fan out and surround our position. The narrow doorway was a choke point. It limited how swiftly they could attack the room.

A clump of dirt fell from above, disturbed by the vibrations of their movements.

"Not all of this is charted. I think we're somewhere past here." The woman spoke English with a Down Under accent.

"They were here," said the man with the device.

"Take some of the boys forward." She made a crisp, sharp gesture toward a passage I hadn't seen in the darkness. "That path might box up with this one." The man with the laser sight stepped out. In a lower voice, she spoke to the man with the radiation detector. "What do you see?"

"Looks like they rested here or were unsure of where to go next, but then moved on. That way." He pointed toward the back of the room.

Renika took my hand again. I waited for her message. It came all at once, not traced in letters, but packaged neatly in a round object.

I gripped the grenade, and with the index finger of the same hand, slipped out the pin. The metal ring felt cool against my knuckle. I waited, my other arm trembling with growing fatigue.

"Let's move three by three, five meters apart," ordered the woman. Light swept the room again. "Look out for booby traps. Wires, newly dug dirt. They had one IED, they could have others."

She let a man with a rifle-mounted flashlight take the lead. The man with the detector went next.

I let her pass before I rolled the grenade toward the door. After a few seconds, the next trio of jackboots entered. Six in the box. I'd take those odds. They stepped right over the grenade. I braced myself, my head down, a hand covering one ear, the other pressed into my shoulder. Two, one. The blast lit up the darkness, and for an instant like a flash photo, the image of Renika, Phoebe, and Daniel, limbs outstretched, faces up, was burned into my vision. In that illuminated instant, I saw the shaft was broader and deeper than I expected. Daniel had to be twenty feet below me, the opening at the bottom another ten feet.

The air was choked with dust. There was muffled shouting. Bullets strafed the wall. Dirt and pebbles showered down on me. I couldn't protect my face without falling. My ears rang.

More shouting came as the woman screamed for the idiot blasting away to hold his fire. But the bullets continued until the weapon clicked empty.

I raised myself to the edge, daring to take a look even if it meant revealing myself. The idiot stood there, a stupid look on his face. Ricocheting bullets had hit one of his own men. Correction. Two were hit, counting himself. He fell to his knees, then pitched forward, hitting the ground face first. The concussion of the blast had left the woman and the three men dazed, stumbling, hands to their ears.

The room brightened as the aerosolized dirt settled. The doorway was plugged with fallen rock. Faint streams of frantic light cleared the top of the rubble. The space was too small for anyone to fit through. Calls from the other side went unanswered.

The blast had fogged my brain as well. It took me a moment to realize most of the light in the room was emanating from a source inches in front of me. Before I could boost myself higher and snatch the woman's flashlight, she scooped it up as she desperately tried to clear the dirt and debris from her eyes.

We were a foot away from each other. She never saw me.

Then…Renika purposely made a noise. The woman whipped around, aiming the beam toward the sound. I lashed out and grabbed the woman's feet, pulling her into the shaft. The flashlight came down with her, spiraling out of her hand, hitting Daniel on the shoulder. He caught it.

The woman fought and clawed and clutched at the walls, losing the battle and disappearing into the abyss. I didn't witness her hitting bottom. I had other things to worry about.

Renika charged out of the hole, racing toward the staggering figures. I sprung up behind her. She slammed into the men, bowling them over like tenpins. She reached her arms back. I took them, giving her the leverage to kick the first man high in the jaw with both feet. As she landed, I flipped over her, ramming my heels into the sternum of a second man as he tried to stand. I heard a crack. I came down on the third man and finished him.

Hand to hand combat doesn't rage on in real life. It's over too quickly to build dramatic tension. You win or you lose. And a lot of times you fracture your hands.

I howled in pain. The sound echoed down the shaft. My hands were torn up. The wound in my side stabbed me. Short of consuming copious amounts of morphine that would render me incapable of movement, I wondered if, perhaps, a shovel to the side of the face might help. At the moment, I'd gladly make that trade.

I came out of my fog long enough to hear Phoebe and Daniel, their cries for help. I rushed to the edge and immediately saw the struggle taking place. The woman had not plunged to the bottom. She had grabbed Phoebe's ankle on the way down and was now hanging on as she desperately attempted to gain a foothold. Daniel shined the light up, the glare making it difficult for me to see, but the terror on Phoebe's face was clear. I grabbed her hand just as she lost her grip on the wall. I was nearly dragged over the edge but jammed my knee into the stones at the lip.

"Kick her," I said. Phoebe hesitated. "Kick herrrrrr!"

It's one thing to act out of instinct. It's another to be ordered to do harm, then make the decision to inflict injury. We all think it's so easy. We read about our heroes in action, watch them on the screen defending themselves, punching, kicking, fighting, killing.

Of *course*, we'd do the same.

Don't kid yourself.

It isn't easy. It's not effortless, not painless, not simple, not without doubt or regret or guilt. If it is, there's something wrong with you.

Listen, what's coming is going to challenge the good. It's going to test us. Each in different ways and to varying degrees. But we cannot let the ones who kill easily, who rape and pillage, who inflict pain without remorse, who do not empathize, be the *only* ones to survive.

So, prepare for what's coming. But don't for a second think it'll be easy. Be grateful it isn't.

I struggled to hold on. Phoebe could feel my grip slipping even as I squeezed my fingers tighter. She stared into my eyes.

And I was surprised at what I saw.

Rage. Not fear. Rage. She was pissed off. At *me*. Because I had put her here, in this place, in this situation. She glanced at my hands holding hers as if the very act of my rescuing her was an offense, a violation. And then it happened. The decision. To become the master of her own destiny. To own her actions. She kept her eyes on me, but the anger shifted to determination. And I knew she was going to do it, kick the woman on the bridge of the nose and send her careening to the bottom.

"Let go," she calmly said to the woman. "Let go, or I will." Phoebe wrestled one hand free from my grip to prove her point.

"No!" I shouted.

"I'll do it. And when I do, I'll land on you," she said, glaring down at the woman.

There was a long moment. It lasted a decade.

A guttural scream echoed from below, and I was thrown back as the woman released Phoebe's ankle. I had been pulling so hard, I launched Phoebe out of the hollow. The woman's yelling continued longer than it should have. In fact, it grew louder, more fierce.

I scrambled back to the edge. Daniel hadn't been directly beneath Phoebe, so the woman missed him. I expected to see her at the bottom, a crumpled mass, but inextricably, amazingly, she had saved herself a second time. Her hands were bloody, and her face was contorted in a mix of pain and determination. She had halted her descent a few feet above the end of the shaft. Her strength and small frame had made arresting the fall possible, but now her torn up fingers and battered limbs were losing their grip.

Daniel's arms were failing as well. We had to do something to help him. He was too far down for me to reach. Just then, the room got noticeably brighter as debris was pulled away from the pile. The doorway was being cleared. One of three men we incapacitated was coming to.

Phoebe stared down at the crushed scanning device. It hadn't survived the blast. "They followed us right here."

"The radiation," I said.

"It's probably on everything we touch," said Renika.

More light. This time it came from the passage at the rear of the room.

"The passages must connect." Renika cursed, then jumped into the shaft. "C'moooooooonnnnnnnn." The pitch of her call to action dropped as she did.

Phoebe was just catching her breath. "She's not serious."

"Oh, yes she is."

"She just dove into a—"

"She did." I pulled gloves off two of the men. They fit me okay but looked like tennis rackets on Phoebe. "Curl your fingers so they don't slip off. Don't press against the wall, claw at it."

I jumped, disappearing into the dark. I didn't want to leave Phoebe behind, but if I waited for her to go first, she might hesitate. As my hands dragged on the limestone, I glanced up to see her silhouette dropping into the abyss.

The descent was pretty much as exhilarating and as terrifying as it sounds. The vertical drop was more than fifty feet. The gloves helped, but only so much. My knees took a beating, so did my toes. I could feel the friction burning through the soles of my shoes. My *fingernails* hurt. And worst of all, the width of the shaft increased toward the bottom to the point that my legs and arms were close to splitting me apart. Add strained groin to my bullet wound. Renika was kind enough to step out of the way so I could land directly on the hard-packed ground unimpeded. I waited for Phoebe to exit the chute, hoping to catch her or cushion the impact, but she didn't appear for several long seconds. She finally emerged, walking herself horizontally down the last few meters, her hands and feet outstretched. She paused, then did a backflip from the ceiling—not a perfect one, mind you, more of an I'm-falling-with-style maneuver—and stuck the landing.

Daniel slid out, landing ass-first a second later. He labored to his feet rubbing his bruised tailbone. "Show off," he said to Phoebe.

At some point, while we were distracted up top, the woman's grip had failed, and she had tumbled to the ground. She was propped against the wall and had already fashioned a splint from a cracked plank. Yellowish brown streaks ran down her face where sweat and tears had attracted granulated limestone.

Renika stripped the woman of her gloves. Put them on. Then removed her military pack, weapon, and utility belt.

"You won't get away," the woman laughed.

"No one asked for your opinion," Renika said as she gagged the woman with the belt strap, then handcuffed her wrists with a set of restraints pulled from the woman's kit. Renika bound her ankles with fabric cut from her uniform. "They're going to be on us quickly," Renika said, rummaging through the pack. She set a heavy black flashlight on its end, the beam illuminating the ceiling, pocketed a multi-tool, then handed a small utility light to Phoebe. She dumped the rest of the contents on the ground and rolled the bag into itself.

Phoebe shined the light at the shaft. "Can we throw a grenade up there? Would that do anything?"

"Rain down the earth upon us." Daniel stared at her. "Seriously, what is it with you people? Now, Phoebe, you want to blow us up, too? Hey, I know what we can do when we get out of here, let's go jogging in a minefield."

"*That*, Daniel, is a very good idea," I said.

"No. No. No, it's not."

I instructed the others to gather the largest pieces of wood. Several planks were nearly intact. Voices filtered down the shaft as they worked to clear the doorway. I found stones to use as fulcrums, then dug two shallow holes and placed a grenade in each. I rested the wood so that the levers were held in place by the weight of the boards. Once the others were a safe distance, I eased my hand under the planks and pulled the pins.

The woman glared at me as I spun the pins on my finger.

Without a good deal of planning, it would be impossible to exit the shaft without landing on some part of this mosaic. One false step and the planks would rise, releasing the striker levers, setting off the grenades a few seconds later. Not a half-bad makeshift minefield.

I got to my feet, keeping my movements to a minimum. I removed the gag from the woman's mouth and freed one of her wrists. "I'm giving you a chance to save yourself. I'd be screaming for them to stay away from here. And just in case you were thinking maybe you could crawl to safety and they could drop something from above to set this off." I slid the freed cuff through an eye bolt identical to the one a level above, then reclicked the cuff on her wrist. "That would be a terrible idea."

I was about to chase after the others, but stopped, seeing the tattoo on her wrist. It was identical to Mrs. Dunn's and Mrs. Avery's except that it had a dot in the middle of one triangle. My eyes met hers. There was something in her gaze. Something familiar. I ran my hand inside the woman's vest. She jerked away, furious, thinking I was taking advantage of her. I found her ID in her left pocket. It had the A.i. logo on it.

Arcadem International. Virginia. London. Dubai.

Beams of light shone down from above as her comrades considered the shaft and what to do. I held the ID in front of her face.

"Now I know who you are, Alana Gray. Remember that."

I slipped the badge in my pocket. And turned to leave.

"You don't know anything about me," she paused for a beat, "Alexander of Constantinople."

I stopped. Surprised. Her face was barely visible in the dim glow. I saw a smile. Which quickly turned as stones trickled onto the planks from above.

I glanced up at the dusty beams of light. "If you're smart, I'm sure we will meet again."

Without another word, I charged into the dark after my friends.

Navigating a creepy pitch black tunnel is no fun. Doing it alone is much worse.

A moment later, I heard Alana Gray call out the danger to her team.

Renika, Phoebe, and Daniel were standing at the edge of a submerged passage. Our lights glimmered off the water, flashing streaks on the limestone. The ceiling arched down until it touched the surface about a hundred feet away.

Renika grabbed the backpack from Daniel. "Looks like it slopes down gradually."

"But does it come back up?" wondered Daniel.

"Let's see." She took a step and immediately dropped until the water was at her shoulders. "Okay, not gradual." Two more steps and her head disappeared below the surface.

I took the utility light from Phoebe and scanned the water. Bubbles appeared. Then nothing. Then Renika's light faded beneath the surface. Twenty seconds. Twenty-five. I ripped off my shoes preparing to dive in just as Renika popped out of the water, looking refreshed, smiling.

"It's about fifteen feet at the deepest," she said brightly, treading water. "It flattens out right about there." She shined her flashlight on the spot where it looked like the ceiling dipped into the water.

Phoebe stared into the dark pool, an oily sheen covered the surface. "I don't think I can do it."

"I'm not going to lie to you," Renika said, pulling off her top.

"This water tastes…unpleasant. But it should wash away whatever's on us." She reached down, pulling off her pants. "We've been leaving a trail."

"Of radioactive breadcrumbs," said Daniel.

I jumped in. Daniel followed doing a cannonball a second later. What you couldn't see until you got in the water was that the ceiling never touched the surface. There was about six inches of clearance that ran for twenty feet and then angled up.

I swam out until I could touch the ceiling with my hand.

"Your turn," I said to Phoebe, aiming the light at the limestone above, bathing the submerged corridor in a greenish-yellow glow.

She stood at the edge, her arms tight against her body. "I can't."

"It's not that bad. Honest."

Daniel surfaced spitting and hacking like a five-year-old that had just eaten Brussel sprouts topped with caviar. "This is disgusting!" He struggled with his shirt, which got caught halfway over his head, the wet fabric making it difficult. He lurched, smacked his head into the ceiling, wrestled at his clothes some more, and began sinking.

Renika swam over, rescued him from going under, and helped him remove his clothes in the water.

"Thanks," he said. "You know, if the surroundings were a little nicer, I might be enjoying this more."

She floated the backpack at him. "Seems like you're enjoying it now."

Daniel was beyond embarrassment at this point.

This distracted Phoebe for a moment. "I wouldn't feel too flattered."

"He's not my type," Renika said.

"Oh yeah, what is your type?" he asked.

"Much older."

I'm sure Daniel figured she was talking about me since she was staring right at me, but all I could think about was her and my father.

Renika dove under and a moment later resurfaced well beyond where the ceiling angled up again. She waded toward the other shore, rising gradually out of the water, a silhouette in the dim light.

From my vantage point, I could see Renika *and* Phoebe, but it was impossible for them to see each other. Renika removed her bra, tossing it into the water. It floated on the surface like flotsam from a pool party gone horribly wrong or terribly right. She checked the waterproof seal on the flashlight and set it down, then ran her hands through her hair, wringing it dry, her naked body sending droplets of water onto the packed dirt.

Our presence had stirred up a nest of Norway rats. Dozens of gray-brown creatures scurried along a decorative ridge that jutted out a few inches from the wall. As the ledge dipped below the surface, the rats baled into the water furiously churning their little legs until they could scratch and claw themselves to where the ridge reemerged. My clothes were weighing me down, but I had no desire to take them off while the rats swam around me.

"Phoebe, we're not leaving without you," I said.

"We are if she doesn't get moving," Renika shouted.

I made eye contact with Phoebe. "We are *not*. I'm going to stay in this water until you jump in."

"I can't."

"We have to move," said Renika. "What is the problem!?"

"What *is* the problem?" I asked.

"She almost drowned when we were six. In a pond behind her grandmother's house," Daniel said.

"Is that true?"

"Yes."

"We've been at a half-dozen pool parties together. I never saw one hint of fear in you."

"Because the water was clear," she said. "I got stuck in the mud and couldn't get free. Couldn't see. My brother dove in and grabbed me. I almost pulled us both down."

"How do you know this," I asked Daniel

324 | EDWARD SAVIO

"I told you. We used to be friends." He dove under the ceiling.

I tried to come up with words that might help her. But all I could think of was something Yang Lu-ch'an would say to me over and over again.

"In the struggle between the stone and water, *kōhai*, in time, the water wins."

I reeeeally disliked Lu-ch'an.

"Phoebe, there are only two ways to deal with fear. Avoid it. Or face it. You don't have the option to avoid it right now."

She stared into the black liquid. But did not move toward it.

Daniel emerged on the other side, his bare white skin iridescent in the dim light. "C'mon, Phoebe! I just swam through disgusting, rat-infested water. Me! Do you really want to be the only one who can't do this?"

I glared at him. Before I could offer more positive encouragement to Phoebe, she dove in.

She broke the surface, gasping for air. I wrapped her in a scissor hold with my legs. The rats were pouring out in waves. Dozens and dozens. They spilled into the water. With the ledges unable to hold the hordes, they scurried toward us. They crawled over us, over each other. I felt no bites, no stabbing pains, just hundreds of tiny paws trying to find purchase on my body. Phoebe was screaming. I tried to backstroke, but the added weight was pushing us under. Phoebe choked on water. It was the only thing squelching her screams.

I felt a hand at my collar, dragging me, and another hand sweeping away the living mass swarming my chest.

Being rescued shuts down the survival override, the switch in the brain that allows you to walk over dead bodies, run through fire, eat putrid, rotting flesh without hesitation, without getting sick. Once the do-or-die veil was pierced, I wanted to vomit as tiny feet continued to crawl over my skin. Somehow, I managed to keep down the bile.

My foot briefly touched bottom and I scrambled until something solid was under me. As we stood, the remaining rats bailed off of us and broke for dry land. But more were coming. Waves and waves of wriggling, writhing bodies. A slender, pretty arm passed over me. I watched the grenade hanging in the air before disappearing into the black water. A few seconds later, the surface jumped half a foot for just an instant, then a ball of fire erupted. Clouds of dust and pebbles fell as part of the ceiling collapsed. Flaming rats twitched while others turned from the heat and headed back toward their nest.

Phoebe coughed water out of her lungs.

I stepped out, the air heavy with the stench of burnt hair and smoldering flesh. I struggled to unbutton my jeans, my fingers shaking.

"It's easier if you do that in the water," said Renika.

Bubbles boiled up, roiling the dying rats on the surface. It had the look of a witch's cauldron.

I waded back in and quickly removed my clothes, remembering just before letting go of my pants to take Alana Gray's ID card.

In the shallows, we used the pulverized limestone to scrub our bodies clean while avoiding the occasional drifting rat.

Phoebe emerged naked. I unconsciously averted my eyes. In doing so, I ended up staring at Daniel's neon nudity. An unhappy alternative.

As I stood, Phoebe rushed over and embraced me. She was shaking. From the cold and the fear. "I'm freezing," she said, squeezing me tight, her head buried in my chest, her shivering body vibrating against mine. When her teeth stopped chattering, she glanced up. It took forever for her to speak. "Not the way I expected to be naked with you."

I swallowed hard. As much as she was shivering, her skin felt hot.

Daniel gazed at Renika, his arms outstretched. "You must be freezing, too."

"Don't even think about it." Renika tossed the sopping wet military pack at Daniel, hitting him in the chest.

"You sure? Not many chances like this in life."

Her dismissive glare elicited a shrug from him. This from the guy who couldn't get up the nerve to ask anyone to Homecoming. Either everything we'd overcome had given Daniel a new sense of confidence, or he was so sure he was going to die in the next few hours that it didn't really matter. Might as well go for it.

"Perv," Phoebe whispered.

"He's just jealous."

She let out a satisfied snort into my chest. When her fingers found the tape covering my wound, she glanced up at me.

"I'm fine. Just a scratch."

My hand ran down Phoebe's wet hair. Her curves fit into mine. A rare moment of peace. The sensation traveled down my body, deep into me. And it reawakened in me a feeling I had put away. The need to be part of something more than a passing fling. She held me close, biting her lip and chuckling just a bit as she felt me against her.

As Daniel transferred the contents of the backpack to the clean military pack we'd taken off Alana Grey, a grenade got away from him and came to rest at our feet.

"Ahhhh," Phoebe howled at him.

"My bad," he said.

I booted it, sending it rolling back toward its siblings.

Renika was studying the map that had remained remarkably dry in the backpack. "We've got to get back to the main level. They dug a second tier in very few places. We'll hit a dead end a lot faster down here."

Not more than sixty feet away life was going on as it always did. Men and women pouring out from offices, smiling, grumbling, laughing, spilling in all directions, into restaurants, into cafés, into bars, into homes. Sixty feet. A fraction of a block. Two-thirds of a run to first base. But when that distance is vertical rather than horizontal, it's the difference between going two doors down the street or descending into this dark alien landscape.

The only items we put back on were our shoes. And only after rinsing and scrubbing them thoroughly.

"There was a woman in Boston," I said.

"Someone else you told?"

"No. Like us. Late twenties looking. Seems older somehow. About this tall. She tried to recruit me. Coax me into joining with her and Elam Khai."

"Eleni," Renika said.

"She called herself Elle."

"You call yourself Alexander *Grant*," she said, her shoes squishing with every step as we marched away from the submerged passage. "Don't let her soothing personality fool you. She's led armies. And her warriors will lay down their lives for her. Gráinne O'Malley. Anne Bonny. Eleanor of Aquitaine. Those are the identities I know."

"Eleanor of Aquitaine." I squeezed my forehead. "I didn't get that one. Every king and pretender in Europe wanted to marry her."

Renika laughed. "*Yeah*, she controlled a quarter of France. And unlike most brides that came with gigantic parcels of land, she was beautiful."

"She's still hot," Daniel said.

"She would lash you to a mast."

"Thanks, I've already been lashed to something this week."

Unlike the rest of the catacombs, there were no signs of life in this passage. No graffiti, no trash, no empty liquor bottles, no piles of crushed soda cans, no pools of wax from spent candles. There were no offshoots. No stairs, ladders, or crawlspaces. We had to squeeze by a square pillar of concrete that blocked most of the passage and seemed to plug a shaft to the main level.

"So, who did she end up marrying?" asked Phoebe.

"Basically all of them."

I shook my head. "Not *all* of them."

"She was married to the king of France for fifteen years. Had that annulled, then married the king of England. Gave him three sons.

All who became king. All were fearless warriors, especially Richard The Lionhearted."

Which made sense considering what Elle had told me. "According to her, all her children have been fathered by Elam Khai."

Daniel grew agitated. "So, you're saying, these two are making *super* babies? Their own people-who-live-forever factory?"

"Having two Eternal parents makes it more likely. But it's still at best one out of four or five." Renika was calculating something. "Good news is…I figure the earliest she could have had a child like us, they'd probably be a few hundred years younger than you."

"Oh, that is good news," said Daniel. "Megalomaniac middle schoolers running around unsupervised. What could possibly go wrong there?"

"She said I was the only one of my generation in my family."

"And you believe her?"

I glanced at Renika. "I don't know."

The passage opened up, and with this change, came the first signs of life: A metal table and two steel chairs.

On the wall, a rusted electrical box sat open. Bare bulbs and empty sockets, useless without power, hung from above. Stenciled in black on the grimy and chipped gray-painted wall were the words, "Nicht Rauchen."

I tilted my head. "That's strange."

"Because it's in German?" asked Phoebe.

Renika followed the wall to the corner, shining her flashlight into the next passage. "That's not strange. Both the Nazis and the French Underground used the catacombs during the occupation."

"Wait. The French Underground in World War Two was *literally* underground?" asked Daniel.

I ignored him. "I get why it's here, but that says, 'No Smoking.'"

Renika raised an eyebrow. "The Germans didn't want a bunker full of soldiers puffing away down here. No ventilation. Fire hazard. They did it anyway."

"No, *Nicht Rauchen* is a literal translation of those red circle-and-slash 'No' signs. The Germans didn't use this phrasing in the nineteen forties. It should read *Rauchen Verboten*. 'Smoking Forbidden.'"

"I've seen both," Renika said dismissively.

"Not back *then*. Someone tried to make this wall seem older than it really is." The lack of clutter suddenly took on an ominous meaning. The hairs on the back of my neck stood up. Literally. "Something's not right."

As I moved closer to the wall, It wasn't just the hairs on the back of my neck. My clothes, the hair on my arms. It was the same sensation I'd had on stage with the Tesla coil. I grabbed Daniel, thrusting him toward the gray wall. Even two feet away, the hair on the left side of his head looked as if it was being sucked into the rock.

Everything moved in slow motion as my mind raced to solve the problem. What was creating a charge of static so strong it could be felt through stone walls?

"Alexander. You need to see this." Renika's voice echoed from around the corner.

Entering the next passage, the roughness and littered debris made their return. The tunnel emptied into a gigantic vault. It was vast, but the ceiling was relatively low overall. Three shaky-looking pillars in a delta pattern held up the expanse. Several fissures spidered along the ceiling. The most significant was a V-shaped crack across half the space that came to a point just beyond the three pillars. Water dripped from the crevices.

Renika held out the map, trying to get her bearings.

Daniel glanced over her shoulder, unaware of how close their bodies were. "I don't see that Nazi area on the map," he said, motioning to the upper part of the page.

"That's because we're over here." She circled a point in the middle marked by a tiny swastika.

"We never went that way. We're well beyond this point." He pointed toward the northern fringes of the catacombs.

Renika took note of his proximity and elbowed him a few inches away. "There aren't catacombs beyond here."

"I have a really good sense of direction," he said. "We started here in the public area. Then after blowing up *this* gate, we meandered west-ish." Daniel moved closer again. This time she didn't react. His finger serpentined through passages and rooms. "This is about where we hit that Beach thing." He accurately tapped the area making up La Plage, even though it was marked "La Vague" on the page. "We've been heading north-northwest ever since."

"I've been down here dozens of times, and I'm not sure where we are," she said.

Daniel looked at her. "I'm sure."

Last fall, me and Daniel and a group of friends visited some corn mazes where people pay money to get lost in the twists and turns carved into vast fields. This is what you do in a place like Great Barrington. Watch leaves. Trek through corn. Most people end up cutting through the thick rows to find their way out. Not Daniel. He never got lost. Always knew where we were. Could retrace and backtrack any misstep no matter how complicated the pattern.

"I've seen him do this before," I said.

"After all this mess, we hit another straight passage that put us at the shaft." He slid his index finger up to the northern end of the Southern carrières. "We went down a level, then continued moving *north*." He stabbed his finger, indicating a spot beyond the Seine at an outline that had the general shape of the room in which we stood. No tunnels connected where we had started to where he was pointing.

"That's west of the Louvre. By the Tuileries," I said.

Renika shook her head. "The catacombs don't go under the river."

"Maybe they *didn't*," I said. "But that Nazi bunker is a fake. And the passage from the submerged area to here doesn't look the same age as this chamber."

"I know I'm right about this," Daniel said as we moved deeper into the cavern. "Just like I know there's something hidden in the file Maaaarcus gave Renika," he said, imitating the way she spoke my father's name. "My mother forces me to give her the password to my computer. You can hide a ZIP file inside a JPEG. It's preschool level hacking, but it's how I keep certain files private."

"How you hide your porn, you mean?" said Phoebe.

"And *other* things," he said. "The image your dad sent is fairly high-res, but as a JPEG, the file size shouldn't be anywhere near as large as it is. There's something else in there. Then there's the date issue. The file's five weeks old when you've had this for ten years. It must have gotten updated when we opened it."

He started to remove the backpack to get at the laptop.

Renika stopped him. "You can look at it later. Right now, we need to find a way out of here."

We walked the perimeter of the cavern. There were no exits other than the way we came. Remnants of a World War II-era staircase dangled from the highest part of the ceiling, giving the impression of a drill bit boring through the rock. Beyond being out of reach, dirt and debris packed the stairwell core. At one time, it probably led to other paths out of here.

At the other end was a passage that had never been completed or had been closed off. It was little more than an alcove.

I placed my hand on the chamber wall around the bend from the Nazi bunker. I could feel the charge through the rock.

"Whatever's on the other side is functioning. If we could get in there, maybe there's a way to the surface."

But we found no doors. No access.

The A.i. team would clear my jerry-rigged minefield soon. Then it was a straight path to us. They'd be slowed a bit by the collapsed ceiling.

Ten minutes. Maybe, fifteen. That's all we had.

Renika dumped the contents of the pack onto the dirt. The laptop fell out, and Daniel went to grab it. "I told you, later," she said, knocking away his hand.

We sifted through the items. We had three strings of lights, a roll of duct tape, twelve grenades, a glass resin knife, the utility tool, two flashlights, and just about all the rocks we could hurl. There was also the Babe Ruth baseball, which I was perfectly willing to throw at someone if necessary.

"There is one more item I picked up," she said, unzipping the outside compartment of the bag.

We worked in phases. Breaking the plan into small, fully operational tasks so that if we had to abandon our efforts at any point, we'd have something to work with.

"This seems like an Alamo situation. One of your pink highlights, by the way," Daniel said eluding to the American history test that seemed in the ancient past even though it was only a week ago. "I still don't know why a car rental company would want to associate themselves with everyone dying, but…whatever."

"I thought you were behind this idea. You said, 'That ceiling looks like it could come crashing down at any second.'"

"That ceiling *looks* like it could come crashing down at any second. That's not a plan, that's a warning!"

"If we really are in this area, as you say," Renika pointed to the map, "And we can get to that staircase, clear it, I'm hoping the rumbling we're hearing means we're under the roadway beneath the Place de Concorde or the Cours La Reine or the tunnel to the Louvre parking garage."

"You're basing our survival plan all on me?" Suddenly, Daniel's confidence in his directional abilities vanished.

"You were very sure of where we were five minutes ago," Phoebe said, annoyed.

"I am sure. I'm just not sure I'm *don't-wanna-be-dead* sure."

"Listen, you two can walk out that passage any time. But for me and Alexander, that isn't an option."

Phoebe sighed. "Give me the duct tape."

Daniel sighed. "Give me a grenade."

As Phoebe secured the grenade Daniel was holding against a pillar, I showed Renika Alana Gray's ID.

"She knew who I was. Called me Alexander of Constantinople."

"How does someone build an army if you don't have a country?" Renika waited only an instant before continuing. "Arcadem International is the second largest private employer in the world," she said. "Three-quarters of a million people. The only company with more workers is Walmart."

"Wait. A private army is that big?" said Daniel. "That anybody can hire?"

Phoebe removed her shoes.

"I know that Marcus controls several large PMCs," Renika said as she and Daniel lifted Phoebe onto my shoulders. "Not that one."

Her bare feet pressing against my clavicle, Phoebe was steady—more steady than I was—as Renika passed grenades up to her. You realize the awesome, terrible power of a hand grenade when you see one in the palm of the charming girl you sit behind in history class.

"Are you saying Elam Khai might control Arcadem?"

"I'm not saying anything."

Phoebe glared down at us. "Can you shut up for a moment while I'm handling the explosives?"

We shut up for a moment.

Eventually, we heard the rumble of marching boots. We doused the lights. Daniel and I continued our work in the dark, untangling the last string of lights as Phoebe put her shoes back on and got into position.

I froze as flashlights raked the room. The panning stopped when the beams found the beautiful woman standing naked in the middle of the cavern. There were whistles and catcalls.

The man at the lead quieted his team with an annoyed grunt.

He was medium build, but strong. Not Chechen. French maybe. Italian. Greek. Arab. Israeli. Hard to tell.

"If one more person steps in this room, I will blow it to pieces," Renika snapped.

All movement stopped. There was a long, awkward silence.

"There's nowhere for you to go," said the man finally, his voice echoing in the vault. His accent was nondescript American, which surprised me.

"Maybe not. But there's nowhere for you to go, either. Unless it's back the way you came. Which if you value your life, you should do immediately."

"Listen," said the man, sounding fatigued. "I've got people here who have come up with numerous scenarios where you all 'accidentally' end up dead. But me, despite the understandable inclinations of my team members, I give you my word. I won't cut you to pieces like you did our colleagues." He stared at Renika, taking her in. "Because. That. Would be a waste."

"That's the best banter you can come up with?" She needed to keep him talking so Daniel and I could finish. "Your foreplay is disappointing."

The man chuckled. He was stalling, too, I realized. Probably trying to assess the situation. I hoped the buried wiring wasn't obvious.

I could hardly see what I was doing. The tiny bulbs kept catching on the release pins. I closed my eyes and pictured slipping the wire through the metal ring. It went more smoothly doing it blind.

"I think our foreplay would be anything but disappointing," the man said.

My hands worked carefully, threading the wire through the next pin. Then the next. Done.

Renika's tone changed seconds after I tied off the third pin. She must have heard me take my first breath in over a minute.

"Every time you speak you get less interesting and less attractive," she told the man.

"Enough!" His bark caused me to jump. "Where are the others?"

"We're not playing anymore? I thought we were playing. Just the two of us." Her voice was smooth, inviting.

"I'm losing my patience."

I imagined Renika smirking.

"One's right over there." The enchanting tone in her voice

remained. She pointed a light at Daniel who looked absolutely terrified. He must have just dropped the wires because his hands were frozen as if playing an invisible piano. She clicked off the bulb.

Lights were aimed at the spot, but Daniel was gone, hidden. The beams crisscrossed the room reflecting nothing but limestone walls and the pillars. Three guesses where we were.

"That's not the one I want. My job is to bring *him* in. There's no reason the rest of you have to come if you hand him over."

"See, I'm rather fond of *him*. We go way back. Even if he can be an idiot."

The man lifted a gun. Suddenly, a dozen weapons came to attention. "I could just shoot you unless he comes out."

I bit my lip until I tasted blood to keep from shouting out a surrender.

"You could," said Renika. "But that would be unwise."

She held out her hand. In it, wavered a bowling ball-sized rock with a light string taped securely around the surface. The wire ran to the roof of the chamber, passed through the eyelet on the handle of the resin knife, then along the ceiling to a set of grenades wedged in crevices above the man.

"You shoot me. I drop this rock, which I'm barely able to hold now." She feigned feebleness that quickly receded. "Which yanks the wire and pulls the pins, which set off the grenades that blow up over your head."

Flashlights from several directions aimed toward the ceiling, finding the explosives.

"That ceiling looks like it could come crashing down at any second," she said, parroting Daniel's words.

The man's arm went up to make sure none of his people moved. And that's when I saw his wrist. He had the same tattoo as Alana Gray, as Mrs. Dunn and Mrs. Avery.

The painting of Alexander at Achilles' tomb came back to me. The characteristic that had tickled my brain was the steep angle of the pyramid marking Achilles' resting place. The same angle as these deltas coming to a point.

"Phoebe!" Renika called. "Come hold this for a moment."

Phoebe emerged from the shadows and took the rock. She stood there under the lights, under their gazes. Naked. Stoic. Unflinching.

Renika stepped closer to the man. "Take off your clothes."

He laughed. "As much as I'd love to…" He eyed her body hungrily.

"Take. Off. Your. Clothes." She extended her arm, waiting for compliance.

The man took her hand and shook it. "Kydell Black. Perhaps, we could do this over drinks."

"I'm not going to ask you again." Renika tugged gently on the man's belt, undoing it as she lowered to one knee in front of him.

He smiled, enjoying the sight of her kneeling before him. He clearly didn't understand. She reached for the wire leading to the column I was hiding behind. She got to her feet with the cord in her grasp, but it had less slack than she expected. The wire zipped out of the dirt. A wake of disturbed soil raced toward the string of explosives attached to the pillar at my back. I stepped into the open and slammed my foot on the ground, arresting the wire an instant before it snapped tight and pulled out the pins.

Kydell followed the movement with his gaze. I stood there, unprotected, my chest heaving, hoping the weight of my foot on the cord wouldn't pull the pins while I was only a few feet away. Renika took a step back, and the slack returned. I ducked behind the column.

"Any one of us can pull the pins on the grenades attached to all three pillars."

"You pull those pins, and we all die," he said.

"You're assuming we haven't engineered this demolition." She pressed her finger into his flak vest. "I think I engineered the hell out of it."

I tried to listen to the conversation but kept getting distracted. Daniel had pulled out the laptop. Into the root terminal, he typed:

```
cd Desktop
```

He hit return, then continued:

```
unzip image.jpg
```

He hit return again.

Lines of text flowed down as several operations were tasked. He went to the desktop. Three files appeared as each was decompressed.

Daniel opened the first one. Gibberish text filled the screen. He opened a photo application and dragged the gibberish file into it. An image appeared. A schematic of a sphere. I couldn't read the content at this distance. Daniel scrolled down, and a simple, flat map of the world appeared with more unreadable captions and inscriptions.

Daniel pointed frantically to the screen, mouthing something I couldn't understand.

I put my fingers to my lips.

"You want him alive," Renika said. "And despite you trying to make it seem like you were holding back your revenge-seeking team, you know that if something happens to him, you won't be around long enough to know why he's so important. And you know that if you see someone with this," she pointed inside of her left hip. The man let his gaze linger. "If that person dies, you and you and you and you and you and you and you," she pointed to the man and the half-dozen closest to him, "will pay for it with your lives. And know this. Even my enemies would be obliged to hunt you down. Even with your nice tattoo."

That's when I heard the sound. The sound of defeat. It sighed out of him. "How do you figure this plays out?"

Now Renika was the one losing patience. "There's no play here. Give me the clothes or I swear I will give you *no* warning before I set the world crashing down on you."

"Say I give you my clothes."

"And his and his and hers."

"Then what? You still have to get by us. I can't allow that. The client wants to speak with him. He's on his way here."

Elam Khai was coming.

"And you're right. Maybe we can't kill you, but I have no orders that tell me I can't hurt you."

Renika didn't flinch. If anything, her shoulders relaxed.

"Listen," he continued, his tone softer. "We're here to do a job. I don't want any more of my people getting hurt. I'm thinking you don't either. So let's make nice." He pulled off his clothes. Now both of them were standing toe to toe naked. "Isn't this nice?" he asked.

She glanced him up and down, cocking her head to one side. "Okay, you're slightly less disappointing now."

He smiled. His confidence matched hers.

"Clothes," she said.

Kydell gave an order. More clothes were tossed out of the darkness. Renika picked them up, kicking some items to the side. "We're not interested in your underwear, but thanks."

"You don't want our weapons? Our lights? The endless supply of chewing tobacco my team has stowed in their packs."

"You keep your guns. And your toys. But why doesn't everyone toss them on the ground for now. Since we're playing nice."

Phoebe's voice wavered. "I can't hold this much longer." Her arms shook violently.

That's when I stepped out of the shadows and grabbed the rock out of Phoebe's hand just as her muscles were about to fail. She fell to the dirt, kneading her arm until the feeling returned.

Renika glared at me. I was only a lunge away from Kydell.

"Ah, the guest of honor," Kydell said. Then he tapped his earpiece. "And our host has arrived as well."

Toward the back corner, I could make out joggling beams of light, crisscrossing the darkness. My stomach tightened. I was not prepared for Elam Khai. I looked at Renika. We may have missed our opportunity to separate ourselves.

The lights emerged from the passage and stopped. A dark, impressive figure continued walking toward us, the backlighting making his entrance that much more dramatic.

I blew out air in short bursts, like a woman about to give birth having contractions.

"Get back behind the column," I told Phoebe.

Watching him march closer, I replayed our first meeting in my home. The unyielding confidence. The power of his body and his will. Then came the memories of Wonderland Park. His impassioned argument that could not easily be dismissed. The empty feeling as he ripped my world apart by revealing my father's past. The image of the flaming pipe through the torso of the Scotsman. And in that moment, rather than make me weak, I grew more resolute.

"Very well done." His voice echoed in the cavern as he approached.

My heart skipped a beat as I saw his face.

‒ FOURTEEN ‒
Lights Out

I've been in the presence of kings and queens, prime ministers and presidents. Known generals and chiefs, warriors and artists, geniuses and visionaries. The famous, the infamous, the forgotten. And every time I meet one of these great women or men, it surprises me how much I am still affected by it. Not in a stammering, nervous way, but with a sense of joy and excitement and even delight.

When Elam Khai came to my house, I felt this way. And when the naked merc named Kydell stepped aside for him, I felt it again. But only for an instant.

Renika laughed. Long and hard. "Of course, it's you."

"I don't think we've had the pleasure of meeting." He put out his hand.

"I'm Bonnie. This is Clyde," she said. "You'll forgive me if I refuse your hand."

His outstretched palm wavered for a moment before slowly moving to his chest as if he was pledging allegiance. In greeting, he dipped his head. "Peter Krol."

Late forties, but looking younger than that, with a physique built in the gym by a celebrity trainer who knew he wasn't coaching an Olympian but a billionaire, Peter Krol had a piercing stare made all the more penetrating by his slightly larger than normal eyes. He had a mouth that was too small, and a nose that fit with neither of his other two features. He was at angles handsome and a little odd looking.

"I know who you are," said Renika. "You're the idiot who thinks most of our problems started when women got the right to vote."

His small mouth curled up into a small smile. "That's not exactly my position. I don't believe voting by *anyone* is helpful. Freedom and democracy cannot coexist. The mob doesn't allow true freedom." He finally took in Renika's body. There was nothing sexual in his gaze. "You look incredible for your age. What are you? A hundred? Two hundred years old?"

"That's the kind of question that gets people killed," she said.

My mind was still recovering from this man not being Elam Khai. Was Krol responsible for the men in Boston tasked with shooting down Elam Khai's jet?

"I don't understand," I said, not really meaning to say it out loud.

Renika kept watching Krol. "He's got a thing for young things."

"Don't be crass. That's not who I am."

"Right, I forgot, you just love the blood of young things. You with your eighteen-year-old boy blood circulating through your body. That doesn't sound creepy at all, keeping a cross-matched kid on the payroll, drawing blood every few days, spinning out the plasma so you can dump it into your veins. A little vampirery, don't you think?" She turned to me. "See, he doesn't believe in the inevitability of death."

"Or taxes," he said with a smirk.

"You're hilarious." Renika motioned toward the others. "Listen, I don't want to kill these fine people. But erasing you from the planet would ease my conscience about it."

"I'm trying to save humanity."

She laughed in his face. "You believe everyone should fend for themselves. Do you really think humanity survived all these thousands of years by adhering to libertarian beliefs with everyone 'doing it on their own?'"

"You can't believe everyone is created equal. Just look at you."

"Just because people aren't the same doesn't mean they aren't equal."

He squeezed his fist. "The strong, the smart, the driven should be our legacy."

"Oh, yes, oh wise one who got insanely rich being at the right place at the right time—internet stuff, right? Why don't you billionaire-explain it to me. Because you're not the first self-indulgent idiot to try selling this bullshit. Being smart, lucky, and selfish doesn't make you a genius. What was that quote of yours? 'We wanted flying cars and an end to disease. We got texting and cat videos.' So profound."

"Humanity should strive for something better than placating the masses, don't you think?"

"I do. But it's a little hypocritical when what made you rich was placating the masses. Don't worry, when this is over, I'll be sure to strap you into a chair, eyes forced open Clockwork Orange-style with those fucking cat videos on an endless loop."

"Charming. I already have his blood," Krol said, looking at me.

I unconsciously ran my hand along my side. "I think if you had my blood, you wouldn't be here. I think the vile broke and mixed with everyone else's blood."

"Oh, I have it." He held up the tiny vial. "But I want more than a few drops. And I want more than just your blood. Imagine the kind of healing power and tissue regeneration you must possess. You can't look like her if the only thing that's modified is the aging clock. Wear and tear alone would take its toll on that perfect face." Krol's tone regarding Renika's beauty seemed clinical, as did his gaze. "More samples, more chances for success. Frankly, I don't need you alive. I just need your bodies."

That was when I noticed figures at the passage entrance carrying cryo-bags, which were placed on the ground behind Krol.

Renika glared at Kydell. "Do you work for him?"

"He's the client."

"That's not what I asked you. Do you work for *him*?"

Krol was getting impatient. "He just told you. I've paid a lot of money for this moment. It's your choice. You can walk out. Or be carried out."

Renika ignored Krol. Her stare bore into Kydell. "Do. You. Work. For this. Piece. Of. Shit?" She lowered her eyes to the tattoo on his wrist.

Kydell glanced at it as well. "I work….for…this piece of shit."

Krol didn't know how to feel about this. Happy, sort of.

Renika blew a chuckle out her nose. "You are a well-trained liar."

Before anyone could say another word, she grabbed the pistol taped to her back. The one she'd taken off Alana Gray. She lifted the muzzle and pointed at Kydell.

He was startled by this. "You know what this means," he said, pointing emphatically at the two dots inside the triangles on his wrist.

"Yes. It means I shouldn't do this."

And then she fired a bullet into Kydell.

He staggered back and dropped to one knee.

There were angry shouts from team members itching to pick up their weapons and start firing. They restrained themselves as Renika swept the room, ready to discharge the weapon again if anyone moved.

She slowly backed away, her arm pushing me back as well. "I would leave now," she said looking down at Kydell. "This is that warning I was talking about."

"There's nowhere for you to go," said Krol. "We've got every exit covered."

"We're not leaving through the exits," Renika said. "Now…I told you to step back."

Renika knocked the rock out of my hand. Wounded and bleeding, Kydell lunged for it but he was too late, and the chunk of stone fell to the ground, yanking the wires and pulling the pins overhead.

Then Renika did something really stupid. She went forward, the opposite way I was moving. She swept Krol's legs out from under him, sending him hard to the ground. Only then, did she turn and follow me.

It all happened in slow motion in my head.

For an instant, the PMCs watched us running away, naked. Then as if shocked by electricity, they jolted into action. Most fled, some gave chase. Krol was seized by several mercs and dragged toward the exit.

I stumbled over stones and depressions in the floor as I headed toward the alcove.

Flashlights swung wildly. The light strobed off the walls. Bleeding, his left hand pressed to his chest, his face a mask of pain, Kydell was closing. I didn't see Daniel, but he'd pulled his pins and was no longer by the pillar. Kydell had the angle on Renika. He reached for her. I lurched to the side and purposely tumbled, my bare flesh grinding into the gritty floor. My sudden dodge gave him no time to react. Renika escaped Kydell's desperate grasp as he tripped over me and crashed to the ground. I rolled to my feet, stumbling forward, churning my legs. I was less than ten feet from the protection of the alcove when the world ignited.

The explosion was deafening. The grenades overhead went off. There wasn't a huge fireball crawling across the ceiling like you see in a movie. In fact, I don't remember any flames at all, just a bright flash, a loud bang, and an expanse of dust and rock. I instinctively covered my head with my arms. Small pieces of debris pelted me. Then the pillars exploded. Pop, pop, pop. Sending another cloud of dust and more fragments of rock our way.

A second later, a more powerful trembling shook my bones.

I scrambled in the direction of Phoebe's screams, dragged her several feet, then fell on her, covering her with my body.

This rumbling wasn't a handful of grenades exploding. This was the sound of sixty feet of rock and soil, a thousand, million pounds of earth crashing down.

Limestone blocks the size of subway cars fell to the floor, the tumult piercing my ears. Stones slammed into my back, one after another. Phoebe's frame felt so fragile under me. Could my own body withstand the punishment to protect her? And if we did survive, would the debris clear from the abandoned stairwell?

Could we even get to the stairs? I winced as a cleave of limestone stabbed me in the back.

Ears ringing, I couldn't hear anything for several minutes. My eyes were filled with dust. I had shielded my face aggressively. Not just to protect myself from the rubble, but to create a pocket of air to breathe.

When the ground stopped shaking and I felt no more falling debris, I allowed myself to open my eyes. There was a faint light. I felt something drip from my forehead, and I wondered if I was bleeding.

Phoebe was motionless beneath me. But her body was tense, not limp as it would be if she were unconscious, or worse. When my pulse settled, I felt her heartbeat.

I struggled to press myself up, the hardest pushup I've ever done. More than a hundred pounds of rock rolled off my back. A piece slammed my fingers, which was the most painful part of the ordeal.

I felt wetness again. And this time I knew it wasn't blood, but water, pouring down from above. The collapse had busted a water pipe or unleashed an underground spring. On my tongue, a tang of sourness, a noxious order filled my nostrils, and I felt a wave of hope. It might be a sewer. That could mean a way out. A disgusting path, but I'd take it.

Phoebe and I had only gotten to the archway of the alcove, but it had been enough to protect us from the worst of it. I got to my knees and realized the ground behind me was gone. A massive block of limestone stood in its place.

Phoebe got to her feet. We were still naked although pulverized limestone covered our skin, making us barely discernible from the rock around us.

As the moisture fell on us from above, droplets etched away lines of dust.

We found the scattered pile of clothes Renika had acquired. I wasn't sure we'd be any less conspicuous running around Paris in paramilitary gear than running around naked, but it would protect us as we struggled to climb out.

Renika stood over the leader, Kydell. He was alive, the wound in the upper pectoral bleeding, his lower leg twisted at an odd angle.

"Help me," he said, his voice calm, his right arm held up. Perhaps so she could give him a hand, perhaps to present the tattoo to her again.

"The fact that I didn't put the bullet between your eyes is all the help I'm willing to give you." Renika kicked him across the face, knocking him unconscious.

Phoebe's hand was bleeding. I tore some fabric and wrapped it. As my eyes adjusted, I realized the beams of light were coming from much farther up, outside light refracting down to reach us. The dust was clearing.

I walked toward Renika who was at the edge of the mountain of rock, staring down at something. She hadn't gotten dressed yet. The uniform hung from her arm. I couldn't help it, but my eyes went to her midsection. The scar, small, but distinct, between her pelvic bone and her hip. It was the symbol. The fact that I had never seen this mark on her bothered me for a couple of reasons.

Distracted, I almost stepped on what she was looking at.

Glancing down from her hip, I saw a white-dusted forearm sticking out of the debris, the military pack clutched in his hand. A thousand pounds of rock crushing the rest of his body. The Babe Ruth ball was visible through the half-zipped opening. The laptop was partially open, his hand blocking it from being closed.

A wave of rage washed over me. I tried to move the largest of the stones. Even in my adrenaline-fueled state, I couldn't budge it. I felt a hand on my shoulder.

"We need to move," Renika said. "There's no way to know how stable this is." She pulled on her clothes and watched me as I fought with the stones and debris. "You can't do anything, Alexander."

"I can't leave him here." I thought of Braeden and again felt the agony of abandoning him, consigning him to die alone.

"You can. And you will."

It took Phoebe a moment to understand what she was looking at. "Daniel…" she said, calling to him. "Daniel!"

She went for him, and I grabbed her as the ground moved and more of the wall crumbled.

"We have to go," insisted Renika.

I thrust Phoebe—protesting, yelling, screaming—toward Renika. Once she had Phoebe moving up the mountain of debris, I fell to my knees, shards of rock cutting into my flesh through the fabric. I didn't feel a thing. I laid myself next to Daniel, caressing the only part of him that remained unearthed. The pendant Braeden had given him, its thin leather cord snapped in half, rested on his palm. I uncurled his fingers, letting my hand drag along his. "I'm sorry," I whispered as I squeezed his flesh. "I'm sorry." I felt the tears on my cheek as my thumb rested on his wrist. There was no pulse. No life. I slid the pack out of his grasp, his skin gritty and rough from the dust.

I tried again to dislodge the block crushing his body, but it refused to move. Renika called to me several times, each more agitated and farther away than the last. When I had barely strength left to pull myself up, I stood. I felt my legs give out. Not the floor giving way, but the emotion hitting me.

I reached for the laptop. I absently wiped the dust from the screen. It still worked although the display was cracked.

The image of the sphere I'd seen was a schematic of the earth, viewed from above the North Pole. I closed the lid and put it in the rucksack.

I touched Daniel's fingertips to mine one last time, took the pendant, and involuntarily inhaled a sob. A single breath that I held for a long moment.

I pushed the anger and pain and sorrow down, swallowed it, buried it, and switched into warrior mode. I zipped the pack closed, slung it over my shoulder, and summoning my last reserves, I stepped over my friend and climbed atop the slab that was too heavy for me to move, adding my weight to his burden, and I began moving in the direction of the staircase.

That had been the plan. Set the charges in a way that would clear the stairs of debris and hope that the rubble would be high enough for us to reach them.

But a chunk of limestone at least twenty feet wide blocked access to the stairs. That was the bad news. The good news was that the collapse had opened a hole in the ceiling. I found Phoebe and Renika resting in a hollow a moment later. From here, the path toward the surface meandered in a zig-zag of vertical clefts large enough to slip through. I pressed my back against one side and used my hands and feet to apply pressure to the opposite vertical. After chimneying up forty feet, I came to a pocket thirty feet across. Renika and Phoebe were staring up at the foundation of a massive pillar hanging precariously over our heads.

Then something bizarre happened. A car fell into the hole. Dove, actually. Nose first. A perfect swan dive. The traumatized driver's eyes were wide with fear, his face disappearing as the airbags deployed.

Phoebe touched the warm hood of the car which came to rest a few feet away.

There was honking, lots of honking. Then the sound of metal and glass. More crashes. But no more falling vehicles.

We used the side mirrors, the wipers, the doors, the wheels, and the fenders of the car to gain footholds and bridge the gap to the shaft the sedan had plunged through. We helped the stunned driver escape. He kept apologizing in French as if the entire thing had been his fault. Shaky at first, he climbed quickly, assisting Renika and Phoebe. I fell behind, demonstrating just how tired I was.

I could see rays of light growing stronger as we—hacking and coughing—made our way higher, climbing now through soil and crumbled concrete, pipes, and chunks of asphalt. I caught the harsh, artificial scent of natural gas. Even as everything within me screamed to hurry past the toxic air, we had to move slowly and carefully to avoid creating a spark that could set off an inferno. Dirt and debris trickled down on me as the others climbed. I tried to breathe through my shirt until the path was clear for me to follow.

My feet dangled as I pulled myself up on a broken gas main, my body weight taxing my grip, the noxious vapor fouling my lungs and sapping my strength.

I scaled the last few feet, coughing uncontrollably, my lungs barking as I found a pocket of fresh air.

We emerged into the glaring, searing sun from a cavernous hole, a crater more than a block in diameter, and stood at the edge of the Place de Concorde just west of the Louvre and the Tuileries. Almost precisely where Daniel had predicted we were.

As onlookers pulled us from the crater to the street, I gazed up at the obelisk at the plaza's center that had been removed from the Temple at Luxor and brought to Paris. It stood somehow undamaged in the midst of the destruction.

The Eiffel Tower rising to the southwest looked like the skeleton of a distant relative.

The two Arcadem helicopters circled overhead in an ever-widening radius.

"Well, at least there's that," I said.

Renika nodded. "We're no longer leaving a radioactive trail. We should try to blend in."

Black is the color of Parisian fashion. Black pants, black sweaters, black shoes, black coats, black hats. *Le noir, ça amincit.* The black, it thins. Strange as it may seem in a capital of fashion, exuberance of style offends Parisians. They want to impress you with their minds.

And so we found ourselves draped in black in a sea of black. On the ground, the three of us stood out in our ill-fitting paramilitary garb. From above, we were indistinguishable from the rest of the locals.

I glanced down at my chest, at the name "Black" in black thread on the black name patch. I was swimming in Kydell Black's urban fatigues. "Why did you shoot the merc? The marks on his wrist, that's supposed to offer him protection."

"Not when he points a gun at me just moments before."

"I've never seen dots in the triangles."

"It means he has a parent who's an Eternal. One dot. One parent. Two dots. Both parents. How do you not know this?"

"I don't know. So, how do you think shooting someone with two Eternal parents is a good idea?" I said.

"I sent a strong message to those parents. Let's see who answers."

The shrieking sirens of at least a dozen police cars arriving at the massive crater mirrored what was going on inside my head.

I pulled out the laptop and studied the images Daniel had uncovered.

Nine dots circled the wireframe of the earth. A note indicated these objects—Z-AXis (Zirconia Communication Satellites)— were three-hundred-twenty-six miles above the surface, about half again as high as the International Space Station. A flat map of the continents showed the BROADCAST AREA projected from each dot. Two-thirds of the planet's landmass and ninety percent of the population were within one of the intersecting ovals.

"What am I looking at?" asked Phoebe.

"A terribly bad idea," said Renika.

"Communications satellites," countered Phoebe.

Renika pointed at the notes on the image. *Yield, Rads, Coverage=Effect.* "Communication satellites that appear to be carrying thermonuclear devices into low-Earth orbit."

Phoebe's face drained of color. "I don't understand. Is Elam Khai planning to irradiate all these areas?" Great Barrington was clearly within one of the spheres.

Renika shook her head. "That high up, the fallout is insignificant. These are EMP effect zones."

I nodded. "The EMP would knock out anything with a chip or circuit board that wasn't shielded."

Phoebe's eyes widened. "That sounds significant to me."

I stared at the screen. "Daniel was right."

There was an instant, a fleeting moment, where the warrior left me, drained away like blood from a gaping wound, when the truth I had abandoned underground to focus on getting to safety rushed to the surface. That Daniel lay beneath us, beneath a city block of earth and stone.

My friend, Daniel Lang was—

I couldn't say the word. Not out loud, not in my head. Couldn't bring myself to do it. He was not with us, that's all I could manage.

Phoebe gripped my body tightly. "I don't want to know any of this. I just want to go home, Alexander. I just want to be with my family, whatever's going to happen." She wiped her tears on the fabric of my shirt and stifled a sob.

"They're not going to let you." Renika said it without malice and without looking up at the helicopters, whose blades slicing through the vortex broadcast their presence. "I told you you'd get one of them killed," Renika said into my ear before she pushed through the crowd.

As I stood at the center of the half-destroyed Place de la Concorde, grieving my friend, I did not want Phoebe Amara to go home.

"I'll get you home," I said, not sure if I really could.

I closed the laptop and started after Renika. We were nearing the edge of the crowd. More people were heading toward the spectacle of the crater than away from it. We'd lose our cover soon.

"Elam Khai is a lot farther along than I thought."

"Of course, he's ten steps ahead of us. And this is probably just the tip of it." Renika said over her shoulder.

Something about that clicked. I couldn't grab onto it yet. The sounds around me were mixing with my thoughts, the rolling whirr of tires, the growl of engines, the chirp of emergency vehicles, the murmur of voices, the whomp-whomp-whomp of the helicopters searching for us.

And then, I caught it. The thing that had been right there in front of me.

"I never would've found those hidden images without Daniel." I turned to Renika. "Would you have thought to look for something else?"

"In the file, no. In the image, yes."

"You saw something," I said. Renika gave the smallest nod. "Maybe we're supposed to deal with *that*...before dealing with the concealed images."

"You're saying, we're not supposed to do anything about Elam Khai setting off nuclear weapons?" Phoebe voice grew loud.

Renika glanced up at the helicopters that were getting desperate in their search for us, zigzagging, flying low. "I did see something." She opened the laptop and pointed at a symbol in my father's handwritten comments on the original image. A "Y" sprouting from the top of a hexagon. "Where I grew up, there were priests that used this symbol to—"

The screen went black.

It was late afternoon. The sky was clear.

There was no noise. No rumble. No change in air pressure. No flash of light. No warning. Nothing to indicate an extraordinary event. But something happened. Both black helicopters fell from the sky, scattering the crowd in a brief stampede. Another helicopter, a French military craft, also plummeted, splashing down in the Seine. Cars were paralyzed. Buses, trucks, mopeds, boats. Some crashed, some skidded, some drifted, some ground to a halt. Streetlights and walk signals went dark. Sirens and horns fell silent. People tapped at their phones, imploring them to work. In an instant, everything came to a standstill. The only thing moving were the people.

A man in his sixties clutched at his chest and went down to one knee, his face contorted in agony. Several bystanders came to his aid as the man desperately, feebly pounded his sternum with his fist.

Renika grabbed Phoebe. Without the threat of being seen from above, we abandoned the anonymity of the crowd.

I ran toward the ancient Egyptian obelisk at the plaza's center. Using the power cables leading to the floodlights, I pulled myself onto the base.

Renika frantically waved for me to get down.

I put up a hand that said, *give me a moment.*

I surveyed the landscape.

The streets were clogged. The familiar sounds of the city, the traffic, the horns, the music, the buzz, had been muted.

I felt lightheaded.

Slightly sick to my stomach.

Daniel.

I couldn't process it yet.

Over the last five days, I had lost a stepbrother I didn't know I had, and a friend I'd grown to care for like a brother.

I held my hand up to block the sun hanging in the western sky. In every direction, for as far as I could see, it was the same.

No lights.

No power.

This was a taste of what Elam Khai had in store for the world.

As my focus narrowed from the surrounding streets to the back of my hand, I noticed my posture—arm outstretched, palm slightly cupped, standing atop a pedestal. Like the statue of Elam Khai being crowned First Emperor of Rome.

The ancient among us, my father, Elam Khai—the ones four, five, six, seven, eight, *nine* thousand years old—they were as different from me as I was from Phoebe and Daniel. Thousands and thousands and thousands of years of fighting, scheming, surviving, of being worshiped as Gods and near-Gods had altered them in ways I couldn't comprehend, and was only to imagine.

As I climbed down from the pedestal, Phoebe threw her arms around me, her lips brushing against my neck, her breath on my skin.

"Did he do this?"

"I don't know."

We'd seen no flash, no aurora caused by charged particles colliding with Earth's magnetic field, giving me hope this wasn't the execution of the plan Daniel had uncovered.

In the catacombs, when Peter Krol emerged from the shadows, I was surprised. I was relieved. I was…disappointed.

Because I had to face Elam Khai.

I was *born* to face him.

But only if I became more than the long-restrained high school student taking History instead of making it. Only if I shed Alexander the Pretty Good and became the *Something Greater* I was meant to be—a Saladin, a Pershing, a Napoleon, a Leonidas.

Achilles' weakness was not his heel, but his pride. His stubborn refusal to fight alongside anyone else.

You do not achieve greatness on your own, no matter how great you are. I would have to forge an alliance of equals to stand beside me to have any chance of succeeding.

Children of Eternals, a man of untold wealth determined to live forever. We'd have to deal with them. But Elam Khai…if he got his way, Daniel would be just the first of *millions*.

I have been running away. It is time for me to run toward.

I will not stop until I stop them or I stop breathing.

I'm coming for you, Peter Krol.

And *you*, uncle.

And anyone else who gets in my way.

I'm done being polite.

THE BATTLE FOR FOREVER EXPANDS...

VOLUME III:

LEAGUE OF AULD

(COMING 2020)

ENHANCE THE EXPERIENCE.
LISTEN TO THE AUDIOBOOKS READ BY WIL WHEATON.

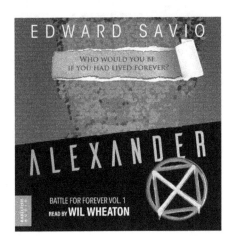

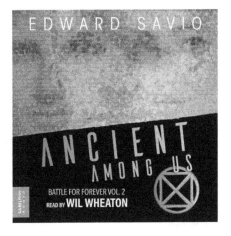

About the Author

Edward Savio grew up in Connecticut. He has written numerous film projects for Walt Disney Studios, Sony Pictures Entertainment and others. He is creator of the political cartoon, "Ourmageddon." He makes his home in San Francisco with his family.

Follow him on Twitter and Instagram @edwardsavio

Visit edwardsavio.com
for more on his books and comic.

Other books by Edward Savio

Adult Contemporary Fiction:
Idiots in the Machine
Love on Haight
The Velvet Sledghammer (2019)

Sci-Fi/Action:
Alexander X
Kids:
The Stupor Heroes vs. Dr. Earwax

Get Exclusive Content.

Post about the book on social media through **edwardsavio.com/AXBonus**

When you do, you'll get a link to exclusive content, including bonus short fiction, lost chapters, that will take you deeper into the **Battle For Forever Universe**, future, present, and past. Post a pic with the book and the best pics will get you the audiobook for free.

Your support means a lot. Thank you.

CPSIA information can be obtained
at www.ICGtesting.com
Printed in the USA
LVHW101005270323
742698LV00009B/50